Stately Pursuits

Also by Katie Fforde

Living Dangerously
The Rose Revived
Wild Designs

Katie Fforde

St. Martin's Press ❧ New York

Library of Congress Cataloging-in-Publication Data

Fforde, Katie.
    Stately pursuits / Katie Fforde.
      p.   cm.
    ISBN 0-312-18668-1
      I. Title.
    PR6056.F54S83   1998
    823'.914—dc21   98-17463
                                                     CIP

First published in Great Britain by Michael Joseph Ltd, a division of the Penguin Group

First U.S. Edition: July 1998

10 9 8 7 6 5 4 3 2 1

To my mother,
Barbara Gordon-Cumming,
1912–1996

ACKNOWLEDGEMENTS

To Richenda Todd, my much-beloved editor. To Miranda Ward-Kirkby, for an idea. To Barbara John, for help with research. And, as ever, Sarah Molloy, my agent.

PROLOGUE

Hetty was humming to herself as she drove up the rutted track to Alistair's cottage. It was a house she loved, a true gem. It had genuine casement windows with diamond panes, a little porch guarding the studded front door, and gingerbread woodwork under the eaves. Hetty would have liked to live in it for ever and longed to see it in summer when the roses that tangled up the side of the building would fill the air with their sweet scent. To Alistair it was an excellent investment.

She parked her car carefully behind Alistair's Porsche and got out, pulling a box of groceries from the back seat. She'd brought all his favourite food: cheese, single Gloucester with nettle, from a specialist cheesemonger in Covent Garden, some wild Scottish salmon, which she had queued half an hour for, and some handmade chocolate truffles. In a freezer-bag she had some ice-cream she had made herself. It was the only way she could afford to give him his favourite kind, and she did like to spoil him.

She'd made excellent time. It was still only ten o'clock. They had the whole, wonderful weekend to be alone together, and although it was January, and the weather was bleak, Hetty loved winter walks, followed by hot buttered crumpets in front of the fire as a reward. She'd bought those, and butter, in case Alistair had forgotten.

Using her key as usual when they travelled down separately, she let herself in, put down her box, and called 'Alistair? Are you in?' She knew he was, because his car was there, and he wasn't an early riser at weekends. He might still be asleep, his soft floppy hair tumbled across his cheek, his eyelashes long and curly, giving him a schoolboy innocence which was quite lacking when he was awake. For a moment she wished she hadn't called, but had just tiptoed up so she could wake him with a kiss. But it was too late.

I

'Come up,' he called, obviously awake, probably surrounded by newspaper. 'I'm in bed.'

Hetty smiled indulgently, wondering whether he'd stayed in bed so he could welcome her there, or was just having a lie-in. She knew he had had to go to a dinner party, unofficially business, which was why he'd been unable to bring her down. If it had gone on late, he would be tired.

She climbed the twisting staircase, lifted the latch of the bedroom door and went in.

There was no heap of half-read Saturday supplements snuggling up to Alistair. Instead, a tall, slim, blonde woman, several years older than Hetty, and several aeons more sophisticated, appeared to be offering him entertainment.

The couple did not spring guiltily apart on Hetty's entrance, as convention demanded. They stayed together, Alistair's arm curled defiantly about the woman's shoulders.

Hetty stared, unable to make sense of the picture before her, which was made more bizarre by the feeling she had that they were waiting for her. Hetty almost expected them to leap out of bed and tell her she'd won some mysterious prize. But they didn't. They stared back, Alistair looking smug, and the blonde more than a shade uncomfortable.

Hetty's disbelief of the obvious melted, leaving behind the sensation that a bad attack of flu was about to claim her. Her head swum, the floor tried to pull her to it with alarming strength. She realized if she wasn't careful, she would faint.

'I'm sorry to spring this on you, Hetty,' said Alistair. 'But there was never anything serious between us, and all good things come to an end. This seemed the best way to tell you.'

Hetty heard her voice come out of her mouth, apparently without any help from her. 'Oh, really? The telephone too conventional for you, was it? You didn't feel you could just slip it into the conversation while we had lunch yesterday?'

Alistair shook his head, still insouciant. 'I had an important meeting in the afternoon and couldn't handle any extra hassle.'

Hetty didn't feel anger, she became anger, as hot and lethal as the white-hot centre of a volcano. She moved towards the bed without knowing she was doing it. She pulled the duvet on to the floor.

'Hey,' said the woman. 'Look, I'm sorry . . . but . . . what are you doing?'

Alistair slept under linen sheets, nothing synthetic was allowed near him, except, Hetty observed as though from a long way off, the blonde at his side. One of these sheets, an antique inherited from his mother, covered him and his companion now. Like its fellows it had monograms embroidered on the corners, and had deep hems top and bottom. She had personally spent two hours ironing it, having somehow omitted to send it to the laundry. From nowhere came the memory that there was a tiny darn near the top.

They should have been warned when she pulled off the duvet, but Alistair and his friend seemed unprepared for any reaction. Hetty twitched the sheet easily from their slackened fingers, causing a horrified scream from the woman and an indignant 'Hey!' from Alistair.

Their modesty was not threatened. Hetty didn't even glance at them as she picked up the sheet and ripped it, her teeth locked on to one half, the other being pulled with her hands in a rolling motion, like a conjuror producing coloured handkerchiefs out of his mouth. The sound as the ancient linen tore was supremely satisfying, drowning Alistair's cries of distress and the blonde's admonishings. Only when the sheet was in two halves at Hetty's feet did she look up.

The woman had picked up the duvet and was cowering under it. Alistair, furious, had got out of bed and was striding towards her.

'You little bitch! That's an antique you've just ruined. You can bloody well pay for it to be mended!'

On a cloud of rage, Hetty felt elated, invincible. But she wished to avoid Alistair's furious onslaught and so left the bedroom and closed the door, shouting through it, 'You're a turd, Alistair. A coward and a turd. You didn't tell me we were finished because you couldn't be bothered to work out how. So you just got your lady friend to help you act it out.'

'There's no need to be rude . . .'

'There may not be any need but there's one hell of a lot of justification!'

She retreated rapidly down the cottage stairs, before Alistair could find his silk boxer shorts and set off in pursuit. She ran out of the front door, leaving it open, found her keys in her coat pocket and unlocked her car.

The first flush of rage was leaving her. It took her a few tries to start the car, and when it did start she put it into first instead of reverse. She shot forward into Alistair's Porsche.

She hadn't meant to do it, and had only hit his bumper and did little damage. But it felt so good that Hetty reversed properly, angled her own car and went faster, so the next bump made more of an impact. The third time actually dented his car, but also caused an unpleasant-sounding crunch in her own. She was reversing for a final onslaught when Alistair appeared in the doorway.

The sheet was bad enough, but she really couldn't afford to pay for the damage to his car. It would be better if he didn't find out what she'd done until she was well out of the way. She put the car into first and escaped.

She had driven down from her London flat early that morning. There was no way she could drive all the way back. Now the corset of rage that had held her together thus far was beginning to disintegrate. She was starting to shake. Any minute now she would burst into tears.

Her parents. Although they lived quite near, and Hetty's mother was always issuing invitations to Sunday lunch when Hetty and Alistair were down for the weekend, they never went. Alistair found parents a trying species, to be avoided unless absolutely essential – possibly for financial reasons. Thus Hetty didn't know the way, but once on the main road she found a signpost to a town she did know. She'd driven ten miles or so when the car started to protest.

'Just get me there,' she implored as steam began billowing from the radiator. 'Please, just get me there.'

It tried, but it was an old car, an ancient Ford Escort, which had taken all her savings and now took most of her spare cash to run. It wasn't accustomed to being used as an offensive weapon and, though loyal far beyond the bounds of duty, it gave out at the end of her parents' avenue.

Hetty just managed to get it to the side of the road, and then got out, hurriedly, in case it exploded. Then she ran down the lane to her parents' bungalow and hammered on the door.

Her mother opened it. 'Hello, darling. This is a surprise. Have you brought Alistair?'

Hetty opened her mouth and started to sob.

CHAPTER ONE

'Now, you will be all right, won't you, darling?' said Hetty's mother. It was more of a command than a question.

'Well, if I'm not,' Hetty muttered, stowing her mother's overnight case in the boot of the Clio, 'it'll be your fault.'

'What's that?' Her mother emerged from putting something on the back seat.

'Nothing.' Hetty forced a smile. 'I'll be fine.'

'I know you will.' Mrs Longden spoke as if there had never been any doubt. 'You should be all right for money for a while. Samuel seems to have plenty. But let me know if you run short. And I'll sort out a car for you soon, then you can visit Samuel and not be so isolated.' She glanced at the narrow country lane that ran through what had once been the park belonging to the big house. It was edged with beautiful huge trees, but there wasn't another property in sight. 'Not that you'll be isolated, exactly . . .'

They both knew she was lying.

'I said I'll be fine,' repeated Hetty. 'And if you don't go now, you'll get the rush-hour traffic going into Guildford.'

Hetty wasn't particularly happy about being abandoned in a crumbling, possibly haunted, pile in the middle of nowhere, but as this was to be her fate, she wished her mother would leave her alone to get on with it.

'The village shop sells everything and you can use Samuel's account. He said you were to. And it's only about ten minutes' walk.' As her mother never walked anywhere Hetty knew this estimate might not be accurate. 'And they're such *nice* people.'

By 'nice' Hetty's mother meant well-spoken and middle class. She had ascertained, while buying a pint of milk and a box of cornflakes, that the owners were refugees from the rat race, escaping from the City just before Black Wednesday, and had swapped urban amenities for rural bliss.

7

'I know. You told me. I'll pop along there when you've gone,' said Hetty. 'I'll need some cat food.'

Her mother frowned. 'Mmm. Samuel should've mentioned the cat. Still, it looked pretty ancient. I don't suppose it'll go on for much longer.' She opened the car door. 'Now, I really must get off.'

After much kissing, finding of keys and slamming of doors, Hetty watched her mother drive away. She sighed deeply and then realized she'd forgotten to remind her mother to get the telephone reconnected. Damn! Fighting a sense of abandonment she made her way back into the house.

The manor had been in the Courtbridge family since the Wars of the Roses, passing down from father to son until the First World War killed off three male heirs and the line was forced to divert to the furthest, spindliest twigs of the family tree. This branch were far less prolific. Hetty's mother's Uncle Samuel, awaiting a serious, possibly life-threatening, operation, had been only distantly related to the previous incumbent. And his heir was not only distant genealogically, but also geographically, last heard of in some part of the world that used to be the Soviet Union.

Hetty's mother was the only member of the family who knew who had married whom and how many times each cousin was removed. She had a strong sense of duty and when her uncle – ('Not really an *uncle*, darling, more a third cousin, but the generations all went wrong.') – became ill, it was Hetty's mother he contacted. He wanted her to get in touch with his quasi-nephew and ask him to come and look after the house. On no account must it be left empty for more than a few days.

But after many days with her ear glued to phone and fax machine and receiving only ear-splitting shrieks for her pains, even Mrs Longden's determination expired. She put down the phone for the last time and turned to Hetty.

'I don't suppose he'd have come anyway. He never turns up for family occasions or we would have met him. He's probably far too busy making money to do his duty.' It was then her gaze narrowed. 'You're not doing very much at the moment, darling. I don't suppose you'd care to house-sit for a while? It's a beautiful old house, in a lovely part of the world. Do you remember when you were a bridesmaid? The house made a great impression on you.'

'Mother, I was five years old . . .'

It was thus that Hetty's misfortune, in the shape of a devastating love affair, became the ill wind that blew somebody some good.

'If you can't be happy you may as well be useful,' her mother had said, when Hetty had demurred. After three weeks of trying to 'bring Hetty out of herself' she had despaired of ever hearing her daughter laugh again.

Hetty, on the blunt end of these efforts, felt that if she had to smile brightly to any more of her mother's buddies while they did Meals on Wheels or manned the WI stall together, she really would have reason to end it all. And, having fled the independence of her London flat along with her job and her involvement with Alistair, she was finding it hard to go back to living at home. She welcomed this opportunity to be miserable in private, if not the attendant anxieties. She agreed to look after the house until either her mother tracked down the heir, or her mother's Uncle Samuel was fit enough to return.

It certainly needed someone, she thought as she went back into the kitchen, distracted from her misery by the awfulness of her surroundings.

The kitchen was chock full of original features, chocker full of rubbish, and absolutely minus anything remotely resembling a mod con.

Multifarious cupboards surrounded the walls, keeping work-surfaces to the minimum. Some of the cupboards were chipped Formica, others might have been pine underneath the layers of paint – one, badly battered, was mahogany. They were all thick with dust, and too full of china for the doors to stay shut unless wedged.

A large kitchen table, the only flat surface apart from the ridged draining-board, was completely covered with things. Stone salt jars, rusty bread bins, several copper milk cans, sweet jars, an ancient glass butter churn, left there, not to add character to the room, but because no one had ever bothered to move it, flower-embossed biscuit tins, antique storage jars and an old-fashioned typewriter – possibly an early prototype – all jostled uncomfortably with a rack of bistro cutlery and a tower of very new-looking stacking plastic boxes. The Portobello Road meets a Tupperware party. Even in her state of misery, Hetty couldn't help smiling at the bizarre juxtaposition.

Among the tat, Hetty realized, might be some gems, collectibles that would fetch hundreds in the right London shop. In there, without any doubt at all, were myriads of weevils, flour mites, silverfish and woodlice. As this was where she was expected to make her solitary snacks, she'd fairly soon have to sort some of it out. It was just as well she was less fastidious than her mother, who had so blithely sentenced her to living in a cross between an overstocked junk shop and a sanctuary for invertebrates.

Still, she was here now, she'd just have to cope. Hetty turned her gaze from the table and regarded the cooking arrangements.

Where once a range had reigned over the kitchen and numerous attendant skivvies there now stood an obscure make of stove. It shivered in the fireplace of a much larger beast, but, unlike its noble ancestor, it was oil burning and had been left on a low flame to stop the pipes freezing. Hetty and her mother had managed, after a lot of experiment, to turn it up to full power. It was while they were fiddling with taps and levers that they opened fully the door of the lowest oven and an aged cat staggered out. After finishing the milk that Hetty instantly gave it, it went back whence it came, and apparently stayed there all night.

Now Hetty glanced round the kitchen to see if the cat had re-emerged. She wanted to give it her leftover cereal. It was still curled up in the oven.

Deprived even of this bit of company, Hetty gathered the couple of plates and cereal bowls she and her mother had used and put them in the crazed porcelain sink. There was something very depressing about washing up for two when now you were only one, and would be for the foreseeable future.

And the state of the kitchen did not help her spirits, although there was nothing wrong with it that a thorough clean and Smallbone of Devizes couldn't put right. Too small for a baronial hall, it could have been a wonderfully ample family kitchen, provided your family was at least the size of the Von Trapps, she thought.

Still, no point in feeling sorry for oneself. Not knowing quite why, Hetty took a breath and let the first few notes of 'Little Girl Blue' emerge into the dusty air.

Unlike her voice, which was husky from lack of use, the acoustics in the kitchen were good. The high ceiling, dusky with ingrained dirt, fly droppings and cobwebs, gave the small sound a pleasing echo.

It had been such a long time since she'd done any singing. Before leaving home for London, it had been her hobby. She and a friend would sing together, jazz for preference, but almost anything except grand opera. They led the local carol singers, and did sing-alongs for old people's homes and anyone else who asked. They both thoroughly enjoyed it.

But Alistair had made it plain, very early on in their relationship, that he was an opera buff. Amateurs (and Hetty definitely came under this category) set his teeth on edge. Since then, she only sang in the car, and definitely only when alone. And since her car's sad demise and her own devastation, she had had no opportunity or desire to sing.

Wishing she'd chosen a slightly less melancholy number, but still humming, Hetty moved to the window to see if the dirt was mostly inside or out. Her damp tissue came away black but made no impression on the dirt. It was both sides, and ivy rampaging up the outside walls had encroached well over the glass. What she needed was a jolly, local window-cleaner who would cut the ivy as well as polish the glass. But, as such characters were as fictional as Father Christmas, she'd have to look out a good bucket, a rag and a ladder.

Her song over, she peered into the oven. 'Come on, Puss,' she called. 'Come and see your Aunty Hetty. Let me know you're still alive.' A stiffened little corpse in the place of a cat would send her back down into the depths of depression.

The cat obligingly stretched out a tentative paw. But, although the warming oven was now almost hot, it declined to venture into the kitchen. Hetty could see its point. The stove had been going full blast all night but you could only sense the difference in temperature between the kitchen and the great outdoors if you got caught in a gust of wind. And as it was February there were plenty of those.

'Oh, come out, do,' she stretched her hand towards it. 'Come out and tell me who's been feeding you.'

The cat mewed, almost silently, deigned to come towards Hetty's hand and, before Hetty realized its intention, had clawed its way up her jean-covered legs until it reached her shoulder. It purred, very loudly, into her ear. Hetty, somewhat overwhelmed, was grateful that the cold had made her put on every stitch she had brought with her, and noticed that the cat had extremely bad breath.

'I don't suppose that the village shop sells breath freshener for cats, even if it is as wonderful as Mum says,' she said to it. 'But I'd better find it anyway.'

The cat stayed on her shoulder while she found her bag and sorted herself out. It was a warm, comforting, if somewhat weighty, presence. Hetty hummed in harmony with its purr. It was hardly singing, but this tentative stretching of her vocal wings lifted her spirits.

Hetty unhooked the cat and shrugged on her father's Barbour, purloined without his knowledge, then set off down the tree-lined road towards the small collection of cottages, shop, church, what had once been a school, and pub which made up the pretty end of the village. The council houses, garages, and a bit of light industry were kept out of sight of the conservation area.

At the end of the lane, Hetty paused and looked back at the house. It had been dark when she and her mother had arrived the previous evening, and this was the first chance she'd had to take a good look at it since she had last been there, nearly twenty years ago.

Three unequal gables of grey-gold stone thrust upwards towards the sky. From one protruded three tiers of bay windows topped with a little balcony of castellations beneath the pointed roof. This, she guessed, was the newest part, when the wool trade filled the area with wealth as well as sheep and the family must have felt flush and ostentatious. She imagined the begowned lady of the house in the sixteenth century – rather like her own mother – demanding that her lord have a bay put in so she would have somewhere sunny to do her needlework.

The middle gable was wider and shallower, the original core of the house, which contained the great hall and the kitchen. They had been there since the Dark Ages, and judging by the kitchen hadn't altered much since. The end gable was smaller and had a bay window, designed to catch the sun in what was once the morning room, since demoted to the sitting room. Slates, the same grey-gold as the walls, could be seen under the swathes of ivy that clambered to and round the chimneys, which clustered in groups of three. When had they last been swept? she wondered.

It was not a house for purists. Too many unauthorized changes had been undertaken for its history to be evident. It was no Perfect Example of any period. But for those who liked a mystery, the puzzle of what came when and where, it was a delight. When Hetty had last seen it, it had been a warm summer's day. There had been a large marquee in the garden, and some relation was getting married. Hetty, dressed in a Laura Ashley version of Bo Peep, had run through the house with her partner-in-glazed-cotton, thinking how huge it was, and how mysterious. Oddly, it hadn't got any smaller or less mysterious with the passage of time.

The village, when she got to it, a good twenty minutes later, showed signs of a battle for its survival. The school, placed diagonally across the green from the pub, had recently become a private residence, a fact made plain by the raised beds on the tarmac playground, and the embossed-iron name-plate with THE OLD SCHOOL painted on it.

The church, where she had been a bridesmaid so long ago, was still functioning, as was the pub. But as more and more local people moved to where the work was, their houses bought up by weekenders who didn't go to church much anyway, life as it had been lived for centuries was under threat. Samuel had bewailed the decline of rural existence when they had visited him.

'Soon every house will have two cars and no children,' he had complained. 'No one spends their money locally any more. I just hope those young things in the shop make a go of it.'

'Those young things' had certainly tried hard, but their window was papered with notices that seemed to confirm Samuel's fears. The WI had combined with the next village, the vicar had duties in other parishes, and the bus service had been reduced to two days a week. No wonder everyone had two cars and no children, thought Hetty, then bravely opened the door to the shop.

13

Even when she was not suffering from a compound fracture of the heart Hetty was fairly shy. But the thought of entering a small grocer's wouldn't usually make her uncomfortable. However, Hetty's mother, on the principle that a trouble shared is a trouble halved, reckoned that the more people you shared it with the better, and was unlikely to have held back in the village shop. Everyone, from the 'nice' proprietors to the passing salesman stopping for a *Sport* and a packet of fags, would have been given, in carrying tones, a detailed account of how Hetty's wicked, lecherous boss had shamelessly seduced her, breaking her heart and ruining her career at a single stroke. Knowing this, with her morale already at a subterranean level, made popping out for a few tins of cat food an act of some courage.

But Hetty reasoned that she was so miserable already, not even this public humiliation could make her feel worse. And there was the chance, very slight of course, that her mother might have kept her mouth shut. It would be a shame to let the cat starve to death unnecessarily.

In spite of these bracing thoughts, she still felt as though she were entering the dentist's waiting room as she opened the door and the old-fashioned bell announced her presence with painful lack of discretion. However, there were no fanfares, and Hetty was able to slip into the shop almost unnoticed.

It was divided into two halves. One half was a supermarket, which sold life's staples – sliced bread, tinned soup, corned beef and packets of biscuits. The other half was an up-market delicatessen. This was fighting back with a vengeance – if this shop went out of business, it would go with sun-dried tomatoes and porcini flying.

Home-cured hams rested on china plinths, handmade sausages stuffed with truffles and dried cranberries sat fatly next to dishes of kalamata olives and local sheep's-milk cheese. Olive oil in wine bottles, arborio rice in linen sacks, and organic chocolate bursting with cocoa-solids were all appetizingly arranged in willow baskets. There was a stack of tissue-wrapped loaves, dark brown and dense with goodness, next to a pile of enriched Italian ciabattas, genuine French *flutes* and a basket of croissants.

The proprietors obviously strove to satisfy all tastes, those of the local population whose children liked their baked beans orange, thank you very much, and the more esoteric requirements of visiting foodies.

The man behind the counter was large and handsome and wore a boater and a blue striped apron. He smiled broadly at Hetty as she came in, but didn't immediately demand to know how she had let that man do those dreadful things to her. This was a good sign. Either he was blessed with a certain amount of tact, or her mother hadn't confided all her daughter's secrets.

She said good-morning, picked up a basket – wicker instead of the more usual wire – and perused the shelves, trying to summon an interest in something her mother would consider nourishing. Hetty had no desire to nourish herself, she just wanted comfort food – hot, sweet and fattening. She took hold of a can of mushroom soup as a gesture to vegetables and then discovered the tins of ravioli.

She was just wondering if the cat had a preferred brand of cat food when a pretty woman in a white overall and long shopkeeper's apron came over and put her hand in Hetty's.

'Hi, I'm Angela Brewster. You must be Hetty Longden? Come to look after the manor?' Hetty shook the hand and nodded. 'Your mother said you were there. We're so relieved that *someone's* there to keep an eye on the place. It's been empty far too long already. Besides, my son's fed up with feeding the cat.'

Hetty smiled. 'Oh, was it him? It's very kind. My mother and I didn't know there was a cat until we opened the door of the stove and out it came.'

'Typical cat, knows how to look after itself.'

'Perhaps you could tell me its name, and what sort of cat food it likes?'

'He's called Clovis and he likes the very cheapest kind.' Angela picked up a tin. 'Unfortunately.'

The shop bell jangled again and a thin, athletic woman with a lot of thick grey hair and a ruddy complexion came in. 'Oh, here's Mrs Hempstead, I'll introduce you,' muttered Angela. 'She's one of the guides.'

'Guides?' Hetty lowered her voice to match Angela's. 'Girl Guides?'

Angela shook her head, confused. 'No, no. For when the house opens. To the public.'

Comprehension dawned. Hetty remembered her mother mentioning that the house was open to the public in the summer. 'Oh, yes. I don't expect I'll still be here by then.'

Angela looked surprised. 'Won't you? I thought Easter was early this year? Still, you mustn't mind Mrs Hempstead,' she went on. 'She's a wonderful woman, but she can be a bit domineering and does rather feel she owns the place. She's a keen local historian and has lived here for ever. She'll bully you to death if . . . Mrs Hempstead! How handy that you've popped in. You can meet Hetty Longden. She's come down to look after the house.'

Hetty allowed herself to be led up to the woman, still wondering why Angela had mentioned Easter in that unnerving way.

Mrs Hempstead grasped Hetty's hand, testing her handshake for signs of weakness of character. 'Goodness me, you're young!'

'I'm twenty-four,' said Hetty.

Mrs Hempstead tutted. 'And what do you know about looking after a great house?'

'Nothing.'

Mrs Hempstead exhaled. 'Still, you're bound to be better than that Awful Nephew. At least you won't change the place into a *Funfair*.' The emphasis she gave the word indicated she really meant 'Den of Iniquity'.

'Er, no,' said Hetty. 'I'm only here while my mother's uncle is ill.'

Mrs Hempstead shook her head as if predicting the end of the world. 'He's an old man who's led a dissolute life. Might pop his clogs any minute.' Before Hetty could react, Mrs Hempstead turned her attention to the bacon slicer. 'Could you do me half a pound of smoked streaky, cut very thin?' She turned back to Hetty. 'I'll do everything to help, of course. But you won't find it easy, not at your age.'

Hetty, who recently had hardly been able to muster the initiative necessary to brush her hair, found her courage rising to the challenge. 'Oh, I don't know. I expect I'll manage . . .'

Mrs Hempstead pursed her lips. 'Managing isn't quite enough. And Easter's early this year.'

Hetty escaped while Mrs Hempstead inspected a goat's cheese over the top of her glasses. She found herself by the cat food and filled her basket with quite an impressive array of tins before happening on the freezer. The thought of being bullied by Mrs Hempstead gave her long-missing spirit a metaphorical kick. Perhaps, she reflected, as Angela checked out her shopping, I'm getting bored with being a victim.

She was just leaving the shop when a muddy white sports car drew up and parked somewhat askew. Out of it climbed a blonde woman in leather trousers and a dashing hat. Hetty's small revival of spirit sank back to where it had come from. No one would reject a woman like that, she thought sadly, sharply reminded of how her own rejection had been for a woman equally glamorous, with very long legs. Hetty's legs were not particularly short, but they did not make her tall. And although her hair went fairer in the sun, it was a boring brown colour at this time of year. It also needed cutting, but beyond keeping herself and her teeth clean Hetty had done nothing to enhance her appearance since Alistair's betrayal.

To get her mind off this depressing topic she planned what she would say to her mother on the subject of just when the house was supposed to open to the public when either the phone was put back on or she located a phone box. But she knew it wasn't her mother's fault. Uncle Samuel, for all his gentlemanly ways and generosity of spirit, could be conveniently vague at times.

When she had first come across him, when she was a bridesmaid, and Courtbridge House was *en fête* for some distant cousin's wedding, Hetty remembered him describing her as 'a taking little thing'. She had been horrified, thinking he must have seen her take a strawberry from the mountain of them piled on the buffet. It was only years later that she realized he'd paid her a compliment.

She'd met him a couple of times since, once at another wedding, and again at a funeral. She liked him enormously, prejudiced no doubt by his good opinion of her.

Hetty and her mother had visited him in hospital before their descent on the house, a couple of days before he was due to be operated on for a faulty prostate gland. His lawyer had been present and he had drawn up the documents giving Hetty limited power of attorney.

'You must be able to write cheques, my dear,' Uncle Samuel had said, when she had shrunk from the thought of such responsibility. 'Or you won't manage at all. You'll need to open my post, too. I've a feeling there may be a few bills. The telephone people have been pestering me lately.'

'You can only sign cheques up to two thousand pounds,' the lawyer said firmly, his deadpan expression telling her not to get carried away. He handed Hetty his pen. 'There's a fairly healthy balance at the moment, but we'd like to keep it that way.'

'Hetty must spend whatever she needs,' said Uncle Samuel. 'It's very kind of her to help out. I don't want to keep her on short rations.'

'Well,' the lawyer relented. 'Any reasonable expenses will be allowed.'

'And I don't suppose the phone bill will be that much, will it?' Hetty's mother had said.

Samuel's eyes suddenly took on an ancient, rheumy look that Hetty suspected was deliberate. 'There may be Other Expenses,' he said. 'Hetty, if I might have a word . . .'

At that moment a nurse, who up till then had been fairly tolerant of all these people taking up space in her ward, rustled up in her plastic apron. 'I'm afraid I really must ask you all to leave. I've other patients to see to.'

'Oh, yes,' said Hetty's mother. 'Bye-bye, Samuel. Hetty'll be in to see you the moment she's got transport.'

Hetty's eyes met Samuel's and she saw that they were no longer vague, but demanding. He had something of great importance to say to her. But, instead of holding her back and saying it, he just gave her a rueful smile and submitted to the nurse's cajoling commands.

CHAPTER TWO

Braced by her encounter in the shop, Hetty walked briskly home and was somewhat disappointed that the house was no less gloomy than when she had left it an hour before. But, reminded of Mrs Hempstead by a packet of streaky bacon she unpacked from her bag, she felt the faint stirrings of her returning spirit, a memory of what she had been like Pre-Alistair.

Pre-Alistair, she had often heard herself described as bubbly and enthusiastic. It always made her cringe, it sounded so like a chocolate bar. But it wasn't inaccurate. She did rise to a challenge and occasionally get carried away by a new idea. Whether she would have stayed with the firm of management consultants so long if she hadn't fallen in love with her boss, Alistair Gibbons, she doubted. But she had, and she stayed, until he abandoned her for an older woman.

She was just about to see if she could get Uncle Samuel's supplementary cooking source, in the form of a two-burner camping gas-stove, to work when there was a knock on the back door. After a few false starts, Hetty got it open. It was the glamorous woman with the sports car.

'Hi! I'm Caroline.' The woman smiled. 'Can I come in? I've been longing to get a proper look at the house for ages, and when I heard you were here on your own I thought it was the ideal opportunity.'

Hetty stepped back automatically and Caroline came past her into the kitchen.

'Here,' Caroline burrowed in the pocket of her shiny leather jacket and produced a Cadbury's Creme Egg, 'I've bought you a present. Just the thing for a broken heart.' Hetty's descending spirits made it down another couple of notches. This long-legged beauty had heard everything and had come to patronize her. 'Sorry.' Caroline did actually look sorry. 'I wasn't supposed to say that.'

Hetty sighed resignedly. 'Does the whole village know?'

Caroline, who had pulled out a chair and seated herself at the kitchen table, shook her head. 'Shouldn't think so. But your mother told Angela Brewster, and Angela told me. Not to be gossipy, but she knows I'm an expert.' She produced another Creme Egg and started to unwrap it. 'I attract shits like black attracts cat hairs.' Caroline brushed at her sleek, leather-covered legs, as yet unsullied. 'But even if she told everyone, no one will remember. They're all more worried about what you're going to do while you're here.'

'Oh, I'm not going to do anything. I'm just house-sitting until my great uncle's out of hospital.'

'How boring! And bad for you, darling. You'll just die of misery living here if you don't *do* something.' Caroline wiped away a glob of yellow-and-white goo that had landed on her chin. It didn't go with the image created by the perfectly made-up face, the Hermès scarf knotted casually round her neck, and the large gold earrings that looked imposingly real. 'Perhaps what I really mean,' she went on, 'is *I* will die of boredom if I don't do something. My husband – not a shit by the way – is abroad an awful lot and I need something to do to keep me out of trouble. Or so he says.'

Hetty hadn't yet worked out if this woman was impossibly bossy and interfering – a younger, up-market version of her mother – or irresistibly attractive. But she didn't seem patronizing.

'I'm afraid I don't think I can help you,' she said, hedging her bets. 'I mean, the only sort of staff I'm likely to be needing are cleaners, and I shouldn't think you'd be interested in that.'

Caroline shook her head. 'Not really, though I am actually quite a good cleaner if I put my mind to it. But I don't want a job, I want a *project*.' The glint in her eyes was unnerving.

'What do you mean?'

'I need something to get my teeth into, by which I mean you.'

Hetty let out an involuntary whimper.

'Oh, don't worry. I'm not actually a cannibal, I just want to rescue you, cure your broken heart, and send you back into the world a stronger woman.'

Oh God, thought Hetty, looking despairingly at the woman making herself at home at the kitchen table. I come here to escape my mother, only to be hit on by someone even bossier. Talk about out of the frying-pan into the fire.

'Would you like a cup of tea or something?' she said politely, taking control of the situation.

Caroline nodded. 'These eggs are so sickly, I need something. What have you got?'

Hetty rummaged in the box of groceries brought from Hampshire and found some instant coffee. 'Instant coffee or a tea-bag. Nothing fancy, I'm afraid.' Caroline was probably a Lapsang Souchong or Rose Pouchong sort of person.

'Tea, good and strong, please.'

While Hetty made the tea, Caroline got up and prowled around, burrowing into corners, picking things up and putting them down with excited little exclamations. 'Ugh!' she said with a clatter. 'Rat droppings!'

Hetty instantly broke out into a sweat, dropped the teaspoon and tea-bag she was holding and rushed over. 'No,' she said after a moment. 'Coffee beans. I spilt them yesterday.'

'Sorry,' said Caroline, breathless with relief. 'I over-reacted.'

'It's all right.' Hetty felt pretty shaky herself. 'They do look very sinister, scattered about like that. My mother and I couldn't even find a coffee-grinder. And something about this place makes you think the worst.'

Caroline sat down. 'It's got huge potential.'

Hetty handed her a mug of tea. 'You sound like an estate agent.' Family loyalty made her want to say something nice. The facts forced her to keep quiet.

'It's been empty for a bit. The dust is bound to accumulate,' said Caroline with masterly understatement. She took a sip of tea. 'Well, will you give me the guided tour now, or shall we get your love affair out of the way?'

Hetty scalded the roof of her mouth and nearly dropped her mug.

'You don't have to,' Caroline went on, seeing Hetty's distress. 'Not the guided tour, I insist on that, but the love affair. Although telling people does help.' She made a rueful face. 'Believe me, darling, I know. Before I met Jack, I'd had at least three *devastating* affairs.'

'Really? I find that hard to believe.' But Hetty's hackles were coming down. Stunning Caroline may be, but she was also kind. Looking like a model didn't necessarily make you a bitch, supposed Hetty.

'Oh yes. If I hadn't met Jack when I did, God knows what would have happened to me.' Hetty, her sensitivities heightened by her own pain, saw a glimpse of real sadness in Caroline's eyes. Caroline smiled. 'I'll go first, if you like?'

'Of course, everyone knows you shouldn't stick around a man who hits you, but he was so *sexy*, and I liked the excitement. I did see sense in the end.' Caroline ended her confession with a voluptuous yawn. 'Your turn.'

Hetty had intended to give Caroline the expurgated version – expurgated of the pain, the desolation, the sense of abandonment, of how she felt like an outcast, unworthy of love. She had learnt, since it had happened, that people allowed you to tell them your problems only if you could be amusing about it. Weeks of practice with well-meaning old school-friends, her mother's cronies, and people she had worked with, had honed her story to a witty, well-polished little tale that left its hearers smiling their sympathy. Only her sister had been given an ungilded version.

But because Caroline had been so frank with her she found herself leaving out the jokes and allowing some of her hurt to show. She told Caroline how she, the junior secretary, assigned to the many who did not justify secretaries of their own, was lured into the bed of one of the senior management consultants.

It had started when his secretary was away. Asking her to help him rather than booking a temp ('Because my work is important and I don't want it done by some bimbo who's got her eye on the clock and her mind on her make-up.') was a huge imposition. She told him so but, having nursed a secret crush on him from the moment she started her employment, did the extra work anyway. He invited her out to lunch as a thank-you for her 'efficient and intelligent assistance' when his own secretary got back. Then he had to visit a client at short notice and, rather than cancel completely, persuaded her to make it dinner. So blinded was she by frustrated lust, and his elegant compliments, she didn't think to query why he hadn't just suggested taking a rain check and making lunch another day.

'Of course, it was awfully flattering,' Hetty went on. 'And when he suggested spending the weekend at his cottage sometime, I knew what he was asking, and I was *glad*. I went on the pill straight away.'

'Were you a virgin?'

She nodded. 'The last one left in England, I daresay. Someone should have put a preservation order on me.'

'Did you tell him?'

'I felt I had to. He was bound to have noticed.'

'Was he nice about it? He didn't laugh?'

'Oh no. He told me there was no such thing as a frigid woman, only a bad lover.'

Caroline did laugh. 'How *wonderful!* Anyone who can say a thing like that, in all seriousness, has to be a number-one toe-rag.'

Hetty nodded.

'And was he a good lover?'

'Oh yes, I think so. Terribly imaginative, always doing things to my feet.'

'You don't sound terribly convinced.'

'It was fine, really.'

Caroline's eyebrows gave a disbelieving flick, but she didn't press the point. 'So you miss the sex?' she asked instead.

Hetty shook her head. 'No, not really. Not the sex part anyway. That never really worked for me, but I miss the cuddling, the closeness.'

Caroline was silent for a moment. 'So what happened?'

Hetty looked at her fingers, which had clenched themselves round an empty fish-paste jar. 'I was to join him at his country cottage one weekend. He was in bed with another – older – woman. For some reason he thought that was the best way for me to find out it was all over.'

'Shit,' breathed Caroline. 'What did you do?'

'Well, I ripped his mother's antique-linen sheet completely in half, and then I dinged his car a few times.'

'Oh well done! Was he livid?'

'He was about the sheet. I bashed his car while he was getting dressed, and drove away before he knew about it.'

'At least you went out fighting.'

'Yes. Killed *my* car while I was about it, though.' Hetty sighed.

'Of course I could see his point. She was everything I'm not. Lean and sophisticated, and I'm plump and naïve.'

'There's nothing wrong with puppy-fat –'

'I'm well past adolescence, thank you. What I've got is dog-fat.'

Caroline seemed relieved that Hetty was making jokes. 'What I meant was, there's nothing wrong with a little roundness over the hips when you're still young . . .'

'And I'm not going on a diet for Bastard Alistair anyway.'

Caroline handed her the chocolate egg. 'Good for you. And you're better off without him. Aren't you?' she asked.

Hetty shrugged and tried to agree, rolling the egg in her hands.

'I can see I'm going to have my work cut out with you,' said Caroline. 'But I'll have you a raging feminist with a man begging to walk over broken glass for you before you know it.'

'Does Jack do that for you?'

'Well, no, but I'm desperately in love with him, so he doesn't have to. Now, what are you going to do about a car?'

'My mother will get round to organizing one eventually, but I can easily walk to the shop.'

'Nonsense, you need a car, living in a great barn of a place like this.'

'It's not that big,' Hetty assured her. 'Less than a mile between the kitchen and the sitting room.'

Caroline frowned at her. 'I meant, it's stuck out on its own. You need to be able to get about. Why don't you let Jack look out for one for you?'

'I couldn't possibly –'

'Yes you could. He collects cars like other people collect stray cats. Can't bear to think of them left unbought on the forecourt. Do let him. He'll be home soon, and it'll be such a treat for him.'

'Well, as long as it's cheap.' Jack's stray cars might be pedigrees.

'It will be, I promise you.' She glanced at her Cartier watch and got to her feet. 'Damn! I haven't time to see the house. If I don't go now I'll miss my cleaning lady, and I haven't paid her for weeks, poor dear.' She gathered up her outsize leather shoulder-bag. 'But I'm going to find you someone else,' she warned, 'who'll make you forget all about this Alistair person.'

'Oh, please don't!'

Caroline laughed. 'Well, I won't if you really don't want me to, and let's face it, talent round here is pretty scarce. But really, the best way to get over a man is to find another one. You know what they say about falling off horses and getting straight back on.'

'Find me a horse and I'll try my best,' said Hetty, fixing her new friend firmly in the eye.

'I really must go,' said Caroline, chuckling. 'It's been super meeting you. I'll be back, and next time I'll bring lunch. Have you got a microwave?'

'No. My mother and I looked last night.'

'I'll bring you our old one,' said Caroline. 'I've got one now that talks to you.'

'That's really awfully kind –'

'Not at all. It's only cluttering up the place. Mark Twain said there's no such thing as an unselfish act. If you let me rescue you, you'll be doing the neighbourhood a service. Not to mention Jack.'

Alone again, Hetty felt exhausted but exhilarated. Caroline was fun, and while it was unlikely she could actually cure a broken heart she could bring one a little light relief.

Hetty went through to the front of the house and found a pile of mail on the doormat. Remembering Samuel's instructions to open his post, she put the phone bill on one side, for immediate payment, and sorted the rest. Some of it went straight into the bin, the rest in a neat pile.

She drew a breath before opening the first one, she was Samuel's house-sitter, not his secretary, and 'Private and Confidential' usually meant just that. But, as agreed, she found a knife and opened it.

Any letter from any bank made Hetty's stomach churn a bit. This one, from a private finance house, would have made a hardened embezzler reach for the Rémegel. Samuel had obviously taken out a huge loan.

We note that your monthly payment is overdue. May we politely remind you that should your payments be late, the financial penalties stated in your agreement will be enforced. There followed a bewildering calculation, involving A P R rates, percentages and deductions, which ended in a horrifying amount. Surely Samuel couldn't have been paying this amount every month?

She rummaged through her bag for the amount the lawyer had jotted on a piece of paper for her, which was the balance in Samuel's bank account. She realized she had about enough for three payments. Three months' supply of extortion money. But was it just interest, or was it paying off the capital as well? She would have to find out. But whichever it was she had enough to keep the moneylenders at bay for a short time, but no money for anything else.

What she would have to do was visit the bank and explain the problem. Samuel probably had another account, and she could ask them to release some funds for day-to-day expenses into the account she was authorized to use. Or something. Really, if she'd known what a responsibility it was going to be, she'd have left Courtbridge House to its own devices.

Hetty had washed up the mugs, and was debating whether to penetrate the rest of the house, or pack up her nightie and leave, when there was a knock on the back door.

Who could that be? she wondered, feeling besieged. With her luck it would be someone selling something, patio doors or – here she was forced to smile – house insurance. She wanted it to be Caroline, come back for her tour of the house.

On the doorstep was a man – tall, broad-shouldered but slim. Not exactly handsome, but kindly, with dark eyes, eyebrows and eyelashes, and a lot of dark hair. He wore a huge Aran sweater, faded jeans, and Timberland boots.

Before he even had time to say hello, two small brown dogs pulled their leads free of his grasp and shot into the house. Hetty and the man followed them to the door of the sitting room, which they scratched at urgently. Hetty opened it hurriedly and both dogs leapt on to the sofa and started digging in it, woofing delightedly as they tossed cushions on to the floor with their back legs. A moment or two later they flopped down contentedly and wagged their tails, panting happily and grinning at Hetty and the man.

'Do your dogs always do that?' Hetty asked in wonderment.

The man laughed. 'No, never. But these aren't my dogs, they're yours. Or rather Samuel's.'

'Oh my God,' breathed Hetty.

'I'm Peter Lassiter. I live the other side of what used to be the

26

estate, beyond the wood. I've been looking after Samuel's dogs for him. When I heard you were here on your own, I thought you might like them.' He hesitated, observing Hetty's confusion. 'If you don't want them, I can easily take them away again.'

'No,' said Hetty. 'Don't do that. I'll be glad of their company, but I know more about cats.'

'These've got minds of their own, but fortunately they mean well and don't chase poultry or anything embarrassing.'

'What sort of dogs are they?'

Peter Lassiter regarded Hetty gravely. 'Small brown ones.'

Against her will, Hetty smiled. 'I see. What are their names?'

'Talisker and Islay. After Samuel's favourite single malts.'

'Ah.'

'Well, that's me and the dogs introduced . . .'

Hetty took the hint. 'Oh, sorry. I'm Hetty Longden.' She flapped her hand vaguely, not sure if she should offer it or not.

He took it anyway. His was large, warm and calloused, enormously comforting. 'Hello.'

Hetty smiled. He was nice, this man. And while she was far too bruised to dream of seeing him as anything but a friend, Caroline would no doubt see him as a horse to get back on to after her fall.

'Would you like some coffee or tea or anything?'

'I would,' said Peter. 'Very much.'

'I'll go and make it,' said Hetty.

'Would you like me to get the fire going while you do that?' asked Peter. 'The house gets dreadfully damp if you don't light fires every day in winter – up until early summer, really.'

'I'd noticed. And I'd be very grateful if you'd light it. We have central heating at home and I wasn't ever a Girl Guide – or even a Brownie, come to that.'

He laughed sympathetically. 'I'm sure Caroline could teach you how to light fires with dried orange peel. She's the local Brown Owl.'

Hetty, her hand on the kitchen door, turned round abruptly. 'Not the Caroline I've met? Blonde, terribly glamorous, drives a sports car?'

He nodded. 'The very same. You should see her in her uniform – black tights, skirt six inches above the knee. She gets a lot of support from the fathers at Brownie events. Particularly if they involve running.'

Hetty found herself smiling. 'I'll bet.' A hideous thought suddenly occurred to her. 'Did she send you round?'

'No, I haven't seen her this morning. They told me in the shop you were here,' he repeated.

Hetty forgot her manners. 'And did they tell you I was suffering from a broken heart?'

'No. Are you?' His heavy eyebrows rose in sympathetic inquiry.

Hetty could have kicked herself. The one person her mother hadn't actually told, and she went and told him herself. She nodded. 'And foot-in-mouth disease.'

'Why don't you make the coffee and I'll get the fire going? I promise I won't ask a single awkward question.'

She dried the mugs and made coffee, carrying it, with a packet of ginger nuts, into the sitting room. The dogs, Talisker and Islay, were curled up on the sofa. Peter was crouching in front of the fire, which was already roaring, adding lumps of coal. He'd drawn back the curtains and Hetty looked around. The room, brightened by the fire and the daylight, looked a lot better than it had the night before, when she and her mother had peeped in and, put off by the smell of damp, retreated.

'There's a lot of dry wood in the shed,' Peter said as she entered. 'And plenty of kindling. Have you found it?'

'I haven't found anything.' She could only just find space among copies of *Horse and Hound* and *The Field* on an occasional table for the tray. 'We got here quite late yesterday, and I haven't had a chance to explore yet.'

'I'll give you a guided tour if you like. I'm a friend of your uncle's. I used to chop wood and things for him.' He took the offered mug but declined the packet of sugar and the teaspoon.

He seemed quite content to drink his coffee and watch the flames in silence, but Hetty was too much her mother's daughter not to need to make conversation with people she didn't know well.

'So, what do you do?' Not a very imaginative opening, but it was the best she could do. It would be just her luck if he turned out to be unemployed and go all depressed on her.

'I'm a cabinet-maker, wood-turner, bodger, forester, whatever.'

He smiled a kindly, heart-warming smile, not looking at all depressed. 'I make most money doing fitted kitchens. I live behind the stable yard, across the big field. There's a spinney. Do you know where I mean?'

'Erm – not really.'

'It was one of the lodges for the house. Your uncle used to let me use the old smithy as a workshop. I did odd jobs around the place for him in return.'

'Oh. But you don't use it any more?'

He shook his head. 'No. I've got my own purpose-built workshop now. But I carried on doing the jobs after I got it.'

'That was very kind.'

'Not really. I liked – like him.'

Hetty struggled with the thought of Alistair doing odd jobs for an old man because he liked him, but couldn't make the leap of imagination. 'It's still kind.'

'I'm very glad you came to house-sit. I didn't know what relations Samuel had and I was starting to worry about the house.'

If this was a round-about way of asking Hetty for her credentials, Hetty wasn't offended. He had a right to know. 'I'm hardly a relation at all. Samuel's some connection of my mother's, but although she told me how exactly I wasn't concentrating. Some cousin a few dozen times removed, I think.'

'But there's a nephew?'

Hetty nodded. 'Another sort of far-off cousin, actually, but Mum couldn't get in touch with him. She tried terribly hard, but he's somewhere unpronounceable in Russia, or somewhere.'

'So you got lumbered?'

'It's not that, exactly. But I was . . . at a loose end, available.'

'It must be a huge shock for you. Or do your parents have a house like this?'

Hetty shook her head. 'A four-bedroom bungalow overlooking a golf course. I was only living with them temporarily . . .' She faltered and went off in a different direction. 'So, do tell me about the house. If I've got to live here, I'll need to know as much as possible.'

He hesitated as if wondering how much to say. 'You're only here until Samuel's back, aren't you? It might only be for a month or so.'

'Well, for Samuel's sake I hope so. But at his age, he might take a while to recover.'

'I know, but . . . just living here could be problematic enough. You know it's open to the public?'

Hetty nodded. 'At Easter.'

'And Easter's early this year.'

'I know that too.' She smiled inquiringly. 'There's nothing important about the house I ought to know, is there? It's not haunted, is it?'

'I really don't think it's haunted.' Peter sounded very down-to-earth and reassuring on this point at least. 'And Samuel had the roof done last year, or most of it anyway . . .'

'So, what is it?'

Peter sighed and stretched his long legs towards the now blazing fire. 'Did you know that this nephew – or cousin – plans to turn the house into a theme park?'

'Mrs Hempstead mentioned something in the shop.'

'It would be the most terrible desecration.'

Hetty didn't like to contradict him, and she had her share of interest in history and heritage, but given the state of the house the idea of turning it into a theme park might have its good points. 'It would bring a lot of jobs into the area.'

'Not the right sort of jobs! It would employ hundreds of teen-agers, about two of whom would be local. But there'd be no jobs for anyone else – craftsmen, tradesmen, housewives,' he added.

'Are you sure?'

'Yes! Connor Barrabin – Samuel's heir – known locally as Conan the Barbarian, for obvious reasons, stands to make an absolute packet, while the village gains nothing.'

'How do you know that's what he wants to do? Did he tell you?'

Peter shook his head. 'I've never actually met him. He's been working abroad lately, and his visits to Samuel never seem to coincide with mine. Can't help wondering if that was just coinci-dence. Anyway, Samuel told me his nephew felt the house should be turned into a theme park. Samuel had been approached by developers you see, and he consulted this nephew, who said he should go ahead.'

'Oh. But Samuel didn't – doesn't agree?'

'Oh no. He loves the place. He wouldn't have bothered having the roof done if he didn't.'

'It would be sad to see it as a theme park. I remember coming here as a child for a wedding. I was a bridesmaid. It reminded me of the pictures in "Beauty and the Beast".' She paused. 'And that was then. It's gone badly downhill since.'

'You can't blame Samuel.' Peter obviously thought she had been. 'It costs a bomb to keep up.'

'Perhaps that's why his nephew thinks it should be sold.'

Peter shuddered. 'I very much doubt it. He just wants to make a packet out of the place, never mind what Samuel wants.'

'But presumably he won't have much say in the matter until he actually inherits?'

Peter shook his head. 'Samuel seems to respect his opinion. And recently he's been coming to visit a lot more. Checking out his inheritance no doubt.'

'Or keeping an eye on his elderly relative?'

Peter's expression softened. 'You have a less cynical attitude than I have, and you may be right. But somehow . . .'

He didn't finish his sentence, so Hetty couldn't grill him further as to why he was so convinced Samuel's nephew, whom she would now always think of as Conan the Barbarian, was a Philistine, out to make a fast buck from his heritage. She sighed and, remembering the loan repayments, thought the missing nephew probably had justification for feeling as he apparently did.

'I shouldn't have burdened you with all that,' said Peter. 'There's nothing you can do. I don't suppose you can even open the house on your own.' But his eyes were giving quite another message. They said clearly, 'Please contradict everything I've just said.'

He's got nice eyes, she thought. I would like to tell them what they want to hear. 'Oh, I'll certainly do my best to open. After all, it may be for the last time.'

He looked at her very intently and took hold of her hands. 'It's hard for you to understand, but this house, restored and running as a proper tourist attraction, could be the saving of this village.'

Hetty stifled a sigh. Peter obviously didn't have the full picture. He didn't know about the loan sharks. Lovely though the house was, it might indeed be better for Samuel if he were to get rid of it and live on the money in peace.

'I haven't been here long enough to know what I can do, or what is for the best. But I promise I won't abandon the house' – she would have crossed her fingers if he hadn't been holding them – 'without telling you first.'

CHAPTER THREE

'I feel terrible leaving you,' said Peter. 'But, if you're sure. You won't hesitate to phone?'

Unable to break it to him that the phone had been cut off, Hetty, glad now to be able to cross her fingers, obliged. 'Even if it's three o'clock in the morning.'

He chuckled. 'Well, if it's that time it had better be burglars, or at the very least a rat. But you'll be all right for firewood for a few days anyway. And you've got the dogs for company.'

'Yes.' Right now, Hetty craved solitude. With her luck the dogs would turn out to have the gift of speech. 'I really will be fine.'

'If I didn't have so much work on, I wouldn't go.'

'There's really no need for you to be worried about me. I'm a big girl now.'

He would have continued to argue, only she pushed him firmly towards the back door, saving her sigh of relief for when he finally drove away.

He left her with some ancient rugs, which in theory the dogs slept on, their leads, a bag of dog food and a couple of dog bowls. He also gave her a lot of instructions about how to light a fire and persuade it to stay alight all night.

Alone at last, Hetty went back to the sitting room to reread the letter from the loan company, cursing herself for not thinking of asking Peter for a lift into town so she could go to the bank. He'd been so eager to help.

If only she'd actually read the bus timetable instead of just noting how few of them there were. If only she had a car. If only she hadn't let herself be talked into coming to a house that needed not so much a sitter as a financial wizard – something she'd have found difficult at the best of times.

But, she told herself firmly, a broken heart wasn't a good enough excuse for wimping out – not like a broken leg would have been.

And if she had to face an unknown bank manager in an unknown town and explain her distant relation's complicated financial arrangements, she might as well get on and arrange to do it. It would be a baptism of fire. It would be good for her. She decided to take Islay and Talisker – moral support as far as the bus timetable.

'Well, you two,' she said bracingly to them. 'How about a little walk?' Recognizing the word, the dogs leapt off the sofa and sprung about like wind-up toys until she produced their leads. Then they sat stock still, ears pricked, eyes intelligently expectant while she slipped them over their heads. 'You do that part very well, I must say,' she said, praising them extravagantly as per Peter's instructions. 'I just hope you're as good at walking to heel. I don't want everyone to see how little I know about dogs. I bet Mrs Hempstead is an expert on them, as well as on minor stately homes.'

Out of loyalty, or maybe just good manners, the dogs trotted quietly enough along the road, if not at her heels then at least not pulling a couple of paces in front. She found their presence surprisingly supportive. No one would stare at her wondering why she was alone if she had dogs to walk.

The bus timetable was depressingly clear. There were no buses until the end of the week, and Hetty didn't feel she could wait that long. Not wanting to go home without having furthered her end in some way, she tied the dogs to a conveniently placed rail and went into the shop. She bought a packet of biscuits and boldly asked Angela Brewster the best way of getting into town without a car when there were no buses. 'I thought there might be a local taxi firm or something?'

Angela nodded. 'There is. But why don't you ask Phyllis Hempstead? She'd love to help, and I know she goes to town on Tuesdays. It's market day. She gets her organic veg there.' Angela's expression became speculative. 'I must go and see the woman who runs it. If we had really good organic veg . . . Oh, sorry. Yes, why don't you ask Phyllis for a lift?'

Hetty demurred. She'd far rather spend a fortune on a taxi than ask favours from someone she'd only met briefly.

Angela brushed aside her objections. 'Nonsense. Mrs Hempstead would never forgive me if I let you get a taxi when I know

34

she'll be going to town.' Angela made a face. 'Apart from anything else, it's so un-green.'

Feeling like a child packed off to the village miser to ask for alms, Hetty changed the biscuits for a packet of chocolate-and-hazelnut ones, which Angela promised were Mrs Hempstead's favourite.

'She seems a bit of a dragon, but she's got a heart of gold when you get to know her,' Angela told Hetty, handing her a hastily drawn map.

Not much reassured, Hetty left, clutching the map and the biscuits like lucky charms.

Mrs Hempstead lived in a stone cottage, with a stone-tiled roof. A perfect period piece, surrounded by what would be a perfect cottage garden, come spring. Hetty felt slightly sick as she knocked on the door. Supposing Mrs Hempstead hated dogs? Supposing they jumped on her sofa, as they had on Samuel's? Why had she brought them? Why had she come at all? She knocked on the door and stood well back on the garden path, giving herself a head start should she need to make a run for it.

Mrs Hempstead looked at her blankly for a few seconds after she opened the door. 'The girl from Courtbridge House?'

Hetty nodded.

'Hello! I see you've got the dogs.'

'Yes. They seem very good.' She hung on tightly to their leads. 'But I don't know which is which.'

'The dog is Talisker, and the bitch Islay,' said Mrs Hempstead, unable not to sound patronizing, although she tried.

'I had worked that out. It's knowing which one is which. They both –'

Mrs Hempstead snorted, interrupting Hetty. 'Oh, simple, the dog'll cock its leg and the bitch'll squat.'

At that moment one of the dogs obligingly lifted its leg against a lavender bush, and the other immediately followed suit, exactly copying its sibling. No wonder they say dogs are loyal, thought Hetty, seeing them repeat what they had done at intervals all the way from the house.

'Ah,' said Mrs Hempstead, not approving of this display of gender-bending. 'I suppose they've been together all their lives and Islay's picked that up from Talisker.'

'So there's no other way of telling?'

Mrs Hempstead regarded her sternly. 'Look underneath.'

'Oh,' said Hetty quickly, before Mrs Hempstead could tell her what to look for. 'I didn't think of that.' In fact, she had, but it seemed a rather intimate way to behave with creatures she'd only just met.

'Well, come along in then. Don't stand out there. And let the dogs go. They'll be all right. They know the house well.'

Hetty released her companions somewhat reluctantly. At that moment a black Labrador appeared and, after giving Islay and Talisker a cursory sniff, took hold of Hetty's sleeve and led her into the house. It was a kindly, welcoming gesture, which Hetty much appreciated.

'I brought you some biscuits,' she said, offering them.

Mrs Hempstead eyed them warily, as if aware she was being softened up. 'No need to do that, dear. But thank you anyway. Come into the kitchen where it's warm.'

Hetty's dogs instantly settled themselves in front of Mrs Hempstead's battered Aga and Hetty seated herself at the kitchen table, drawn there by the dog. It was only then that the dog released her.

'Now,' said Mrs Hempstead, 'what's the problem?'

'I need to go into town tomorrow. I asked Mrs Brewster at the shop about taxis, but she said you always – she insisted –'

'You mean, she said I'd give you lift? Of course I will. I always go into town on Tuesdays. It's market day. I get my organic veg from there.'

'That's what Mrs Brewster said.'

'Sensible woman, Angela Brewster. Turned the shop around. Dead on its feet, it was, after the school closed. If you have to take your child to school by car it's as easy to carry on to town to the supermarket for your groceries. But it doesn't take account of the people who haven't got cars.' Mrs Hempstead drew breath. 'Sorry. Hobby-horse of mine, rural decline. That's why the house, Courtbridge House, is so important.'

Mrs Hempstead opened a cupboard. From it she produced a wine bottle with the sort of sinister white label, scrawled with the word *Damson*, that indicated the contents were Home Made. 'Little something to keep out the cold? Glad of a chance to have a good talk.' She filled two sherry glasses with viscous purple liquid. 'Here's to a good visitor season.' Hetty sipped dubiously. It was surprisingly pleasant, strong and sweet, and only faintly reminiscent of cough mixture. 'That house could be a little gold mine,' said Mrs Hempstead. 'If we can only keep it out of the hands of that nephew.'

Wondering how on earth they could do that when he was Samuel's legal heir, Hetty said, 'Tell me about him. Peter said something about him wanting to turn the house into a theme park.'

Mrs Hempstead nodded. 'There was a planning application in the paper. We all wrote and protested, and the plan was refused. But it told us how he was thinking.'

'But if the plan was refused –'

'Only the first shot across our bows, I'm afraid. He'll apply again, for sure. His type always do.' Hetty badly wanted to ask her hostess if she'd met him but, even aided by damson wine, she lacked the nerve. 'So, why do you want to go to town? Our village shop is excellent, you know. And you should always shop locally if you can.'

Hetty did know – so many people had told her. 'I need to go to the bank.'

'Ah. Have to go to town for that.'

Having arranged to be collected at eight-thirty sharp the following morning, Hetty weaved her way home, and drank a couple of glasses of water to counter the effects of damson wine on an empty stomach. She then made a sandwich and, with it, a decision: she would thoroughly explore the house and make up her own mind about whose side she was on, that of Peter and Mrs Hempstead, and, according to them, most of the village; or the wicked nephew, a.k.a. Conan the Barbarian.

She decided to do the outside first, and made her way through the maze of still rooms, game larders and pantries, all long unused and full of junk, to the yard at the back of the house.

A huge horse chestnut spread its branches to brush against the roofs and guttering of the buildings that surrounded it. An ancient coach-house butted against a magnificent arch, high enough for a coach and horses to drive through. A few wisps of old man's beard sprouted from the top like forgotten Christmas decorations.

She wandered across to a row of farm buildings and found them, like the spare rooms in the house, full of junk. But the stables were almost empty, and seemed completely unaltered from the days when the house would have kept several pairs of horses for driving and riding, and more draft horses for working the land. There were even wisps of hay in the mangers.

It was sad to see them so empty when once they must have been constantly busy, noisy with the sound of hooves on cobbles. There was even a name still visible above one of the doors. She traced it with her finger. FESTE. Nostalgia swept over her, a longing for a past she could never have known. She was just about to slump into tearfulness when one of the dogs butted her in the back of the leg with its nose. She started, remembering that she was supposed to be clinically assessing whether she thought the house should be preserved, or become a theme park; a plastic, sanitized version of itself. Feeling unable to make an unbiased decision, she went back into the house, where the decay was less attractive.

The kitchen was now quite warm, but it was far from cosy. Now that the daylight was beginning to go, the single bulb that dangled from the ceiling threw shadows into every corner. Her feelings of romantic melancholy threatened to become mundane depression. She slid the kettle on to the hot part of the stove before continuing her tour. The kitchen did not further the cause of the conservationists.

The great hall was a dim, echoing shadow of the room she remembered from her childhood. Cobwebs draped the tops of dusty tapestries and the wall sconces created more shadows than they shed light. The tall windows were overgrown with ivy, and if it hadn't been for the dogs frisking and sniffing, unconcerned by their surroundings, Hetty would have sworn the room was haunted. Perhaps it was, haunted by the laughter and music that had filled it all those years ago. But not, apparently, since.

She didn't explore the other ground-floor rooms. They were gloomy, full of furniture, and needed sunshine. Sunshine being unavailable, she hurried back to the sitting room where the fire crackled enthusiastically, and lit the candles that stood in the tarnished silver candlesticks. The room seemed cosy now, the china in the shelved alcoves reflecting the dancing light of flames.

The house was impossible, she decided. It was in bad order, too large for a home, too small for anything else. It would cost thousands to put in order. Even new curtains (the present ones had torn the moment she tried to draw them) would be impossibly expensive. Why Samuel had bothered to repair the roof when it was quite obvious the place was about to come to the end of its natural life, she couldn't imagine. But nor could she think of the place as a theme park.

It was no good – logic had failed, romance had won. She wanted to preserve the house at all costs. It was foolish, quixotic, ridiculous perhaps, but she felt she had to protect this gracious, dilapidated old house against the ravages of common sense, practicality and progress. Then, remembering the letter on thick, embossed cream paper, she recalled how great the costs were likely to be, and went back into the kitchen to make herself some tea.

In the kitchen there was a sort of background roaring from the stove, which quite likely meant it was beavering away heating hot water for her. She could have a nice hot bath. But the thought of taking all her clothes off in a strange, spooky, probably spidery, bathroom was too unnerving. She could do that tomorrow when, no doubt, she'd feel better.

What Hetty was really dreading was sleeping in the house on her own. She'd never liked sleeping alone in any house, mostly because she'd hardly ever done it. And Courtbridge House was a very different prospect from a bungalow overlooking a golf course.

Her mother had no notion of her daughter's fears. It wasn't something Hetty had liked to mention, it sounded so pathetic. And she'd been pathetic enough since Alistair. Cursing herself silently for being neurotic, she took her cup of tea into the sitting room.

The fire was going well and, in spite of dark, unexplored areas, the table lamps made the room more welcoming than the kitchen, and it felt safer. It could have been a lovely room, given a good spring-clean and some judicious decorating. It had, according to the guide book, which Hetty had picked up from the hall table, been decorated in the early eighteenth century with panelling, wainscots, dado rails and cornices. Two arched niches either side of the fireplace had beautifully carved tops, like shells. Within them, on curved shelves, was a collection of china which might have been very fine indeed if dusted. The ceiling was decorated with elaborate plasterwork.

Hetty noticed that although this room was described, sparingly, in the guide book, it was not, according to the same book, open to the public. Probably, she thought somewhat critically, because Samuel hadn't wanted to go to the trouble of tidying it.

Hetty noticed that the panels were painted in shades of pale grey – either that or the paint was extremely dirty. If it was dirt and not paint, would it be necessary to redecorate in order to open the room to the public? Or would a good scrub do? And if not, could she use ordinary emulsion, or would she have to track down some specially aristocratic paint, deemed fit by those who knew about important country houses? She'd have to ask Mrs Hempstead.

Hetty winced. She had once decorated her bedroom at home without moving even her homework. Mrs Hempstead, without doubt, would be a wash-down-with-sugar-soap, sand-down-with-fine-glass-paper, it's-all-in-the-preparation sort of decorator. Fortunately, Hetty hadn't come there to redecorate, merely be there. Someone else could argue the virtues of paint-stripper versus hot-air blowers, and the best way of 'antiquing' new paint.

She felt tired at the thought, probably because she was tired. But she couldn't go to bed until she had decided where. Should she sleep where she slept last night? Or where her mother had slept, a slightly grander bedroom, with a four-poster bed and a marble wash-stand? Samuel's bedroom had merely been peeped into and then rejected. It had smelt of strange ointments and old books. It was the sort of room that should be faced with a can of air freshener and a good friend, in bright sunlight.

She was comparing rocks and hard places, when the dogs came up and shoved her with their noses. Horrified, she realized she'd forgotten to feed them and Clovis, the ancient cat. She leapt up and went back to the kitchen.

That's what happens, she told herself firmly, measuring the amount of dog food specified into two bowls, when you become wrapped up in your own problems. You forget to feed the animals.

While the dogs pushed their bowls noisily round the flagged

floor, Hetty shook the woodlice out of a saucepan and made herself some scrambled eggs. It really was time she stopped being so feeble.

She settled down to eat her supper in the sitting room, and had shared her toast crusts with the dogs before she remembered that she wasn't supposed to. 'Oh well,' she said, feeling more relaxed after a few sips of Old Sack, 'I don't suppose you'll tell anyone.'

Seeing the dogs so cosily ensconced in front of the fire she thought of the vast, echoey upstairs that she had to penetrate before deciding which bedroom was the least terrifying. Then it came to her. She would fetch her bedding, bring it down, and join the dogs in front of the fire.

The following morning, Hetty awoke early, disturbed by the shufflings and scratchings of her cohabitees, and anxious about what the day would bring. The sofa was not sufficiently comfortable to linger on anyway, so it was no hardship to get up, although it was barely six o'clock.

She let the dogs out into the yard, filled the kettle, and tried to feel as if she really belonged to the house, and was not, in spite of her bed on the sofa, merely camping in it. But it was hard to feel optimistic about Courtbridge just at the moment.

Mrs Hempstead arrived soon after eight. Hetty met her in the yard while she was watching the dogs catching up on the early morning smells, cocking their legs and snuffling up the dew.

'Good-morning. Sorry I'm a bit early. Being a lark myself, I sometimes forget that others aren't so fortunate.'

Mrs Hempstead talked long and hard throughout the journey, not giving Hetty a chance to think about what she was going to say, or even an opportunity to reassure Mrs Hempstead that on matters such as rural decay and community spirit they were on the same side.

In fact, if Mrs Hempstead hadn't drawn up outside a beautiful stone building, announcing that it was Samuel's bank, just when she did, Hetty might have switched her allegiance.

'I'll drop you here. Can't stop, double yellow lines.'

Grabbing her bag in the nick of time, Hetty found herself on the pavement, propelled towards the doors of the bank by the force of Mrs Hempstead's personality. Once inside its gracious portals, Hetty approached the inquiries desk, was directed to a seat, and had plenty of time both to plan her speech and to speculate as to whether the man she was waiting to see would be willing to discuss Samuel's private financial affairs with a girl in grubby jeans.

Not very, was her answer. In fact it took Hetty a good ten minutes to prove to the junior under-manager that she knew enough about Uncle Samuel's affairs for him to get out his file in her presence.

'So,' he said at last, after a lot of tapping into his computer terminal and sending for papers, 'what can I do for you?'

'I think my uncle might have got himself into financial difficulties.'

'Have I explained that I'm not able to discuss a client's private affairs with anyone, even a relative?'

He had, ad nauseam. 'But if I asked you questions, you could perhaps give me yes and no answers, in a hypothetical way?'

'Possibly.'

'Would it, hypothetically, be possible to reschedule a loan? If, for example, someone has borrowed money from a finance house' (she had a feeling that the junior under-manager wouldn't like the term 'loan shark') 'at rather a poor rate of interest. Could you, should they ask, give them a better deal?'

'It would depend on how healthy the account was. It would be unlikely if, hypothetically, the account already had a substantial overdraft, for example.'

Shocked out of her hypotheticals by the implications of this, Hetty became more specific. 'But the lawyer told me there was quite a lot of money in my uncle's account. I've got the amount written down. And anyway, I did you specimen signatures. I can write cheques for him for up to two thousand pounds after the weekend, when you've done the paperwork.'

The junior under-manager tapped in his terminal again. Then he shook his head. 'I've no record of any such arrangement.'

Hetty felt sweat trickle down her front and thought, irrelevantly, that she should have remembered to take off several sweaters before entering a centrally-heated building. 'But I've got a cheque-book. Look.'

He took the offered book. 'Wrong bank, Miss Longden.'

Hetty bit her lip, pleased at least that the colour which now flooded her face would hardly show given that she was already scarlet with heat. 'Oh, hell,' she murmured. 'I think perhaps I ought to go –'

'Not so fast,' said the junior under-manager, who watched a lot of films. 'Am I to understand that there is money available in this other account?'

'Now look,' said Hetty, 'you wouldn't discuss my uncle's business with me. I don't think *I* should discuss it with *you*.'

'Your uncle owes us a lot of money. If he has funds he has a duty to lower his overdraft.'

'Nonsense! You make loads of money out of his overdraft.'

'Only if he pays the interest.'

'Well, I'm only his house-sitter anyway.'

'But you can write cheques?'

'Only for household things. And not exceeding two thousand pounds a cheque.'

'Two thousand pounds is a lot of housekeeping. Or should that be house-sitting?'

'So?'

'Listen, Miss Longden, we have been very tolerant with your uncle, because of his age and infirmities. But should we discover that he hasn't been entirely honest with us we might become less tolerant.'

'That sounds like a threat.' Hetty had seen her fair share of movies too.

'It's not meant to.' He sighed. 'But I'm sure you understand. Banks aren't charitable institutions. We need our customers to pay money in as well as take it out.'

He looked tired, and Hetty suddenly felt sorry for him. 'Mmm,' she said, as sympathetically as she could.

'And the house insurance is due. If you could write me a cheque immediately, I would appreciate it.'

Hetty sighed. 'Lend me a pen. How much is it for?' He told her. 'I'll have to write two cheques.' With extreme reluctance she handed them over. 'Don't cash them until after the weekend.'

'Do you know that if the house is open to the public you have to have a Certificate of Public Liability?'

'Oh.' Hetty's voice was very husky.

'The insurance wouldn't be valid without it.' She got out a bit of dirty tissue. The heat had made her nose run. But the junior under-manager mistook her motive. 'That house could be a gold mine if it was properly promoted,' he said. 'I went there last summer with my partner. It's got real potential. All it needs is someone with a bit of energy.'

Hetty, who'd spent the night on the sofa, got wearily to her feet. 'Thank you,' she said, pushing away her chair. She had got as far as the door when he stopped her.

'About the Certificate of Public Liability. The insurance people will come round and check to see if the building's safe. It might be quite expensive to make the house fit for the paying public.' He looked sad, a little abashed. 'I'll try and warn you when he's coming.'

'Thank you.' Hetty got through the door with her self-possession barely intact.

CHAPTER FOUR

Hetty was so shell-shocked that she completely forgot where she was supposed to meet Mrs Hempstead. Luckily Mrs Hempstead found her wandering aimlessly through the town.

'There you are, dear,' she said, unaware of Hetty's disorientated state. 'Sorry I'm a bit late. I met an old friend. How did you get on?'

'Badly. It was the wrong bank.'

'Was it? Then that's my fault. I could have sworn that Samuel and I had the same one.'

'Oh, he did have an account there, just no money. I had to pay the house insurance. And if we're going to open to the public, we've got to have a Certificate of Public Liability.'

'Oh, dear.'

'They'll check to see if the building's safe.'

'Oh, God.'

'But the man from the bank will try and warn me.' A thought struck her. 'I'd better pay the phone bill while I'm here.'

Mrs Hempstead bore Hetty off to the sort of café that sold home-made cakes, a huge variety of teas, and played Vivaldi to its customers. While Hetty stood dithering at the counter, Mrs Hempstead ordered two slices of Scrumbumptious Chocolate Gateau, a *spécialité de la maison*, and a pot of Assam for two.

'Now, my dear,' she said when they were settled on rush chairs, their elbows supported by the scrubbed pine table, 'tell me all.'

Hetty told if not all then most of it. She left out the loan company, but confessed to Samuel's second bank account, in credit, and his huge overdraft. 'And then there's this wretched certificate.'

'Oh, Lord.' Mrs Hempstead dug her fork deep into a triple-layered cake intersected with butter-cream and melted chocolate. 'I don't suppose Samuel ever had one of those.'

'We will have to decide if it's all worth it.'

'What do you mean?'

'I mean, it might cost so much to get this certificate that we won't get the money back on the gate. I mean, how much did it make last year?'

Mrs Hempstead shrugged. 'Of course, Samuel never kept proper figures, but it was probably peanuts. Though if you're willing to open up more of the house, perhaps some of the out-buildings, we could up the entrance fees and would get more visitors. But you might consider that too much to take on. I'd do everything I can to help – in fact, I'm sure the whole village would back any attempt to save the house, but you would be the one bearing the responsibility.'

Hetty pressed her fork into a whorl of icing and watched chocolate ooze up between the prongs. It had been a long time since she had eaten a gooey cake in a tea-shop. Alistair had been too gourmet and sophisticated for such things, and, until she had come to Courtbridge House, had obsessed her every waking thought. It was such a relief to have something to think about that she could actually affect: no amount of longing would bring Alistair back to her. But Courtbridge House was something she could change.

'I think I might enjoy the challenge.'

Hetty was in the sitting room trying to decide whether or not it would have to be repainted when there was a knock on the back door.

It was Peter. The dogs, delighted to see him, flew across the room and jumped at his legs. Hetty, more restrained, gave him a big smile. 'Hello. How nice to see you. Can I get you a cup of tea or something?'

His smile was even broader. 'Tea would be lovely. I tried to ring to warn you I was coming, but I discovered the phone wasn't working. You should have told me.' He sounded reproachful.

'What could you have done about it? It's been cut off.'

'Lent you my mobile.'

Hetty was touched. 'I paid the bill today when Mrs Hempstead took me into town. It should be on again in a few days.'

'Good.' Peter regarded her seriously. 'I don't like to think of you alone here without a phone.'

She opened the biscuit tin and shoved it across the table towards him, suddenly keen to confide. He was kind, and very fond of Samuel and Courtbridge House. 'I went to see the bank.'

'Oh? Samuel's finances a bit rocky are they?'

She nodded. 'There's also something called a Certificate of Public Liability we've got to have before we open. To make sure it's safe for the public to come.'

'I'm sure Samuel didn't have one.'

'No, but we want to open much more of the house than he did. Make it earn its keep. You know yourself there's a lot here that would be fascinating to visitors.'

He nodded. 'But it might not be worth opening at all if you don't earn enough extra to cover the cost of whatever needs doing to qualify for this certificate.'

'I know. It's a risk, but I think we've got to take it. For Samuel's sake, really. But also for the house's. I mean, if it can't sustain itself it deserves to be turned into a theme park.'

Peter regarded her with thoughtful brown eyes. 'The market economy, eh? Red in tooth and claw.'

'That's about it.'

'I really don't think you should take it on, Hetty. It would be too much for you.'

Hetty smiled, her liking for Peter a little diminished. 'I need something to do. I can't just sit here, keeping away burglars, looking at the dirt.'

'You mustn't let Phyllis bully you about the house. She's expecting too much of you.'

Hetty shook her head. 'She's not expecting anything. *I* am.'

Hetty was up a ladder, applying an ancient feather-duster to a collection of cobwebs that were not so much fairy hammocks as fairy tenements, piled one on top of the other, when a strident ringing told her the phone had been put back on. She clambered down and answered it.

'Hello, Miss Longden? Mark Rhys-Jones, from the bank.'

'Oh yes.'

'I rang to tell you that our man from the insurance company

is planning to visit you the day after tomorrow. Will that be convenient?'

Hetty gulped. She'd only been in the house for three days and, although she'd worked hard, she hadn't made much impression on the grime. 'I suppose so.'

'What he'll worry about most are things like fire exits, doorways not being blocked, having enough fire extinguishers, and the wiring being up to scratch. So don't bother cleaning up.'

Hetty dropped her feather-duster. 'No.'

'I hope it goes well for you. I really would like to see the house in order.'

'Enough to let me have some money for improvements?'

'I'm afraid that wouldn't be up to me. And even if it was, frankly, I'd have to say no. The house would have to be very much a going concern for us to be able to consider anything like that.'

'Oh well. Thanks for the warning.'

In spite of her brave declaration to Peter, Hetty suddenly felt nervous. She took a deep breath and remembered Mrs Hempstead's promise of support. A search in the region of Uncle Samuel's phone revealed a card with phone numbers written on it. Thanking God that she'd remembered Peter referring to Mrs Hempstead as Phyllis, she dialled the number and was told not to panic, and that she, Mrs Hempstead, would be round as soon as she could, and would definitely be there when the man came.

Still needing moral back-up, she rang Peter. He was out, and unfortunately Uncle Samuel didn't know Caroline.

Frustrated and tired, Hetty went into the kitchen and put the kettle on. Just as it boiled, like an angel from heaven, Caroline arrived.

'Hi! Is this a good moment for a guided tour?'

They talked as they walked, and while Caroline opened cupboards and exclaimed at the beauty of dusty bits of furniture, some so large they must have been built *in situ*, Hetty found herself telling Caroline that the house, while very romantic, was also deeply in debt. The whole story apart from the loan sharks came out, ending with the imminent visit from the man from the insurance company.

'Do you want me to be with you when he comes?' Caroline offered. 'For a bit of moral support?'

'No thank you, though it's sweet of you to offer, but Mrs Hempstead's coming.'

'And her support is more moral than mine. Point taken, sweetie.'

'It's not that –'

'I know. Only joking. I'll come into my own when you want people to do the work. We had so much done on our house I've got the names and numbers of practically every known trade. Most of them are Brownie dads, and they're all willing to knock bits off if you pay them in cash.'

'I haven't got any cash.'

'But you will have. If you do a bit of fund-raising.'

'We could never raise that kind of money.'

'Of course we could. Before we moved here I was always organizing events for the local hospice. Car-boot sales are the best fun. You could have one in the yard.'

'I think that's the last thing I could possibly take on just now.'

But three days later, after the man from the insurance company had pulled the house apart, figuratively and – in the case of the upstairs fuse-box, which he declared was ready to burst into flames at any moment – literally, she changed her mind.

After he'd gone, Mrs Hempstead collapsed on to the sofa while Hetty poured out the last of Samuel's sherry.

'It'll cost a fortune,' said Mrs Hempstead.

'Caroline said we should have a car-boot sale.'

Mrs Hempstead opened her eyes. 'You know, that's not a bad idea. We've got to do a lot of clearing out anyway. We might as well sell the junk and make money.'

'It just seems like such hard work.' Hetty had her eyes closed now.

'You know, this village is full of people wanting a good cause. After we fought off the motorway that was due to come right through the middle of the village. You must have heard about it? We were on the news several times.' Hetty murmured noncommittally. 'Well, after we'd won we were thrilled, of course, but we all felt a bit flat. Having to fight for our way of life was awful, but it did mobilize and motivate us.' Hetty resolved to start taking vitamin pills. 'And we've got to pay for all those fire extinguishers and that rewiring with something.'

'You know, Mrs Hempstead, Samuel has got a little money –'

Mrs Hempstead snorted. 'And a lot of things to spend it on, I'll be bound. If he didn't borrow money to have the roof done, I'm a Dutchman. And do call me Phyllis, dear.'

Phyllis regrouped her army of energetic women of a certain age, while Caroline assembled her pack of little girls under eleven; smaller, uniformed, and no less indomitable. Not an attic, cupboard-under-the-stairs or cellar was to go unsearched for saleable items.

'Everyone's always thrilled to have an excuse to get rid of all those unwanted presents in aid of a good cause,' Caroline said.

'Is it a good cause?' Hetty wondered. 'It's not the same as starving children, or dear little donkeys.'

'Of course it is. It's Heritage.' Caroline gave the word a capital letter. 'I'll get the girls to make posters, too.'

'Well, only if we give some of the money the Brownies raise to Brownie funds.'

'But what do we need it for?' Brown Owl argued, against her beloved troop.

'I don't know! Outings, new premises, a minibus, anything!'

Caroline sighed. 'If we want to go on an outing, I just ask Jack. He pays. Our premises have just been done up to the nines, and if we need a bus, Fred Lovings lends us one for half nothing. Really, we're a very well-off little group.'

'Well-off or not, it's good for children to raise money for their treats, not just be given things.'

'So how come you know so much about children all of a sudden?'

Hetty shrugged. 'I read it somewhere, I expect. But seriously, I'll be so glad of the Brownies' help. Don't make me feel bad about it.'

Caroline muttered something and committed her pack to making cakes for a tea-stall, which they would also run. 'The mummies can help. They'll love it. Everyone loves car-boot sales.'

Hetty gave in.

★

50

Mrs Hempstead, whom Hetty tried hard to call Phyllis, helped Hetty sort through Samuel's cupboards for junk. She knew what was precious and what wasn't, salving Hetty's uneasy conscience by insisting that the space was more useful than the china, most of which was chipped.

'He used to buy up sets of cups and saucers for when he gave garden parties in aid of the church. It's all rubbish really, but people will buy it if they think it comes from a stately home.'

'What's this hideous thing?' Hetty held a particularly garish vessel which could have been a vase or a container for one's loved one's ashes.

'Clarice Cliff. Worth a fortune. Put it in the pile we're taking to an antique dealer.'

'But Samuel might love it dearly. If it's valuable I don't think we should sell it.'

'A fire extinguisher's a lot more valuable to Samuel, believe me. And I know he doesn't like that piece, he told me.'

Hetty made a mental note to ask Caroline if she knew an antique dealer who wouldn't rip them off. By now, Hetty was convinced that the parents of Caroline's Brownie pack represented all the most useful professions. And if there wasn't an antique dealer among them, she'd eat a Brownie standard issue baseball cap.

The man who came to do the wiring was most obliging. His estimate was enormous, however. Partial rewiring, which was all Hetty felt they could afford (although the man from the bank would have preferred a complete job), would cost a few thousand pounds, and that was a reduced rate.

'I'll pay you the moment we've had our car-boot sale,' Hetty promised. And sold off a few heirlooms, she added silently.

'In cash?'

She nodded.

The electrician grinned at her.

It was a contact of his who could provide fire extinguishers at a cut rate. He too wanted to be paid in cash. Hetty couldn't afford to refuse his offer, but wondered if one car-boot sale and some antiques could possibly raise enough. She might have to dip into the loan money. Her fears, partially expressed to Caroline, were dismissed by her friend.

'Don't you worry. You've got a Brownie pack behind you, not to mention Mrs Hempstead.'

'And her army.'

Which proved formidable, but fun. Many of the women who came to the house offering help had memories of the place, either of their own or of their parents.

'My mother used to work in the dairy. Used to make wonderful butter and cream.'

'The dairy! Where's that?' asked Hetty. And, when she was shown, saw that it had been left completely untouched since it was last used, and would therefore only need a thorough clean and some redecorating to be made useable again.

'I don't suppose you know anything about dairying?' she asked the woman who'd shown it to her.

The woman laughed. 'Reckon I do. You get this place in order, I'll come and do demonstrations for you when you're open. I suggested it to the old boy, but he'd got rather depressed lately, and wasn't really interested.'

Hetty was just wondering if the whole thing had got totally out of hand when Caroline appeared. 'Hi darling! Sorry I haven't been around for a few days, Jack's back. He's got you a car.'

Hetty insisted on writing a cheque for the bright yellow 2CV instantly. No amount of protesting from Jack and Caroline could stop her.

'Don't worry, my mother will give me the money,' she said. 'She promised me a new car as a bribe for coming here. And so I could visit Samuel. It's just she's not as good at finding them as Jack is.'

Jack bowed in acknowledgement of this compliment.

Hetty's first act, now she was mobile, was to visit Samuel, who was not in good form. He was pleased to see Hetty, but didn't want to hear about the house, beyond the fact that preparations for opening were going well and that Hetty and Phyllis had become friends. Hetty got no hint of what he might have wanted to say to her in private when she had visited him with her mother. Perhaps he realized she must have found out by now.

In fact, a few days earlier, Hetty had received another communication from the moneylender.

It was addressed to her, the bank obviously having noted it was she who'd signed the last cheque. They were inquiring as to whether there was any problem regarding the loan, and reminding her of the penalties should the loan not be paid in full by the specified date. Unfortunately, they didn't give any details regarding either the penalties, or the date the loan was due to be paid, or whether she was paying interest only each month, or the capital as well. She wrote back a brisk letter requesting instant enlightenment. But another wrestle with the figures gave her hope that it was not just interest, unless Samuel had borrowed millions.

Clear skies and biting winds had swept away the remnants of winter, but hadn't yet replaced it with spring. The sun shone, lambs frolicked in the field next door, and violets and primroses peeped unexpectedly from the greenery that had burst forth almost overnight. But it was still icy cold.

Notwithstanding the temperature, Hetty was full of optimism for the success of the following day. There were six tables'-worth of bric-à-brac from the house and the Brownies – a good five hundred pounds' worth on Mrs Hempstead's reckoning.

Hand-painted posters, laminated by a Brownie father, lined the drive and had been stuck to every tree and post within ten miles. Hetty had put advertisements in the local papers, and Caroline had persuaded every licensed premises in the area to put up a poster. Caroline had even talked sweetly to the local police, persuading them that, as this was a one-off and they were not going to make a habit of having car-boot sales, any infringements of local by-laws that might occur would hardly be worth pursuing.

Hetty had been all for finding out what permission, if any, one should ask for, and of whom. Caroline was against it.

'If you know the regulations, you have to obey them. If you don't, you can plead ignorance.'

If Hetty had had less to organize, she would have protested that ignorance is no defence in law, but she still had to ask the farmer who grazed the two fields next to the house for his permission for them to be used; one for a car park, the other for cars with boots full of loot. Fortunately, it transpired he had most to lose if Conan the Barbarian's theme-park idea went ahead, so he was most co-operative.

Peter, whose help she needed to prepare the fields, was less so.

'If it's muddy, they'll all get stuck,' he protested, having been dragged off to survey the field by Hetty.

'It won't be muddy. It hasn't rained for days. And you could earn a few bob pulling them out with your Land Rover.'

Peter, feeling, justifiably, that the whole thing was a terrible gamble, refused to take part in the spirit of optimism shared by the rest of the village. But he did agree to take the money, and direct people into the car park. He also said he'd contact his friend from Somerset who made real cider. 'For you, Hetty. Not for this hare-brained scheme.'

Hetty rewarded him with a kiss on the cheek, which he would willingly have worked up into something more passionate given the chance, but she wasn't ready for Peter to change status. She needed him as a friend. Although she hardly thought about Alistair these days, the words 'boyfriend' or 'lover' rang alarm bells. She laughed when Caroline referred to Peter as her S N A G – Sensitive New Age Guy – but she wouldn't let his lips stray from the chastity of her cheek.

The night before the sale, convinced she'd never get to sleep, Hetty found a copy of *Pamela* by Samuel Richardson. Her plan was that either the print would be so small and the light so bad and the story so slow-moving that she would drop off. Or, if her eyes still refused to close, she would at least enhance her education. In fact, she was so tired she didn't get past the first page.

Unsure of how long she'd been asleep, but aware that it was pitch-dark outside, she slowly woke up. With great reluctance she allowed her brain to register an unfamiliar noise. It was faint, and sounded oddly like someone clashing pots and pans together. It must be some leftover junk blowing in the wind, she decided. And then listened again. There was no wind, and the noise was coming from inside the house, from the kitchen.

She would have to go and investigate. It was probably something perfectly innocent, like a window blowing open and a breeze playing on the pots and pans. The dogs, who were now sitting up, ears pricked, would protect her.

She disentangled herself from her bedding, picked up the poker, tiptoed down the passage, and very, very slowly, making as little noise as possible, opened the kitchen door.

CHAPTER FIVE

There was a man standing with his back to her. He had opened the fridge door and was staring into it. He was wearing corduroy trousers and a very hairy sweater, the sort of clothes that could see off Cape Horn without bother. The dogs, on seeing him, pushed past Hetty, ran up to him and jabbed their noses into the backs of his legs. He jumped, turned, saw Hetty, and made a sound like someone in a film who'd been shot, which he swiftly turned into a string of very bad language.

'Who the fucking hell are you?' he demanded hoarsely, after what seemed a long time.

Hetty pulled herself up, trying to feel dignified in her Damart pyjamas. 'More to the point,' she said stiffly, 'who are *you*?'

But she didn't need to ask. She knew who he was. He was Conan the Barbarian.

He was tall, wide and crumpled. His rugged features were screwed into a combination of extreme fatigue, irrascibility and irritation. He had the tough, roughened look of a man who could wear Shetland wool next to the skin and not itch.

More swearing followed Hetty's question and she observed how very badly she must have frightened him. 'Connor Barrabin,' he said, huskily. 'What the bloody hell are you doing here?'

'House-sitting,' said Hetty.

He gave a sort of grunt, which acknowledged the need for a house-sitter but didn't actually express enormous gratitude for her giving up her life to look after his inheritance, and turned back to the fridge. 'So who *are* you?' he rasped over his shoulder, bringing out Hetty's cheese and a couple of tomatoes.

'Hetty Longden. Marjorie Longden's daughter. You know? Who left you all those messages.'

He grunted again. It was easy to see how he'd got his nickname – it was his size, his limited vocabulary, and his extreme uncouthness. But then, it was two o'clock in the morning. 'Don't suppose you've got any whisky? Some in the car. Can't face getting it. Got some lurgy. Sore throat.'

It sounded sore. Hetty put down the poker. 'Samuel's got some. I'll get it. I've got lemon juice, too.' She hesitated for a moment. 'I could make you a hot toddy?' she added reluctantly; reluctant because Alistair had had a bad cold shortly before he'd abandoned her. The thought that he'd hung on to her until his cold was better – she made such good toddies – had crossed her mind.

Conan the Barbarian may have smiled. Or it could just have been a random rearrangement of the stubble-covered creases and folds that surrounded his mouth, though there was a glimpse of white, which was almost definitely a set of teeth. 'That would be great.'

Hetty went back into the sitting room to get the whisky, her mind racing. The car-boot sale was tomorrow. What should she do? Tell him about it? Let him find out? Spirit him away in a sack and not bring him back until after it was over?

Her reasonable self told her that she should tell him about it. After all, it wasn't illegal, and it was for a very good cause. But somehow she didn't think Conan the Barbarian was likely to be overjoyed at the thought of a car-boot sale going on in the grounds of his uncle's house, not when he'd just got home from the ends of the earth, and had a cold. But was it possible to have a car-boot sale secretly? She thought of the posters, the advertisements, the people, and decided it wasn't. But she still wasn't going to tell him about it, not tonight anyway. He might turn violent. She clutched the whisky bottle tightly and returned to the kitchen.

She sat him down at the other end of the table while she poured lemon juice, sugar, a lot of whisky and a splash of water into a pan. While that was heating, she boiled the kettle. Could she make it strong enough to knock him out for twenty-four hours? Or even twelve?

'Things seem different,' he croaked, peering around him, his thick hair obscuring his view somewhat. 'Less cluttered. Have you put some stuff away?'

Hetty gulped, thinking of the boxes and boxes that she and Phyllis had sorted for the sale. 'Sort of.' She stirred the contents of the pan to check if the sugar was dissolved.

He grunted again.

Hetty tested the toddy and added a splash more lemon juice and a splash of boiling water. When she was sure it was very nearly boiling, she poured it into a mug. Her mother complained that making them as hot as she did killed all the vitamin C. Hetty claimed that hot toddies did nothing to cure your cold, they just made you feel better. If you wanted vitamin C, you should take pills. She handed Connor his brimming mug and sat down to watch him drink it.

His first sip caused a lot more facial action. Hetty could almost feel the toddy searing its way down, like molten lava. Then he made the same sort of satisfied groan that Alistair had made when he was content. Something else about him reminded her of Alistair, though it wasn't easy to see what it was. He was much more coarsely made, larger, not at all handsome, and, at the moment, extremely unkempt. But he had all of Alistair's arrogance. Hetty forced herself to remember that he was in pain, had probably been travelling for hours, and that she ought to refrain from hitting him with the poker. She didn't want to antagonize him.

'Have you come from far?' she asked, after several scalding sips had had time to do their work.

'Turkmenistan.'

Hetty was none the wiser. 'Oh. My mother tried hard to contact you.'

He nodded. 'Why I'm here.'

'I've been here four weeks.'

'Good for you.'

'I mean,' said Hetty, annoyed, 'you didn't come immediately.'

'No.'

'Well, why not?' Hetty was quite prepared to accept his reasons, but he should at least give them to her.

'Turkmenistan's a long way away. Communications not good. Contract to finish.'

'Oh.'

'Look,' Hetty watched him make an effort to talk in whole sentences. 'Which bedroom are you in? I need to sleep. Can't remember when I last slept in a bed.'

'Well, which bedroom would you prefer? Uncle Samuel's? I could put some sheets on in no time.' She didn't really want to explain that she'd been sleeping on the sofa with the dogs, who were now snoring loudly in front of the stove.

'Fine. I'll get my bag in from the car.'

Hetty forced herself not to feel frightened at the thought of going upstairs in the dark on her own, wishing she could turn on all the lights. She picked up the torch Peter had lent her, and faced her fears.

Actually she found herself feeling perfectly calm burrowing about in the linen cupboard for sheets. She and Phyllis had been through the cupboard pretty thoroughly looking for things to cover tables with, so she knew where all the good linen was. Uncle Samuel still had blankets and eiderdowns instead of duvets on his bed, which made things harder.

'Why don't any of the damn lights work?' demanded Connor, thumping up the stairs.

The bed was nearly made by this time. Seeing it, Connor forgot about the lights and flung himself down in all his clothes.

'The wiring's unsafe,' said Hetty. 'There could have been a fire at any moment.'

'Oh shit!' In the torchlight, Hetty could see him close his eyes, as if in pain. 'I knew this bloody hell-hole should be pulled down.'

Hetty harrumphed her disapproval. 'You don't mind if I take the torch, do you?'

His eyes were closed, his mouth was open, and his chest rose and fell rhythmically. With a sigh, she took off his shoes, covered him with the blankets, and went quickly back down the stairs.

Back in the welcoming light of the kitchen, Hetty felt wide awake. It didn't take much thought to conclude that a hot toddy for herself was a good idea. She made it nearly as strong as she had for Conan the Barbarian, and while she sipped she considered the situation. Even with reality blurred by hot whisky and lemon, things didn't look good.

Did he, or did he not, know about his uncle's loan? What would he do when, half-way through the following morning, he woke from his sick-bed to discover a car-boot sale in full cry in his uncle's backyard? Would he throw her, neck and crop, into the proverbial street, possibly suing her for misuse of relative's property *en passant*? Which would not only be hugely embarrassing, but also a terrific waste. The village had put an enormous amount of hard work into the car-boot sale, and tomorrow they would put in even more. For it all to be ruined by Samuel's wicked heir would turn farce into tragedy. But, try as she might, Hetty couldn't see what on earth she could do to prevent this potential calamity, short of slipping her nocturnal intruder a Mickey Finn.

'And where do you get them at this time of night in the middle of the country?' Hetty asked Clovis, who was confused, and thought it was breakfast time. He looked at her blankly, rightly regarding her question as rhetorical.

Hetty doled out a minimal amount of cat food and realized that she desperately didn't want to leave Courtbridge House – not now that she had committed herself, and most of the village, to its rehabilitation. But if Connor Whatever-it-was asked her to leave, what could she do? The house was his responsibility, after all. She was only there because he hadn't been able to look after it. She had no right to stay if he didn't want her to.

And why on earth would he want her to? She'd sold some of his uncle's ugly but valuable antiques, the Clarice Cliff urn being the ugliest and most precious. And she planned to sell an awful lot of other stuff to raise money to restore the house that he wanted to turn into a theme park anyway. It was unlikely she would be his first choice of house guest.

Gradually, however, the toddy began to kick in, and Hetty accepted that there was no point in trying to make a plan when she had no idea of what might happen. 'Sufficient unto the day is the evil thereof,' she told the dogs as she summoned them, picked up her drink, and retired to bed.

When she awoke, barely three hours later, she hurried into her clothes in a panic, terrified that the first car would arrive at the very moment that Conan the Barbarian appeared downstairs. By the time she had washed, let the dogs out, and made a cup of tea, she discovered it was only six o'clock.

Her first priority was Connor. Thinking it best to confront him armed, she made him a cup of tea and took it upstairs. The sound of snoring issued from his room, confirming that he was still asleep. Reassured, she went in and put the tea down. It didn't seem likely that he'd drink it.

He was lying on his back, still dressed, but with the bedclothes strewn about him. He didn't hear her enter, and when she placed a tentative hand on his forehead he didn't stir. He felt terribly hot. If it wasn't for the sale she might have called a doctor. As it was, she had more important things to think about than poorly cousins-many-times-removed. However, she decided he'd be more comfortable – and therefore less likely to wake – if she could get him out of his clothes.

He weighed a ton. At first it seemed as if she would never be able to drag his cords from under him. As she tugged and heaved she realized how deeply asleep he was. It might mean he was seriously ill but, more importantly, it might ensure his keeping to his room for the whole day. When at last he was naked, but for his boxer shorts, she made the bed over him and tucked him in firmly. Not because she cared if he lived or died, she told herself, but because she wanted him out of the way.

She went downstairs and put three soluble aspirin into a glass of orange juice. Three were unlikely to kill him – he was the size of an ox – but it might take three to keep him comatose for the required length of time. Fluids were a good idea too, not just because he had a temperature, but also because he would be less likely to wake from being thirsty. Back in his room, she made a determined effort to rouse him.

'Drink this!' she shouted into his ear. 'It'll make you better!' She put an arm behind his shoulders and dragged him upright.

Conan the Barbarian, who had begun to return to consciousness, scowled at Hetty and then at the glass. 'I'm fine,' he whispered hoarsely. 'Leave me alone.'

'You're not fine. You've got a temperature. Drink this!'

Fortunately for Hetty, he was too weak to fight for long and soon opened his mouth to let her tip the spiked orange juice into him. She wiped his mouth with the sheet.

'Well done.' She spoke more gently now, soothing him back to sleep. 'You just stay here. I'll be up to see you later.'

She brought up a glass of water and more aspirin, which she left by his bed. But there was no sign of him waking. He lay on his side now, no longer snoring, and seemed cooler. Satisfied that her nursing had done some good, and reasonably confident that he would stay safely asleep for most of the day at least, she left him.

★

Caroline had told her the cars and vans would arrive early, well before the ten-o'clock start advertised. She wasn't really expecting them at eight in the morning, but it was then that the first ex-Post-Office van drove into the yard, eager to claim the best site and the best bargains.

Fortunately, Hetty had already put up trestle-tables, borrowed by Mrs Hempstead from the village hall, all along one wall, so the Brownie and WI stalls would be in pole position. Peter had wanted to help her put them up last night. Thank goodness she'd refused, or Conan the Barbarian would have had to crash through them to put his car away.

Seeing the dealers get out of their cars, Hetty prayed that, for once in her life, Caroline would be punctual.

'Mornin', love, where's your mum?' asked a pony-tailed, ear-ringed, tattooed man with a substantial beer belly.

Hetty reached a personal Rubicon. She could either blush and stammer and apologize for not being older, or more experienced, or even just for breathing, or she could give back as good as she got. A month ago she would have slunk back into the house with some excuse. Not any more.

'At home asleep, I hope. Where's yours?' She grinned broadly. 'It's good you've come early. You can get the best site. Tell your mates to park next to you.'

The man, an experienced dealer, and in the habit of eating girls like Hetty in between pints of beer, was a little taken aback. 'You in charge, then?'

'Yup. I'll be round for the money later. Oh, look, here's another lot. Quick, or they'll take your place.'

The sight of several more vans filled with stuff that appears regularly at car-boot sales, changing owner from time to time, made the man hurry back to park neatly and start unloading.

Phyllis Hempstead arrived shortly after this. She bustled up to Hetty, full of energy. 'I say, we've got a grand day for it, haven't we? And all those vans already!'

'I know! It's amazing, isn't it?' There was no point, Hetty decided, in telling Phyllis about Connor's arrival. She couldn't do anything about it any more than Hetty could. There was no point in them both being worried sick.

Once during the morning, in between directing Brownies and

WI members to their allotted spaces, taking money, and seeing Peter's friend with the cider press had a good spot, Hetty dashed upstairs to visit her patient.

He was showing signs of waking when she got there so, terrified he might come round completely, she fought with the foil wrappings of three more aspirins, tipped them into the water, and virtually forced the liquid down his throat. 'This'll make you feel much better.' She rubbed her hand across his forehead. 'You've still got a bit of a temperature.' She had no idea if he had or hadn't, but her mother had always said this to her when she was little, and it sounded caring.

Connor grunted. He still looked terrible. There were dark circles under his eyes, fierce gold stubble covered the lower part of his face, and his lips looked dry.

'I'll be up to see you again later. There's water if you want it, but don't, whatever you do, get out of bed.'

Guiltily she fled, before he could ask about the unaccustomed noise, resolving to find time to get some more aspirin.

The car-boot sale was a huge success. Buyers and sellers flocked to it, partly from nosiness, and partly because they assumed that as the setting was stately the junk would be also.

'They came here for antiques, and they got chipped china,' Hetty said somewhat ruefully to Mrs Hempstead, when she had a moment.

'Never mind *why* they came – they came. And some of the china's very nice. If not actually antique.'

Her spirits flagged only when five o'clock came and there were still a few buyers haggling over the price of some hideous handmade pottery on Mrs Hempstead's stall. But eventually even Phyllis packed up and went home, handing Hetty a bag full of notes and change before she went.

'Well done, dear. You've done extremely well.'

'It was you, Mrs – Phyllis. Sorting all that china and getting your friends to help.'

'Didn't mean that, so much. I meant well done for grasping the nettle like you have. You're plucky and brave. A lot of girls would have run home and said they couldn't cope. You didn't.'

Hetty was touched. And pleased. And while Mrs Hempstead

was pleased too, she thought she should tell her about Connor. But Hetty couldn't bring herself to. She was too tired, and Mrs Hempstead would no doubt expect her to poison Connor as he slept. Plucky and brave she might be, but neither her pluckiness nor her loyalty to Courtbridge House extended to murder.

'I couldn't have done any of it without you, Phyllis, you and your friends.'

'Nonsense child! We've enjoyed ourselves!' Mrs Hempstead went off, string bags bulging with bargains.

Caroline and Jack, who left soon afterwards, had tried very hard to persuade Hetty to join them in the pub. If it hadn't been for Connor, a time bomb in human form, Hetty would have gone. It took a lot of precious energy to convince Caroline she wanted to stay at home.

After checking on her patient, who was now sleeping soundly without the aid of analgesics, Hetty sat down at the kitchen table to count the money. She had enough to pay Caroline's pet electrician who was due to redo the wiring tomorrow, and almost enough to pay for the fire extinguishers, on order, and due to arrive later in the week. 'Good eh?' she said to Clovis. He mewed, giving her a whiff of halitosis powerful enough to kill a canary.

Hetty cleared up the kitchen carefully, getting rid of all hints that any commercial undertaking had gone on. It was unlikely she could remove all traces of the car-boot sale, but there was no point in rubbing Connor's nose in it.

He showed no sign of waking, however, so Hetty eventually went to bed herself, glad to be spared any awkward explanations or confrontations.

She went up to see him again first thing in the morning, but he was still asleep, though he had drunk the water and taken more aspirin. Bored of waiting for the Sword of Damocles to fall, she decided to walk across the fields to Peter's to thank him for his help, to tell him about Connor, and to ask him to give her breakfast.

It was a truly lovely morning – the sort of early spring day when people tell each other, 'This is summer, better make the most of it.' Primroses were starting to appear in the hedgerows, and a green fuzz was beginning to blur the outlines of trees. The dogs seemed to feel the vibrance in the air, and frolicked about, woofing and rolling each other over. Hetty got soaked to the thigh as she kicked up dew with her wellingtons. The beauty of it all caught her by the throat. She didn't want to leave it and go back to London or, worse somehow, the quasi-country where her parents lived. Nor did she want to think about these ancient fields being torn up to be replaced by manufactured fun-machines, made of metal and plastic instead of living things.

She wouldn't let it happen she decided, and turned her mind to thoughts of bacon, brown toast and coffee, trusting that Peter would have them. He was sure to. He was so reliable.

It occurred to her, as she raised her hand to knock on his back door, that perhaps she was using Peter just like – well, not just like, but in the same way morally – as Alistair had used her. She rejected the notion as she knocked. Peter liked helping people.

'Hi, Peter. Am I too early for you?'

Peter looked attractively ruffled. He'd obviously just come out of the shower; his hair was wet, and he hadn't got a shirt on under his jumper.

'Er, no. Well, a bit. Are you all right?'

'Fine. I've got some news. I thought I might beg breakfast off you.'

'Come in. I'll just go up and finish getting dressed.'

'So.' Peter had ground coffee, sliced mushrooms, and was now laying slices of bacon under the grill. 'What's this news?'

'Conan the Barbarian's come.'

Peter turned, a rasher of bacon hanging off his knife. 'What?'

'In the middle of Friday night. He turned up. He must have got all my mother's messages at last.'

'You mean, while there was all that commotion, with the car-boot sale, Samuel's heir was upstairs somewhere?'

It did sound bizarre. 'Yes. Fortunately he's ill and he slept through it.'

'Good God! Does that mean you'll go home?' Peter put the last slice of bacon under the grill and moved the kettle on to the hot part of the Aga. He seemed worried.

Hetty shook her head. 'I don't know. I really hope not.'

'And is he going to start turning Courtbridge House into a funfair?'

Hetty shrugged. 'I don't know. Two o'clock in the morning isn't a good time to ask those sorts of questions.'

'What's he doing now?' A couple of tomatoes joined the bacon on the grill.

'Still sleeping off flu and jet lag, I hope. But really, until he wakes up, I won't know anything. And I've got one of Caroline's men coming to do the wiring this afternoon.'

'On a Sunday?'

She nodded. 'He's moonlighting – or Sunday-afternooning.'

He didn't smile. 'What will you do if the Barbarian asks you to leave? I'm just asking because if he does,' he went on quickly, 'you'd be more than welcome – to move in here with me. Spare room or my room. One egg or two?' he added to cover his embarrassment.

'That's really, really kind of you. And, I must admit, running to you was my first thought.'

Peter put down the eggshells. 'Was it?'

Hetty realized he'd got hold of more stick than she'd intended to offer. 'I mean, I knew – I felt I knew – that if I was really in trouble, you'd take me in.'

'You don't have to be in any kind of trouble for me to take you in, Hetty.'

Hetty licked her lips and made a big effort to look directly at him. 'I know, Peter. You're very kind. I don't know what I'd do without you.' She was trying to be honest but she realized that every word she uttered was leading him further in a direction she had no immediate intention of going. 'I'm nowhere near ready for a new relationship yet. But if I was, you'd be the first – I mean . . .' She didn't know what she meant, so she shut up.

Peter regarded her for a long time. Then got a plate out of the warming oven and put her breakfast on it.

'Thank you,' said Hetty, gratefully.

CHAPTER SIX

Back from Peter's, Hetty entered the kitchen cautiously, like a character out of a James Bond film, scanning it for signs of an alien presence. There were none. Conan the Barbarian was obviously still asleep.

She trod quietly up the stairs, still feeling like a spy, to see if he'd moved from his bedroom. He had. He'd been to the bathroom and left the seat up. Reassured by this sign of life, though not by the sign of carelessness, she tiptoed into his bedroom. He lay like a log, but the water jug she'd left was empty. She refilled it from the bathroom and left.

She was disappointed. She'd braced herself for a confrontation, and it had been denied her. Now the car-boot sale was safely over, she needed to find out how much he knew about Samuel's dire financial state.

And she wanted to get back to hating him. The trouble with looking after someone, she thought, even in the minor way she was looking after Conan the Barbarian, was that you inevitably started to care about them.

Upstairs, she decided that now was as good a time as any to pick herself a bedroom and move into it. It would be staking a claim. If he found out she had been sleeping on the sofa, it would make her seem more ephemeral, temporary. A bedroom would be territory. Besides, if Caroline's electrician came as arranged, there would soon be light upstairs. And however dreadful her distant cousin might turn out to be, he was extremely solid and unghostlike, and, as far as she could tell, had the sort of sceptical personality that would scare away anything not made entirely of flesh and bone. She chose the room she had slept in on her first night there, when her mother had been with her.

She hummed softly to herself as she made up the bed and plumped up the pillows, looking out of the window from time to time to see if the electrician had arrived. She ran down to pick a bunch of primroses for her room, put candles, matches and a book on the bedside table, singing throughout. By the time she had finished she realized she had probably been making quite a lot of noise. But, to her relief, there was no sound from her patient.

It was good to feel her voice working its way back to what it had been like before she left home. In the safety of the kitchen, she let her voice soar to the dusty, fly-blown beams and reverberate off the greasy, dirt-streaked walls as she washed up, and cleared another corner of old jamjars.

It was only when she heard thudding from the upstairs landing, declaring that the Kraken had Woken, that she remembered the money on the kitchen table. How could she explain six margarine cartons filled with carefully sorted small change, and a cloth bag bulging with banknotes? She piled the cartons in a cupboard, cramming them behind jars of crystallized jam and dried-up Marmite, and forced the cloth bag into a drawer, which was already full of supermarket carriers. She had just stuffed the last bag on top of the money when Connor entered the kitchen.

'Good afternoon,' she said brightly, certain she was looking as guilty as sin. 'How are you feeling now?'

'Bloody awful.'

He did look ill. All those hours in bed had done little to clear the shadows under his eyes, and nothing to lift the scowl from his features. Although that probably had more to do with personality than jet lag or a strep throat.

'Shall I make some tea or something?'

She didn't want to adopt a subservient role to keep him sweet, she'd made that decision last night. But, on the other hand, it might be a good idea to soothe the worst of his ill-feeling away before she attempted to extract information from him. She really needed some potion that would make him tell her everything he knew, but would leave him with no memory of having done so.

'Thanks. Picked up a bug on the way home. Feel like death.'

'Shouldn't you go back to bed?' Hetty heard her mother's voice come out of her mouth and hoped he wouldn't resent it.

He nodded. 'Needed a hot drink. Go back later.'

'It's a bit early in the day for a hot toddy –'

'No it's not. If you'd make it?' His features didn't lend themselves

67

to asking favours, he was obviously more accustomed to giving orders. But a sore throat was a strong disincentive to barking out commands. 'Got some duty-free in my bag. Still in the car. Do you need it?'

She hesitated. Her instinct to nurture was almost overwhelming. He looked so ill. But so had Alistair looked ill when he had a cold, and what good had nurturing him done her?

But Connor had more than a cold, and although she knew nothing good about him, all the bad she had heard about him was, so far, only hearsay. There was time enough to be assertive when Connor was in a state to cope. 'It's all right. There's still plenty of whisky. Would you like a bath? It might make you feel a lot worse. But if your muscles are stiff, it'll help.'

'Is the bath usable?'

Hetty nodded. 'I tell you what, I'll go and run it while you watch the saucepan, then you can drink your toddy while you're in it.'

She was rewarded by the glimmer of teeth appearing briefly among the stubble and tortured folds of his face. Hetty had a sudden desire to iron him.

Hetty spent the afternoon waiting for the electrician to arrive, rearranging ornaments in the drawing room, and speaking to her mother, who rang her. After a few minutes Hetty, who had the receiver tucked under her chin and was still playing with Meissen shepherdesses as she talked, realized her mother had just told her she'd arranged something but Hetty hadn't taken it in. 'Can you just run that by me again?'

Her mother sighed, and gave her daughter a potted version of what she'd said before, leaving out most of the extraneous detail.

'So, it's a ruby wedding, but you're not sure when?' Hetty asked.

'That's it. She's going to ring you – not Mrs Graham – the woman with the wedding. You don't sound very pleased, darling. I thought you needed the house to earn money.'

Hetty thought of Connor asleep upstairs and of his gasped, husky words as he first lay down that Friday night. She decided not to mention him to her mother – she'd only panic. 'Yes, I do. It's just we're not really ready for that kind of event yet.'

'It may not be for ages. People like to get things organized well in advance.'

'Mmmm.'

'She's going to ring you anyway. I told her you were . . .' There was a pause while Hetty's mother realized she'd put her foot in it and tried to pull it back out.

'Mother, you didn't!'

'I didn't say a word about Alistair, I swear. I just said . . . you didn't know many people in the area.'

It was Hetty's turn to sigh. If only that were true!

Hetty, having concluded that the electrician wasn't going to turn up, took the dogs to visit Phyllis Hempstead – ostensibly to tell her how much money they had made, but also, if she could slip it into the conversation without causing too many fireworks, to tell her about Connor.

'My dear girl!' said Phyllis, sloshing damson wine into glasses. 'Are you telling me that all the time that car-boot sale was going on, Samuel's Godforsaken nephew was asleep upstairs?'

Hetty nodded. 'He slept right through it. He must be quite ill.'

Phyllis harrumphed. 'Not ill enough, in my opinion. Have you confronted him about his plans?'

'I haven't confronted him about anything. He's been too ill.' Hetty, sensing that Phyllis was about to suggest that Hetty turned it into an illness he never recovered from, possibly with the aid of some ancient horse pills they had found, went on, 'You can't hit a man when he's down, can you?'

Phyllis's nostrils flared disdainfully. 'Speak for yourself! But I suppose, as you have to share a house with him – temporarily at least – I must leave it to you to behave as you think fit.'

'Well, yes, and he might send me packing after all, and then where would we be? I only came to house-sit.'

Phyllis sighed, the fight gone out of her for a minute. But only for a minute. 'You could always come and stay with me, use the money from the boot sale to fight a rearguard action. I can see the banners now, SAVE COURTBRIDGE HOUSE, NO THEME PARK HERE.'

'I hope it won't come to that. The enemy within, you know? Far more powerful.'

Shortly afterwards Hetty left, realizing that the damson wine was fairly powerful too.

★

Connor stayed in bed all Monday, Hetty bringing hot drinks and cold water at intervals. She discouraged him from moving as, a day late, the electrician arrived.

All day Andy had worked with the power turned off, tapping away at the plaster, pulling ancient flex away from the walls, drilling holes with a power drill, and through it all, Connor had slept, oblivious of the chaos. Now, at six o'clock, Hetty was in the hall saying goodbye to Andy when the hairs on the back of her neck stood up. Her reprieve was over.

She heard footsteps on the upstairs landing and tensed, then relaxed as she heard them turn up the passage to the bathroom. Have a nice hot bath, dear, she urged him silently. Hot enough to make you feel faint and send you back to bed. Just until I've had a chance to get rid of Andy.

'You've been absolutely great.' She took hold of Andy's arm and walked him a few paces nearer the door. 'Will you be back tomorrow?'

'And the next day, love. I've a few days' work to put in yet.'

Oh, God! A few days! She had no chance of keeping his presence concealed that long. 'But it won't cost more than we agreed?'

'Oh, no. Not unless I come across something really dreadful.' He chuckled in the light-hearted way people do when they're talking about someone else's property, not their own. 'The good thing about these old places, the plaster comes off really easily.'

Hetty tried to join in his cheerfulness. 'So I'll see you tomorrow?' She heard the bathroom door open. Would Connor go back to bed? Or did he feel better now?

'About eight. You'll be up, will you?'

'Oh, yes.' She'd have agreed to be up at five, or even stay awake all night, if it would keep Andy's presence secret from Connor.

She opened the door and nudged him further towards it. 'I mustn't keep you. You're an angel to come in your spare time like this.' She realized she was gushing.

'That's OK, love. Anything for a friend of Caroline's.' He had his foot well over the threshold, seemed about to go, and then stepped back again. 'Let me know if there's anything else wants doing that I can help you with. And if you've got any guttering wants seeing to, I've got a friend who's good at leadwork.'

Hetty almost pushed him out of the door. 'Fine, I'll bear that in mind.' At last he was gone.

Connor was in the kitchen when Hetty returned there. The dogs were frisking about him as if he were their dearest friend instead of their temporary mistress's bitterest enemy. He petted each one briefly, but he didn't bother to greet Hetty. There was no, 'Hello, how are you?' Or even, 'What was that man doing here?' – he just said, 'How are you going to pay him?'

Hetty fought the urge say, 'With my body.' However tempting, she knew childishness would not help. 'With cash.'

'Whose?'

It was a good point. Whose cash was it, stuffed away in a drawer under a bundle of supermarket bags? 'Well, I'm not planning to go through your pockets for it. Unless you're offering?'

'No chance. What did he do?'

'Started rewiring the house.'

Connor's eyebrows arched scathingly. 'Was that necessary?'

'Yes! It was dangerous. They won't let us open to the public with wiring that could explode at any minute. They're funny like that.'

'Does Samuel know about this?'

'No.'

'Don't you think you should clear it with him before you spend vast quantities of his money? Possibly unnecessarily?'

Hetty was aware that perhaps she should have consulted Samuel, but it would have been hard to ask about the rewiring without mentioning money, and he was depressed enough. 'I didn't want to bother him. He's ill and he's old.' Although she tried to sound self-righteous, she actually felt rather guilty.

'So, where are you getting the money to pay for it? Is your mother paying?'

'No!'

'Then who is?'

Hetty was getting tired of this – tired and not a little uncomfortable. 'If it's not you – and I don't see you reaching for your cheque-book – why worry about it?'

'I'm just concerned in case you've nagged Samuel into paying for things he can't afford. There's no point in spending money on the house. It would take far too much to put it in order.'

Didn't he know about the new roof? Hetty resolved to try and hunt out some bills, so she would know when it had been done. She realized that as he'd arrived in the dark, the new bit of roof wouldn't have been very noticeable. 'So you're prepared to just let it fall down?'

He nodded. 'When Samuel dies, I shall have it pulled down.'

Hetty felt sick. She hooked a chair out from under the table with her foot and sat on it. 'You can't mean that,' she breathed.

He seemed almost amused at the effect his words had had on her. 'Selling the reclaimable materials will help considerably with the death duties.'

While Connor had been ill, gruff with jet lag and a debilitating bug, Hetty had clung on to a faint hope that when he was well he wouldn't turn out as bad as everyone had said. She'd hoped there might be a heart of gold under that unpromising exterior. Now she wished she *had* stabbed him in his sleep, or crumbled the ancient horse pills into his tea.

'Surely if the house is in such bad order, it won't be worth much? And the death duties won't be all that high.'

Connor shook his head. 'The site is extremely valuable. To put money into the house itself would just be throwing good money after bad.'

'Samuel didn't think so, or he wouldn't have had the roof done!' Too late Hetty remembered she hadn't been going to mention this.

But Connor didn't flinch. He must have known all about it. 'Samuel wanted to die in the dry. Doing the roof was a mistake. I'm not going to compound his error.'

Suddenly Hetty felt that anything was better than having the house demolished. 'I'd heard you were planning to turn the place into a theme park. Wouldn't the house be one of the main attractions?'

'It's not a very big site. Obviously it wouldn't be up to me. But the feeling is that the developers would rather have the space than the house.'

'What does Samuel think about this?'

Connor pushed his hand through the thatch of hair that was making it difficult for him to see. 'He doesn't think he'll live to see it. He may be right. I trust you won't mention it to him?'

So he did have a small sliver of conscience. 'Of course not. But the whole village knows about the theme park. When he comes home, people are bound to ask about it, especially –' Just in time she managed to stop herself adding 'when they know you've arrived'.

'Especially what?'

'Especially when it's open to the public,' she improvised. 'They're bound to want to know what's happening.'

Connor shrugged. 'He's knocking eighty. He's had major surgery. People may not get the chance to ask him. He may never come home.'

All their hard work, their dreams and plans, seemed about to crumble. 'But supposing he does? Supposing he is dying, and the doctors all think it would be nice for him to end his days at home! Would you want him to come home to a house with no wiring, no light upstairs, no . . .' Frantically she tried to think of things Courtbridge House lacked that Samuel might miss. He wouldn't be bothered by the thought that there were no smoke alarms or fire extinguishers. '. . . with the place looking uncared for,' she finished.

'It doesn't take vast sums to make a house look cared for.'

Hetty took a breath to protest, but on this particular point she agreed with him. She felt tired and despairing and realized a lot of it was hunger. Her mother's genes meant it was impossible for her to cook and eat without offering him something, so she pushed aside her animosity and asked if he wanted any supper.

'Have you any soup? My throat is still a bit sore.'

That was simple enough, in theory anyway. 'Tinned soup?'

'Fine.'

That was a relief. Alistair would only touch soup that was home-made or from an expensive carton. She must stop thinking he was the same as Alistair. She had enough reasons to dislike Connor without adding that one.

'You go and see if the fire's all right in the sitting room, then.' What she meant was, 'Get out from under my feet.' She had a feeling he understood the subtext perfectly well, but didn't take orders from anyone.

'I'll have a quick bath first. If that's all right with you?'

She dismissed his sarcasm with a saccharine smile.

While she was alone in the kitchen, Hetty fiddled about with bowls and bits of toast, analysing her feelings. Part of her wanted to run away from the whole situation. Connor's plan was worse than anyone had thought. No one had imagined that the house would be pulled down, just hedged about by monstrous cafeterias and acres of car park. And no one but her knew about the awful debt.

The other part of her made her want to chain herself to the front door in the path of the wrecker's ball, and get herself on the *Nine O'Clock News*. In fact, to do anything to stop him tearing down the house. But what, in reality, could she do to stop his plans, now that he had made them?

She set the tray, poured the soup, and made her way into the sitting room. The fire was obligingly active. Connor and the dogs were snuggled up on the sofa together, making what could have been a cosy picture had the human element not been so fatally flawed.

What a shame Connor had to be Samuel's heir, she thought as they sipped their soup. If only Samuel had married, or if his younger brother hadn't died, then the house might have gone to a nice stable person, with a nice wife, keen on keeping the family going.

On the other hand, Connor might be married. He might have the sort of wife who would appreciate a quasi-stately home to live in. Connor might not have mentioned Courtbridge House to her just because he didn't want to live there. There was only one way to find out. Caroline would have had no qualms about coming straight out with it. But it took Hetty several gulps of hot soup before she could put her question.

'Are you married?' In the flickering firelight, his features seemed to register horror. 'Living with anyone?' she amended.

'No. You?'

'No. So no children then?'

Connor shot her a strange look under his heavy eyebrows. 'No. You?'

Hetty bit back an irritated 'Of course not!' and snapped 'No.'

'Why the curiosity? Or are you just checking out the opposition?'

'What do you mean, "opposition"?'

'You want to know about my private life to see if the coast is clear. So you can have a go with a clear conscience,' he added.

Hetty was too angry to be embarrassed. But she held it back. Any evidence that she objected to his suggestion would only give him more ammunition with which to bait her. 'What a quaint idea,' she said eventually.

Connor laughed. 'Not as quaint as you might think. In my experience women get married either when they're very young or when they want to have children.'

'I'm planning on doing it when I'm old. Very old.'

'So, what are you now? Eighteen?'

'Twenty-four.'

'Ah. First affair just over, then?'

Hetty went hot and cold. Surely not even her mother would leave that information on an answerphone? No. Calm down. He doesn't know. He's just guessing. 'What on earth makes you say that?'

'Why else would you be here, looking after a crumbling mansion that's not your responsibility? If you're just unemployed, it's not the best place to job-hunt.'

'I was at a loose end,' said Hetty firmly. 'My mother asked –'

'Your mother –' Connor began.

'What about her?' Hetty broke in. She was allowed to criticize her mother, and so were her father and sister, but no one else. Only people who loved her.

'Is an interfering old bag,' he said mildly.

Hetty waited for the rage to rise to a suitable level for physical violence. It didn't. He was so matter-of-fact, non-judgemental, as if interfering was something a person couldn't help being, like having big teeth. 'She means well,' she mumbled into her polo-neck.

'Exactly,' said Connor.

Hetty finished her soup without any further attempts at conversation. Anything she said would reveal either her youthful naïvety or her curiosity.

'So, how much is this rewiring likely to cost?'

Hetty told him. Connor raised his eyebrows. 'Cheap. But still a waste of money.'

'Not if Samuel's going to come back and end his days here. Even you wouldn't want him burnt in his bed.'

'Nor do I want him spending his last days worried about a debt he can't pay.'

Which is precisely what he is doing. But if Connor didn't know that, Hetty couldn't tell him. Nor could she face telling him how she did plan to pay for the improvements. She shut her eyes. 'If we opened more of the house, it would pay for itself.'

'Opening the house is the last thing anyone ought to be doing. Whatever Samuel says.'

'Why?'

'It's a waste of time.'

'Whose time? Yours? Well if you think anyone is expecting you to put *your*self out, think again. We'll do it.'

'Who's the "we"?'

'Me. Mrs Hempstead, Peter, Caroline – the whole community.'

'What makes you think that?'

'We had a car-boot sale –' Too late, she remembered she hadn't been going to tell him that.

'You *what*?' He seemed to increase in size as he said it.

'We had a car-boot sale, on Saturday, while you were asleep.' She lowered her voice in the faint hope that he wouldn't hear. 'Everyone in the village did something to help. The WI, the Brownies, the Gardening Group, the Church, the pub, everyone. They all donated things and manned stalls, baked cakes. Bill Winters let us have his field for parking – they all helped because they all care! You can't just behave as if you live in a vacuum. What you do here affects everyone.' Her volume increased with her passion. She took a deep breath and went on. 'Though I don't suppose you'd care if the whole village went into mourning – if the whole *county* did. You wouldn't be here to notice. You'd either be in some Godforsaken part of the world earning more bloody money, or in some tax haven living off the money you sell this place for.'

'Why should you care? You won't be here either.'

It was rather a mild response after such a passionate speech, but then, she hadn't really expected him to clap his hand to his head and say, 'My God, you're right. I never saw it like that until now.'

'I care because I've lived here for a few weeks. Something I don't suppose you've ever done. And I care about the house, too. It's beautiful. And although it does need a lot of money spent on it – and I'm sure you're right in that it would take a lot to keep up – it has so much potential. You could have functions here, open much more of it to the public, let out the stables as workshops, all sorts of things. OK, so you won't make as much as you would if you sold it to some developer, but you'd be doing some good in the community – providing jobs for local people –'

'Not as many as I would if I turned it into a theme park –'

'Not the right sort of jobs! Only for students, or temporary summer labour. But if the house was open more, there'd be jobs for the people of the village. Not just a lot of blow-ins.'

'I don't think so.'

'This is a beautiful building. You could make lots of money out of it. But you would have to put some effort in, and you wouldn't make a quick profit. So you justify selling it by saying it would provide more jobs.'

'I didn't. I merely said there'd be more jobs if I sold it.'

'Comes to the same thing.' Hetty picked up her soup bowl. She felt exhausted, like a gnat trying to make an impression on an elephant. And angry. It was all pointless. She'd lost her battle for the house before she'd properly begun. Before they'd even opened to the public. She got to her feet, eager to get away from the man she was in danger of hitting with a poker. 'If you've finished, I'll take your bowl back to the kitchen.' She snatched it up and stalked out of the room.

She crashed the bowls into the sink and turned on the cold tap. She was burning with unexpressed fury and splashed her hot cheeks with water before burying her face in the roller towel. It smelt faintly of onions and washing-up liquid, and she was regretting plunging her nose into anywhere so malodorous when she heard Connor come into the kitchen. Hetty groaned quietly into the towel. Couldn't she even have a temper tantrum in private?

CHAPTER SEVEN

'You know, you may have a point . . .'

Hetty lifted her head. Had those words really come out of his mouth, in that combination?

He pulled out a stool and sat down at the kitchen table. 'I didn't realize, until you told me, how much this house must mean to the community. My work has kept me out of the way, particularly recently, so, although I keep a fairly close eye on Samuel, I don't spend a lot of time in the village itself.' Hetty looked up, mystified. She was about to fling her arms metaphorically round his neck, when he went on. 'But even though I do have some idea now, I can't change my plans.'

Disappointed that his conversion was not complete, she muttered into the towel. 'Well no. It would cramp your style no end.'

'But I will undertake to keep the house going until Samuel dies.'

Now was the time to ask him if he knew about the loan. But if he didn't, and she told him, he might change his mind again. 'You mean, you won't have his house pulled down while he might still want to live in it?' she said instead.

He clenched his teeth, leaving Hetty thankful for small mercies. Unclenched, his teeth would probably bite. 'I said, I'm prepared to keep the house going, keep opening it, until Samuel dies. And then – go ahead with my original plan. But I'm not prepared to authorize huge cheques for patching up the place when it needs demolishing.'

He couldn't know about the huge cheques she was authorized to write, and now was definitely not the time to mention it. 'The house needs some things doing to it or they won't let us open it.' She said this in the vain hope that he might cough up for a few fire extinguishers.

'Who's "they"?'

Hetty prevaricated. She didn't want to go into too much detail.

'There are regulations.' That at least was true. 'We have to have smoke alarms and fire extinguishers, things like that. Nothing that couldn't be sold on,' she added quickly. 'But we can't just carry on in the way Samuel was doing. Because of the regulations,' she added, for emphasis. 'He obviously didn't care about them.'

'Probably not.'

'The thing is . . .'

'What?'

'How long are you going to stay? Do you want to open the house, do all the things that need doing, or would you want someone else to?'

His expression of disgust was almost risible. 'Well, I'm sure as hell not going to tell three elderly ladies fibs about the Civil War while I show them round the great hall every second Saturday.'

For the old ladies' sake, Hetty rejoiced. 'Does that mean you're going away again?'

'Sorry to dash your hopes, my dear, but no. I haven't another contract for a while, I've sublet my flat, and I thought I'd spend my time near my nearest relative. If that's all right with his house-sitter, of course.'

He wasn't the only one who could be sarcastic. 'I'm sure Samuel will greatly appreciate your presence at his bedside. Just don't hasten his end too obviously, will you? I don't want my name in the papers.' And I'm not at all sure I want to stay here if you're here too. She kept this to herself, but had a feeling he could read her thoughts.

Connor got to his feet and Hetty braced herself, like a tennis player facing a potentially killing serve. But before either of them could say anything there was a knock on the back door and in came Peter.

He stood on the threshold, looking from one to the other. 'I just came to see if you were all right,' he said, as if finding Hetty 'all right' was the last thing he had expected. He shot Hetty an anxious look before turning to Connor, hostility showing in every muscle, and beneath that protective instincts ready to spring into action were detectable.

Hetty was annoyed. Peter had no right to barge into the house with his hackles up. He knew Connor was here, after all. And if he did want to check up on her he could ring first, like a civilized human being. While she was thinking how to calm Peter down, Connor answered.

'Well, I haven't raped her yet, if that's what you were worrying about,' he said in a manner not calculated to set anyone's mind at rest.

Hetty felt like an old bone which, in the presence of two dogs, suddenly becomes interesting.

'Peter's been keeping an eye on me,' she said quickly, feeling that, as it was almost Connor's house, he was the more entitled to an explanation. 'While I've been alone here. Terribly kind of him. He looked after Samuel's dogs until I came. He's a friend of Samuel's.' She turned to Peter, knowing she had to introduce Connor. She took a breath, searching for his surname. It was something like Barbarian, but not. 'Connor . . .'

'Connor Barrabin.' Connor held out his hand to a still-hostile Peter.

Peter took it, sizing him up. 'Peter Lassiter. As Hetty said, I'm an old friend of Samuel's.'

Connor nodded, but didn't reply. Hetty, terrified that he was going to say something inflammatory, burst in with the traditional oil for troubled waters.

'Would anyone like a cup of tea? Or coffee?'

'Or whisky?' suggested Connor. 'Peter, would you like a drink?'

Peter hesitated, as if wondering whether accepting a glass of duty-free from this man would compromise his integrity. 'Yes, thank you. That would be nice.'

'Hetty? What about you?'

'Yes, please.' A stiff drink seemed like a very good idea.

Connor poured whisky into three glasses while Hetty found a little jug and filled it with cold water. When Peter had his drink, Connor handed a glass to Hetty. 'You are old enough to drink, I presume?'

Hetty almost snatched it. 'You know damn well I am.'

'I just wouldn't want Peter thinking I was leading you into bad ways.'

She returned his amused gaze sternly. 'I'm sure Peter knows you couldn't lead me anywhere.'

For a moment, their eyes locked and some spark – of admiration or animosity, Hetty wasn't sure which – passed between them.

80

'Couldn't I?' he said softly.

Hetty turned away, hoping that, in the inadequate light of the single bulb, no one would notice her blushing, and wondering why on earth she was. 'Some water, Peter?' She waved the jug at him and he took it. 'I'm going to find some biscuits or something. You two go in by the fire. We can't sit in here.'

A little later Hetty brought a plate of crackers and cheese through to where the men were comfortably established, long legs stretched out. Peter was sitting on the one decent armchair, and Connor was on the sofa. Rather than sit next to him, and be thrown up against him by the missing springs, Hetty sat on the floor. She took a sip from her glass and noticed Peter looking at her. He seemed a little shocked to see her drinking neat whisky.

The fire crackled and the dogs shifted about, but no one said anything. Hetty searched frantically for a neutral topic of conversation, which cut out the house, Samuel, village life, and everything else all three of them would know about, apart from the weather.

'Did you finish that woman's kitchen?' she asked Peter eventually. 'Peter is a joiner – he makes wonderful kitchens.'

'Really? And do you earn a decent living, making kitchens?'

'Sorry?' said Peter, wondering if he'd misheard.

'I mean,' Connor went on, 'if you're courting Hetty, I'm the nearest thing here to a family member, I ought to find out what your prospects are.'

Hetty would have liked to kill Connor at that moment, but with a supreme effort she hung on to her temper. 'Oh, Connor,' she said, as blandly as she could manage, 'you've got it all wrong. Peter isn't courting me at all. I expect he's got a girlfriend the other side of the village, haven't you, Peter?'

'No, actually.'

'He and I are just good friends.' She shot Peter a look that was more glare than friendship. 'Aren't we?'

'Don't knock it,' said Connor. 'A good friend is harder to find than a lover. Don't you agree, Peter?'

Hetty wanted to die or groan very loudly.

'I would hope that one thing might lead to another,' said Peter.

'Ah, the romantic view. I'm afraid I'm old-fashioned. I see men as friends and women as lovers, and I don't like to mix them.'

'That *is* old-fashioned,' said Hetty. 'Not to mention wildly politically incorrect. Men can have friendships with women, even if they are heterosexual.'

'Believe me, sex always rears its ugly head sooner or later. Women may think they can be friends with a man, but sex will always be there somewhere, for the man at least.'

'I'm sure that's not true,' Hetty insisted, knowing that in Peter's case it probably was. 'And anyway, aren't we getting a little heavy? How about another drink?'

Peter got to his feet. 'Well, actually, I've got to go. Things to do. I just popped in . . .'

'. . . to see if Hetty was all right,' Connor finished for him.

Hetty got up too. 'Oh shut up, Connor,' she muttered. 'I'll see you out.' And she pushed Peter to the door before Connor could make any maddening comments about them kissing good-night.

'How long is he staying?' Peter asked, when they were safely out of earshot.

'*I* don't know. And I don't suppose he does either.'

'I don't like you being here alone with him. I don't trust him.'

'Oh for goodness' sake, Peter! He's not going to jump on me or anything. I'm perfectly safe. And it is practically his house; he's entitled to live in it.' Even if he does plan to pull it down.

'And will he let you stay?'

'I think so. He's not keen on showing old ladies around the place.'

'But do you want to go on living here? In the house, with him?'

Hetty exhaled slowly. 'I don't really know. He's been in bed most of the time since he arrived. I want to stay here, yes. But I don't know if we can live together. On the other hand, I'm not going to let him stand in the way of our plans if I can help it.'

'But how are you going to do that? If the place is practically his?'

'I don't know, Peter. I'm just going to hang on if I can. Now can you please go? You're letting all the heat out.' And driving me completely mad with questions I can't answer.

Hetty went back to the sitting room, wondering how to face Connor. Her mother would have offered him a nice piece of cake, on the grounds that men usually got irritable because they were hungry. But Hetty didn't have a nice piece of cake, and she didn't think a stale fairy cake left over from the car-boot sale would quite do. Nor did she think Connor's awkward temperament was anything to do with hunger. He'd just eaten a plate of cheese and crackers, and as there weren't any more she was forced to confront him unarmed.

He was standing with his back to the fire, his whisky glass refilled. He handed Hetty her glass, equally replenished. 'Don't you want it?' he said. 'Sorry, I didn't think.' Hetty was quite happy to accept it. It was such a relief to see him being unconfrontational. 'So, that was Peter.'

'Yes.'

'Very protective.'

'Yes.' She took a bracing sip. 'He was asking whether I'll stay, now you're here.'

'And will you? I'm sure the idea of us sharing a house makes Peter feel very uncomfortable, but how does it make you feel?'

Hetty bit her lip. 'I don't know. I suppose it depends on whether you want me here or not.'

Connor shrugged. 'I don't feel strongly either way. You don't take up much room.'

'So?'

'Well, what do you want, Hetty? Do you want to stay? Sort out the visitors and Mrs Hempstead? Or do you want to go back to your parents?'

It seemed that no one had asked Hetty what she wanted for a long time. Lately, people had mostly told her what she had to do, what was expected, or what was good for the community.

Connor perched on the edge of the sofa. 'I imagine Peter would like you to stay,' he continued.

'I'm sure he doesn't care one way or the other –'

'Oh come on! He's half-way in love with you. Anyone can see that. But Peter aside, are you happy here? Or do you want to get out while you still have the choice?'

Hetty didn't want Connor to think there was anything going on between her and Peter, even if, one day, there might be. 'Peter aside, I'm busy and I feel useful. I came here more or less against my will, but when I got here and saw what needed doing, I got involved. I would like to see things through.' She took a rather large gulp of her drink. 'Although I do realize that now you're here, things are a bit different.'

'In what way?'

'Well, the house doesn't need a sitter. And your . . . plans . . . for the place are quite different from my dreams.' If it hadn't been for the whisky she wouldn't have used a word like 'dreams' in front of someone like Connor.

'My living here needn't make much difference. As I said, you don't take up much space, although that's the one thing this damn house has got plenty of. As for your dreams . . .' he hesitated and almost smiled, '. . . you're young, you're entitled to them, however impractical they may be.'

'They're not impractical, not really. I mean, my plan probably wouldn't make as much money as other options might, but eventually, when everything was up and running, we'd earn enough to keep the house going.' Now was the time to mention the loan for the roof, while he was being comparatively nice. She found she couldn't do it. 'If that was what . . . anyone . . . wanted to do.'

Connor was silent for so long that Hetty had finished her whisky and the dogs had stopped begging for the cracker crumbs by the time he next spoke.

'I'll go and see Samuel tomorrow – see how well he's coped with the operation – and then decide what I think is best. But quite frankly, Hetty, if I think he's on the way out, I'm not going to let you play Stately Homes. I'll only let you stay if I think he's got a chance of coming out of hospital.'

'Hang on.' Hetty's mind was not at its clearest. 'Who's doing whom the favour? Who came to keep your inheritance from being burgled, or burning down? And now you're talking about *letting* me stay?'

'I can do without you, Hetty. You're not here for me. I didn't ask you to come.' He spoke softly, with painful truthfulness.

She thought for a moment. 'OK. So I can stay and play Stately Homes if Samuel looks like recovering? If not, I'm – free to go?'

'You're free to go at any time. As I said, you're not doing me any favours.'

'It was Samuel I came to help.'

'Then stay as long as Samuel needs you.' He took Hetty's glass from her. 'And now I think we need to eat. A few crackers might

84

be enough for you, but they barely filled the holes in my teeth.'

Remembering that he hadn't eaten for days, Hetty followed him out of the room, prepared, in view of his illness, to cook him something. Once in the kitchen she saw him open the fridge and pull things out, muttering under his breath about how little there was to cook with.

'Can I help?' she asked, watching him cutting the soft bits out of a couple of tomatoes and a green pepper.

'Only if you can make toast proficiently.'

She snarled at him, cut two slices of bread and put them in the toaster. She stood over it. Knowing her luck the thing would burst into flames or burn the bread if she didn't.

While guarding the toast, she watched him make a meal out of what was available. Scrambled eggs, baked beans, tomatoes cooked in the oven, half a green pepper singed on the gas and chopped, and the one remaining rasher of bacon snipped on to the eggs. For someone so aggressively macho, he was very handy about a kitchen.

'You're very resourceful with your cooking,' she said, as he handed her a plate.

'I have to be, in the parts of the world I spend most of my time.' He loaded a fork with eggs. 'Mind you, conditions aren't that much better here. How does Samuel manage without a grill?'

Hetty shrugged.

'And you're obviously no budding Mrs Beeton, judging by what there was to cook with.'

'Sorry about the sun-dried tomatoes.' Her voice dripped sarcasm. 'Somehow, I clean forgot to get any.'

He ignored the sarcasm and accepted the apology with a gracious nod. 'I don't suppose you could have got them locally, could you?'

Hetty gave up. 'Actually, the village shop sells more or less everything except meat. They're expensive, but very handy.'

'Isn't the butcher there any more? By the post office?'

'The shop *is* the post office, and there's no butcher.'

'Ah. Shame.'

The combination of tension and whisky meant that Hetty couldn't think of how to capitalize on this glimmer of sentiment for times past. But she stored it away for future use.

★

85

The following morning Caroline waltzed in, dressed to kill in leather trousers and a short jacket, which showed off her tiny waist and slim thighs. She flung her handbag on to the table, among the less aesthetic clutter. The village grapevine being as efficient as it was, Hetty wondered what had kept her away so long.

Caroline beamed at Connor. 'Great car! Whose is it? And what is it?'

Hetty, not so car-minded as Caroline, hadn't noticed that the car, parked in an empty stable, was anything special.

Connor gave Caroline a rare and splendid smile, transforming his been-round-the-block-a-few-times looks into something dangerously close to charm and sexiness. 'It's mine and it's a Citroën DS Decapotable.' Caroline was not only extremely attractive, she also said the right things.

'Jack will die with envy when he sees it. He's just gone away again, which is why I haven't been over. So who are you?' She directed her long-lashed gaze towards Connor. 'Hetty obviously isn't going to introduce us.'

She was right there. Once more, Hetty was trying to erase the word 'Barbarian' from her mind and replace it with Connor's surname. She was having no luck.

'Connor Barrabin,' he said, his eyes crinkling with pleasure. 'Who are you?'

While Caroline told him, an act that involved a lot of swishing of blonde hair from her, and a lot of crooked smiles and eye contact from him, Hetty cleared up the breakfast things. Unsurprisingly, she thought, his attitude to Caroline was as friendly as it had been hostile to Peter. Hetty felt displaced, both from the kitchen, which had been her territory, and from Connor's attention. But Caroline couldn't help flirting any more than she could help breathing. And Connor, obviously possessing a normal quota of male hormones, couldn't help responding.

'So, darling.' Caroline turned her attention to Hetty. 'Did Andy come?'

'He's putting the light back on upstairs as we speak. I hope.'

'And you've got enough money to pay him? Otherwise I can easily . . .'

'I've got plenty.' Hetty didn't want the M word used in front of Connor. He still didn't know how many of his uncle's things had been sold to raise it.

'So what are you going to be doing with yourself all day?' Caroline turned back to Connor.

'Today, I'm going to visit Samuel. Then I've got a report to write.'

'Let me know if Samuel's well enough for non-family visitors. I'd love to pop in and see him. I met him at a village do – he's such a sweet old boy.'

'I'm sure a visit from you would cheer him up. I'll let you know how he is. And, if possible, get some idea of when he's coming out.'

Hetty didn't know if she wanted him better or worse. If he came home, she might have to go, and then what on earth would she do with herself? She rinsed the bowls and put them to drain. 'Anyone want a cup of coffee?'

'Not for me,' said Connor. 'I must go. I've got to see the bank after I've seen Samuel. I'll do some shopping while I'm in town, but I'm not sure when I'll be back.'

He patted Hetty's shoulder as he passed, appearing not to have noticed her jump when he said 'bank'. Which bank?

Connor waved to Caroline. There was a moment's silence after he left.

'Mmm. He's not at all bad, in a sort of caveman way. He might clean up very nicely.'

Hetty tried to put banks and loans to the back of her mind. There wasn't anything she could do even if she knew which bank he was going to. 'He's a Barbarian,' she said.

Caroline raised her eyebrows. 'He hasn't thrown you over his shoulder and carried you upstairs to bed, has he?'

'No!' said Hetty indignantly. 'He's just planning to pull the house down before Samuel's cold in his grave!'

'Pity,' said Caroline, far too calmly.

'Which is? That he hasn't raped me, or that the house is going to be pulled down?'

'I don't think he'd ever need to rape anybody. I should think he's quite subtle as a lover.'

'So what? I wish you'd concentrate! I said he's going to pull the house down. How can we stop him?'

87

Caroline shrugged. 'I don't suppose we can, if he's dead set on it. When is he planning to do it?'

'Not while Samuel's alive, unless he's terminally ill and not likely to come home. But he says the house is too far gone to save.'

'It's not, is it?'

Hetty shrugged. 'I don't know. It's got a new roof and Andy doesn't think it's too bad. But perhaps we ought to get outside advice. Preferably before Connor has time to get back from town. You haven't got the right sort of architect tucked away in your bag, have you?'

'Sorry, no. But why the rush?'

'Well, we can hardly get in an expert to evaluate the condition of his inheritance while Connor's here, can we? If it's bad news, we don't want him to know.'

'I suppose not.' Caroline lapsed into silence. 'I still think we could get round him, persuade him to change his mind.'

'You might be able to. Don't include me in your plans.'

'You've never learnt how to manipulate men, have you?'

Hetty closed her eyes and shook her head. 'No.' She didn't know whether she should be proud of herself or ashamed.

'I'll set up a course. You can be my first customer. Now, I must go and do something useful.' She pushed herself off the table on to the floor. 'I only called in to get a squint at the young master.'

'You won't say anything about Connor demolishing the house, will you? I don't want people hearing and getting upset unnecessarily.'

'Not if you don't want me to. And Hetty, don't get too upset yourself. We'll get round Connor.'

'Is that the Royal "we", or do you mean me as well?'

Later that morning Hetty was looking through the Yellow Pages, searching for someone who might be able to come and tell her if the house was worth repairing or not, when Connor came home. He came in through the back door, his arms full of supermarket bags. 'There's more in the car,' he said.

Hetty shut the phone book and went to get the shopping in. As she might have expected, his car was as battered as he was. It was old, possibly old enough to be considered classic, though Connor obviously didn't treat it as such. It was a two-seater convertible with leather upholstery and a long bonnet. It looked as if it had once been at home speeding down to the South of France. Now, it had a bash in the driver's door and badly needed a respray. Alistair's Porsche, as she had last seen it, came into her mind. She knew that if she wanted to hurt Connor, she'd have to find another way of doing it.

She took the remaining bags, leaving a box full of bottles. Connor waved the phone at her as she came in. 'It's for you. Some woman.'

She took the phone, praying it wasn't Phyllis Hempstead. She couldn't tell her about Connor while he was listening. 'Hello?'

'Is that Hetty? It's Felicity Makepiece. I spoke to your mother. About our ruby wedding celebrations?'

'Oh, yes.' Hetty found a pencil and prepared to make notes.

'I do want to speak to you about that, but really why I'm ringing is to invite you to dinner.'

'Oh! How kind.'

'On the Thursday after next. Can you manage that?'

That was two days before they were due to open, but Hetty said, yes, of course.

Felicity Makepiece was just about to hang up, having confirmed that Hetty had a car and given her pages of directions, and many other items of extraneous information, when, in between breaths, she dropped a bombshell. 'Oh, I nearly forgot.' She laughed. 'Rather fun! One of the young people who'll be down for Easter. Says he knows you.'

'Oh? Who is it?'

'Alistair Gibbons.'

Hetty reeled for a few moments, coming to just in time to catch Mrs Makepiece before she rang off in a hail of 'find a moment to talk about the ruby wedding', and 'looking forward to seeing you's.

'Can I bring someone?'

There was a moment's pause. 'Only if it's a man, dear. I've already had enough trouble getting my numbers right.'

'Oh – it is a man.'

'That'll be lovely. See you then, then. Byee.'

CHAPTER EIGHT

To her relief, Hetty realized that Connor hadn't overheard her conversation, so she wouldn't have to explain it. He put the box of bottles on a chair, there being no space left on the table.

'So, how was Samuel?' asked Hetty, before he could ask her about the phone call, or tell her about the bank.

'Ah.' He paused, pushed back his hair and bit his lip. 'The jury's out on Samuel, I'm afraid. As you probably know, he came through his operation all right. But he's not making the progress they'd like.'

Much as Hetty thought. 'Was he pleased to see you?'

'Not particularly.' He gave a quick grin. 'But he was glad I was here to keep an eye on the place.'

'But he knew I was here.' Hetty was indignant.

'I know. But he felt it was a bit much, expecting you to live here on your own.'

'He seemed quite happy for me to live here on my own when there was no choice!' Hetty furiously muttered, grinding coffee beans in the hand-operated grinder she'd finally unearthed.

'But now there is a choice . . .'

'You mean, he wants me to go?'

'No. He just wants me to stay. With you.'

Hetty poured boiling water into the coffee jug to warm it. 'But what about the house? Is he going to be well enough to come home or not?'

'As I said, the jury's out. But talking of the house, Hetty . . .' He fixed her with a stare that made her heart sink.

'What?'

'I saw the bank managers – both of them. And I found out about a lot you should have told me.'

Hetty felt herself redden. 'Oh.'

'The first one told me the extent of Samuel's overdraft, which was bad enough. He then told me you paid the house insurance with a cheque from another bank.'

'Oh?'

'Having discovered which bank it was, I went on to learn that you had the power to sign cheques up to the value of two thousand pounds.' He emphasized the words. 'And that you had already used up a large proportion of the money in the account.'

'Oh,' did not seem an adequate response this time. 'Well, I don't know how you got all that information out of them. I could hardly get them to admit Samuel had an account.'

'What did you spend the money on, Hetty? If I find that you've been rewiring the house, decorating, playing about, with Samuel's money . . .'

Hetty had unconsciously started to huddle in her chair. 'I used the money to have the phone put back on and for the loan.'

'What loan?'

'The loan Samuel took out with a moneylender, presumably to have the roof done.' She spoke very quietly and kept her eyes shut.

Connor's voice was hardly any more audible. 'What?'

Hetty opened her eyes. 'Didn't you notice? The roof at the back part of the house has been repaired –'

'Do you think I'm blind? Of course I knew about the roof being fixed, but I didn't know about any loan to pay for it. What are the terms and conditions?'

'I don't know, I'm waiting for them to tell me.'

Connor turned away abruptly. 'How did you find out about it?'

'I opened Samuel's post. He'd been late with a payment. As I had the cheque-book and limited power of attorney, I made it. A few days later I got a letter, addressed to me, not Samuel, warning me about penalties and about the loan having to be paid by the due date. I wrote back asking them to tell me what these were. I haven't heard yet.'

Connor swore, under his breath at first, but as his anxiety grew, so did his volume.

'So you didn't know anything about it?' Hetty said, when at last he'd stopped.

'Of course I didn't. Do you think I'd have let him get involved with loan sharks? Why didn't he ask me for the money for the roof?'

It was a rhetorical question, but Hetty felt she had the answer. 'Could it be that he thought you wouldn't want to lend him money to spend on the house, knowing your feelings about it?'

Connor brought his fists up to his head. 'Surely he couldn't have thought I wouldn't have lent him the money?'

'Perhaps he thought you wouldn't have that sort of money to lend?'

Connor uncovered his face. 'He may well have been right. He knows I've been working hard to pay for my damn car. If only I'd known he'd do this, I would never have brought the bloody thing.'

Hetty was starting to feel sorry for Connor. 'Well, you can't read people's minds.'

'You've got a better chance of doing so if you're there.'

'And I'm sure he wouldn't want you not to have a car.'

He gave her a glowering look under his brows. 'There are cars and cars. Mine was particularly expensive.'

'Don't worry,' Hetty murmured very quietly. 'It doesn't show.'

He glared at her but didn't react. 'That settles it. The sooner I sell the property the better.'

'No!'

She got the full force of his piercing gaze. 'Then what do you suggest?'

Hetty took a breath. 'Look, I know this has all come as a great shock to you, but I've had time to think things over. I reckon – hope – we could keep up the payments on what we earn from the house.'

'How are we going to pay off the capital when we don't even know how much it is?'

'I think we're already doing that. Given the size of the payments, if it was only interest we were paying he would have had to borrow enough to have the house completely renovated. And – unless he's spent it on something else – he hasn't.'

'But you don't know for sure? Why didn't you try and find out?'

'I didn't like to. It seemed like prying.'

Connor tutted at her scruples and together they went through Samuel's desk, drawer by drawer, until they found a bill for the roof. It was a comparatively small amount. Mystified, they hunted some more until they found the original loan agreement.

Connor whistled. 'Fucking extortionists.'

'Why do you think he borrowed so much, when the roof bill isn't half that?'

'Look at the rates of interest. He borrowed enough to make most of the payments, but not quite all.'

'But why?' Hetty studied the paper again, as if it would tell her. 'It doesn't make sense to borrow money you can't repay in full. Making a few payments won't help much.'

'I'm sure he knows that. But I don't think he thought he'd need to worry about it.'

'What do you mean?' Hetty sat on the floor, surrounded by paper. She was developing a headache.

Connor glanced at the letter in his hand. 'The final payment is due on the third of June. I expect he thought, by then, it would be my problem, not his.'

Hetty massaged her scalp. 'I still don't understand.'

'Poor Samuel. He obviously decided he'd make it through the spring, but die before midsummer.' Hetty groaned. 'He knew he was ill,' Connor went on. 'Thought he was dying, and wouldn't go to the doctor until I dragged him.'

'Oh, poor Samuel.'

'And now he's had his operation, he should last for years. If he wasn't so depressed.'

'And the reason he's so depressed is worrying about this loan?'

Connor nodded. 'Probably.' Hetty buried her face in her hands so she could think. 'What a choice,' said Connor. 'I could sell the house now and break his heart, or wait until he's worried himself into an early grave and then sell it.'

Hetty looked up. 'That's not the only way out, you know.'

'No. I can sell that damn car –'

'Forget the car! Concentrate on the house! It's beautiful, it's interesting, it could attract hundreds of visitors. I've already got some woman wanting her ruby wedding celebrations here. If we worked hard, we could make up the extra payments. We've got until the third of June.'

'You know what the payments are. Do you really think the house can earn enough to make up the shortfall?'

'This is no time to think! This is the time to *feel*, to hope, to work. If we fail, and the house has to go in the end, at least Samuel will know we've done our damnedest. And even if we don't quite make it, we could ask them to reschedule. Hell! If we were a going concern we could get a proper overdraft and pay off the loan that way! You're so defeatist!'

'Am I? Well you're living in cloud-cuckoo-land.'

'Maybe, but at least I'm not doing the next best thing to giving Samuel a lethal injection! Tell him you know about the loan! Tell him you've got it all in hand, and that we can pay it off, at least he won't die of despondency!'

'It would be a lie.'

'No! Not a lie, more . . .' she searched for the right words, '. . . an over-optimistic speculation. You don't know we *can't* do it, any more than I know we can. But we both know we can try. And with the village behind us, we've got a good chance of success.'

'Oh – the village. With Mrs Hempstead on our side, how can we fail?' His voice dripped with sarcasm.

'How indeed? But even if we do fail, at least we won't have lain down in the mud to let ourselves be trampled to death by property developers.'

Something like a smile disturbed the severity of Connor's expression. 'Count me out. I still think we should cut our losses and sell.'

'And break Samuel's heart?'

'Hearts don't break that easily.'

'No, they don't,' said Hetty, who was an authority. 'But they do get dented, and I don't think he could take much of that at his time of life.'

Connor sighed. 'Luckily for you, nor do I. But don't expect any help from me. I intend to tackle the problem a different way.'

'But you won't actually obstruct us?'

'Not unless I have to. But I really don't want Samuel's private financial business being the talk of the village. So please don't tell anyone about the loan.' Hetty nodded. 'But you have to promise to tell me everything I might need to know, not to lie to me.'

Hetty nodded. 'Not unless I have to.'

'If I find you have,' he went on in the same, calm voice, 'I will be extremely annoyed.'

Hetty resolved not to annoy him unless she really couldn't help it. It wasn't likely to be a pleasant experience.

After lunch, which Connor made, scorning Hetty's offer of help, he disappeared upstairs with his laptop. Hetty cleared up and then set off with the dogs to see Peter. She would feel reasonably confident about seeing Alistair again with Peter at her side. As the songs all went, she was no longer the frightened little girl she had been when they'd parted. It may not have been long since that terrible morning but, in terms of experience, she was years older.

Peter was, as usual, pleased to see her. 'Come in. Have you come for sanctuary from that oaf?'

Hetty felt instantly defensive of Connor. 'He's not that bad. And he's said I can do whatever I need to to get the house open.'

'Big of him. To whose advantage is that, I wonder?'

'Well, not his. When Samuel dies, he's planning to have the house knocked down.'

Peter dropped the kettle he had just filled. 'What!'

'Didn't I tell you?' she asked in a small voice, realizing she hadn't meant to.

'No you didn't! Is there anything else you haven't told me? Like that you and he are having an affair? Any little detail like that?'

'There's no need to be angry, really. I only didn't tell you – immediately – because I hoped I might be able to talk him out of it.'

'That's asking rather a lot, even of your powers of persuasion, isn't it?'

'Not really. I mean – yes – you don't understand.' And, as she didn't plan to tell him about the loan, understanding would be difficult. She took a deep breath and prepared to be economical with the truth. 'He went to see Samuel today. Connor's plans for the house depend on how well Samuel's recovering.'

'Oh – and how is he recovering?'

'Not as well as they'd hoped. But he's not dying either, so we've got a bit of time.'

'So, what did the Barbarian agree to?'

'That I can carry on with my plans until we know. If Samuel's going to recover, everything will be all right, at least until he dies, then God knows. But if he isn't going to come home, well, Connor says there's no point in doing anything to the house.'

'I see. Calling him a Barbarian doesn't even begin to sum him up, does it?'

'I really don't want this getting out, Peter – about pulling down the house. I told Caroline –'

'You told *Caroline* when you don't want it getting out! Put your secret in the local paper, why don't you?'

'I didn't mean to tell her. I was upset at the time. I swore her to secrecy.' Peter snorted. 'But I don't want the village knowing. Not when it's only a vague plan.'

'They'll lynch him. Or resurrect the stocks.'

'Can't have that,' said Hetty primly. 'Think of the scandal.'

Peter regarded her ruefully, his head slightly on one side, his anger dissipating. He mopped up the spilled water and refilled the kettle. 'Sorry, I didn't mean to shout at you. I was upset.'

'Of course you were. So was I. I'm still hoping – I mean, he's not totally unreasonable – that I may make him see what a horrible idea selling the site is.'

'Well, don't feel obliged to sleep with him to make your point.' He held up a soothing hand. 'Only joking. I know you wouldn't do anything like that.'

Hetty was just about to complain about Peter being possessive when she realized that she needed him on her side. He handed her a cup of tea she didn't want, and she smiled, gratefully.

'Changing the subject, Peter, well sort of, we might have a booking for a ruby wedding sometime soon. I gather it would be a very plush affair; could earn us thousands. Well, one thousand, possibly more.'

'That's good. Biscuit?'

She shook her head. 'The thing is, I've got to be briefed about it. At a dinner party.'

'That's a bit odd, isn't it?'

'Well, yes, but the woman's some connection of my mother's and she feels obliged to entertain me. She knows I'm on my own here . . . and things. It's what my mother's told her.'

'I see.'

'The thing is, and it's really the most ghastly coincidence, she let it slip just as we were ringing off, that Alistair is going to be there.'

'Alistair?'

'Yes, you know, the one who – behaved so badly. You must have known . . .'

'Yes, vaguely. You mentioned having a broken heart when we first met.'

'So I did. When I so didn't want people to know, too. But anyway, Alistair's him. And he's going to be at this dinner party.' She closed her eyes. 'And I wondered whether you would possibly come with me to it.'

'When is it?'

'A week next Thursday.'

'Hetty, I'm terribly sorry, but I'm away all that week. I'm putting in a kitchen in Shropshire.'

This was awful – awful and totally unexpected. 'Couldn't you come back for the evening?'

'It's an awfully long way.' He regarded her sadly, his brown eyes compassionate but unrelenting. It flashed into Hetty's mind that it was the way dentists look when they tell you that you need a little filling, and that it won't hurt, much.

Hetty frantically tried to think of ways of persuading him to undertake a round trip of a hundred miles or so to take her to a dinner party. Ripping off three layers of clothing to reveal a greying bra probably wouldn't do it. And Peter fancied her. If she couldn't make Peter do a little thing like that for her, how did she even dare to hope that she might be capable of changing Connor's mind about the house?

'Listen, it is terribly, terribly important that I don't go alone.'

'Caroline would go with you.'

'Yes, but when I asked if I could bring a friend Mrs Makepiece said it had to be a man. She's spent long enough getting her numbers even.'

'How ridiculous. Who is this woman?'

'One with a lot of money to spend on a party, at Courtbridge House.'

'There's no need to prostitute yourself, Hetty. The money's not that important.'

Hetty wanted to throw her mug at him. 'It's very important now. Even more important than it was before.' Hetty wished she could tell Peter exactly why. 'If we can show Connor that money's coming in, fairly regularly, that the place is a going concern –'

'But it's not, is it?'

'Not yet, no! But we could make it one.' If only I wasn't surrounded by negative, nit-picking, no-I-can't-take-you-to-a-dinner-party sort of people.

'I'm sure we could.' Now he was being soothing. Hetty wanted to throw something even more. 'But you going with someone to this dinner party isn't going to make a difference either way.'

Hetty licked her lips, sipped her tea. 'It'll make a difference to me.'

Peter shook his head. 'I'm very sorry. I wish I could help. But I'm afraid this time I can't. You know I'd do anything for you, within reason.' He didn't need to add that this request didn't qualify.

It was hopeless. If she'd had to go to hospital he would have found a way of taking her. The trouble was, he was a man, so he didn't see the occasion as important. She debated having one more go, but decided against it. It was very bad for her confidence, failing to get someone who was very fond of her, if not actually in love with her, to drive a few hundred miles and spend a boring evening, just for her.

She smiled stiffly. 'That's OK, Peter. I know you'd help if you could. I'll ask Caroline. She's bound to know any number of presentable men who would go with me. I would just rather it was you, that's all.' She looked sadly down into her mug and hoped he felt a pang of guilt.

Conveniently, Caroline was at Courtbridge House when Hetty got home. She was charming away at Connor in the kitchen as if he wasn't the man who planned to sell his birthright, desecrate his heritage, and offend every conservation group in the country.

Connor was doing his share of charming, his crooked smile revealing his crooked teeth, under his crooked nose. You could write a nursery rhyme about him, thought Hetty, and then remembered that somebody already had. But it was amazing how much good humour improved people. Connor would never be handsome, but he was almost attractive when he smiled.

'Hi!' said Hetty brightly, hiding her resentment at their devious pleasure in each other's company, highlighted by her recent failure with Peter. 'What are you two gassing about?'

'This and that,' said Caroline.

'Samuel,' said Connor.

'No more news, is there? You haven't had a phone call?' Hetty felt her heart dip, and a second later felt remorse as she realized it wasn't only Samuel's health she was worried about – she had selfish reasons of her own for wishing him better.

Connor shook his head. 'No. No need to get worked up. Is there a decent-sized saucepan to be found anywhere? I want to make some stock.'

Hetty was fairly sure she'd sold the only really big saucepan. 'Have a look in that cupboard at the end,' she suggested, merely because that cupboard was furthest away and she wanted him out of earshot. 'Caroline, you wouldn't be an angel and come up and look at the bedroom with me? The one with the four-poster I want to open to the public?' She jerked her head towards the door as people do when they want to speak to someone privately, but don't want to tell the whole room.

'Oh!' Caroline was not slow on the uptake. 'Having trouble with your SNAG?' She spoke very quietly, but not quietly enough.

'Her what?' demanded Connor, straightening up.

There was a moment's pause while both women independently wondered if there was a lie they could get away with, and then Caroline decided that there wasn't. 'Sensitive New Age Guy.'

'Oh, you mean Peter.'

'Actually, it's just the sheets that are bothering me,' said Hetty. 'Should we have antique linen, or won't they show under the quilt?'

'It depends who's going to wash them, Hetty,' said Connor. 'If Peter's going to do it, I'd stick to polycotton. They'll need changing fairly often, I imagine. You don't want the poor chap up all night ironing.'

Hetty closed her eyes for a moment. 'As usual, Connor, you've got it all wrong. I'm talking about the bedroom upstairs. Peter's sheets are no concern of mine.'

'Oh, a lovers' tiff? I'm so sorry.'

Hetty stalked out of the room, trusting that Caroline would follow. How could he get it so wrong and so right, both at the same time?

'Well,' said Caroline, when they reached the bedroom, 'is it sheets, or is it Peter?'

'Well, it's both, really. But Peter is the more urgent.'

'Why? What's he done?'

'It's what he's not going to do. I've been invited to a dinner party, and I absolutely have to take a man with me.'

'Oh, why?'

'Because Alistair is going to be there.'

'Holy Shit!' said Caroline, forgetting her *alter ego* as Brown Owl.

'I asked Peter and he's working and won't come. Do you know anyone I could take?'

'You mean, anyone single, trustworthy and half decent-looking?'

'If possible.'

'Well, yes, I do. But you're not going to like it.'

'Why not? Who do you know like that, who I know too?'

Caroline turned round. 'Conan the Barbarian.'

Hetty closed her eyes. 'You have got to be kidding. Lying too. He is not half decent-looking.'

'He's not handsome, but he doesn't need to be. He's gorgeous being ugly.'

'Do you think so?'

'Well, don't you? I mean, I know his nose is crooked, and he's got that little scar on his upper lip, and his hair wants cutting. Stuff like that. But he's got bags of sex appeal. Surely even a broken-hearted woman can see that?'

'Caroline, I would rather die than go with him, even if he'd take me. You know how he's always making embarrassing remarks, he'd have an absolute field-day.'

Caroline shrugged. 'If Jack were home, I'd lend him to you. But if Peter won't go with you, I don't see you've got a choice. Unless you'd like me to ring round the Brownie dads and ask them?'

Hetty began to smile in spite of herself. 'You could offer a badge for it. A little picture of a man in a dinner-jacket with a woman in a long dress on his arm. The Escort badge.'

Caroline nodded. 'It could fit right in between Hostess and House Orderly. But seriously, I'd do that if you wanted me to, but I can't think of anyone remotely suitable. There's Alan Brewster at the shop, I suppose. But as he gets up at five in the morning, it hardly seems fair to ask him.'

'I wouldn't dream of it!' Hetty was horrified. 'But are you sure there's no one else? You must have loads of suitable friends.'

'No one who lives remotely locally. And their wives are my friends too. Some of them might not be too keen on lending their husbands to an attractive young woman.'

'Oh, come off it!'

'You come off it, darling. You just come downstairs now and ask Connor. If he says no, we'll think again.' She hesitated. 'You couldn't possibly not go yourself?'

'I wish. But no. The hostess is planning to have her fortieth wedding anniversary here. She wants to tell me about it and, as she's a sort of friend of my mother's, wants to offer me hospitality. Besides . . .' She paused. 'If I don't go, Alistair is bound to find out I was invited, and he's bound to think I couldn't face him.'

'And can you?'

'Yes, but not alone.'

'Right,' said Caroline. 'What about Connor? Do you want to face *him* alone, or shall I stay?'

'No. He's bound to be embarrassing, and it'll be better without an audience.'

She waited until that evening when they had eaten the lamb chops, new potatoes and green beans, which he cooked perfectly, followed by the chocolate soufflé, ditto. Hetty was beginning to understand how some women felt disenfranchised by men who cooked.

'You go and sit down in front of the fire. I'll make coffee,' she suggested.

He gave her a strange look. 'Why, what is it you want to ask me?'

'Just because I offered to make coffee . . .'

'Well?'

'I've got to go to a dinner party, and I really need someone to go with me.'

'Why? Don't you like driving at night?'

She didn't, particularly. 'It's not that, it's just . . . someone is going to be there –'

'Ah. The ex-boyfriend.'

'Just what do you know about him?'

'Only what you've told me.'

'But I haven't said a word about him!'

'That's how I knew he'd hurt you very badly.'

'Yes, well, he did. And for various reasons, I can't face seeing him on my own.'

'Pride?'

'That, and other things.' She didn't want to go into what had happened to Alistair's car, or explain why he might present her with a huge bill.

'Presumably you've asked Peter?'

'He's fitting a kitchen somewhere.' Hetty's tone made it clear where she'd like to fit his kitchen.

'And there's no one else you can possibly ask?'

'No.'

'Well, I really wish I could help. But I don't want to.' Hetty closed her eyes. Why did she ever think he would put himself out for her. He didn't need her – probably found her a nuisance – why should he drive thirty miles there and back to be bored out of his skull for an evening? 'On the other hand, I can't let you face this bastard on your own, so I'll come.'

'How do you know he was a bastard?'

'He let you down, didn't he?'

CHAPTER NINE

Hetty was singing merrily as she put the finishing touches to the second-best bedroom. She was feeling exceptionally pleased with herself. Not only had they received the vital Certificate of Public Liability, but also a few compliments too. The man from the insurance company, probably warned by the bank manager and expecting to find a crumbling ruin, had been pleasantly surprised to find the makings of a beautiful period home. She was just reliving Connor's look of utter surprise as the man had delivered his verdict, when Connor appeared in the doorway.

'I'm going into town for a haircut, and Caroline's downstairs.' Connor didn't comment on her singing. He was probably tone-deaf.

'Oh. Hell!' Hetty's triumph dissipated as she remembered the dinner party, which she had successfully blotted out of her consciousness. 'I was supposed to be going round to sort out something to wear for this thing tonight. What are you going to wear?'

'Clothes,' said Connor, and stalked off.

He might at least have given the bedroom a glance, she thought crossly, now it was almost ready. It had been repainted, most of the furniture removed, the bed-hangings had been handwashed, painstakingly ironed, and rehung. The floor had been polished with something Phyllis Hempstead had concocted from an old edition of Mrs Beeton. It looked a perfect example of a young girl's bedroom. Before opening-day, Hetty was planning to drape a nightie across the bed, put a vase of flowers on the window-sill, and find a book of poetry that was both romantic and in period. There was bound to be some Herrick somewhere.

'Hetty!' Caroline shouted up the stairs. 'Do you want to go to this thing in your dungarees?'

Reluctantly, Hetty left the bedroom, making a mental note to check the date of the pictures before she finally declared it finished. She didn't want Phyllis telling her that silhouettes weren't popular until *much* later, my dear.

Hetty had been extremely busy, so the fact that she'd bought nothing with her except jeans and jumpers flitted into her list of anxieties only occasionally. Now, she had to face it. She had a hot date, nothing to wear, and Caroline determined to give her 'a whole new look'. She shuddered, and turned her mind back to what she had managed to achieve lately.

She had drawn up a master plan of what needed doing for the grand opening the following weekend. Mrs Hempstead had allocated tasks to all her friends who had volunteered to help. Hetty had to make sure that whoever appeared at the back door or front had whatever paint, cleaning materials or tools they needed. She spent quite a lot of time chugging about in her car, cadging power tools, or buying more sugar soap and white emulsion. But as the house always looked a little better whenever she returned, she was quite happy being the gofer.

When not on the road she had her own restoration agenda, which was confined mostly to bits of cleaning you couldn't ask anyone else to do. People are happy to recreate a working dairy (at least, the two people detailed for this task were) but no one wanted thankless tasks with little visible effect, such as washing skirting-boards in corridors. Hetty started by the front door, washing the trail of paintwork along the path the visitors would take. Nowhere they wouldn't see got so much as a wipe. She sang as she went, and managed to resurrect most of her repertoire. She had just been struggling to remember a bit of opera that had been used in a television commercial while tackling some beading with a toothbrush, when Connor came up to tell her the man had come to inspect the house. Hetty had stopped singing mid-breath, horribly embarrassed at being caught with her tonsils showing.

'The little black dress is an awful cliché, but it does work,' said Caroline. 'Do you want to look sophisticated, or sweetly pretty?'

Hetty, wearing Caroline's bathrobe, regarded Caroline's open wardrobe with dismay. She'd never seen so many clothes, except during the sales. Caroline didn't keep her clothes in her bedroom.

She had a special room for them, quite a large room, but it was still crammed.

'I don't know. What do you think?'

'Let's go down and have a drink and think about it.'

'It's only five o'clock.'

'Is it! Hell! We'll have to think fast then. I wonder if I could do your make-up while Susie's doing your hair?'

Susie breezed in, refused a glass of wine, and wrapped a gown around Hetty. She fingered her wet hair.

'Mmmm. Now do you have any ideas about how you want it? Just a bit off the ends, or something more exciting?'

'Something more exciting,' said Caroline. 'Trust her,' she said to Hetty. 'She's a genius.'

Indeed, by the time Susie had taken off quite a heap of hair, and blow-dried the remainder, Hetty felt a lot better.

'All that extra length was weighing the hair down,' Susie explained, as unexpected curls appeared from under her skilful fingers. 'Now your natural curl can come through. When you wash it, just put on a dollop of mousse and scrunch it.'

'It looks wonderful, Hetty,' said Caroline. 'Now you run along upstairs and find something to wear while I see Susie out.'

Hetty knew that Caroline had paid Susie, but she was so shooshed by Caroline when she suggested that she paid for her own haircut, she shut up.

Caroline was right about the little black dress being a cliché, and besides, Caroline's dresses might be a bit *too* little for Hetty. What should she wear? Alistair's woman, whether she was the same one or a new model, was bound to be sophisticated. Hetty had been but a short foray into *naïveté* for Alistair, she was sure. So did she want to compete, or be sweet? She was trying to improve on this potential song lyric, when Caroline came in.

'Well, you can't wear that bra, that's for sure.'

'I know it's a bit grey, but it won't show.'

'Hasn't anyone ever told you that bras show through your clothes? If they don't give you a nice shape, there's no point in wearing one. I've got every sort. Uplift, downlift, backless, topless, you name it, it's stuffed in that drawer. Now,' she gestured to the open wardrobe, 'which of these do you fancy?'

'God! I don't know! I may not fit into anything. I'm not as slim as you.'

'Yes you are, but if you feel like that, let's not go for anything too tight over the hips. But I insist we go for sexy.'

'Why? I don't want Alistair back, you know.'

'You'll feel confident if you feel sexy.'

In the end Caroline found a rather revealing black number, which Hetty agreed to wear under a scarlet silk jacket with black velvet revers, which she loved. The decision made, Caroline started on Hetty's make-up.

Connor was sitting on the sofa in Caroline's sitting room, drinking ginger ale and reading last week's Sunday papers. He stood up as Hetty and Caroline came in, but although he looked Hetty over, he made no comment on her appearance.

Hetty found it hard to swallow her disappointment as she tottered across the room in Caroline's black suede stilettos. He was usually so forthright, she was expecting him either to say she looked fabulous or like a tart – probably the latter. But to go to all that trouble and for him not say anything was galling.

'You look very smart,' she said to him, determined not to be mean-spirited.

Like her, he was dependent on borrowed finery. He had had a haircut and his thick, sisal-coloured locks had been trimmed and tamed, revealing, thought Hetty bitchily, that he had a forehead. Quite a high one. His eyebrows seemed less shaggy – surely not Vaselined into shape? And his nose, still crooked, gained nobility from being in less close proximity to his hair.

Jack's dinner-jacket did his looks no harm, either. Hetty was used to seeing him in ancient jeans or cords and baggy sweaters – very similar to the clothes she lived in herself. All that sleek black flannel and gleaming white cotton smoothed out his creases so he seemed almost civilized. Not handsome, of course, but . . .

'Very tasty,' said Caroline frankly. 'Almost as beautiful as Hetty, don't you think, Connor?'

'What are you asking me? Do I think I'm beautiful, or do I think Hetty's beautiful?'

'Either.'

'I don't respond to loaded questions. If you want a drink,' he turned to Hetty, 'have it quickly. We ought to go.'

Upstairs in Caroline's bedroom, with Caroline's bra and Caroline's make-up on, she had felt some of Caroline's self-confidence. Connor's lack of interest was demoralizing. She declined a drink.

'Come along then. Get your coat. Thank Jack very much for the DJ, Caroline – after you tell him you lent it to me.'

Caroline smiled and hugged Hetty. 'Good luck, darling. It'll go really well, I'm sure. You look wonderful, believe me. And as for you, you gorgeous hunk,' she prodded Connor in the shoulder, 'you don't deserve a kiss. But do look after her, won't you?'

Hetty slid into Connor's battered, beautiful car, hoping the heater worked. Her legs felt bare with only a pair of tights to cover them up to her knees and, sitting down, the skirt rose several inches. Hetty hoped Mrs Makepiece had large napkins, so she could feel decent. At least in the dark of the car, Connor couldn't see her lower thighs spread out.

She wished she was wearing her own clothes; it would have been nice to have some old and faithful garment about her to give her confidence. But perhaps she should take on Caroline's persona along with her clothes. That would give Alistair something to think about.

Connor drove without speaking, handling the car gracefully, fast but safe. He didn't accelerate up to junctions and then brake hard, or zoom away from them. She was grateful that, unlike Alistair, he would get her to their destination without making her sick.

'Do you want directions?' she asked at last, uncomfortable with the silence.

'Not till we're in the actual village. I know my way until then.'

'It's very kind of you to take me.'

'Yes.'

'Of course, I could perfectly well have taken myself – '

'If Alistair hadn't been coming. Yes, I know all that.'

Hetty gave up trying to make conversation. If they'd been a couple she could have appealed to him to be more supportive. This was an important occasion for her, he should back her up, not sulk. But they weren't, so she had no right to ask anything of him.

'So why are you so worked up about seeing Alistair again, then?'

He broke into her resentful thoughts. 'Are you likely to burst into tears at the sight of him with another woman?'

'Certainly not. But I am a bit – frightened of him.'

'Why?'

'Well, when we parted, I sort of – ran into his car.'

'What do you mean?'

'I was in my car at the time. His was a Porsche. I hit it several times.'

'Bloody hell!' He hadn't been on her side before, now he was definitely on Alistair's. 'I'm not surprised you're frightened. If you did that to my car, I'd certainly beat you. Not that I'd wait this long to do it, of course,' he added grimly.

She struck him a verbal blow where she knew it would hurt. 'I could do much, much more to your car and it wouldn't even show.'

His scowl was magnified by the moving shadows as they passed through the sporadic lights of a hamlet. 'Don't you believe it. I know every dent and every spot of rust, and when I've got time I'm going to restore it to the thing of beauty it once was.' He shot her a glance as ugly as anything Quasimodo could produce. 'And if you even look at it wrong, I'll wallop you.'

Hetty ignored the threat and followed up on the passion. 'Why can't you feel like that about the house? It could be a thing of beauty with a little attention.'

'A lot of attention, and a small fortune, which I haven't got. And don't change the subject. You want me there tonight to protect you from Alistair doing what you justly deserve to have done to you?'

'I'm not frightened of him hitting me. He's not a violent person.' She shot a look of accusation at Connor, who didn't notice. 'I just don't want the bill for the damage.'

'I'm not surprised. You must have cost him thousands of pounds.'

'The car was insured.'

'But still. He'd have to pay the excess, and he'd lose his no-claims bonus.'

'Well, my car died in the fight.'

'Serve you bloody well right. You should treat cars with more respect.'

'I was upset.'

'That makes it all perfectly all right, of course.'

'No, but it does justify the – violence of my actions.'

'I doubt that very much. No one likes being dumped, but there's no need to react like that.'

Hetty clenched her teeth. 'He didn't just dump me. He wanted to, but he didn't want to just tell me, so he very carefully and deliberately arranged for me to catch him, and her, in bed.'

The car swerved slightly. Connor got it quickly under control and then brought it to a smooth halt under the lights of a pub.

'We're here. Give us a look at those directions.' He snatched them from her.

At that moment, she hated Connor as much as she had ever hated Alistair, and wondered if there was any way she could possibly go home, now, without asking him to drive her. She had ten pounds in her evening bag, put there by Caroline for emergencies. It probably wasn't enough for a taxi.

He tossed the directions at her. They landed on the floor. 'Come on, Cinderella, let's get you to your ball.'

He found the house quickly and easily, and parked his car on the gravel drive, the last in a chain of expensive company cars. He took her arm as she staggered on the thick gravel in her heels, and held on to it as they went up to the house. He rang the bell without giving Hetty time to renew her lipstick, or run her fingers through her carefully tousled hair.

'Next time,' he murmured as they heard the door being opened, 'put sugar in his petrol tank. That would really bugger up his engine.'

When Mrs Makepiece opened the door, she found one of her guests looking very surprised indeed.

Hetty had been hoping that Alistair wouldn't be there. It was a perfectly reasonable hope – if a more exciting invitation had come up he was quite capable of not showing up. But as she took off her coat and saw to her hair, Hetty noticed that her surroundings, though not large and indeed a little shabby, were grand. And Alistair cared about grandness. She sighed, angry with herself for still minding.

She knew what she had seen in him. He was handsome, power-ful, and his attention was extremely flattering. What annoyed her was that she gone on being spellbound long enough to fall in love with him, to give him her virginity, when her brain should have told her he was a self-seeking snob long before either of these things could happen.

To her relief and surprise, she found Connor waiting for her at the bottom of the stairs. He took her arm and took her into a drawing room where people were drinking champagne.

The room was full, but she saw Alistair immediately she entered it. She waited for the familiar stab of pain which thoughts of him had created for so long, but it never came. She still felt angry – incredibly angry – with him, but there was no churning in her stomach, no aching longing for a look or a smile she had once felt. It was such a relief that, when he caught her eye, she smiled at him. It was satisfying to register his surprise at her reaction. Then she remembered his car, and developed butterflies.

She was glad she'd gone for the little black dress and scarlet jacket. There are times when one wants to stick out from the crowd, make a statement, be individual. And there are times, like tonight, when there is safety in wearing more or less the same uniform as everyone else. It made you less likely to be picked off by the hyenas.

Mrs Makepiece introduced Connor and Hetty to a young couple who were part of the group staying for Easter. Alistair came up while they were talking about gliding. At least, Connor was talking, Hetty was warming up her champagne in her overheated hands and nodding politely.

'Hetty,' he said, significantly. 'You look very . . .'

'. . . Well?' she suggested.

Connor turned towards Alistair. 'Who's this, darling?' he asked, and put his hand on her waist, as if staking his claim.

Hetty managed the introductions, although she was taken aback by Connor's form of address, not to mention his hand.

Alistair noticed the hand, too. 'You cost me an awful lot of money, Hetty.'

'She costs me an awful lot of money, too,' said Connor. 'But I reckon she's worth it.'

'She certainly does look . . .' Alistair couldn't bring himself to pay her a compliment either – he and Connor did have similarities – '. . . well cared for,' he finished. Which was, Hetty decided, an insult.

'Oh yes, Hetty's got *me* looking after her now.' Connor gave the words a weight that almost made them a warning.

'So, where's your girlfriend, Alistair?' asked Hetty. 'Is she here?'

'Yes. Not the one you – met.'

'Oh, don't worry. I wouldn't have recognized her with her clothes on.' Hetty had to bite back a smirk at having managed to work this old joke into the conversation. Clichés certainly had their uses, be they little black dresses or ancient put-downs.

Mrs Makepiece – she had told them her Christian name but Hetty couldn't remember it – was making waving gestures.

'Come and eat, everyone. I've done a *placement*, so just find your places and sit down. It's a bit of a squash, I'm afraid.'

There were twelve people sitting down to dinner. The dining-table had been made up of several tables, not all quite the same height, butted up together, and covered with sheets. It filled the small but lovely dining room and involved everyone in a lot of pulling in and pushing past. Hetty could see why Mrs Makepiece wanted somewhere bigger for her major celebration.

It was inevitable that she should be sitting near Connor, but having him plumb opposite, able to scrutinize her every move, was a little unnerving. Mind you, she comforted herself, Alistair would have been worse.

The food was distributed by a collection of young people, the children of the guests. Tottering piles of Melba toast, slabs of butter and huge bowls of pâté fought for space along the table. Bottles of red and white wine fitted in where they could. It was the kind of occasion that Hetty would normally have enjoyed, but with Alistair and Connor there, it might not be such fun.

Hetty's neighbour poured her a glass of red wine. He had pleasant but unremarkable looks, and seemed not to be with anyone.

'So, what do you do?' Too late, she realized he would be bound to ask her the same question, and she would have to explain about Courtbridge House. With Connor sitting opposite. She took a glug of wine.

'I'm an architect.'

'Oh? What sort?'

'Oh, nothing exciting like Richard Rogers I'm afraid. I deal with old buildings mostly.'

This gave them something in common, at least. 'I'm living in an old building at the moment,' she said quietly, checking to see that Connor was engaged in conversation with the blonde on his left.

'Oh?' He didn't sound intrigued exactly, but he was prepared to go on with the conversation.

'Mmm. I'll tell you about it – ' She was just about to launch into the story of the lovely old house and the wicked heir to it when she felt Connor's gaze upon her.

His eyes, she noticed for the first time, were hazel, and looked extremely perceptive, which could explain how he so often managed to come out with statements that were frighteningly near the knuckle. She gave Connor a brief smile, picked up the pâté and offered it to the man. 'Have some. And some toast.' Under cover of handing him the butter, and scraping it off the knife for him, she muttered, 'And give me your card, if you've got one. I could do with a good architect.'

The good architect raised his eyebrows, not unflattered by Hetty's attention. 'But how do you know I am? Good, I mean?'

'Quite frankly, I can't afford to be fussy.' Then, realizing she'd sounded rude, smiled and patted his hand, just like Caroline would have done. 'Have you known Mrs Makepiece long?'

'Felicity? All my life. She's my Godmother. She asked me down to cheer me up. I got divorced last year.'

'Oh, I am sorry.'

'Don't be. Felicity has my convalescence well in hand. She's a closet fairy godmother, always being nice to people she thinks might be lonely.'

'Oh yes. I think I might be one of those.'

He smiled. 'I think you must be the girl she invited for me. She had to drag another one up quickly when you wanted to bring a friend.'

'Good God! Why didn't she say I couldn't?' Hetty had forgotten all about Alistair, and the agony such a situation would have caused her.

'She probably thought it was a long way for you to come on your own. By the way, I'm James Taylor.'

'Hetty Longden.'

'So who did you come with?'

She nodded in Connor's direction. 'I came with him, but we're not a couple. What about you? Who did Felicity get for you when I messed things up?' He gestured to the blonde who seemed to be greatly appreciating Connor's attention. 'Oh.' Hetty felt responsible. Connor had taken this man's partner. 'I am sorry. Do you want me to call him off?'

James shook his head. 'Not at all, I'm very happy with the way things have turned out.'

Felicity Makepiece's husband bellowed from the top of the table. 'Pass your plates down, chaps. It's time for the beef stew thingy.'

'Did you have a card?' said Hetty in the resultant confusion. 'I really need someone like you.'

A moment later she met Connor's eyes. He had not only heard this slightly rash remark, but had also seen her slip James's card into her bag. Judging by his expression, he was not pleased.

CHAPTER TEN

'So you see, there's not really enough room for a big party. But I don't want anything too formal,' she went on. 'You do catering?'

Hetty and Mrs Makepiece were seated in the hall, on the sofa normally occupied by dogs. They were having the 'little chat'.

'Er – yes,' said Hetty, trusting fervently that with contacts in the WI she could.

'And how much will it cost?'

Hetty cleared her throat. 'To hire the hall – the whole house, really – would be in the region of a thousand pounds.' She waited for an exclamation of horror. There wasn't one. 'Catering would be extra. It would depend on the menu.'

'And would you provide the wine, or would we?'

She thought quickly. Would they need a licence? Perhaps there was time to get one. 'We would. But we'd get you a special deal, and not charge you through the nose for it.' This was Jack's territory. He was bound to know how to organize that sort of thing.

'Right then. I'll come along one day when you're open – look the place over. And then, when I've thought what we'd like to eat, we can sort out prices.' Mrs Makepiece got up. 'There's just one other thing . . .'

Hetty spotted Connor coming from the dining room through to the sitting room, where coffee was being served. 'Which is?'

'Entertainment.' Mrs Makepiece made a gesture with her hands. 'I think a little entertainment to break the ice is a good idea, don't you? Just to get people going, you know.'

Hetty gulped. 'If you say so.'

'I was wondering what you could offer in that line?'

Insane suggestions such as karaoke, balloon-sculpture and conjuring sliced through her mind like paper darts. All equally unsuitable, but what other sort of entertainment was there?

'Cabaret,' said Connor from behind her. 'Hetty does cabaret.'

'What?' squeaked the cabaret artiste.

'Oh, she's terribly modest about it,' Connor went on. 'Doesn't like to suggest it. But she's got a lovely voice, a wide repertoire, and comes very reasonably.'

'It sounds ideal! Why didn't you say you sang, silly girl? A few songs and a piano, what could be nicer? Oh!' Mrs Makepiece's attention had been caught by something going on over Connor's shoulder. 'Someone can't flush the lavatory and they'll have the handle off if they keep trying. Do excuse me. I'll get back to you about this one, Hetty. It's all right,' she called out to the cloakroom, 'I'll do it!'

When she was out of earshot, Hetty turned on Connor. 'What the bloody hell do you think you're doing?' She was shaking with fright and rage. 'How dare you tell Mrs Makepiece that I sing when I don't?'

'But you do, I've heard you. You've got a very sweet voice.' She waited for a sting in the tail, something on the lines of, 'You'll get them going all right – going straight home.'

When this didn't come, she went on. 'But I don't sing in *public* – at least, I haven't for ages. And then, not on my own. I had a friend with me, and a pianist. You had no right to suggest just me doing it.'

'She wanted entertainment, I was just providing it. It's called adding value to the package.'

'Oh, for goodness' sake! My "hits from the shows" hardly counts as value! I'm not Cleo Laine, you know.'

'Don't be so modest. And you're the one who's so determined the house can earn its own living. It's only fair that you should help it.'

'Me singing will not help! It'll hinder! The windows might break!'

'Now you're fishing for compliments. You know you sing very well.'

'There's still the little matter of an accompanist! Even if I could drag my friend over, our pianist has emigrated.'

Connor narrowed his gaze. 'I'll accompany you.'

Hetty's head spun for a few, sick-making moments. Then she remembered. 'But there isn't a piano at Courtbridge House!'

Dizzy with relief she beamed at Mrs Makepiece as she returned from the downstairs cloakroom. Finding another form of entertainment would be a happy dream compared with providing it herself.

Mrs Makepiece beamed back, possibly a little surprised by the breadth of Hetty's smile. 'Do go and have your coffee, you two, or there won't be any left.'

There was plenty of coffee, but very few seats. Connor's dinner partner had saved one for him, which she patted urgently as he appeared. Hetty saw that she would have to perch on the arm of James's chair, though he gallantly offered it to her, but she declined, preferring to perch than disappear into a mire of cushions. 'I'll be fine, really,' she assured him, pulling her skirt down.

'If you won't have my chair, let me get you some more coffee.'

'Lovely.' After he had refilled her cup she went on, 'Sorry to be so furtive, but I don't want the man I came with to see me talking to you.'

James shot an agitated glance towards Connor. 'He's not going to get possessive, is he? I wouldn't want to be on the wrong end of him in a fight.'

'It's not like that. I said, we're not a couple. But I need an architect – to tell me whether this house where I live – he lives there too actually – is really in such bad repair it would be better – cheaper anyway – to pull it down.'

'It would have to be pretty bad for that. Where is it?'

Hetty gave the address. 'It's not in danger now, but my great uncle is old and in hospital. His heir,' she avoided looking at Connor in case he caught her eye and sensed he was being plotted against, 'is planning to pull it down and sell the site for a theme park.'

'Well, isn't it listed? The house?'

'Sorry?'

'Old buildings, even quite dull ones, are usually listed – Grade II most often – to stop people from pulling them down or doing anything dreadful to them.'

'You mean, pulling it down would be against the law?'

'Yes.'

'Good God! Why didn't I know about this sort of thing?'

He struggled to find an excuse for such ignorance. 'Well, I suppose if you're not in the business, it's not something you pick up until you start house-hunting.'

'Some were born in houses, some acquire houses, some have houses thrust upon them,' she misquoted glibly. 'I didn't exactly hunt Courtbridge, rather the reverse.' The same being true for Connor, it might mean he was similarly ignorant. 'Does it mean he – it couldn't be turned into a theme park either?'

'Not necessarily. It would depend on what the developers planned to do. But I should think the house is safe.'

'Listen, the house is opening to the public this Saturday. I don't suppose you could come along, have a quick look, and tell me what you think about the house's condition? I wouldn't mind your opinion on whether or not it's architecturally interesting enough for people to come and see.'

'Well I could, but it would be better if I could bring some equipment with me and get a proper look. Besides, I'm busy on Saturday.'

Instantly remorseful, Hetty put her hand on his sleeve. 'I'm so sorry. I'm so involved with the house I forget other people have different lives.'

'Is it open on Sunday too?'

'Oh yes,' said Hetty. 'It'll have to be open pretty much all the time. I'm dreading showing people round, I know so little about it. A million times more than I did when I first went there, of course . . .'

He smiled. 'Sunday it is then.'

'Brilliant. And I'll do my best to get Connor out of the way.' If he thought he might not be allowed to pull it down he might panic and sell it immediately before anyone could stop him. And she was still extremely angry with him for offering her singing as entertainment. Not for the first time she regretted her misplaced morality, which meant she hadn't murdered Connor when she had the chance.

'Why must you get him out of the way?'

'Oh – he's the one who wants to pull it down.'

'Oh my God.' said James, instantly regretting his generous impulse.

'It's all right. He won't be there.' She smiled at him, trying to make him feel better, wishing she wasn't so hot.

A quick glance around showed her that most of the other women had already removed their jackets, but on the whole their black dresses were not nearly as little as hers. But she was also aware that by now her cheeks must be clashing violently with the scarlet silk.

'You look awfully flushed,' said James. 'Can I take your jacket?'

The decision was made for her. She was too embarrassed to admit her fear of exposing too much flesh: besides, such a remark would only draw attention to it.

'Thank you. That would be kind.'

The dress did at least have sleeves – small, short ones – and, at the front, it showed only a little more than an average amount of cleavage. But it had no back at all. And, owing to some law of physics which had passed Hetty by, Caroline's backless bra had pushed up her front, adding a couple of letters to her cup size. The consequence of it all was that Hetty felt very well-endowed, and naked.

This seemed to attract male attention as if she were a moth sending out pheromones. Alistair's gaze veered towards her like a searchlight, ignoring the blonde, who could quite easily have been the one Hetty had seen him in bed with, and leaving her delivering the punch-line of the joke she was telling him to the side of his head.

Connor, too, looked up from James's unattached female to turn his lazy gaze in her direction. His gaze stopped being lazy the moment it made contact. Hetty smiled weakly at him, and put her shoulders back.

James was fetching Hetty another cup of coffee when Alistair came over. Hetty sat up very straight, and wished her position, back against the wall, wasn't so symbolically significant.

'Hello.' She fixed him in the eye, daring her dress to move an inch.

'You really do look wonderful, Hetty. Far better than I expected. For a moment there, in the winter, I thought I broke your heart.'

'For a moment there, you did. But spring came, and I got over it.'

'And who is it you're with now?'

Hetty opened her mouth to say she wasn't 'with' anyone, but remembered Connor's possessive behaviour when they'd first arrived. She didn't want to dismiss it as never having happened, in case she needed it to again.

'You met him.'

'He looks like a gorilla.'

Hetty wanted to jump on his feet with Caroline's heels. Connor was not conventionally handsome, she would be the first to admit. But he wasn't a gorilla. 'No,' she said silkily, 'he's just a little less effete than your friends. He doesn't need to watch his weight, or work out. Unlike you, he doesn't spend twelve hours a day behind a desk.' Hetty actually had very little idea what Connor did, but she was fairly sure desks were only a small part of it.

'You seem harder,' said Alistair. 'You were a sweet little thing when I knew you.'

'Was I? Well, people change.' She tried hard not to sound sarcastic, but he'd obviously expected to find her a heap of damp brown feathers, and was curious to know why she wasn't.

James appeared, holding her coffee cup.

'But, on the whole,' went on Alistair, ignoring James, 'it's an improvement.'

Hetty took the cup from James and took a sip, wishing she could spit it in Alistair's face without causing either a scandal or a stain on the carpet. She wanted to deny his compliment, it was so insulting. And yet she and Caroline had gone to a lot of trouble to make her look as unlike a broken-hearted wretch as possible, and she'd been furious when Connor hadn't commented. She swallowed the coffee, and bared her teeth in an artificial smile.

Their enthusiastic hostess bustled into the room. 'Right now, everyone, we've cleared the hall. I want to see all you people dancing.'

Most of the people froze into immobility as their collective heart sank into their collective, uncomfortable shoes.

Except Hetty. She owed Mrs Makepiece. She was going to risk vast sums of money and her reputation as a hostess by using Courtbridge House. If she wanted Hetty to dance, that was what Hetty would do. 'Come on, James. Let's hit the floor.' She took him by the hand and led him out of the room, her bare back hot from the gaze of every pair of male eyes. She caught a glimpse of Connor looking surprised, and not pleased. Serve him right, telling Mrs Makepiece she could sing.

Startled, but sheeplike, the rest of the guests followed her and James into the hall. Music burst out from somewhere, and James took Hetty into his arms.

It was difficult for him. There was no way he could avoid touching her bare flesh, but he was shy, and reluctant to do this on such brief acquaintance. He compromised by placing one finger where her dress started again, a couple of inches below her waist. But as the floor became more crowded, and he relaxed more, he pulled her closer, and let his hand drift down. Hetty didn't care. The whole evening had been a series of nightmares anyway. It couldn't get worse.

It could. Alistair cut in and tried to re-establish old territories. It was hateful, but Hetty didn't want to make a scene. How could his touch ever have turned her to jelly? Now it felt like jelly on her flesh, though, to be fair, it was hot.

'I really think it's time we were getting home,' said Connor loudly, in her ear.

Hetty had been tired before the party, and now felt drained from being sparky and outgoing. But she didn't want to obey Connor's summons absolutely immediately. 'OK. I just want to dance with James one more time.' She disengaged herself from Alistair and went over to James, who was leaning against the wall, looking in need of a little positive reinforcement from a friendly woman.

'James, would you mind? Just one last dance?'

Connor practically forced her jacket on her while her fingers were still entangled with James's. 'Come along. Let's say our goodbyes. And make them brief,' he added, when they were out of earshot.

Mrs Makepiece was in the sitting room, her shoes off and a glass of whisky in her hand. 'Are you off, dear? So nice of you to come. I am looking forward to seeing Courtbridge House. I'll be in touch about when.'

'Goodbye, Felicity,' said Connor smoothly, kissing her cheek. 'It was a splendid evening. Fabulous food.'

Hetty couldn't possibly call Mrs Makepiece Felicity, although she had been invited to. 'It was lovely. All of it. I just hope you're not too exhausted.'

Her hostess made a face. 'I shall go up soon, and leave these young things to themselves. But I am glad you enjoyed yourselves. And Hetty, I am so looking forward to hearing you *sing*.'

'How could you do that to me?' Hetty began, as soon as they were in the car. 'How could you commit me to singing without even consulting me?'

'I didn't think consultation was much in your line. You haven't bothered to consult me about the house once.'

She dismissed this. 'You weren't there! I had to make all those decisions by myself. Besides, you're not interested in the house, except as a means of making money.'

'It seems to me your interest is exactly the same. Why else would you be opening it for ruby weddings? You'll be having medieval banquets with "pinchable wenches" next.'

'You know perfectly well why. I just want to get Samuel out of debt. And to make it profitable so you won't tear it down.' She looked at him out of the corner of her eye. Did he know that this was probably not an option?

'You should be grateful to me for enabling you to add another couple of hundred to the bill, then.'

'I won't do it. Besides, as I said, there isn't a piano. You don't know much about your inheritance, do you?'

Connor shot her a look of triumph. 'There's a grand piano, actually.'

'There bloody well isn't! And even if there is' – there was the remote possibility of there being one in a disused out-building she hadn't properly explored – 'it'll be in such bad condition it would be unusable.'

'That's all you know.'

Hetty sighed deeply. 'You're being very childish. Why say there's a piano when there isn't?'

'I keep telling you, there is.'

'But where, for goodness' sake?'

'Phyllis Hempstead's got it.'

'What!'

'Samuel lent it to her on permanent loan because he knew it would deteriorate if it stayed in the house.'

'Good God! Really? Still, if it's at her house, we can't use it. Unless you're suggesting the guests all troop a couple of miles and cram into her parlour.'

'It was moved out, we can move it back.'

'It's not just a question of moving it. Even if Phyllis has kept it in tune, moving it will put it out again.'

He changed gear and made the engine growl. 'Just which of us is the pianist here? I'm playing for you, don't forget.'

Hetty buried her head in her hands and groaned.

She dozed on the journey home, and when they arrived she awoke with an awareness that she and Connor had been quarrelling, and that she was going to have to thank him profusely for taking her. In many ways she *was* grateful. He'd been wonderful with Alistair. It was just everything else he'd done that made gratitude hard to express.

They fought their way past the welcoming dogs, and Hetty pulled the kettle across to the hotplate. She took off the jacket and hung it where it couldn't get stained, and quickly pulled on her cardigan, which was hanging on the back of a chair. It felt odd next to her bare skin, and inadequate. She pulled it closely around her.

Refreshed from her nap, she felt too jizzed up to go to bed immediately. Besides, she needed to woo herself into seeing Connor as someone she was grateful to, and not someone she wanted to kill, slowly and painfully.

'Would you like a drink?' she asked him.

'Don't you think you've had enough?'

'No! And what's it to you how much I have to drink?' Oh God, this wasn't what she'd intended to happen. 'I meant tea, or cocoa.' She was lying. She wanted the kettle for her hot-water bottle, the offer was purely symbolic.

'Just as well. You ought to drink a couple of pints of water, or you'll have a hell of a hangover in the morning.'

'What on earth makes you think I've had too much to drink? I only had a couple of glasses of wine at dinner.'

'Really? I thought you must be drunk the way you threw yourself at that man.'

'Which man?' she asked, before she realized how much worse this made her look.

'So many you can't tell them apart, eh? I meant the man you sat next to at dinner. Though Alistair got a good look-in, so to speak.'

It occurred to Hetty that Connor was physiologically incapable of talking to her without enraging her. Perhaps he should have hormone-replacement therapy.

'I did not throw myself at anyone,' she said as calmly as she could. 'Certainly not at Alistair.'

'OK, I absolve you of flirting with Alistair, but that other man didn't know what had hit him!'

'Nonsense! We were just chatting.' It was the chatting that had so unnerved poor James.

'You let him put his hand on your bottom.'

'Only when we were dancing! He had to put it somewhere, for God's sake! And anyway, what's it to you? If it was your bottom you might have grounds for complaint.'

'You mean you had no objection?'

'No, I meant that you have no right to have any.' She was getting a bit confused as to what she did mean. Perhaps she had had too much to drink.

Connor crossed the kitchen and, before she realized what he was going to do, he picked her up and sat her on the narrow cupboard next to the stove. 'Now, listen you . . .'

CHAPTER ELEVEN

He leant towards her, more angry than she felt was reasonable. 'I'm *responsible* for you . . .'

'No you're not! *I'm* responsible for me. You may be male, and live here, but you're not my keeper . . .'

She relapsed into silence. It was hard to shout at him when she felt so unsteady, perched up there. He was so near, he would have caught her had she fallen, but his nearness also prevented her from jumping off. And it would have looked as though she was running away – which she would have been. She clung on to the edges of the cupboard and leaned back slightly, to adjust her point of balance. The single kitchen bulb threw everything into shadows, altering the room she knew so well into somewhere more sinister. She could smell his aftershave and a faint whiff of cigars. Had he smoked one himself, or had he just been near someone who had?

'I promised Samuel I'd look after you.' His tone had changed. He was no longer haranguing her, he sounded tired and anxious. 'Make sure nothing dreadful happened to you.'

'What can possibly happen to me at a perfectly respectable dinner party?'

'The dinner party may have been respectable, but you weren't.'

'What on earth do you mean?'

'You flirted shamelessly. I know your pride was at stake, and you didn't want that prat to think you were nursing a broken heart, but you took it a bit far.'

She gave an indignant squawk.

'I saw you exchanging billets-doux with that man you were sitting next to.'

'So what? Whoever I exchange whatever with is none of your business!'

'Then why look so hellish guilty about it?'

She flushed, not knowing how to answer him. 'I didn't . . .'

'Yes you did.'

Hetty bit her lip to prevent herself from starting a did-didn't session, which would add nothing to her dignity.

'Like it or not, Hetty, you're my responsibility.'

'No I'm bloody well not! I'm responsible for myself!'

'It would make my life a whole lot easier if you behaved as if you were.'

Curiosity began to overcome her indignation. 'Why? What did you promise Samuel exactly?'

Connor's expression became grim. 'I promised him that no harm would come to you while you're under this roof. I also promised . . .'

'What?'

'Not to seduce you.'

Hetty swallowed. He was leaning so close to her she could see a tiny thread caught into a loop in his lapel. She could see the movement of his breathing as he leaned on the cupboard. It seemed fast for someone who was so fit. She shifted back an inch and the cardigan gaped. She let go to pull it together again and slewed violently as she lost her balance. Connor took hold of her waist and pushed her backwards so she was sitting more solidly. His hands felt warm and firm. 'That's not likely to happen is it?' she asked him, as if he alone had any control over the matter.

He shook his head. 'I don't know. It depends a lot . . .'

'On what?'

'On my strength of character.'

He looked down, and for some reason she put her hand on his shoulder. It felt strong and cool under her hand and she knew she should remove it, but she couldn't. 'The kettle's boiling,' she told him, giving him an excuse to go away.

'Is it?' He didn't move and she didn't want him to. She sat up straighter and put her other hand on his other shoulder. This time she didn't worry about her cardigan falling open.

Connor kept his gaze lowered. 'I don't think you should do that.'

'What?'

'Hold me like that.'

'If I don't, I'll fall off. You put me here,' she added. 'And it's not very safe.'

He cleared his throat and straightened up, removing her hands from his shoulders. 'I'll make some tea.'

Hetty, still clinging to the edges of the cupboard, watched him. He moved about, finding mugs and milk, and she wondered why she had never noticed how graceful he was. There was an economy of movement as he went about the task that was very attractive.

'It's ready.' He didn't look at her.

'I can't get down.'

Now he did. 'What do you mean?'

'My feet have gone to sleep. If I jump, it'll be agony.'

He moved across the kitchen and picked her up. For a moment, he held her close, and then let her slither down to the floor. Even lowered so gently on to them, her feet hurt. 'Ow.'

'What's the matter?' He took hold of her shoulders again and looked at her, concerned.

'Nothing, it's just my feet hurt. You know how they do? Something to do with the blood supply.'

Connor kept hold of her. She could feel the wool of her cardigan prickle on her skin where the weight of his hands pressed it against her. 'I think we should have the tea,' he said.

'Let's take it into the sitting room.' Hetty suddenly wanted to prolong the evening, and she didn't want to stay in the kitchen.

'No. I'm not sitting on that sofa next to you.'

'Why not?'

He turned sharply away from her and picked up a mug of tea. 'I just don't think it's a good idea to sit next to you in that dress, in the mood you're in.'

Hetty felt indignant. 'What do you mean? What sort of mood am I in?'

'Dangerous.' She started to protest and he interrupted her. 'I warn you, I'm within an inch of throwing you over my shoulder and carrying you upstairs to bed. Just like Peter and Samuel and everyone else in this damn village thinks I already have.'

'I'm sure no one thinks anything of the kind,' she breathed, trying to banish the picture his words had created from her mind.

'Get real, Hetty, they all think it. And, as I'd prefer not to sink to the level of their expectations, I'd be grateful if you didn't do anything else that means I have to come near you.'

'Are you saying you *want* to go to bed with me?'

'I'd have to be dead if I didn't. Surely even you're not so naïve you haven't realized that!'

She hadn't consciously realized it, but now she had been told, she discovered she wanted it just as much. She put it down to wearing Caroline's clothes. This sudden wave of desire for strong arms, for danger, for the smell of Connor, was something to do with her clothes.

She moved briskly across the room, picked up her mug and sipped. It was scalding hot, enough to bring anyone back down to earth.

'The good old cuppa,' he said, watching her drink. 'Works every time.'

'What do you mean?'

'Every emergency, just have a cup of tea, and everything's instantly all right.'

'Is this an emergency?'

He nodded. 'Narrowly averted.'

Hetty lowered her eyes as she lowered her mug, not sure what message he would read in them should he look. It must be because it's been such a long time since I had sex, she thought brutally. It's purely hormonal, nothing to do with feelings or love or anything pure. I just want him so badly because I haven't had anyone for so long. She took another sip of tea. Why couldn't it have been Peter who made her feel this, instead of Connor? Nice, safe Peter. She tried to transfer her desire to Peter, but found it quite impossible to summon up any of the excitement she felt in Connor's presence.

She took a couple more sips from her mug. 'I think I'll take this upstairs. I'm very tired. I'll drink it in bed.'

'Hang on . . .'

Hetty's heart did a forward roll, half fear, half desire.

'You forgot your hot-water bottle.'

'Oh. So I did.'

'I'll do it for you.'

'That would be kind.'

Numb with disappointment, Hetty watched him take her hot-water bottle from where she had hung it on the kitchen door and pour boiling water into it. How much more mundane and unsexy an action was there?

'Here.' He moved across the room to hand it to her.

Now, do something, kiss me, touch me, anything – just to show you're not as much in control as you seem, she willed, looking at her feet. But he didn't. He just handed her the bottle.

'Good-night, Hetty.'

'I suppose a good-night kiss is out of the question?'

'Yes. Good-night, Hetty.'

Hetty sighed, annoyed that she'd exposed herself, but not feeling as rejected as she might have done. She knew that Connor would have liked to kiss her good-night very much indeed.

It was only upstairs in her bedroom that she remembered she had discovered a means of ruining all his plans. She sat on her bed and hunched herself into a ball, contradictory feelings causing adrenalin to course round her veins. What would have happened if she'd got her way, and they had gone to bed? Could she still have gone on plotting behind his back? Had Alistair turned her into the sort of woman who could use men just for sex? Or had she always been like that, but just hadn't realized it before?

Of course, it wasn't surprising that Samuel had told Connor not to seduce her. It was just the sort of thing he would do, possibly primed to do so by her mother. What was surprising was how much Hetty wanted him to do just that. She yearned to feel his hands on her breasts, his lips on her mouth, his strong arms around her. She had had an inkling of the strength of his arms while he was lifting her, now she longed to feel the hard, smooth shape of them without the intrusion of cloth. She longed to press her cheek against his chest and hear his heart thumping, strong and solid beneath her ear.

She washed her face in cold water to rid herself of all warm feelings and, back in her bedroom, she wandered about naked to make herself really cold. The sheets were icy as she slid between them and should have purged her of any sensual feelings. But she didn't have the strength of character to abandon the hot-water bottle Connor had filled for her.

'Typical bloody Connor,' she muttered, trying to summon up her safe, familiar feelings of anger towards him, and finding a jumper to wrap round it. 'Can't even give me a hot-water bottle that's safe to touch.'

★

Neither Connor nor Hetty made any reference to what had happened after the dinner party, though they entertained Caroline with a full account of the party itself. Hetty's account was longer than Connor's, and mostly conducted at Caroline's house after she had returned the clothes.

'. . . and he's an architect, who specializes in old buildings. He's going to come on Sunday to have a good look. And he says the house is probably listed, which would mean Connor couldn't pull it down. So that's really good news, isn't it?'

'Why do I get the impression there's more "really good news", and that it involves me?' asked Caroline.

'Mind-reader! We need Connor out of the way, so James can have a good poke about.'

'And you feel I'm the person to get him out of the way?'

'There's no one better. You know how much he . . .' she faltered on the word 'fancies', '. . . likes you.'

'Oh, hell! I am awfully fond of Connor – I know I'm not supposed to be, but I am – but I really don't know how I could keep him amused all afternoon; decently, that is.'

Hetty thought hard. Caroline could hardly suggest it was the perfect afternoon for a country walk when she was well-known for hating country walks. Nor could she express a desire to see a stately home, not if she wanted Connor to take her. What else was there to do in the country on Sunday?

'I know! The very thing! Why don't you ask him to look at a car for you? A special sort of car, like he's got; say you're thinking of buying it for Jack and you need an expert to look it over for you.'

'He'd tell me to contact the A A.'

Hetty considered. Caroline was right, it was just the sort of thing Connor would say. 'Well, say you want Connor to test-drive it. That if he likes it, Jack will.'

'And if Connor likes it, I have to buy it?'

'Of course not! You just tell him there turned out to be something dire wrong with it. You only have to *look*. Dead simple.'

'How will I find a car to look at? It's Easter Sunday!'

'Car people aren't religious, and you look in *Exchange & Mart*! Honestly, Caroline, don't you know a simple thing like that, and you married to a car buff?'

129

'*Exchange & Mart* is a national paper. There might only be a suitable car in Scotland, or the other side of London!'

Hetty beamed. 'You see how good my plan is?'

It was only after she'd gone home to Courtbridge House that Hetty realized how unhappy she felt about Connor and Caroline spending the day together. Connor hadn't promised Samuel he wouldn't seduce Caroline. And although she didn't think Caroline would cheat on Jack, she hadn't known her long enough to be certain. Hetty had sensed last night that Connor wasn't as immune to her as he made out, and she didn't want this little bit of feeling wiped out by Caroline's eighteen-carat sex-appeal.

She dismissed her feelings as ridiculous and selfish and concentrated on trying to get Connor and Mrs Hempstead on speaking terms before opening-day.

Connor had condemned Phyllis Hempstead as an interfering old bag long since, and had tried to avoid actually meeting her for a while. Several times he had seen her Volvo pull up in the yard and escaped, but eventually Phyllis had been too quick for him. Hetty had made introductions, seeing each wince as they were forced to touch the enemy's hand. Since then, they had avoided each other whenever possible. Mrs Hempstead had made a few pertinent remarks about 'strong men too idle to help their heritage', but, as Connor was out of earshot, they produced no result.

The day before the grand opening, Connor was absent from early morning. If he'd been present, not even he would have been able to avoid the person known secretly to Hetty and Peter as the Clipboard Queen.

Phyllis Hempstead had missed her vocation. She really should have been a general in the army, or a captain of British industry, or at the very least the leader of a revolution. Her organizational skills were second to none.

For opening-day, every woman was assigned a task and a position for the moment when untold numbers of people would surge through the old front door. From there, with luck, they would stream through the sitting room, which for the purposes of the public was now called the drawing room. Then they would move on, in an orderly fashion, to the morning room, which had probably caught the early sun in the days before the chestnut trees had grown so large, and thence to the great hall. After that, they would be allowed upstairs to see the three bedrooms that Hetty had worked so hard on, and the bathroom, a late entry. It wasn't an awful lot to see, but Hetty hoped it was enough.

Hetty was not given a specific duty, beyond checking that nothing unsightly protruded from under the beds. She was detailed to do what she could with the out-buildings, and decide which, apart from the resurrected dairy, were fit for viewing. Hetty, who had a lot on her mind that didn't directly involve the house or its contents, was pleased to be away from the main field of battle and able to dally about on the fringes of the action.

Hetty had swept the forge and was wondering whether it was worth trying to move anything, or if it was time for a cup of coffee, when Peter appeared.

'Hi! Have you come to help?' Hetty asked, pleased to see him. He was so nice and reliable, such perfect son-in-law material.

'Yup. Do you want that shifted over here, then people can see the bellows, and, if they're strong enough, pump them?'

They worked companionably all day, sweeping, painting, knocking things together and writing signs. It was tiring but satisfying.

'Do you really think we'll get all the people Phyllis thinks we will?' asked Hetty, holding the post while Peter banged in the NO PARKING ON THE GRASS sign.

Peter delivered a final wallop, causing the sign to lean sideways a little. 'Who's to say? There have been adverts in all the local papers, and some of the not-so-local ones. And people are always curious. Although the house has been open for years, no one's ever been aware of it.'

'Well, I hope they do. Apart from the gate money, the first lump of which needs to complete payments to Andy, there's a woman in the village who's been bullied into making two hundred scones.'

'Can you freeze scones?' Peter was also sceptical about the need for so many. 'At two scones each, that would be a hundred people.'

'At three pounds each, that would be three hundred pounds – people, I mean, not scones.' Peter still seemed confused. 'We're not selling the scones at three pounds each, we're charging the people three pounds.'

Peter shook his head. 'That's a lot more than Samuel used to charge. A pound for adults and fifty pence for children.'

'It's a lot less than we would be able to charge if we had a bit more to see. Phyllis is still on at me to open the kitchen.'

'That's a bit of an undertaking, isn't it? It's in a terrible condition.'

Before Connor's arrival she would have flung herself into the task with enthusiasm and dismissed Peter's caveats. But now, with the house's future uncertain, she felt less enthusiastic. 'We'd have to ask Connor, and I can't see him agreeing to having the kitchen messed about with. He loves cooking.'

Peter made a rude noise.

'I'm worn out,' said Hetty, before Peter could deliver his opinion of the heir apparent. 'Let's go and have something to eat.'

'Opening-Saturday' dawned with all the good portents it could possibly manage. Phyllis, she decided, must have a hot line to the Almighty, and had arranged it so.

Sun, lack of wind, and the right number of magpies all greeted Hetty as she came downstairs just after six. Phyllis was due at eight, to finish off the cleaning and do the flowers. Hetty would have liked to do the flowers herself, but as Phyllis had worked so hard, doing all the co-ordination, not to mention organizing the weather, it only seemed fair to reward her by letting her fill the vases with catkins and early daffodils. At ten, God willing, the first visitors would arrive.

Hetty took advantage of the quiet to visit each room and try to consider how it would look from an outsider's point of view. There was one room, now full of all the least aesthetic furniture, which Phyllis told her had been the music room.

'I've got the piano, by the way,' she had said. 'If you want it back, just say the word. It's a pretty room, pity to fill it up with junk.'

Not sure whether she should be pleased or sorry about this generous offer, Hetty tentatively explained that she might indeed need it, and why.

'I used to sing a bit before . . . I went to London to work.'

Phyllis nodded. 'Good idea. Have to do it in the great hall of course, for that many people, but anything we can offer to add to the price must be encouraged.'

Hetty had nodded back, cravenly not mentioning whose idea the cabaret had been, and who was going to play the piano.

Now, alone, she tested the acoustics in the great hall. She shut her eyes and sang, softly at first, and then louder, until her voice would have reached everyone in the room, had it been full, even those sitting at the back. The tapestries deadened the sound somewhat, but it wasn't a huge space – she should manage to be heard well enough.

Now her only concern was what sort of a pianist was Connor? Could he really play more than 'Chopsticks', 'Heart and Soul' and the first five bars of the Moonlight Sonata? Hetty determined to audition him the moment they got the piano moved and tuned.

The house, Hetty concluded, after her private tour, was beautiful. A gem; shabby and idiosyncratic, but a gem, nevertheless.

Phyllis, who arrived fifteen minutes before she'd said she would, agreed with her. They heaped thanks and congratulations upon each other for a while and would have hung on each other's necks had Mrs Hempstead not been of an era when touching and hugging were largely considered to be unnecessary.

'I suppose the Barbarian's still in bed?' she asked, when they returned to the kitchen.

'Connor? I expect so. He was working on his report until late last night.' She had been unable to sleep and had heard him come upstairs after two.

Mrs Hempstead harrumphed. 'I'm a lark, always have been.' Not for the first time, her opinion of owls was made perfectly clear.

At ten past ten the first car drove into the designated parking area. Hetty, watching from an upstairs window, was suffering from stage fright. She had been called in from behind the scenes to fill in upstairs for one of Mrs Hempstead's cronies, and she was terrified. Supposing she wasn't able to speak to the people as they came upstairs to view the bedrooms? Mrs Hempstead had told her what to say, and she had a crib-sheet, giving the dates of all the furniture and the history of the house.

By four-thirty, speaking to people about the house had made

133

her feel tired, but no longer anxious. And she found that she liked sharing the house with people. They were mostly so appreciative and enthusiastic. They all loved visiting a house where people actually lived. They loved the little quirky windows, the wood floors, the planks of different widths butted together, with fillets of timber making them complete. Even things not intended to be part of the show were admired. The bookcase in the passage, full of books from the twenties and thirties, attracted a lot of attention, and it was only there because Phyllis had deemed it out of period for the four-poster bedroom.

Hetty staggered down the stairs, exhausted, but happy. Their work hadn't been in vain. The people had come, and they would have made money.

Phyllis was counting it when she got into the kitchen. 'Look at that!' she said triumphantly. 'Who says this house can't support itself!'

She shot a look of venom at Connor, who had come back before the house was closed, and had been skulking in the kitchen.

'Yes.' He got up from the table and went to the door. 'But now all the locals have been, who is there left?' Without waiting for an answer, he stalked out of the room.

Phyllis and Hetty regarded each other across the piles of pound coins, silver and coppers.

'Much as I hate to agree with him,' said Phyllis, 'he might be right. Most of the people who came today were local.'

'Never mind,' said Hetty. 'We can pay for the newspaper adverts and Andy. The car-boot sale paid for the fire extinguishers. If we earn anything tomorrow, we'll be ahead. And Caroline knows the man from one of the papers who writes about stately homes. She's going to tell him about us.'

Phyllis had no faith in Caroline's press connections. 'He won't come. But if we made this much each weekend, and something during the week, we'll eventually make a profit. But we might never see as many people in the house again.'

'It's not like you to be so pessimistic, Phyllis.'

'I know, dear. I'm tired, I expect. And Peter told me a rather depressing item of gossip.'

Hetty was alerted by Phyllis's expression and the mention of Peter. 'Oh? What?'

'The Barbarian wants to pull the place down.'

For a moment, Hetty wanted to pull Peter down, and savage him.

'He can't do it, of course,' went on Phyllis. 'It'll be listed. But it shows the way he's thinking.'

CHAPTER TWELVE

✿

'You owe me,' muttered Caroline. 'Getting me up at this time on a Sunday morning.'

'I know,' Hetty began, and then Connor appeared.

'Hi!' said Caroline. 'This is so kind.'

Hetty retreated, and watched Caroline get into Connor's car. Caroline was well wrapped up in Hermès scarves and was wearing sunglasses. He was in his scruffy leather jacket with the sheepskin collar. The car had its top down. They looked the epitome of a glamorous young couple going for spin.

Hetty refused to feel envious or cast down by Connor's grim predictions of the previous day. He may be right, people may only come out of curiosity, and once they had been, never come near the place again. But the house was in far, far better order than before. Circumstances had forced them to get their act together.

Having waved off Connor and Caroline, Hetty went back to the bedrooms, ready to explain the sampler on the wall, and the patchwork quilt (modern by Courtbridge standards, but pre-War and beautiful). In between groups of people (of which there were a gratifying number), she looked out for James. He arrived at eleven. Hetty deserted her post and rushed down to meet him.

'No! No! Don't charge him!' she said to the lady on the door. 'He's my guest.' Hetty kissed James's cheek to avoid the point of non-recognition when she appeared in jeans and a jumper instead of a short black dress and a scarlet jacket. 'Come on, let me show you round.'

James took a moment to register that the girl who had embraced him so fondly was the same sophisticated woman he had dined with, then kissed her back. 'I'm really looking forward to this.'

James was extremely impressed. Not by the arrangements of flowers, furniture and family photographs, which Hetty felt gave the rooms their character, but the two-storey bay window, which he said indicated the original 'solar', or main upper room, and might date from 1400. 'This room should be opened to the public,' he said.

Hetty regarded her distant relative's bedroom, now occupied by Connor. 'That may not be possible.'

'Ah,' said James. 'Shame. It's a fascinating house. Do you mind if I poke around on my own?'

Hetty went to warn the women who were dotted about the house to prevent people from doing just that. 'He's an architect,' she explained to Mrs Hempstead, on duty in the great hall.

'Is he?'

'He specializes in old buildings, and he's going to tell us if it really is in bad order.'

'A house that's been standing for nearly six hundred years would have fallen down by now if it was.' Phyllis turned away to explain the tapestries to a group, which included a two-year-old. 'Try not to let your little boy tug on that hanging. It's very old.'

Hetty could understand Phyllis's shortness of temper. She too was tired after their mammoth effort to get the house finished, and depressed at the thought of what might happen if things didn't work out. Even the fact that the house could be listed didn't rule out the possibility that Connor might sell it, and the thought of people living in it who may not love it as much was just as dampening to the spirits.

James came into the kitchen after two hours of exploration. He was filthy dirty and extremely happy. 'It's unusual to find a house so untampered with. Usually some Victorian worthy has tidied up the little imperfections.'

'If Samuel's ancestors were anything like Samuel they wouldn't have, although the house hasn't been passed through a direct line.'

'It's had all sorts of alterations and add-ons done to it until the beginning of the nineteenth century, but since then it's just been lived in. The stables . . .'

'I know,' said Hetty as James paused for breath, 'you feel the horses have only just left for the fields.'

'And those farm carts, just left where they were kept, no one restoring them and filling them with bedding plants.'

'Did you see the forge? I really want to get that put back in working order. Peter thinks we could lend it to a blacksmith and have him work in there, the fire going, making things.'

'Wonderful idea. What you've done in the dairy is splendid, but you want to get demonstrations going in there.'

'That wouldn't mean we'd have to keep cows, would it?'

'I shouldn't think so. There are plenty of cows about. What you need is a farmer's wife who'd like to try her hand at dairying. Mind you, you might have to pay her.'

Hetty handed James a mug of tea. 'Do I have to pay you? It would be only fair. Your professional advice, on a Sunday?'

'Don't be silly, Hetty. It's been a privilege.'

It was a pity that James and Hetty were sharing a chaste farewell kiss when Caroline and Connor swept into the yard. Connor didn't comment, but he shot Hetty a look of disapproval, letting Caroline out before putting the car away. Caroline was far more friendly. Hetty was forced to introduce her. 'This is James, the architect I told you about.'

'Oh, yes! The one I had to keep Connor away from. Sorry we got back a bit earlier than I'd hoped. I did find a car, but it was only a hundred miles away, and Connor drives like the wind. He says he's got some work he must finish.' Caroline's well-groomed eyebrows drew together in a frown. 'I'm not entirely sure I believe him.'

'Did you manage to make an excuse not to buy the car?'

'No.' Caroline sounded quite cheerful. 'But it's just the thing for Jack's birthday.'

'Caroline! How will you get the money to pay for it?'

Caroline made an airy gesture. 'Tell him I must have a new pond, or dress or something. I'm always dreadfully extravagant when he's away. Comfort-spending, you know.'

Other people ate for comfort, thought Hetty. Caroline, with her perfect figure and fabulous wardrobe, had a less destructive method. It was a pity chocolate was so much cheaper than designer clothes.

James was intrigued by her, and in a desire partly to get him to go, and partly to reward him, Hetty found herself saying, 'We must all get together for dinner some time. When Jack's home.'

'That would be wonderful, Hetty,' said James.

'It's the least I could do. There's just one other tiny thing . . .' She led James away from the siren appeal of Caroline to his car. 'Could you just check the house is listed? I know I must sound completely neurotic, but – well – I am.'

'Honestly, my dear, the chances of a house like this slipping through the listing net are as near impossible as makes no difference.'

'But you will make sure?'

James sighed the sigh of a man who had been asked to check the gas had been turned off for the fourth time. 'If you really want me to.' He got into his car shaking his head. He clearly thought Hetty was mad.

Later that day Mrs Makepiece rang Hetty to confirm her booking, as James had been so enthusiastic about the house. Hetty was delighted, but also anxious. The bits of the house that enthused James might not have the same effect on Mrs Makepiece. However, a booking was a booking, and she decided to reinstate the piano forthwith.

Connor was surprisingly helpful about getting the piano moved. He arranged a firm of movers and had standing by a man to tune it when it was *in situ*. The moving took for ever, but even the removers were forced to admit that if the piano had been moved out of the house, it must logically be possible for it to be moved back in again. There was a nerve-racking half-hour when they insisted the leaded bay window would have to be taken out. It took Connor that long to convince them that such windows didn't come in units that could be put in and out at will.

Hetty, who had to find somewhere to put all the furniture the piano was displacing, as well as move all the furniture they thought was out of the way but turned out not to be, was exhausted by the time the piano was finally installed, and it was only lunch-time. While it was being tuned she took the dogs for a long walk, leaving Connor, the piano-tuner and Mrs Hempstead to look after each other. Fortunately it was mid-week, and what visitors there were enjoyed the spectacle.

When she finally risked returning to the scene the tuner had gone, and Connor and Phyllis had not yet murdered each other. But only just.

'You've been marvellous, Phyllis,' she said, compliments oozing from her. 'I just couldn't face it. Did it get damaged?'

'Yes,' said Phyllis.

'Very slightly,' said Connor. 'And they'll send a man to repair the french polish.'

'It's not good enough. The men who took it out of here didn't damage it. Why should this lot make such a Horlicks of it? Mind you,' she went on, glaring at them both with equal disapproval, 'it did come out of the music room. Putting it here,' she indicated her beloved great hall as if it were a public lavatory, 'is a complete anachronism. All that varnished wood looks quite wrong with the stone and the tapestries.'

Connor, who'd spent the entire afternoon with Mrs Hempstead, strode off, leaving Hetty to do the placating. 'It's a fabulous piano, it seems a shame to tuck it away in the music room when hundreds – well dozens – of people could benefit from it in here.'

'You could have a nice little soirée in the music room,' said Phyllis. 'Chamber music. Ideal.'

'Mrs Makepiece has invited an awful lot of people and they wouldn't all fit in the music room.'

'They would if she wasn't so set against rows of chairs. Can't see what's wrong with them myself.'

Hetty, who was quite anxious enough about singing to an audience again after so long, didn't want them without a drink to distract them. 'I like the table idea myself. More relaxed.'

'It sounds thoroughly vulgar to me.'

Hetty decided not to tell her about the ruby-coloured helium balloons, the miniature teddy bears dyed maroon to go in the party bags, and the cake that Felicity was having made: white on the outside, but a rich, blushing red inside. 'I'd prefer not to be the only focus of attention. What do you think, Connor?'

Connor, who had just come back into the room, declined to comment. 'I'm putting the kettle on. Does anyone want a cup of tea?'

'I'd kill for one. My mouth feels like the bottom of a parrot's cage,' said that pillar of genteel society.

'Phyllis!' said Hetty, glad that the atmosphere had lightened at last. 'I never thought I'd hear you use an expression like that!'

★

When Phyllis finally went, Connor got out some very strong farmhouse Cheddar, some Stilton, so ripe you could spread it, both bought from the village shop, some crusty bread, a bottle of red wine and some salami. He loaded it all on to a tray with a bowl of farm butter and some cherry tomatoes. Seeing it, Hetty realized why the Brewsters in the shop, while supportive of the efforts to save the house, were the only people in the village who spoke well of Connor.

'Do you fancy taking this lot through and trying out the piano?' he asked. 'Or is it too chilly in there?'

'I'll put on another jumper. Have you got any music?'

'Don't need music. Do it all by ear.'

Hetty, following him down the passage carrying the glasses, was at once both impressed and terrified. How was he going to accompany her if he couldn't read her music?

Hetty curled up on a historically correct, but rather uncomfortable, chair and pulled a rug over herself. She sipped her wine, ate her bread and cheese, and listened to Connor.

He played beautifully. He started with some Dave Brubeck numbers, went on to his own version of Jacques Loussier and Keith Jarrett, and then the show tunes of the twenties and thirties.

'Come on,' he said eventually, without stopping. 'I know you know this one.'

Hetty got up and joined him at the piano, starting softly, but becoming bolder as the wine relaxed her and all her forgotten skills came back. They operated instinctively as a pair and, in spite of the sound-deadening tapestries, filled the great hall with music.

'You're good,' said Hetty, when at last Connor paused, giving her a chance to draw breath.

'Good yourself. We'll have to get rid of those wall-hangings, they kill the acoustics.'

'We can't! What would Phyllis say?'

'Blast Phyllis. They're not old tapestries anyway. Samuel got them in the fifties. He told me.'

'That's quite old enough for me. And Phyllis.'

'Nonsense. Phyllis's Golden Age was in the twenties. She'd think the fifties modern.'

Hetty was about to continue arguing – after all, Phyllis must know they weren't old – but Connor put his hand on the back of Hetty's neck and propelled her towards the door. 'Come on, I'm cold. Let's see if we can resurrect the fire and eat the rest of this in comfort.'

It took quite a lot of bellowing and extra kindling to get the fire to blaze up, but at last Connor felt able to sit back on his heels and leave his creation. He stood up, stretched, and saw Hetty curled up on the sofa, her wine glass to hand, a piece of bread and cheese on its way to her mouth.

She thought he was going to sit next to her on the sofa, and prepared to curl her legs tighter to give him room, but after a moment's hesitation, he pulled a small armchair nearer to the fire and sat on that.

Hetty considered it, but decided not to feel offended. She was happy enough. And the past hour had been perfect. They had followed and chased each other, one song leading to another. Sometimes he would abandon Hetty, leaving her holding the tune and play a descant, or even a whole different song that somehow swooped and dipped about the melody, like swallows on a summer evening, never colliding or clashing, always in harmony.

Sometimes Hetty took the bit between her teeth and tried her hand at improvising, occasionally joining the piano in a phrase, but otherwise weaving threads of anarchy in and out of the ordered notes. She felt liberated, as if she could sing anything. No note was too high or too low, it was impossible for her to be sharp or flat. Her confidence in his playing and her own voice moved her along uncharted paths and led her to perfect resolutions.

Music had never been so perfect or so free before, and she doubted if it would ever be so again. They would choose a selection of songs for the ruby wedding. He would play and she would sing, each according to their parts, neither deviating. At least, she hoped he wouldn't deviate. She wouldn't dare.

Hetty sipped her wine and stared into the flames. She felt happier than she had since she could remember – since before she'd left home. Singing had that effect. It occupied every cell of concentration and released feelings and thoughts that never consciously surfaced. She was exhausted, partly from moving the furniture, but mostly from breathing properly and deeply again. She closed her eyes.

'So, where did you learn to play the piano?' she said, her eyes still shut.

'At home. My aunts had a piano, and I spent a lot of time strumming on it. I kept it up because it's a good way of communicating with someone if you don't have a common language. People will always buy the piano-player a drink. Talking of which, you've drunk all the wine.'

Hetty opened her eyes again. 'Sorry. Get another bottle.' She closed her eyes again until Connor returned, an open bottle in his hand.

'I'm not letting you have any more.' He filled his own glass and returned to his seat by the fire.

Though almost asleep, Hetty could see he was glowering at her, and she forced herself out of her doze. 'What's the matter? Why are you looking so grumpy?'

'I'm not looking grumpy.'

'Well come and sit by me then.' She swung her legs to the floor. 'I can't see you properly over there.'

'No.'

'Why not? It's so unfriendly. We've spent a lovely evening together, and now you won't sit by me.'

'You know perfectly well why not.'

'No I don't.'

She hadn't until that moment. She had understood that dressed in Caroline's skimpy black dress and push-up bra, her make-up smudged into come-to-bed shadows, with her hair shiny but tousled, she might have been considered a threat to his vow of chastity. But today, she hadn't done more than wash her hands since lugging chairs and tables out of the path of the movers. She was wearing filthy jeans and layers of T-shirts and ancient, baggy sweaters. Her hair felt gritty with dust, and her only perfume would be the remnants of her unscented soap.

'Seriously, Connor,' she went on, 'Samuel wouldn't mind if you sat next to me. If he could see me now he'd know you couldn't possibly be tempted to seduce me.'

Connor stood up, and for a moment Hetty's heart lifted as she thought he was going to join her. But he didn't. Instead he put his glass down firmly on the mantelpiece, in among the carefully-spaced Meissen figurines, and picked up the tray.

'Come along, Hetty. It's time for bed. We've both had a long day, and I for one am bushed.'

Hetty sighed. 'Oh, so romantic. He plays the piano like an angel and makes love like a civil servant. A married civil servant,' she added.

'I'm not making love to you, and you know it. But if I did,' in spite of his best resolutions, his male ego had to protest, 'it wouldn't be civil anything. Or married anything. Now get out of here.' He took hold of Hetty's hand and heaved her, against her will, to her feet. 'If you go to sleep on the sofa you'll wake up stiff as a board.'

'No I won't.'

'Come on. If you can't take it, you shouldn't drink it. You go up, I'll take the dogs for a walk and lock the house. And have a bath,' he added. 'You're filthy.'

To prove she wasn't drunk, Hetty took the tray, having removed the glass from the mantelpiece. 'If Phyllis saw that,' she reproved him, going to the door, 'she'd have a fit.'

'She can have a litter of kittens for all I care.' He opened the door for her and followed her down the passage, close on her heels. 'Dogs! Time for a walk.'

He and the dogs disappeared into the night in what looked suspiciously like an escape attempt.

Upstairs, Hetty wondered at how things had altered between her and Connor. She had hated him before he arrived and she had quarrelled with him since. Now, suddenly, she was trying to seduce him and he wasn't playing. Was she a harlot? Was he a monk? How had this humiliating state of affairs arisen?

The bathroom was icy, although the water was scalding hot. Hetty breathed in the steam, wondering if she could bear to take her clothes off and whether it wouldn't be better to just get into bed, dirt and all. But she resisted the temptation. A bath would relax her, sooth the agitation that had replaced the delightful languor she had felt before Connor had spoiled it all.

She pulled off her clothes and kicked them into a heap in the corner of the room. They would have to be removed before the next lot of visitors, since Phyllis had claimed that, in spite of its lack of comfort, the bathroom had visitor potential.

The hot water was delicious. She lay there with only her face above the water, her eyes closed, enjoying the heat, the stretch of her muscles. She felt her eyes closing. When she realized she was dozing off she reared up from the water like a dolphin, grabbed her towel and got out quickly.

Still dripping she dragged on her dressing-gown, brushed her teeth and pulled out the plug. She left the grimy water gurgling down the drain, not stopping to clean the bath or even swill it out. Connor always had a bath in the morning. It would do him good to find it dirty for once. His own attempts on the ring were sometimes very half-hearted.

Typically, the moment Hetty was more or less dry, and tucked up in bed in her tartan pyjamas, all desire to sleep left her. Connor must be in bed by now, she thought. It should be safe to go downstairs and make some hot chocolate. It wasn't that she didn't trust Connor. It wasn't that she didn't trust herself. It was just that when they were together she felt uneasy.

CHAPTER THIRTEEN

Connor hadn't gone to bed. He was leaning on the stove, staring into a glass of something when Hetty came into the kitchen.

She felt awkward seeing him, as if he had read her thoughts, but tempted as she was to scoot back upstairs she couldn't do it without looking a complete fool. 'I'm just going to make some cocoa.' Her voice sounded husky after the singing. She cleared her throat. 'Do you want some?' she added, trying to pretend that there was nothing between them except a little enmity.

He didn't reply, so she took a half-empty bottle of milk from the fridge and tipped it into a pan from the drainer.

'You don't make cocoa like that.'

'Oh?'

'No. You mix the powder with boiling water until it makes a paste, and then add condensed milk and bring it to the boil. Preferably over a camp-fire.'

'It sounds disgusting, and we haven't got any condensed milk.' A joke about the stove being perfectly straight flickered into her mind, but it wasn't the moment for feeble puns.

'You'd better make hot chocolate then. But not for me. It's insipid after the real thing.'

Hetty wondered how on earth she had felt desire for this dis-agreeable man. 'Would you mind moving, so I can put the pan on the stove?'

'Why don't you use the gas cooker?'

'It's extravagant to use that when the stove is going anyway. Besides, if I put this on the gas I'll have to watch it like a hawk and I want to make a sandwich.' He stayed where he was. 'We only had bread and cheese for supper, you know.'

She waited another couple of seconds but then, when he still didn't move, she went to move him out of the way bodily.

He caught hold of her wrist. 'Don't push me around.'

'If you'd shift yourself I wouldn't have to.' She glared at him, milk-pan in her hand, extreme dislike in her heart.

Like territorial animals, neither of them would give an inch. She could feel her pulse leaping under the pressure of his fingers, although his hold wasn't tight. He looked down at her, his mouth compressed with annoyance, his eyes narrowed. With his free hand, he took the saucepan from her and put it down without looking where it went. It landed at the back of the stove, leaning at a dangerous angle.

She took a breath to complain about his carelessness – but didn't. Breathing was all she was up to, and that suddenly seemed quite difficult. In and out, she reminded herself. In and out. It's quite simple, you've done it before.

The saucepan abandoned, he put his hand on the back of her head and pushed his fingers into her hair, still slightly damp from when she had washed it. She let herself sway towards him, although he was applying no pressure. Her nose landed on his breastbone. His sweater smelt of woodsmoke and was rough against her skin. A tiny piece of lichen had caught in the wool. She examined it closely.

After what felt like a lifetime, he released her wrist and lifted her chin. 'I shouldn't be doing this,' he murmured, and, very gently, lowered his mouth to her parted lips.

She closed her eyes and didn't move. She just surrendered to the languor that swept over her as she felt his kiss, so chaste it barely counted as a kiss, merely the lightest brush of his lips against hers. From her lips he moved to her cheek, releasing her chin. At her cheekbone he closed his mouth and applied enough pressure for her to feel it.

She opened her eyes and saw that his were closed. He looked as if he were praying, his lashes a dark semi-circle on the sharp angle of his cheek. He seemed suddenly vulnerable, and, moved, she put her arms around him, hugging his large, rough torso. She heard his heart thumping and then his chest rumbled in protest.

'Don't do that.' It was the growl of a bear, but he didn't pull away.

She shifted so her feet fitted into the spaces between his, her body flush against his, and rested her head against his jumper. She could feel the muscles beneath the wool, hard and well-defined. It seemed a very long time since she had held a man in her arms. Alistair was much slenderer than Connor, and hadn't gone in for hugging much.

Connor's arms came round her now, and they remained together, him leaning back against the stove, Hetty leaning forward against him. For a long time neither of them moved, for a long time she didn't want anything more. But his hands felt warm through her pyjama top and suddenly hugging wasn't enough.

'What about my hot chocolate?' she breathed, when she had despaired of him doing anything other than just hold her.

'Damn your hot chocolate.' This time his lips weren't gentle and they landed full on her waiting mouth.

Her senses, held in check for so long, leapt to meet his kiss, which was hard and angry. She had her own axe to grind and kissed him back just as fiercely. Then old grievances were forgotten as passion took over.

Hetty's neck and back were arching under his onslaught, she swayed slightly and he felt it, and straightened up. Terrified lest he decide the kissing was over, she pushed her hands under his sweater and shirt and found his waist, then the part where his belt and trousers gaped from the small of his back. She took a firm hold of his belt, making it difficult for him to run away, but he was still too far away from her, and her neck was still at a horrible angle.

'I'm terribly uncomfortable. Let's go into the sitting room,' she suggested when he stopped for breath. She was panting slightly.

Her suggestion brought him to his senses. 'Don't be ridiculous. We shouldn't be doing this at all, let alone horizontally.'

'But we are, so we might as well do it in comfort. Unless you don't want to?' She hadn't realized coquetry was in her nature until that moment. Up to then, it hadn't needed to be. Now, she looked up at him, her eyes wide with innocent pleading, one hand creeping up to caress the back of his neck.

He grunted, caught her wandering hand, and frog-marched her along the passage to the sitting room, where the fire was finally going well.

He stopped in the doorway. 'Seriously, Hetty . . .'

Hetty took hold of his hand this time and pulled him to the

sofa. 'I've spent too much time being serious lately. Let's be silly.' She sat down and tugged at his hand.

Connor let out a long-held-on-to breath, and with it went a lot of good resolutions.

Hetty found the Connor who wasn't inhibited by scruples very different as a lover. He picked her up and sat her on his lap, organizing her body so her head rested in the crook of his arm, her bottom was comfortably on his lap, and her feet were on the sofa, clear of the draughts. Then he turned his attention to the matter in hand.

She had been kissed before, lots of times, but with Alistair it had always been the preliminary for sex. Connor kissed with surprising dedication and thoroughness. This was the main course, not the appetizer.

Hetty's insides began to melt almost immediately as his teeth grazed the tender inside of her mouth, and his tongue drew hers into loving interaction.

She sighed when he drew away and dotted little kisses tenderly about her face and neck. She inhaled the musky, sexy smell of him, which owed more to nature than Yves Saint Laurent and further inflamed her increasing passion. She willed him to lower his head a bit and kiss the little vee of skin that was all her pyjamas revealed. But he wouldn't go below her tartan collar.

She couldn't complain of neglect, though. His mouth was creating a wave of sensation that none of Alistair's fancy techniques had produced. She would have been content just to lie there on the sofa being kissed for ever. Almost.

His fingers dangled beneath her collar at the back of her neck, finding the little short hairs and causing them to stir. Having done that, they found their way round the front, and he stroked the little hollow behind her ear, her lobe, wandering down towards her collar-bone. There he stopped, touching nothing that wasn't exposed, uncovering nothing that was not already revealed to him.

Perhaps it didn't matter. Everywhere became an erogenous zone under his roughened fingertips. But it was too tantalizing.

She placed his hand over her breast in a way that caused one of his fingers to land under the lapel of her pyjama top. He didn't pull away immediately, but he wouldn't let her move it further.

He distracted her with kisses and then removed his hand, transferring it to her right foot.

Here, he allowed his fingers enough liberty to creep up her pyjama trousers to her ankle-bone, encircling it with delicate caresses until she squirmed with a half-ticklish pleasure, which seemed to penetrate all the most intimate parts of her body.

Although his hands on her feet did have magic properties, there were other points on her body which would have appreciated such dedicated attention.

'I wouldn't think you were raping me if you undid my pyjamas. In fact, I think I'd quite like it.'

'I can't. I promised Samuel I wouldn't seduce you. I only have so much self-control.'

So did Hetty, and all this restraint, though admirable, was starting to get on her nerves. 'Just a couple of buttons wouldn't hurt, surely?'

'You know perfectly well it wouldn't end with a couple of buttons. I promised Samuel.'

Hetty muttered a curse in the direction of her sick relation. 'It's all right. I didn't promise him anything – except to look after the house. I could seduce you.'

Connor regarded her for what seemed like an age, and then a slow, infinitely sexy smile started at the crooked corner of his mouth and spread until he was grinning. 'Go on then. If you dare.'

Any remaining doubts she had were banished by this last utterance. She had never taken the initiative in love-making before, and had certainly never planned a seduction, but she felt quite certain that she dared. The only question was, where? She felt sure if she and Connor moved, she would lose her nerve, and he would discover more of the scruples with which he was so amply supplied.

'Get up a minute.' She tugged at his jumper. 'I need to make a few adjustments.'

He got up and watched as Hetty pulled the sofa cushions on to the floor and arranged them into a mattress. She took the rug that lay over the back of the sofa and spread it on the cushions. Then she lit the candles that Phyllis had put in the candlesticks, strictly for decoration. Hetty dismissed the momentary flicker of guilt that thoughts of Phyllis caused, and continued her preparations. She gathered all the loose cushions from all the surrounding furniture and piled them around the makeshift bed.

'There,' she said when she had finished. 'What about that?'

'It would be more comfortable on a bed. Why don't we go upstairs?'

If she told him how she felt about moving, he would think she had changed her mind and back out.

'Mine's only a single. Much narrower than this.'

He nodded. 'And I can't possibly take you to Samuel's bed. We'll have to make do on the floor.'

He seemed to sense that her bravado had been leaking from her as she gathered cushions, and drew her gently down to join him, as he knelt on them. He took her face in his hands and kissed her.

'Are you sure about this?'

Hetty nodded. 'Quite sure.'

At first he kissed her with all the gentleness he had shown at the beginning, but as she relaxed he led her back to the passion she had felt earlier. Their kneeling figures threw huge shadows on the walls until she pulled him down on top of her and tugged at his clothes.

When he was stripped to the waist, each muscle and rib shadowed in the firelight, she moistened her lips, yearning to feel his skin against hers, with no cloth or buttons between them. Her pyjamas were still done up to the neck.

'You could undo my top,' she said, remembering that last time she suggested it he had refused.

She thought he was going to refuse again, he looked at her for such a long time. 'You undo it,' he said eventually. 'You're the one in charge.'

She took up his challenge and pushed him down so she was kneeling above him. She almost tore her buttons off in her haste to rid herself of her jacket, and then thought that she should have undone each one with tantalizing slowness, making him wait for the sight of her breasts.

But her assertive gesture made her feel powerful, exciting her and him. She felt in control, of her pleasure and his. She leant forward to brush her nipples slowly across his chest. Now, she would make him wait.

He groaned.

'Am I hurting you?' She thought she must be kneeling on some part of him.

'No,' he said hoarsely. 'Just don't stop.'

After a while, he took one of her nipples into his mouth, the other he caressed with his hand. It was her turn to groan, and she slumped down beside him, surrendering herself to every sensation their bodies could give each other. She sighed with satisfaction when he pulled off her pyjama bottoms and she was naked at last.

A little later he raised his head and took hold of her hands, which were fumbling with his belt buckle. 'What are we going to do about contraception? Are you on the pill?'

She blushed to think that contraception hadn't occurred to her until he mentioned it. One of the first positive things she did after Alistair's betrayal was to flush away three months' supply.

'You haven't got any condoms, I suppose?' he asked.

'Of course not!' She was indignant. 'Why should I have?'

He gave a shuddering sigh. 'It was a long shot.'

'What about you? Haven't you got anything?'

'No! I'm promised not to lay a finger on you, remember?'

'But you might have laid a finger on someone else. Samuel didn't ask you to take a vow of chastity, did he?'

Connor pulled himself up so he was sitting on his heels. 'No, but I really didn't foresee myself having any sort of affair while I was in England. And they're not the sort of things I buy just in case.'

'Oh.'

'It's too late for the pubs to still be open, or I'd raid a machine.'

'You mean – we have to stop?'

'We can't have unprotected sex. I'd never forgive myself, and Samuel would disinherit me.'

She dismissed the thought that this might have its advantages – for the house anyway. Briefly she imagined herself telling Peter and Phyllis that the reason the house was no longer under threat was because Connor had made her pregnant and been struck out of Samuel's will. Would they think she'd sacrificed her virtue in a noble cause? Or that she was a slut?

She turned her mind back to the insoluble problem. She felt

bereft, unbearably cheated. She knew she would never have the courage to do anything like this again, and he wouldn't touch her because of his stupid promise.

'We couldn't just – take a chance?'

'No.'

He certainly wasn't going to let her take it, even if she was foolish enough to risk it. 'Could you just hold me?' She knew she sounded pathetic, but she couldn't bear the thought of them putting their clothes back on and going up to their cold, separate beds.

'I can do a little better than that.' He lay her gently back down, pulled her to him and kissed her until she had forgotten her disappointment. Then with gentle, subtle fingers, he found her secret places and tended them until at last she shuddered to a climax. Afterwards he held her shaking body, pulling the blanket round her so she wouldn't feel cold.

She bit back her tears, unabearably moved by his tenderness. Even her limited experience told her that he'd been exceptionally unselfish, that he must be aching with unfulfilled desire. But he just murmured into her hair and, later, found her pyjamas.

'Come on,' he said eventually, when he'd put his shirt and sweater back on, 'I'll take you up to bed.'

'I feel so guilty. I seduced you against your will, and we couldn't even make love properly.'

'I was very willing. If I hadn't been you wouldn't have got past first base, I assure you.'

'I've never known what the bases are – do you?'

He chuckled. 'One day I'll show you.'

'I do feel so bad.'

'Because of what happened?'

'Because of what didn't happen. I should have thought about contraception. It's so unfair for you.'

'It's just as much my fault. I thought about contraception when I first sent you off to bed. If I'd mentioned it then, you wouldn't have come near me.'

'But you didn't.'

He shook his head. 'The road to hell is paved with good intentions. Now, come along upstairs.'

She got stiffly to her feet. 'I'll have to sort out the room. If Phyllis sees it like this –'

'She'll know what we've been up to. Don't worry, you go to bed. I'll tidy up.'

She placed her hand shyly on his chest. 'Will you come in and say good-night?'

He gave another shuddering sigh. 'If you're not asleep. Now off you go. I've only got so much will-power.'

Hetty went quickly to the door, and paused on the threshold. 'You won't forget the dogs, will you?'

'Just go!'

She heard him come up to bed, go to the bathroom, pause at her door and then go to his own room. She knew he probably realized she wasn't asleep, but he didn't come in.

She hoped it was himself he didn't trust, but she had a horrid feeling that it was her. He had shown such incredible restraint, when she was showing none, would have taken any risk. Her feelings for him were so uncontrolled. With Alistair she had put herself on the pill, had waited until she was fully protected, and even then insisted that Alistair wore a condom.

He had complained that it was belt and braces – she had told him firmly that the pill didn't prevent infection. She could hear herself now, sounding sensible to the point of prissiness. At the time she had wondered at Alistair even suggesting a condom might not be necessary, but then remembered that he knew she was a virgin. He had nothing to risk. She had everything.

With Connor it had all been the other way round. She had been the initiator right from the beginning, and he had held her off as hard as he could. For her sake.

It took all her will-power not to wait until he was asleep and creep into his bed. Not for the sex they hadn't shared, but for the closeness, the tenderness that they had. Her last conscious thought was that she was in danger of falling in love with Conan the Barbarian.

CHAPTER FOURTEEN

Inevitably, Hetty felt acutely embarrassed at the thought of seeing Connor the next morning. Everything that had happened or not happened had been her fault. Being assertive, taking the initiative, was all very well in theory. In practice it could land you with a whole chicken-farm of egg on your face.

She opened the kitchen door wondering what on earth she could say to him, having decided that a simple 'Hello' would have to do. To her relief she was spared saying anything because he was on the phone.

She put the kettle on, trying to listen in without appearing to, but as his end of the conversation consisted mostly of grunts and uh-hus she could make little of it. She looked up when he put the phone down.

His expression was serious and gentle and made her heart sink. 'Hetty? I've got something to tell you.'

Her mouth went dry and she felt the blood leave her face. 'Not Samuel?'

He smiled a little. 'No, it's good news, in some ways, but I've got to go away.' He smiled a little more. 'Of course, you might be thrilled.'

She was relieved enough to smile back. 'I might.' But she knew she wasn't. 'Where are you going, and how long for?'

'Not sure how long. But I've managed to get another contract where I was before. It won't be much fun, but it's very well-paid. It should pay a couple of instalments.'

'When do you have to leave?'

'As soon as I've got some things together. I'll take a taxi to the airport.'

'That sounds very extravagant.'

'They can afford it.'

'What about your car? Wouldn't you rather take it?'

He shook his head. 'It'll be safer here – unless you have any particular reason to be annoyed with me?' He gave her a little teasing smile she could only just respond to.

'Will you be back quite soon? Or will you be gone for a long time?' The thought of facing the anxiety of the loan on her own was suddenly devastating.

'Of course I'll be back.'

'Do you know when?' She forced the wifely anxiety out of her voice. 'I only need to know in case I have to find another pianist for the ruby wedding.'

'I can't be very precise, but I should be back well before then. If it takes that long the country deserves to remain a desert.'

Hetty realized she had no idea what Connor did for a living; while this probably wasn't the time to ask, she felt she needed to know. 'What is it that you do, exactly?'

'I'm a civil engineer. I help to sort out the problems caused by years of bad ecology.'

She nodded. 'I see. Would you like me to make you some breakfast? If you need to pack?'

He flashed her the kind of charming smile he usually reserved for Caroline. 'That would be kind.' Then he whooshed out of the kitchen like a comic-book hero. Hetty could almost see the go-faster lines streaming after him.

She found eggs and bacon, some mushrooms and tomatoes, and set about making him the best breakfast she could manage. She realized it was the first time she'd cooked for him, if you didn't count hot toddies, and for some mixed-up, unfeminist reason, she wanted to make a good job of it. She had everything sizzling away, and was waiting for the right moment to start the eggs, when he appeared in the kitchen again, almost unrecognizable in a suit.

Hetty cracked two eggs into a saucer and managed to add them to the pan without breaking the yolks. Just now, busyness was protecting her from having to confront either Connor or the fact that he was leaving her. She warmed the old enamel coffee pot. Filter coffee would require her to keep her back to him for ages.

Eventually she had to present him with a plate of eggs and bacon, toast and coffee. She was about to wash-up the frying-pan when he ordered her to sit down.

'I've got a few things to tell you about. Sit there, eat some toast, and listen.'

She pulled out a chair and sat on it, but ignored the toast. 'Fire away.'

'Sorry to be so brusque, but there's not much time.' He referred to the sort of watch guaranteed to keep going on the top of Everest or a thousand leagues under the sea. Hetty had never seen it before. 'The taxi'll be here in under an hour.'

'Don't let me hold you up.'

Connor scowled. Hetty was trying to keep her expression bland, hide any hint that the moment he left she might become very upset. She didn't feel she was making a good enough job of it.

'I want you to promise me not to do anything dreadful while I'm away.'

She was affronted. She was the guardian of his inheritance and it didn't give much scope for dreadfulness. Some devil nudged her into being provocative. 'Like what? Running off with Peter?'

He was not provoked. He took another bite of toast and spoke to her through it. 'No. That sounds a very sensible idea. He's a good man, he'll make you very happy. If bored out of your skull.' He finished his mouthful. 'I meant, to do with the house.'

Hetty, reeling from the blow he had just delivered with such insouciance, forgot to be bland. 'What do you mean, to do with the house? You're the one who plans to pull it down!'

'I mean, don't sell off any more antiques or anything.'

She gulped, appalled and indignant that she had been found out. 'I don't know what you . . .' She couldn't stammer out the rest of the lie.

'Yes you do. Oh, I don't mind about you selling off half the crocks at the car-boot sale, we needed the space, and that Clarice Cliff vase was hideous. But there's nothing else around that I won't miss, and I don't want you selling off any more of my birthright.'

Hetty picked up his coffee mug and took a scalding gulp. It was hideously strong. 'You know perfectly well, I was raising money to keep the house going. For Samuel's sake.'

'I know.' Connor's teeth crashed together on a wholemeal crust. 'And I said, I don't mind. But I really don't want to come home to any more unpleasant surprises.'

'And would me running off with Peter be pleasant or unpleasant?'

He should have been shocked into paroxysms of jealousy, but wasn't. 'It would be rather a pity. He's very dull.'

'I thought you said it would be sensible.'

'It would. But is "sensible" enough to last you the rest of your life?'

She wanted to ask him if he was offering anything better, but knew she didn't have the right.

He put a hand on hers. 'I'm really sorry that we haven't got time to sort out what happened – or didn't happen – last night. But it's not something you can do in' – another glance at the fantastic watch – 'under three quarters of an hour. So just promise me, nothing awful with the house, and' – the corner of his mouth lifted – 'nothing irrevocable with Peter? You'll break his heart and he'll break my shins.'

'Why on earth would he think it was your fault?'

'We've been living in the same house. The whole damn village would say it was my fault if you lost a filling, let alone turned down their pet eligible bachelor. Let's face it, if the church tower was struck by lightning, they'd point the finger at me.'

'The Brewsters like you.'

'They're the only ones who've made any attempt to get to know me.'

Hetty attempted a smile. 'I tried quite hard to get to know you, with no great success.'

He sighed. 'Only you could make that sort of pun at this sort of moment. That's why . . .' He stopped.

'Why what?'

He looked at her, half in sorrow, half in sheer bewilderment. Then he lifted his hand to her cheek and cradled it. She leant into it, loving the warmth, the feel of his fingers, which nestled in the hollow behind her ear. A faint smell of Imperial Leather rose from his wrist and she knew she would never smell it again without feeling sad.

'I'm coming back, Hetty. We're going to sort everything out. But please, promise, nothing dreadful while I'm out of the way?'

She promised in a voice that croaked and was barely audible.

His chair screeched on the stone flags as he sprung to his feet. 'I must finish packing.'

He was packed and back in the kitchen before Hetty had had time to clear the table.

'That was quick. Are you sure you've got everything?'

'Yup. It doesn't take long to pack when you're used to it. I'd better leave you some numbers.' He took a sheet off an A4 pad, flicked through his Filofax until he reached the right page, and started writing. 'These are just in case of an emergency. It's not always easy to get through –'

'I know.'

'– And I don't know which of these numbers I'll be at. The people on the other end don't speak much English, but you'll just have to do your best.'

'What language do they speak?'

'Russian's the official language, but it might be anything.'

'Oh.'

'And it's best to ring about midnight, then the lines are less busy.' At last, he finished writing. 'Anything about Samuel, ring me. I'm not saying I'll cross three continents to get to his funeral, but if he's likely to be still alive when I get there, I'll come. Understand?'

'I do, but the village would be terribly shocked if you didn't come to the funeral.'

'Stuff the village. It's Samuel who matters.'

'You're not telling me this because Samuel's worse, are you?'

'Oh no. It's just, he is old and frail, and I'm going a long way away.'

Hetty's throat closed and she gave him a little smile in reply.

'Keep up the singing, won't you?'

Hetty, who felt she would never so much as hum again, nodded.

'Good girl. Now I'm going to ring the hospital and leave a message for Samuel. Call me if the taxi comes.'

Obedient little creature that she'd recently become, she did.

Connor delivered a hard, rasping kiss to her cheek just before he swept out of the door, his laptop under his arm. Hetty murmured her goodbyes somewhere in the region of his armpit, and then she was alone, feeling more devastated than she had when her mother had dumped her there, and Alistair had filled her thoughts. She rubbed her cheek where he had kissed her and wondered if he'd ever learn to shave properly.

But by the time she'd dealt with congealing bacon fat, eggshells and coffee grounds, she felt better. Connor had gone away on business, he hadn't betrayed her. And who was he to her anyway? Someone who threatened this beautiful house and got in the way of all her plans.

Conan the Barbarian – the man who had demonstrated so frustratingly that he was anything but barbaric in some respects – she put firmly out of her mind. She was just about to take the dogs out when the phone rang.

She had a split second of hope that Connor was ringing to say it was all a mistake and he was coming home, and then she picked up the receiver and knew it wasn't Connor.

'Hetty? James Taylor here.'

The architect. Face and name connected just in time for Hetty to be effusive. 'James! How lovely to hear from you.'

'Not all that lovely, actually. I've got some rather unsettling news.'

'What?'

'I've looked up everything I can think of, checked every register of every county you might have been in before the boundary changes, but I can't find Courtbridge House on any list.'

'What do you mean?'

'It isn't listed. I can't think how it slipped through the net. I can only suppose everyone thought this area was covered by someone else. It is rather in a backwater.'

'You mean, there's nothing to stop Connor pulling the place down?'

'Not at the moment, no. But the good thing is, you could get it listed yourself, or, at least, I could arrange it for you. Then he couldn't. Is Connor likely to be out any day soon? I could come round and we could talk about it?'

Hetty screwed her eyes shut and bit her lip. 'Umm – can I get back to you on that? I'd need to do some thinking.'

'Sure. Have you got my number?'

'Give it to me again, just in case.' She found a tiny space on the piece of cardboard which was stuck under the phone and jotted it down. 'It's awfully kind of you to go to so much trouble.'

'It was a pleasure. A house like that deserves a lot of trouble.'

Hetty refrained from commenting that it had caused more than enough trouble already.

When they'd said their goodbyes and rung off, Hetty picked up the receiver again and rang Phyllis. She told her she had to go out urgently and could she let herself in? Then she found her car keys, and took the dogs to visit Caroline.

'Hi! Fancy coming with me to walk the dogs?'

Caroline was wearing a cream knitted garment that wrapped around her in a mysterious but surprisingly sexy way. 'You know I never walk anywhere if I can help it, and certainly not for pleasure. Aren't you on house-duty today?' She watched resignedly as Talisker and Islay trotted down her hall and into her kitchen.

'Phyllis is doing it, and there's no problem exactly, but I hadn't seen you for a while and thought you might like a walk.'

'Come into the kitchen and tell me all about it. Do you like my thingy?' She tugged at the garment, which dipped and clung in all the right places. 'It was quite expensive, but such good value. You can wear it in so many ways. When Jack says, "Not another new dress?" I can say, "What, this old thing? It's just my cardie."'

'It's wonderful.' Hetty pulled out a stool and sat at Caroline's antique refectory table, which took up one end of her enormous kitchen. 'Connor's gone away.'

'Good news or bad?'

'Oh good, definitely. It means he won't be around to interfere with things. You know what a pain he can be.'

Caroline, who had been making coffee, spun round. 'Sweetheart, you're not carrying a little torch are you? I mean, I know I'm the only one around here who seems to notice how fantastically sexy he is, but you do sound a little – sad.'

'Do I? Tired maybe, but not sad. He's terribly domineering, a totally unreconstructed alpha-male. Not even just not "new" but Cro-Magnon.'

'I thought he did all the shopping and cooking?'

'He's a foodie, and a pig. Doesn't trust anyone else to cook the pasta *al dente*.'

'And you're in love with him.'

'What! Don't be ridiculous. Where on earth did you get that idea?'

'Something you said, darling.'

'Nonsense! I never said anything like that at all.'

'You did actually, but not on purpose. Love, I'm so sorry. Is he going to come back?'

'Yes, but really, Caro, I know you're desperately romantic, and it would just suit your ideas about what people should do, but I promise you . . .' her words got slower and slower as she realized she was lying '. . . I'm not in love with him. At least,' she added for truth's sake, 'not very much.'

Caroline sat down opposite her, abandoning the coffee and a first-class opportunity to say, 'I told you so.' 'Does he feel the same way about you?'

Hetty was horrified. It was bad enough discovering her own feelings without having to think about Connor's. 'For God's sake! Of course, not! Talk about sleeping with the enemy!'

'Don't exaggerate.'

'And if he did have a soft spot for me, how on earth would I know about it?'

'He's definitely got a soft spot for you. But calm down. I'm only asking.' She inspected an ancient knot-hole in her table. 'You haven't had unprotected sex, have you?'

'Really! Do you ask your Brownies such personal questions?'

'No. Have you?'

'No! All right?'

'That's a relief. You won't get pregnant then?'

'No.' Hetty found herself close to tears. She would have found it far easier to tell Caroline about it if she had had sex, protected or otherwise. But what had happened between her and Connor last night seemed too personal, far more intimate than if they'd simply made love.

Caroline came round the table, sat next to Hetty and put her arm round her. 'Does he know – have any hint – what you feel about him?'

Hetty shrugged. 'He might. He might not.'

'Well, has he kissed you?'

Hetty nodded.

'More?'

She nodded again.

'All the way?'

She shook her head vehemently.

'Sorry to pry, but I need to know . . .' She paused, making Hetty wonder why, and what torture she would inflict to find out. 'How the hell did you keep your hands off him?'

Hetty, feeling somewhat better, turned to her friend. 'When's Jack coming back? It seems to me he's been away too long.'

Caroline sighed. 'Me too, darling.'

'But you don't want a nice brisk walk to take your mind off it?'

'No. My mind's perfectly happy as it is. I might take a nice bad book and a box of chocs on to the sofa with me later, but now I've got a stunning catalogue to go through. Fabulous clothes, a bit pricey, but absolutely darling. Can't tempt you to join me? We can have a spot of lunch later.'

'Fresh air and exercise is what keeps me going,' said Hetty. 'Not expensive catalogues and lunch. I'll leave you to your sybaritic existence. Come on, dogs, Caroline wants to rot her mind in peace.'

'That's most unfair. I may watch *Countdown* later!'

Hetty reflected that Caroline was one of those rare souls who managed to get an awful lot done, most of it for other people, without appearing to be busy. Usually, with most people, it was the other way round.

She marched through the woods around the village, sensing the coming spring with every step. She went further and faster than she would have done if she'd had Caroline with her, though she would have enjoyed her company.

But even in that short visit, Caroline had managed to cheer her up, even if she had forced her to face up to the uncomfortable knowledge that she had fallen in love with Connor. If it hadn't been for her recent débâcle with Alistair, she would have admitted it to herself earlier. As it was, she tried to kid herself it wasn't so. Quite how she managed to do that so well, she couldn't guess.

Up till now she'd almost managed to convince herself that what she felt for him was lust, that it was just his bulk and dash that attracted her. After all, it could hardly be his chivalrous manners and charming compliments that made her weak at the knees. But Caroline had brought it home to her that, for her, desire only followed where her heart led.

★

163

Hetty parked her car, let the dogs out of the back and walked into the kitchen, her cheeks flushed with the cold and the exercise. Phyllis was busy relabelling jars of marmalade she had brought from home so they said more than just MARM and the year, and she could sell them to the public. She tutted as the dogs pattered their muddy feet on to the kitchen floor.

'You really should train those dogs to wait until they've had their feet wiped,' she said.

'I know. But they're not my dogs and I'm not much good with them.'

'Yes you are. Too indulgent, of course, but you could learn. With a little application. By the way, there was a telephone call for you.'

Hetty turned, her heartbeat quickened. 'Oh?'

'Yes. That architect who came round. James Taylor.'

'Oh, him again.'

'He left rather a peculiar message.' Hetty waited, but Phyllis wasn't to be hurried. 'First of all, he left a different number to the one he gave you. Then when I asked him what he was calling about, he said to tell you that it would be better if you could let him know sooner rather than later if you want him to list the house.' Oh, James! Why couldn't you have just left the number? 'Naturally,' Phyllis went on, 'I asked him what on earth he was talking about. And he told me the house, Courtbridge House,' she glared at Hetty as if the whole thing was her fault, '*wasn't* listed. And that anyone could do anything they liked to it.'

CHAPTER FIFTEEN

'I don't think they can do *anything*,' said Hetty. 'I mean, there are all sorts of building regulations, local-planning laws, stuff like that.'

'But, my dear girl, don't you realize what a terrible thing this is? Our beloved house under even greater threat! Thank goodness we've discovered it in time.'

Hetty spooned coffee into mugs, wondering how on earth she was going to keep Phyllis from going off in all directions. She handed her one of the mugs. 'Biscuit?'

Phyllis shook her head. 'No thank you, dear, haven't got time to waste on biscuits. Where is he?'

'Who? James? I'm not sure –'

'Not James! The Barbarian! If we could just get him out of the way . . .'

Hetty was tired and sad and wasn't at her mental best. 'He *is* out of the way. He's gone back to –' Where had he gone? '– wherever he was before.' The moment she'd finished she wished she'd kept her mouth shut. The threat of his imminent appearance might have kept Phyllis under control.

'Thank God! That means we can act without him having to know anything about it. What a relief! I was really quite worried for a while there. He could have had the bulldozers in before anyone could lift a finger to prevent it.'

'But he didn't.' Hetty concentrated very hard on sounding calm and emotionally disinterested. 'And therefore it means we can't do anything behind his back.'

'Dear child, are you mad? What do you mean not "do anything behind his back"? What do you think all that sorting out and selling the unwanted pieces was all about? Of course we must do it behind his back.'

Hetty shook her head. 'I promised him, before he left, that I wouldn't do anything – irrevocable' – the word 'dreadful' would only set Phyllis off again – 'about the house while he was away. He'll be back quite soon. We won't have to wait long.'

Phyllis obviously felt she was dealing with a dangerous lunatic. 'If we wait, he'll prevent us. Or worse, damage the house before we can stop him.'

Hetty shook her head. 'No he won't, or he would have done so before now. He won't do anything to the house while Samuel's still alive.'

'But how long is that going to be? The dear man looked pretty groggy last time I saw him.' Phyllis made a gesture, which would have been a reassuring pat from anyone more demonstrative. 'I don't mean to worry you, dear, but he could pop off at any moment.'

'I know. He didn't look too well when I saw him, either. I must go and see him again. There never seems to be a moment.'

'You do that. And let *me* worry about getting the house listed.'

'Phyllis, please. I swear to you I will do absolutely anything it takes to get Connor to agree to having the house listed. But I can't allow anything to be done behind his back.' Knowing she had no power to stop Phyllis from doing anything she thought right, she pressed on. 'You must understand my situation. I gave my solemn word. He would never believe me if I said it had been nothing to do with me. It was only through me you discovered the house wasn't listed. It may not be me who told the authorities, but it would only be a technical detail, I'd be just as guilty.'

'Guilty? My dear child, you're forgetting the rights of the matter. That man is at present in a position to destroy this beautiful house, all it contains, and a lot of beautiful countryside as well. Just who would be committing the crime?'

'I said that he won't do anything while Samuel's alive.'

'And we agreed that might not be for very long. Red tape takes time to get tied up if it's something you want doing, believe you me.'

'OK, I accept we might not have very long, but Connor will be back soon. I'll get him to do it.'

'How on earth do you propose to do that?'

Hetty shrugged. 'Reasoned argument, appeals to his better nature . . .'

Phyllis smiled somewhat cynically. 'If you were a different sort of girl I'd suggest you go to bed with him.'

'But, as it is,' replied Hetty, somewhat tightly, 'you don't think that would be enough of a bribe?'

'Of course I didn't mean that, Hetty. I just meant you weren't that sort of girl.'

That was all *she* knew. 'But you'll give me a chance to persuade him?'

'Of course, I don't want to do anything that will distress you, but what on earth makes you think he'll agree to having the house listed when, up to now, his plans have been for demolition?'

'I don't know!' Hetty felt close to tears. If only she hadn't promised to keep Samuel's financial problems private, Phyllis might be less insistent. 'But I can try. And I'd rather fight him face to face, or in the courts, or anywhere, than act without him knowing what we were up to.'

Phyllis took agonizing seconds digesting this. 'How long is he away for?'

'He said he'd be back for the ruby wedding.'

Phyllis sighed. 'Well, I suppose it'll have to wait until then. But I hope we don't live to rue the day.'

'And you won't say anything about all this to Peter?'

'Say anything about all what?' said Peter from the door-way.

Hetty closed her eyes tightly and counted to ten to stop herself screaming. The man had an uncanny ability to know when Connor wasn't about, thought Hetty. He doesn't come near the place for days, and the moment Connor's gone he's in through the back door like a stray cat. She wished all these people would get out of her kitchen and leave her alone. She opened her eyes again and tried to smile.

'Oh come in, Peter. You might as well know, I suppose. Phyllis will tell you everything.'

While Phyllis did so, Hetty stared out of the kitchen window, detaching herself from the character assassination that was going on behind her.

Clovis, the old cat, was picking his way across the yard with surprising agility. Connor was one of the few people who allowed Clovis to sit on him. Most found his breath too offensive. Even

167

Peter had muttered that it might be kinder to have him put down. But you couldn't just kill an animal because it smelt.

All this occupied her mind on one level; the rest was filled with resentment for Peter and Phyllis, the people she was so fond of, and who had done so much to help her. The trouble was, having helped her, they now felt they owned her and could tell her what to do.

'Any chance of a cup of coffee?' Peter drew her attention back into the room.

'Sorry, I was just thinking. Another one, Phyllis?'

'No thank you, dear.'

Hetty put water in the electric kettle, which Connor had bought as back-up. The water would take too long to boil on the stove.

When at last she carried a cup of coffee across to the table, Phyllis and Peter were regarding her as anxious parents do before they tell their wayward child she is going to be sent to boarding-school. You're going to be miserable, they were going to say, but it's for your own good.

'I think I'll have a cup,' she declared, not wanting to hear their homily. Too much caffeine would make her jumpy, but then, she already was.

Phyllis waited until Hetty had her mug full. 'Come and sit down, dear. We must make a plan.'

Hetty sat. 'I think I explained to Phyllis,' she said for Peter's benefit, 'I can't do anything behind Connor's back. Anything that's irrevocable. And I can't let you two do anything either.'

'At the risk of sounding like a bully, how do you propose to stop us?' Peter stirred the coffee that Hetty had forgotten to put sugar in.

'I can't stop you, not really. But I can remind you that the house doesn't belong to Connor yet. I'm pretty sure Samuel would have known whether or not his house was listed. And if he'd wanted it listed, he'd have done something about it. You can't go behind the back of someone old and sick.' Phyllis had played this card, so she could too.

Peter and Phyllis regarded each other. The child had made a point they'd really have to consider.

'And I don't think now is quite the time to ask Samuel about it. Do you? I mean, he's pretty frail, and reminding him of his mortality, which such a subject is bound to do, wouldn't be very kind.'

Hetty sipped her coffee so they wouldn't see the triumph in her expression. She might not have won the war but, with luck, this would hold them at bay until Connor got back.

'Don't you want the house listed, Hetty?' Peter's brown eyes were full of reproach and confusion.

'Of course I do. But not in an underhand way that is likely to upset Samuel or Connor. I promised Connor I wouldn't do anything behind his back.' She turned to Phyllis. 'He knew how much stuff we'd sold, about the Clarice Cliff vase and everything.'

'Oh dear, awkward for you, was it?'

'Not really. He didn't mind. But he said he wouldn't put up with anything else being sold or disposed of.'

'She is in a very invidious position.' Phyllis addressed Peter.

He turned to Hetty. 'Is there any way you can get in touch with him, so you don't have to act behind his back?' He winced as he sipped his coffee.

Hetty thought of the list of numbers, the instructions, the time difference, the fact that no one spoke English. 'No. What we have to do,' she went on, having delivered this convincing lie, 'is get the place in even better shape so, when he comes back, it's a going concern, and not a drain on Samuel's limited resources.'

Phyllis drew a clutch of marmalade jars towards her. 'I see your point about not acting behind anyone's back. But the usual rules of decency can be suspended in exceptional circumstances?' Her upward inflection made the statement a tentative question.

Hetty shook her head. 'Not in this case. And isn't that someone arriving?'

That night Hetty took the dogs up to bed with her, but really felt too tired to worry about being along in the house. 'As long as the burglars come quietly, and don't wake me,' she told Islay, who, being female, was more likely to worry than Talisker, 'I don't mind.'

One of Caroline's pet tradesmen had arrived that afternoon and fitted a security system, a fact that made Hetty simultaneously glad that Connor was out of the way, relieved that the contents insurance would now be valid, and anxious about how the man was to be paid. He had waved away her inquiries on the subject with an airy gesture. 'I'll let you know,' he'd said glibly.

'Could you just give me a rough figure? So I can have it ready for you?'

'I'll pop it in the post, when I've worked it out.'

Hetty wrote '£500?' on her pad and resolved to ask Caroline about it.

She slept like a log.

Hetty had very little time to miss Connor. The house had plenty of visitors. Various workmen came, some of whom were paid in cash, others who promised to send their bills in later. There was also a follow-up visit from the man from the bank, who was flatteringly impressed by their progress.

'Glad to see things getting straight and nothing's likely to burst into flames.' He laughed cheerily. 'Wouldn't like all your good work to go up in smoke.'

A man with a daughter and a pony approached her, asking if they could rent a field she hadn't even known was part of the property. He offered money, or labour in lieu. As the rent seemed very little, she asked him what he did. 'I'm a plumber,' he said. Through him, she got all the dripping taps fixed and the shower working properly.

But after Connor had been gone a week Hetty had another letter from the loan company. They could, it seemed, sense that their loan was insecure, and were threatening to demand it all back – immediately.

Hetty, on her own and unable to consult anyone, wasn't sure they were legally able to do this. She knew ordinary banks could withdraw overdraft facilities without notice, and make firms bankrupt. Did loan sharks have the same powers?

She considered fighting her way through the lists of numbers and asking Connor. But he might not know, and why add to his worry quota when he couldn't do anything to help? She could ask her friendly bank manager. He would know. But Hetty was so busy. And supposing the sharks could demand the loan be paid immediately? It would hardly make her feel better. And although discovering that their demands were illegal would set her mind at rest, she felt the risk was too great: she'd rather live in ignorant hope than certain despair. Consequently, she wrote them a huge cheque, seriously depleting the account, and made tentative inquiries in the village about anyone who might like to buy a nice little 2CV.

And it was not only this added anxiety that made her miss Connor. She missed knowing that any moment he might stride into the room, swearing and cursing, or making some remark guaranteed to make Hetty laugh. She'd rather fight with him than not have him to fight with, and she spent a lot of time humming sentimental songs about preferring to be blue alone without one's loved one, than being happy with somebody else. It was pathetic, but there it was.

She got out of the house as much as she could. Inside the house she felt hedged about with Phyllis and Peter and their unspoken reproaches for the stand she had taken. But she found plenty of excuses.

There were arrangements for the ruby wedding, which marched resolutely nearer. Six weeks was not a lot of time to arrange something like that, Hetty insisted. Having promised caterers and entertainment, they had to be organized, and preferably before the sale of her car left her without transport.

Fortunately, as Hetty had imagined, the WI was a rich source of culinary talent.

'Mrs Makepiece doesn't want anything too complicated, just quiches, salads and gooey puddings, things like that.'

'Oh.' The woman whose kitchen Hetty was standing in when she delivered this intentionally reassuring information seemed disappointed. She was a stalwart of the WI, had four children, a placid manner and, allegedly, an angel's touch with pastry. 'I was hoping for a chance to try something new,' the woman went on. 'I get bored making quiches and the like.'

'Well, I'm sure –'

'I do a very nice raised pie. Hot-water crust. Did some for my sister's wedding. Very popular, they were.'

'That sounds wonderful. I'll speak to Mrs Makepiece, but I expect we'll need about six?'

'And blinis – With a little crème fraîche and some smoked salmon – they go down very well.'

'But you'd have to make so many –'

'Not really. I can knock them up fifty at a time, put 'em in the freezer.'

These ideas seemed a lot more exciting than Hetty and Felicity Makepiece had come up with. 'What else do you have in mind?'

'I'll work out a menu, and let you have a list. How much per head?' Hetty told her. 'And some vegetarians? It's usually at least ten per cent.'

'Yes – well, whatever you think.'

'You want salads? I could do a nice curry pasta, a coleslaw and a Greek salad. Only I use Cheddar. Can't abide that feta.'

Nor could Hetty. 'What about puddings?'

'I'll ask my friend Maureen. She does very good profiteroles and tiny caramel meringues. People are bored with Banoffee pie, don't you think?'

Hetty had stopped thinking anything other than that she should turn the entire catering operation over to this surprising woman. Hetty left the house a little later, waving goodbye to the smallest child, as its mother produced something from the oven that would make a dieter weep.

Later, she rang Felicity Makepiece, ostensibly to tell her about the arrangements and get the new menu approved, and ask when she'd have a clearer idea about numbers, but really she wanted to check that Felicity was quite happy about hiring a venue she hadn't seen, which was run by people who were basically amateurs.

Mrs Makepiece was unnervingly sanguine about the whole thing. 'Of course I'm happy about it. Hotels can be so uninviting and inhospitable. James told me what a lovely house it is, and I particularly wanted somewhere with an informal atmosphere.'

'I think we can guarantee that,' murmured Hetty.

'As for numbers, I haven't sent the invites out yet, dear. But I'm asking about two hundred, providing I don't discover I've left out anybody vital.'

'Right.' Two hundred people, sitting round tables, in the great hall. 'Great' suddenly seemed a huge overstatement.

'But the good thing is, I've decided what to give John for a present!'

'Oh!' And has that to do with me?

'Yes. I want to present it to him at the party, after you've done your cabaret.'

'That should be fine. We can clear a little space for the presentation –'

'It's a cow.'

'Sorry?'

'I said, it's a cow. A Devon Red. They're known in Devon as Devon Rubies. John's always wanted his own cow, and when I remembered about the Rubies I thought, what better present?'

Almost anything! 'And you want to give it to him at the party?'

'I thought I could dress it up in garlands and things. It would only be a calf really, a little heifer. Desperately sweet, don't you think?'

'Could we put a nappy on it?' Hetty suggested, thinking of Phyllis's reaction to fresh manure on the recently-scrubbed coir-matting.

'Oh, I don't think it would like that very much, do you?'

Hetty rang off feeling as if a whole herd of Devon Rubies had trampled on her. Two hundred people, a grand piano and a cow in the great hall. Perhaps she should run back to her mother and let Phyllis and Peter deal with it. If she'd had time to organize it, she would have done just that.

'You're getting clinically depressed. You must get out more.'

Caroline had swept in, wearing pink suede trousers and a jacket, fringed from wrist to elbow. On anyone else it would have been in bad taste. On Caroline, it was stunning.

Hetty sighed. When she saw Caroline she was always reminded of how little time she spent thinking about her appearance, and how much time thinking about the appearance of the house.

'I get out a lot. I'm always trundling across the countryside looking at occasional tables, which always turn out to be too big.'

'Oh, you need beer crates, up-ended, covered with a cloth. Take up very little space, and give people the impression that they could put their glasses down if they really wanted.'

'Caroline, you're brilliant.' Hetty scrawled this down on a piece of paper. 'Where would I get all those beer crates?'

'Ask at the pub. He'll save them for you. But that's not why I came. Have you noticed that spring is here? In fact, it's nearly summer.'

173

Hetty had taken to humming, 'As I Walked Out on a May Morning' as she strode through the woods with the dogs these days, noting that there were now leaves on the trees and birds singing. But the pleasure it brought her tended to be swept away by anxiety the moment she got back to the house.

The third of June seemed to approach faster with every new green leaf's emergence. Another interest payment was due, but although there was just about enough left, she wanted to keep some cash available. She was still trying to sell her car, though didn't want to tell Caroline.

She managed a half-way convincing smile. 'I can never believe that summer's half over at the end of June. May seems too early for it, somehow.'

'Well, it's not the end of June yet. It's still only early May, but you must get out and enjoy yourself. You can't spend all summer in this kitchen.'

Hetty sighed. People still spent a lot of time telling her what to do. It wasn't only Phyllis and Peter, but everyone from the village, and there were many, who came in to do their bit for Courtbridge House. She had got fed up with explaining that it wasn't her house, and really, she had no say in anything, she was just the sitter. None of them took any notice.

Caroline was just as bossy, but at least it was Hetty she cared about, not just the village heritage.

'What do you suggest? Going for a jog? A day on the river with a picnic? That sounds nice.'

Caroline dismissed these suggestions with a flash of French-manicured finger-nails, square cut, white tips, the rest of the nail covered with clear varnish. 'No, darling, can't take a chance on the weather. I meant something fun.'

'Like what?'

Caroline made an airy gesture. 'I don't know. A shopping spree or something.'

'I can't afford a shopping spree.'

'Connor should pay you for all your work.'

Hetty laughed shortly. 'Don't suggest it, unless you're tired of living. Samuel does feed me, but he hasn't got much money, so I try not to spend too much.' This was a masterly understatement.

Caroline considered. 'Fair enough. Now, what can we do that

would cheer you up and not cost much? Have you ever been to a Tupperware party?'

'No. Thank you.'

Caroline took on a mysterious expression. 'I've got an idea.'

'Well, don't keep it to yourself.'

'I think I will for the moment. If you don't mind.'

Hetty protested, but Caroline changed the subject. 'So, when's Connor coming home?' she asked.

Hetty shrugged.

'Do you miss him?'

She shrugged again. 'It's like being permanently hungry. Sometimes you have this great ache in your stomach. Sometimes it fades and you hardly notice it. But the moment you stop being busy, it comes back.'

Caroline slithered off the table. 'Come round tonight for a bottle of wine and a chic flick. Something soppy but with a happy ending.'

'That sounds lovely. Not too late, though.'

'You could stay the night?'

Hetty shook her head. 'No I couldn't. I'd be neglecting my duties as house-sitter. Knowing my luck, the house would get burgled if I spent a night away from it.'

What she didn't tell Caroline was that every night for a while now, she'd been listening out for Connor's arrival home.

CHAPTER SIXTEEN

Connor didn't arrive home in the middle of the night, as Hetty was convinced he would. He arrived at ten to ten on a Saturday morning, in the moment between the arrival in the car park of a coachload of WI ladies, and their appearance at the front door. Hetty had seen the coach from the bathroom, where she had been brushing her teeth. The taxi caught her eye during the final rinse. It took her a moment to take in its significance. She flew down the stairs and arrived in the kitchen just as he walked through the back door. He looked crumpled and travel-stained, desperately tired.

'You might have given me a ring from the airport,' she said, making her way across the room.

'Come here, you.'

Connor pulled her to him, crushing her against his once-elegant suit as if he planned to suffocate her. She gave back as good as she got. Eventually, he allowed enough space between them to lower his head and give her a breathtaking kiss and an intimate encounter with three days' growth of beard. She had just fought her arms up around his neck when she felt herself abruptly dropped.

'Oh,' said Peter, who had been changing light-bulbs. 'Sorry to intrude.' He didn't sound sorry at all. 'Phyllis says the WI ladies have come and they say they ordered coffee, and do you know anything about it, Hetty?'

Hetty fell away from Connor's embrace. 'Oh, yes. I've got it in hand. I was just saying hello to Connor.'

'So I see. Hello. Good trip?'

'Very. Thank you.' He turned to Hetty. 'Is there a bathroom I can use, or are they all full of the WI fluffing up their blue rinses?'

'It's only the main one that's open. Samuel's bathroom isn't, as you know perfectly well. And the shower in there works now.'

Connor grunted, and, picking up his battered leather bag,

pushed his way past the kitchen furniture and out of the room.

Peter looked at Hetty as if she deserved to be tarred and feathered for consorting with the enemy. Connor had reverted to his usual state of permanent disagreeableness, and she was pretty annoyed herself. However, as the woman, it was up to her to try and make everyone feel better.

'Nice to have Connor home,' she said brightly, then, remembering that she wasn't supposed to think it was nice, hurried on, 'I can ask him about getting the house listed.'

'I didn't know you were on such good terms.'

'What do you mean?'

'He was kissing you pretty thoroughly.'

'That was only hello. I kiss you hello.'

'Not like that.'

'That was him – he's sort of – well –'

'Passionate?' Hetty gave an almost imperceptible nod. 'I could be passionate if you gave me a chance.'

Hetty closed her eyes for a moment. 'I wouldn't want you to be, Peter. I rely on you as my good and dear friend. Passion would spoil that.'

He crossed the room towards her. 'Not necessarily. Friendship can grow into love.'

She shook her head and took a step back. Connor had said that men were incapable of platonic friendships with women – heaven forbid that he should be right. 'But not –'

It was too late. Peter had decided that actions spoke louder than words, and had taken Hetty into his arms. His kiss was so much gentler – he had shaved only that morning – and the tang of his aftershave was clean and astringent. She tasted his mouthwash as he parted her lips. She disengaged herself very gently.

'Peter, please, this isn't right. I've got coffee for twenty to organize.'

'Glad to hear it,' said Phyllis, who had come in to ask her about it. 'My ladies have come a long way and are gasping.' She gave Peter a disapproving glare. 'And really, Peter, this is neither the time nor the place for that sort of thing.'

Hetty put her arm round his waist and squeezed it in sympathy. He must be yearning to say, 'Connor did it too.'

'The cups are all out on trays, Phyllis. And both kettles are just about to boil. Do you think they want hot milk? It's a lovely day, though not terribly warm.'

'Thank goodness someone's got their mind on the job. I saw "that man" storming up the stairs with a face like thunder. You'll be able to tackle him, then?'

Peter mumbled something which could have been, 'She already has,' and Hetty spoke louder to cover his mutterings. 'I'll let him get over the jet lag first, I think. He's not likely to be very amenable if he's short on sleep.'

Phyllis snorted. 'Whatever you think best,' she said. 'But don't leave it too long. Samuel was very low when I saw him last – very low.'

'I'll bring the matter up when he's not tired, not hungry, and the house isn't full of people. But I'm not promising anything today.'

Phyllis gave her another scornful glance. 'I think you'd better heat the milk. Put it in that vacuum jug.'

Although she was busy, the rest of the morning dragged by for Hetty, dogged by petty irritations as she was. The WI ladies all asked Hetty questions she couldn't answer, all of them being far more expert than her on antique hangings. Peter, who had finished the light-bulbs, was repairing a bit of skirting. Hetty was not sure it had been arranged for him to do that, and had an idea that he was refusing to leave because of Connor. As he could hardly move into the house permanently, this seemed rather strange behaviour. But since Phyllis might quite reasonably have asked him to do repairs without consulting her, Hetty didn't think she could challenge him.

Feeling that if she didn't get away from everyone soon she would be rude to someone, she told Debbie, who had been one of the stalwarts of the Courtbridge Against the Motorway Campaign and was now a stalwart of Courtbridge House, that she wanted to get something for Connor's supper. There were plenty of tins of beans and lumps of sweating Cheddar, but she didn't want him to have a scratch meal on his first night home, especially when he might not have had a decent meal since he left.

Debbie, who liked Connor because he helped her get her car started, agreed that Hetty could go to the shop if she promised to buy her a Mars Bar. There were only a few visitors, who had trickled along in the wake of the WI, and Debbie could cope perfectly well with them.

Having cleared it with Debbie and her conscience, Hetty took the dogs and made her escape. The dogs, she discovered, were a perfect disguise for not having the car, which she had finally sold last week. She didn't want everyone, namely Caroline and Connor, to find out before they had to, they would both make such a fuss. But, as she remembered from her first day at Courtbridge, no one wondered why you were walking if you had dogs with you. And they were undemanding company.

It was ironic to remember how lonely she had felt when she first arrived at the house. Now she yearned for solitude as then she had yearned for Alistair. Although, she had the honesty to admit, part of her frustration now was caused by knowing Connor was in the house, and that he wouldn't emerge until the coast was clear.

Damn Peter for coming in just when he did. If Connor's kiss had had a few moments longer to establish itself, she could have learnt a lot from it. She had sensed the hostility Connor felt towards Peter, in spite of his previous statements that he would make a good and faithful husband. But then, Connor probably didn't perceive goodness and faithfulness as attractive characteristics. The trouble was, they weren't terribly. But in a husband, they were essential.

Hetty smiled at herself for connecting Connor with the word 'husband', and for her wifely actions in buying something for his supper. She tied up the dogs and went into the shop, hoping Angela Brewster wouldn't laugh too.

Of course she didn't, and Hetty left the shop with some reportedly very nice sausages, some early strawberries and a carton of cream under her arm.

'Sprinkle a little Beaujolais over the strawberries,' suggested Angela. 'It brings out the flavour beautifully.'

'I don't think the heeltap of a bottle of plonk will have quite the same effect.'

'No, but Connor's sure to have a nice bottle somewhere you could open?'

Hetty nodded.

'I gather you're getting plenty of visitors?'

'Not too bad.'

'I'm looking forward to hearing how this ruby wedding goes. It'll be our tenth anniversary this year, and it's such a pretty house, it would be a perfect setting for a do.'

Hetty laughed. 'I don't blame you for seeing how it goes. Mrs Makepiece seemed not to mind I hadn't had that much experience – well, none really. But being in the trade, sort of, you're probably more careful.'

'I don't know about that, and I certainly wouldn't want anything formal. Hotels can be ghastly.'

'That's what Mrs Makepiece said.' Hetty bit her lip ruefully. 'I hope her confidence in me and Courtbridge House isn't misplaced.'

'It won't be.' Angela smiled. 'With so much goodwill behind you, you can't fail.'

When Hetty got back to the house, instead of going straight in she went up the stone steps that led to the upper storey of the coach-house. There was quite a lot of space up there, ideal for letting as a holiday cottage. Like everywhere else, it would take a lot of work to sort out, but the floors were in good condition, the walls didn't seem too flaky, and the roof was sound. Properly done up, this place could bring in several hundred pounds a week during the holiday season. They might even get winter lets, given the setting and people's yearning for country Christmases. She must suggest it to Connor when, if ever, they had a chance to talk.

She went outside to put the CLOSED sign up. It was fifteen minutes early but she didn't care. She was alone at last.

She skipped along the passage to the kitchen. How could she ever have felt lonely? Solitude was bliss. Then, more soberly, she started hunting out some potatoes. She only didn't feel lonely because Connor was upstairs; even when asleep, and not only at the piano, he made her feel accompanied.

She peeled enough potatoes for both of them and then got out the sausages and wished she'd remembered to buy some sort of vegetable. She was very fond of tinned tomatoes with sausages herself, but Connor was such a foodie he was bound to sneer. Then she decided to fry some onion, mash up the tomatoes, add some basil and call it salsa. He would still sneer, but at least it would look as if she'd made an effort.

She was tasting the mashed potato, wondering if it had enough butter in it, when Connor appeared. She lowered the wooden spoon back into the mash, feeling caught out for not using a teaspoon.

'Hi, Connor, you're up! How do you feel? Did you manage to sleep, or did the visitors keep you awake?'

'They kept me awake. There were two of them, discussing romantic fiction in the passage outside my room. Was Ethel M. Dell more erotic that E. M. Hull? I gather we have a stash of classic romance in that bookcase.'

'Have we? Perhaps we can sell it.' She smiled to show she was joking. 'I am sorry you were disturbed. But was it nice to have the shower working?'

'It would have been if I hadn't kept wondering how you'd paid to have it done. You didn't sell anything, did you?'

She flushed guiltily. She didn't want to spoil the moment by telling him about the threatening letter, and her having to sell her car. 'Oh, no. That one's quite legit. I rented the big field to a little girl with a plumber for a father. It's payment in kind.'

Connor snorted. 'And is my car all right?'

Please don't ask me about mine! 'It was when I last looked at it.'

He grunted. 'What about a drink? Shall I open some wine, or would you rather have something stronger?'

'Wine, please.' She was glad she hadn't opened it. 'Then I can sprinkle some over the strawberries. Angela Brewster suggested it.'

'Sprinkle away, but not too much. This is good stuff.'

Connor was quite gracious about the sausages, and ecstatic about the mashed potato. And, unusually restrained for him, didn't comment on the tomatoes. 'I didn't know you could cook, Het. Why didn't you tell me?'

'I didn't want you to think I was trying to find a way to your heart through your stomach.' She meant it as a joke, and she sounded light-hearted, but she suddenly felt she had strayed on to the thin crust that covers a quicksand. 'But bangers and mash aren't likely to do that.'

'Oh, I don't know.' Connor smiled lazily at her.

Hetty suddenly felt she'd bitten off more than she could chew with Connor. The night she'd tried to seduce him seemed light-years away. What had got into her? Starting anything with Connor would be like climbing into a cage with a lion. She'd better get out quick before he noticed there were no longer iron bars between them.

'I was looking at the coach-house today. It would make a great holiday cottage. There's already water downstairs, and you could make two lovely light rooms upstairs. And there's a little room at the end, which would make a super bedroom.' She scraped the last of her mashed potato on to her fork. 'You must have a look at it tomorrow.'

'Why do I get the impression that you're changing the subject?'

'Probably because I am. I mean, there's only so much you can say about sausages, even designer ones.'

Connor's gaze seemed to pierce straight through Hetty's careful façade of blandness to see the nervous tension it concealed. 'You're probably right,' he conceded. 'How's Samuel?'

'He seems to be getting on OK. But slowly.'

'You haven't mentioned the loan?' His thick eyebrows implied a frown.

'No.' Nor had she told him that she'd had to dip into the loan money to pay for repairs to the house, and had had to sell her car to make it up, and that, without a car, visiting Samuel on her own would be difficult. Nor had she asked him if he knew the house wasn't listed. Circumstances had forced her to be extremely secretive.

'I suppose it's hard for you to get away, now the house is open?'

Hetty bit her lip. It was a perfect opening for her to mention the car. But she couldn't. 'Well,' she prevaricated, 'Phyllis would always stand in for me, and for something like a visit to Samuel she wouldn't mind at all. We could go together?'

He nodded. 'Samuel might like that. Come with me when I go in tomorrow?'

'OK.' And, buoyed up by this minor coup, Hetty followed it up with a good word for Mrs Hempstead. 'Phyllis visits him quite a lot.'

'I'm glad she has her uses.'

'Phyllis is a very kind and dedicated person. She has the house's best interests at heart.'

'She's bossy.'

'If she's bossy it's because she needs to be. And she gets things done.'

'Yes, but as most of the things she gets done are my business not hers, I can't be expected to appreciate her.'

'It's Samuel's business, really.'

'Mmm. That's why I don't send them all packing.'

Unsure whether she was included in the 'them', Hetty got up to make coffee, aware that although Connor was being perfectly friendly, he had no intention of becoming anything else, or allowing Hetty to do so. What had happened before he left was a mistake, and one not to be repeated.

The following morning, before the first influx of visitors came through the gate, Hetty took Connor to the coach-house.

'You see? It would convert so well to a holiday cottage. It could bring the estate lots of money.' Connor growled non-committally. 'The house could support itself, given a chance.'

'And a hundred willing volunteers.'

'But there *are* a hundred willing volunteers. All the local people love the house.'

Connor grunted again. They climbed the steps at the side of the building to the upstairs. 'You'd have to have some other way of getting from one floor to another. You wouldn't want to use these in the middle of the night in the rain.'

'No, well, you could put in a staircase. I'm sure Peter would do it. He's got a real feel for wood. He'd put in the kitchen too.'

Connor gave Hetty a look that made her wish she hadn't mentioned Peter. 'I'm sure. But would he accept payment in kind?'

There was no doubt about what he meant but she asked him anyway. She was hurt and angry and wanted him to be too. 'What do you mean? Two fitted cupboards and a peninsular unit in exchange for two nights of passion with me?'

He nodded. 'Except you're pricing yourself a bit high. I think he'd want at least an engagement if you insist on a spiral staircase.'

'Why not go the whole hog? If I agreed to marry him, he'd

build a four-poster bed in that little room and we could christen it on our honeymoon?'

Connor showed no signs of being hurt or angry, and Hetty wondered why on earth she had thought he might be. It was no concern of his who she married. She might fancy herself in love with him, but he was under no illusions.

'What a good idea.' He strode across the empty space, his feet threatening to go through the dusty boards. 'Where is the love-nest?' He found it without difficulty. Hetty, feeling extremely foolish, joined him.

Once there, she forgot her embarrassment. The four-poster-bed idea had been invented entirely to annoy Connor, but as they inspected the space Hetty realized that it was the perfect solution. 'Hey, it's not a bad idea, you know!' She crossed to the window and rubbed at it with her sleeve. 'Look, it gets the morning sun. Ideal for a bedroom.'

Connor looked at Superwatch. 'Not very early morning sun. But I suppose, if you're a honeymoon couple, you don't want it all that early.'

'Admit it, it would make a charming bedroom.'

'If you don't mind scores of people streaming past it.'

'People don't stream past it! It's very cut-off from the house. People park in the field and go round to the front. It's only if we convert the old barn to workshops that anyone will come near it.'

'More plans for my property?'

This was the best she was going to get in the way of openings. Now would be the time to say, casually, 'By the way, did you know the house isn't listed? Don't you think it ought to be?' He was hardly going to agree, considering he thought the house should be pulled down. While she was deciding whether or not to plunge in, she said, 'Not *your* property yet.'

'I know you think I'm very wicked making plans when Samuel isn't even dead, let alone cold in his grave. But nothing can go on unchanged for ever. Not Samuel, not his house. Progress happens whether you want it to or not. You might as well go along with it, rather than shut your eyes and pretend it won't happen.'

'I'm not against progress, *per se*. I just see it differently. I can see how lovely and useful and exciting this house and its buildings could all be, with a little time and effort.'

184

'And a few million quid. Do you do the lottery?'

'No, but you should. You could apply for lottery money – I'm sure you'd get it.'

'Oh, I could, if I had six months to spend filling in forms. But even if they granted me money, they don't just give it to you. You have to match it.'

'We could match it. If we all pulled together, thought of ways to make money. Think what we've achieved already. Oh, I know most of the people we get now are locals, and they probably won't come again once they've satisfied their curiosity, but there's the ruby-wedding party. We could do lots of that sort of thing. We could have actual wedding ceremonies. There are a thousand things we could do to raise money to match a lottery pay-out.'

Connor regarded her with a sort of tender bewilderment, as if she were either an idiot or a very young child, possibly both. 'I don't think you and I live on the same planet.'

Hetty nodded agreement. In those few words, he'd said it all. 'I know. Pity, isn't it? But do let the alien show the earthling the barns.'

She led the way back down and across to where a row of single-storey buildings with very little roof made one side of the square yard.

'You see?' She suddenly felt like a child showing an adult her new swing. 'They could all be turned into workshops. They'd pay rent all the year round, not just in the summer. Mind you,' she went on, 'I'm sure lots of people would rent the coach-house in winter. Imagine Christmas in it.'

'I'd rather not. And I'd also rather not imagine having strangers living just across the way from where I was staying.'

'Do you really hate the house being open to the public?'

'You can't expect me to like it. Not when they troop past my bedroom and I haven't a corner I can work in that isn't entirely without light, or part of the Courtbridge House Experience.'

There was no further argument she could offer, so she offered him food. 'Would you like a cup of coffee and a biscuit before we visit Samuel?'

'No. There are a whole lot of people getting out of their cars, and I want to get away.'

They walked back to the house, Hetty reflecting that no amount of coercion or persuasion could affect Connor's antipathy to the public. If he didn't want his house open to them, what could she do about it?

The answer, she realized, was to ask Phyllis to get the house listed. That way he'd have no choice. But could she do that to him, or, indeed, to anyone? What right had she to force him into a life-style he so thoroughly disliked?

Phyllis met them at the door. 'Hetty, can you give Caroline a ring? And there's something I want to show you. Can you come with me?'

'I'll meet you in the car,' said Connor. 'Don't be long.'

CHAPTER SEVENTEEN

Hetty, tugged one way by a desire to be with Connor and in another by Phyllis's strong hand on her wrist, went with Phyllis.

'Well? Did you manage to say anything?'

'No. At least, not about the listing.'

Phyllis was obviously disappointed in her but didn't mention it. 'Oh. And why does he want to meet you in the car?'

'I was going to ask you, Phyllis, if you could hold the fort here, while I go to see Samuel with Connor?'

'Well, of course, dear. A perfect opportunity to bring up difficult subjects, driving along in the countryside.'

Hetty hid her groan under an artificial smile. 'I'd better ring Caroline.'

She ran upstairs to where she could phone in reasonable privacy, deciding as she did so that a visit to Samuel wasn't a good idea. If she failed to ask Connor about the listing, Phyllis would give her up as a bad job, and if she spent much more time listening to Connor's point of view, she might find herself agreeing with him. Either way, she would end up miserable and in everyone's bad books, except Connor's.

'Caroline? Hi! You wanted me?'

'Just to remind you, darling, that we're going out tonight.'

'Oh?'

'You are coming tonight? You're not going to chicken out? I can't possibly go on my own.'

Hetty was torn. She'd far rather spend the evening with Connor, even if he was likely to spend it biting her head off. But she owed Caroline. 'No, no. I'd love to come. A Tupperware party is just what I need.'

Hetty went back downstairs having concluded that she wouldn't back out of visiting Samuel. If she told Connor she couldn't go to the hospital with him and then went out with Caroline that night he'd think she was avoiding him, and want to know why. Quite how she'd manage to avoid Phyllis after she had failed to sort Connor out was a problem she'd have to solve later.

Connor was drumming his fingers on the steering-wheel in an archetypal gesture of impatience, and was unsympathetic to her insistence that a quick swipe with the hairbrush and a cleaner pair of jeans was necessary for a visit to her aged uncle. 'I can't go into a hospital looking so unhygienic,' she said. 'They wouldn't let me in.'

'OK, OK, enough excuses. Let's go. And don't slam the door.'

It would have been difficult. It was incredibly heavy.

'This is a great car,' she said, after a few minutes.

'Are you trying to get into my good books or something?'

'Good God no! I may tilt at windmills, but I'm not that optimistic. No, it really is great. Leather seats may not be PC, but they smell wonderful.'

The seats were dark blue, scratched and worn, and, at the corner of hers, patched with a piece of sticky tape.

He gave her a look that warned her he was about to be provocative. 'They recline fully, too. A flick of a switch and we're in bed together.'

Hetty didn't rise to the bait. 'I'm sure it's not as simple as that.'

'No, it isn't.' He gave her a grin bordering on the rueful. 'And if it was, the mechanism needs fixing.'

'That's all right then,' she said glibly.

Connor shot her a glance. 'And while we're on the subject of cars, where's yours?'

Hetty gulped.

'I noticed when I came back it wasn't where you usually park it. It isn't in any of the barns. What happened? Have you dinged it?'

'I've sold it.'

'Good God! Why?'

The time for prevarication was past. 'I had a threatening letter from the loan company, implying they could make us pay up the whole amount immediately. I wasn't sure if they could, but rather than risk it, I sent them a double payment. I sold the car to get a little working capital.'

188

To her surprise, he didn't explode. 'Oh, Hetty, why didn't you tell me?'

'I just did!'

'I mean, about the letter, before you sold your car. I can give them a fairly hefty chunk of money when I'm paid. You shouldn't have got rid of your car without telling me. Now we'll have to buy it back again.'

'No! No way. We need every penny. We can't afford luxuries like second cars.'

'Then I'll sell mine.'

'Don't even think about it! You love your car.'

'I do, but it drinks petrol and needs a lot of work to get it as it should be. It's a luxury I can't afford.'

'But you haven't got a wife or a mistress to keep, have you?'

He half laughed. 'No.'

'If you had, you'd have to spend money on them, and I bet the car isn't half as expensive.'

'Well, no, but it's still a luxury.'

'No it isn't. We need a car. It might as well be yours.'

'How will you manage without one?'

'Oh, I've been managing very well. Phyllis lent me her bicycle.'

'And you don't mind being demoted to a bicycle?'

'Not "demoted", Connor. I regard it as a sideways promotion.'

Connor gave her a very searching look. 'You're an extraordinary girl, Hetty.' But from the way he said it she couldn't tell whether he'd paid her a compliment or made a sad statement of fact.

She should, of course, hope it was the former, and follow up on his quasi-approval and tell him about the house not being listed. It was what Phyllis had allowed her furlough for, after all. But having got over one hurdle, Hetty felt she needed time to recuperate before approaching another.

They found Samuel sitting in the day room, looking very small and defenceless in his dressing-gown and slippers. A television, ignored by all the residents, was showing an ancient black-and-white film. Vases of flowers drooped in sympathy with the general tone of the room. The odour of disinfectant and whatever it was supposed to disguise penetrated the smell of institutional cooking.

The moment he saw Connor and Hetty, Samuel brightened

up. 'Connor, dear boy. How lovely to see you. And you've brought Hetty! What a treat.'

Hetty kissed him. 'I hope you're feeling a bit better than you were last time,' she said, thinking he looked it. Perhaps it was seeing Connor.

'There's nothing wrong with me that getting out of this place won't cure. But until I manage to pass all their damn tests they won't let me out.'

'You should revise harder,' said Connor. 'That was what you always told me.'

'And did you ever take any notice?'

Connor shrugged. 'Not much.' He collected a couple of chairs from a stack by the wall and he and Hetty sat down.

Samuel turned to Hetty. 'So, I hope having Connor cluttering up the place isn't interfering with doing up the house?' He glared at his nephew under his eyebrows. 'I know he's not its biggest fan.'

'Oh, no. He's very biddable.'

Samuel gave a crack of laughter. 'I doubt that!'

'Yes he is. He's terrified of Phyllis.'

'Now that I *do* believe. Damned determined woman, Phyllis.' Connor made a face, which his uncle ignored. 'But salt of the earth, and devoted to the house. And if Connor gives you any bother, just say the word, and I'll disinherit him on the instant.'

'I wish you would,' said Connor.

'Not on my account,' said Hetty primly. 'He's quite a good cook.'

Connor looked affronted at this faint praise. Samuel laughed. 'He is. But not too good at showing groups of women round the old place, eh?'

'We all shine in our different ways,' murmured Connor, trying to sound hurt.

'And yours is sorting out the Aral Sea.'

'Not quite,' murmured Connor.

'Well, what do you *do*, exactly?' Hetty asked. 'I know you're a civil engineer, but –'

'I wouldn't want to bore you, my dear.' Connor would have found himself hit on the head with a bedpan had there been one to hand. Sensing this he added quickly, 'Or Samuel. At his time of life, he'd find the details hard to grasp.'

Samuel's shout of laughter caused several old ladies to wake up and look at him. Seeing Connor's manly form, most of them stayed awake. 'I hope he's not as rude to you as he is to me, Hetty.'

'Oh, no,' said Hetty, 'he's always the model of politeness. Aren't you, Connor?'

'Well, let me know if he gets out of hand, won't you?'

'Oh, yes. If he does anything dreadful,' she said, thinking about his plans to demolish the house, 'I'll tell you.' Even though this would probably involve a medium and a crystal ball, she added silently.

'And what will you do about it, Samuel, if she does tell on me?'

'Leave the whole lot to Phyllis.'

'Promises, promises,' said Connor.

Samuel laughed again, and Hetty began to wonder if this sudden burst of high spirits was good for his health. 'She'd certainly look after it,' she said encouragingly. In fact, it would mean Connor would have to spend years sorting out the Aral Sea to pay off the loan, but the house would be safe.

Samuel turned to Connor. 'You couldn't rustle up a cup of coffee or something for us? Those girls'll do anything for you.'

With Connor out of the way, Samuel turned to Hetty. 'Now listen, m'dear. I know Connor doesn't appreciate the old place like we do, but he's a good lad at heart. When the time comes, he'll do all right by it.'

Even if he wanted to, it may not be possible, she thought. But although Samuel seemed so much better, she still didn't want to remind him of the pressure he had put on the house when he'd taken out the loan. 'You know he may pull it down, after you've gone?'

'Well, so he says, but I know him. He protests to the last minute, but he always does the right thing in the end.'

'Do you know the house isn't listed? He *could* pull it down, if he wanted.'

'Of course I know the house isn't listed!' He laughed merrily at her naïvety. 'How do you think it got left off the damn list? A bit of jiggery-pokery at the crossroads, no names, no pack-drill.'

'But that's awful!'

'It may seem awful. But I don't want to land the lad with a minor stately home if he really doesn't want it.'

'You could leave it to Phyllis?'

Samuel shook his head. 'No I couldn't. I couldn't leave it outside the family. I've nothing else to leave, and he's my heir. He's got to have it. But I don't want his hands tied. I'd rather he came round to our way of thinking voluntarily, not because some fellows in some office force him to.'

Or some loan shark? 'But, surely, it's terribly risky,' she said aloud. 'The nation could lose a part of its heritage just because Connor didn't want it.'

'I know it seems like that. And I suppose it is. But it's a hell of a thing, inheriting a house like Courtbridge, and it has . . .' he paused for a significant moment, '. . . a few problems, if that doesn't seem too much of an understatement. If you didn't love it, it could ruin your life. I don't want Connor's life ruined.' Hetty saw the burden that inheriting Courtbridge had placed on Samuel – one which still remained. 'He hasn't had an easy life,' Samuel went on. 'His parents died when he was very small, and he was brought up by his mother's sisters. They were good to him, probably spoiled him to death, but they were too old to be parents. They lived in a mausoleum too, refused to sell it in exchange for a little comfort in their old age so that they'd have something to leave him.'

'Oh?' If he'd inherited a fortune, he'd kept it very quiet.

'Yes, but in the end, all the money went on nursing-home fees. He never told them that their savings weren't enough and that he had had to top up what they paid. You see, he's a good lad.'

'But not hooked on old houses?'

'No. But he's canny. He'll get my bit of local difficulty sorted –'

Just at this moment Connor came back with three cups of coffee, the contents of which were mostly in the saucers. He set one down on the table, within Samuel's reach, and handed one to Hetty. 'What have you two been plotting?' He gave her a warning look.

'Nothing,' said Hetty.

'How disappointing. I was sure you'd've had me disinherited by now.'

'Don't think I didn't try.'

'If I could guarantee she wouldn't marry some bounder, I'd leave it to Hetty. But by all accounts her taste in men is unreliable.'

'Very,' said Hetty and Connor, in perfect unison.

They took their leave of Samuel soon after they'd drunk their coffee, seeing his initial good spirits wilt a little with tiredness.

'He seemed jolly well, considering. Didn't you think?' Hetty asked Connor, on their way back to the car.

'Better than I expected. But I had a word with the sister, and he does need to get a bit stronger before he can come home.' Connor tossed his car keys up and down. 'And peace and quiet when he gets there.'

There was an edge to his voice that stabbed Hetty with guilt. Thanks to her interference, peace and quiet was not a commodity in liberal supply at Courtbridge House. And what Samuel had told her about Connor's aunts made his attitude a lot easier to understand. 'It's all my fault. I shouldn't have let people bully me into doing all that to the house.'

He put a hand on her shoulder briefly. 'Don't worry. It may be a bloody nuisance, but it's what Samuel wanted. I may curse you up hill and down dale, but Samuel won't.' This unexpected support was quite unsettling.

'And she said he'll really need somewhere on the level, at least to begin with,' he went on.

Hetty gave the matter some thought. There were no downstairs bathrooms at Courtbridge, and none of the rooms that might possibly be converted were at all pleasant. 'Perhaps he could convalesce with Phyllis? She's devoted to Samuel, I'm sure she'd be happy to have him.'

He shook his head. 'Over my dead body.'

'She really is a very intelligent, kind and knowledgeable person. If you'd only give her a chance, you'd see that.'

'I might give her a chance, but she'll never give me one, not while she sees me as a despoiler of England's green and pleasant land.'

'You can hardly blame her, given that you are exactly that.'

He unlocked the passenger door and opened it for her, leaning on the car roof while she swung herself in.

'What we ought to do is convert those barns you showed me. We could make a big sitting room, a bedroom, an *en suite* bathroom and a little kitchen, all on the ground floor. And the trippers needn't bother him over there.'

Hetty stared up at him. 'But that would cost thousands. How would we pay for it?'

Connor walked round the car and got in. 'Get a loan.'

'What? Another one? I don't think I could cope.'

'Not that sort of loan; a proper one, from a reputable company.'

'But Connor – if you borrow thousands of pounds converting a barn for Samuel, you'll lose every penny when he dies and you knock it all down.'

He regarded her blandly. 'That's all right. I've been offered enough for the site. Spending a few thou on a barn conversion shouldn't be a problem.'

'But the waste!'

He shrugged. 'Making Samuel's last months happy is not a matter to be penny-pinching about.'

'Months! You think he's only got months?'

'What do you think? You've seen him. I had a word with the nurse – he's still not picking up as they'd like.'

Hetty felt her throat thicken with tears. 'Oh dear.'

'But you knew he was old and ill. We've talked about what'll happen when he dies,' he said gently.

'I know. But his dying was always something vague that might happen in the future. It wasn't only a few months away.'

'I know.' His voice was still surprisingly gentle. 'But see it from my point of view. If he hangs on too long, my buyers might pull out and find some other property to develop.'

For a moment, she thought he meant it. She thought he wanted Samuel to die so he could make a fortune. She looked at him in horror – and, then, she did see it from his point of view. She saw a man who for the second time in his life was witnessing elderly and deeply loved relations get themselves into a financial muddle. And the only way he could see out of Samuel's predicament, was to sell the house.

'If,' she said after a long time, 'I – the house – manages to pay off the debt, without you having to make any huge personal sacrifice – like selling your car – will you promise that you won't sell the house to developers?'

He was silent for a long time. 'I won't make promises I may not be able to keep, Hetty.'

Hate replaced understanding like a tidal river rushing up a

creek. 'With luck he'll live long enough to foul up your deal.'

'He could live ten years and it'd still be a valuable site. However much you'd like it not to be.'

Not so valuable if it's got a listed building on it, she thought, but wisely kept the thought to herself. While there was still a chance, however faint, of changing Connor's mind, she had to avoid making any threats that might just push him into doing something they'd all regret for ever.

Also, silently, she vowed the house would pay off the rest of its loan on its own, with no help from him and his pretentious car. So although he may one day destroy the house, he'd never be able to do it with a clear conscience.

CHAPTER EIGHTEEN

Phyllis was waiting for them when they got home.

'Thank goodness you're back, dear. Mrs Makepiece rang. She wants to change the date of the party.'

Hetty wished she could faint and stay unconscious long enough to necessitate having to be carried away on a stretcher to somewhere where she was spoken to in low voices and given sips of iced water. A moment with her eyes shut told her this wasn't going to happen.

'Oh, God. I'd better ring her.'

'You'd better. I told her it would be very difficult, not to say impossible. She's in a bit of a state.'

She was. It was some moments before Hetty managed to find out what date she wanted the party changed to. Before that she had to hear Mrs Makepiece's profuse apologies for being so stupid as to have muddled up the date of her wedding anniversary with her nephew's wedding. 'It's my new glasses, dear. They make it very difficult to see,' she explained eventually.

'It's an easy mistake to make,' Hetty lied diplomatically. 'So, when *would* you like your ruby-wedding party?'

'Oh, you mean you may still be able to do it? I thought the arrangements had gone too far.'

They had indeed gone too far to be cancelled. 'I'm sure we could rearrange, slightly,' said Hetty.

'In that case, what about the Sunday? The second of June, instead of the first?'

'That would be fine,' said Hetty.

'I can't tell you how relieved I am,' said Mrs Makepiece, and proceeded to do so for some five minutes. And although she added that she'd send Hetty a cheque for part of the amount early, out of gratitude for her forbearance, Hetty decided she'd believe this only when she saw it.

She hoped fervently that she would. The dreaded third of June, when the loan had to paid off, seemed to get nearer with every breath. Could she ask Mrs Makepiece to pay in cash? No. That sort of woman wouldn't have cash to pay the milkman. If only she could have asked Connor how much he had earned on his last trip. But somehow she couldn't. He was determined that the house could never pay its way, and that selling it was the only way out. Admitting that the ruby wedding might not earn quite enough was giving him the perfect opportunity to sneer.

Unfortunately, even having to make a few dozen telephone calls, informing everyone about the change of date, didn't make it possible for her to avoid Phyllis completely. Having asked tenderly about Samuel, she bluntly demanded whether Hetty had insisted on Connor getting the house listed.

'It's not that simple, Phyllis.' Hetty tried not to sound pleading. 'I mentioned it to Samuel, and he said he knew it wasn't listed, and, what's more, it was something to do with him that it got left off. I pointed out that was rather dangerous, but he insisted he didn't want Connor's life ruined by the house, and if he wanted to knock it down he should be able to.'

'Oh, dear. This does complicate things rather. He wouldn't care to leave the house to you, would he?'

Hetty shook her head. 'I have appalling taste in men.'

'Peter's not appalling! He's a very nice young man. One of the best.'

Hetty looked at her fingers. 'He's not quite to my taste. I suggested Samuel left the house to you,' she went on quickly, 'but he wouldn't leave it out of the family.'

'Of course not. Quite right too. Besides, I'm far too old. It needs to go to a young person with lots of energy.'

'And lots of enthusiasm, which Connor most definitely has not got.'

Phyllis thought for a moment. 'But Samuel doesn't want the house destroyed? It seems silly to ask but I feel I have to check.'

'Oh, no. But he wants Connor to come round to his own way of thinking voluntarily, without being bullied by red tape.'

Phyllis made a disgusted noise. 'Where on earth did Samuel get ideas like that from? It sounds to me like a newfangled way of bringing up children. A lot of damn psychological nonsense when a quick smack would do far more good.'

'If you hold him, I'll smack him,' said Hetty. It seemed to her that Phyllis had forgotten for a moment whom they were dealing with.

Phyllis chuckled. 'Well, you know what I mean, dear. But if we can't deal with him straightforwardly, we'll have to employ psychobabble.'

'I hope you're not including me?'

'Well, I am. You'll have to tell him what Samuel said. Apply a lot of moral pressure, and' – Phyllis's eyes took on a gleam, either reflected from the copper saucepan she was cleaning or from pure mischief – 'throw in the thought that it might actually be illegal not to have your house listed.'

Hetty shook her head. 'It sounds like a threat. He'll never respond.'

Phyllis at last put down the saucepan. 'In that case, my dear, you'll have to appeal to his better nature.' Her expression implied he hadn't got one.

If only, thought Hetty, I could tell Phyllis about the loan, and Connor about the listing, and then retire and watch the fireworks from a safe distance. 'I'll try,' she said. 'When I next see him.' And resolved that this wouldn't be for a very long time. She was heartily grateful now that she was spending the evening with Caroline.

But Hetty couldn't avoid Connor for ever and when inevitably they fetched up in the kitchen together she did her best to appear her normal self. Though quite what was normal, she wasn't sure.

He was cooking something. There was a steaming saucepan on the stove, a pile of shredded green stuff on a chopping-board on the table, and a large knife stippled with herbs next to it. Connor was humming to himself – one of Hetty's favourite songs. She took this to be a good omen and decided to broach the L subject, as she had come to think of it.

'Delicious smells as usual, Connor.'

He looked up from a sauce he was beating hell out of. 'What do you want?'

'Nothing. Just commenting, favourably. Are you going to eat it all yourself or share it with me?'

'Would I let my favourite uncle's favourite – what is it? – second cousin three times removed starve?'

'Probably. Shall I set the table?'

He nodded. Hetty also did quite a lot of washing up of the saucepans and little bowls which Connor had used, knowing she wouldn't be there to wash up later. When they were both sitting down to plates of stuffed chicken breasts and spinach she decided to plunge straight in. Caroline would be there to collect her in an hour, so she had a means of escape.

'I was talking to Samuel . . .' she began, hesitantly.

'I know. I was there.'

'He was telling me that he wanted you to like Courtbridge House.'

'But he wasn't telling you that he thought anyone could *make* me like it.' It was a statement, not a question.

Hetty loaded her fork. 'No. He hoped you'd come to like it. On your own.'

'If I was ever here on my own, I'd have a better chance.'

Hetty put down her knife and fork. 'Connor, if you want me to go, just say the word. You're here to look after things now –'

'Shut up, woman, and eat your dinner. Of course I don't want you to go. I couldn't manage everything without you.'

This accolade steered Hetty away from awkward subjects for the rest of the meal. It was only when she had a mere ten minutes before Caroline was due that she dared bring one up again.

'Connor, I don't know if you know this but, strange as it may seem, by some fluke or mistake, this house isn't listed.'

'Of course I knew that. It means I can pull it down if I want to.' His expression became worryingly smug, as if he might pull it down with his bare hands just as soon as he'd had his coffee and brandy.

'But Samuel doesn't want the house pulled down.'

'We've been over all this. What are you getting at?'

Hetty shut her eyes and plunged in. 'The thing is, Phyllis knows – has discovered – that it isn't listed. And if you don't get it listed, she will.'

Connor rose from the table, appearing to grow in stature as his anger grew. 'And just how did she find out?'

'It's not secret information, Connor. Anyone can find out if they look in the right place.'

'Who told her, Hetty?'

There was no point in telling him it wasn't her. 'No one *told* her, but, indirectly, because of me, she found out.'

'Oh. Would you care to enlarge on that statement?'

'Not really, but I might as well. James Taylor, who I met at that dinner party, came round, and he told me it wasn't listed. He left me a message about it, which Phyllis took.'

'You mean, he wasn't just here on a social visit?'

'Well, yes and no. He came because I asked him.'

'And you didn't just ask him for the pleasure of his company?'

Hetty sighed. 'I asked him to look at the house so he could tell me whether or not it was in such bad condition that pulling it down was the only option.'

'And?'

'He said it was a wonderful house, and that we ought to open your bedroom.'

'What!'

'He also told me, because I asked him to check, that the house wasn't listed.'

Connor came round the table at terrifying speed, but adrenalin got her to the door even faster.

'Come back here!' he roared. 'Where the hell do you think you're going?'

'To a Tupperware party. With Caroline!'

It was lucky for Hetty that Caroline was only ten minutes late. Hetty spent those minutes hiding round the corner of the house. She should have taken time to tidy herself up a bit.

'Hey! What's up with you?' Caroline asked, as Hetty scrambled into the car. 'You look like you're fleeing from the Wrath of God.'

'I am. It's Connor. He'll tear me limb from limb if he gets hold of me.'

'That sounds exciting. Why?'

'Because I finally told him – not terribly tactfully – that Phyllis had discovered the house wasn't listed.'

'Hell! How did she find that out?'

'It's a long story, but, indirectly, through me.'

'Christ. And does Connor know that?'

Hetty nodded. 'I told him.'

'Blimey. No wonder you're running away. Though I must say, having Connor angry with you might be rather delicious.'

Hetty shuddered. 'I can't think how.'

'That's because you've got no imagination.' Caroline gave her a quick glance. 'And you stink of Brasso.'

'Oh hell, do I? I know I should have changed, but I wanted to get out of the house.'

'Obviously.'

'Could we go back to your place so I can at least wash my hands? Perhaps borrow something?' Hetty was surprised she had to ask. Usually Caroline would have marched her into the shower by now.

Caroline shot her another look. 'Well, I suppose we'll have to, but we really mustn't be long. I don't want to be late.'

This was a turn up for the books. Caroline was the sort of person who'd rather get to a party when it was half over than risk arriving not looking her best. It was Hetty who liked to be on time.

'What's this fixation with punctuality, all of a sudden? It's not like you at all.'

'I know, but I haven't told anyone what sort of a party it is yet.'

'It's Tupperware, isn't it?'

Caroline shook her head. 'Naughty Knickers. And we really can't have you going like that.'

Hetty spent some moments opening and shutting her mouth. 'Do you mean to say,' she said eventually, 'that not only did you not tell me what sort of party we're going to, but that you didn't tell the hostess either?'

'That's about the size of it. I thought it better no one knew.'

As Caroline sped back to her house, and pulled a skirt and top off their hangers, Hetty reflected that she had had a hell of a day. The only way she could get through a Naughty Knickers party was to get dirty, rotten, stinking drunk.

Given the amount of wine that flowed throughout the evening, this shouldn't have been difficult. But although Hetty drank at least her fair share, if not more, by the time Caroline was finally ready to leave she still felt boringly sober.

'You're a wretch, Caroline,' she said, the moment they were in the car and out of earshot. 'Not telling Amelia what sort of party it was.'

'I did feel a bit guilty when I saw quite how raunchy the stuff was, but honestly, Amelia was thrilled. Everybody bought something, except you.'

'I don't have a man to please. I don't have to waste my money on stuff like that.'

Caroline didn't comment. 'I'm going to have the goods Amelia was given in lieu of commission, and give her the money instead. I do have a man to please.'

'Poor Amelia. Is her husband really dreadful?'

'Yes, but I think they've got their relationship worked out. It might not be perfect, but it functions.'

'That's not a very romantic view of marriage.'

'No, and it wouldn't do for me. But it does for Amelia, or she would have left him.' Caroline continued in agony aunt mode. 'She's swapped romance for security. Compromise is the key to a happy marriage.'

Hetty suddenly covered her mouth with her hand. 'Oh, you've just reminded me.'

'Of what?'

'Keys. I forgot mine.'

'Perhaps Connor will still be up.'

'I do hope not. I'd rather break in than face him now. And it won't be so easy since we had a security system installed. Damn!'

'Would you like me to come in with you? I could help you up a drain-pipe or something.'

'Oh, no. I couldn't face a drain-pipe. I'll have to find some way of getting in on the ground floor.'

'I could help you jemmy open a window, then?'

'No, no. It's terribly late. You must get back. Just drop me off at the corner.'

'I don't think I should. I ought to see you safely home.'

'You have, but I might not be safe if I wake his lordship.'

Caroline looked at her diamond-studded Cartier. 'I shouldn't think you will. I had no idea it was so late. It's two o'clock. He'll be in his deepest sleep.'

'Just stop the car, there's a dear. And thank you for a wonderful evening.'

'It was fun, wasn't it? If a little raucous. Do ring if you can't get in.'

'After I've walked to the village? Sure I will. Don't worry, Caro, I'll get in.' Hetty climbed out of the car and closed the door as quietly as she could. 'Byee!'

Caroline roared off with her usual panache, but, as they had stopped a little way away from the house, Hetty had hopes that Connor hadn't been disturbed. As she got nearer, however, she saw that the kitchen light was on. Connor's shape was visible moving from the table to the stove.

Well, no way was she going to face him, not at two in the morning. Besides, Caroline's clothes had got her into awful trouble with Connor before. But Caroline's talk of jemmying windows reminded her that there was one in the sitting room that had been missed by the man who'd fitted locks on the others. It looked locked, but could be lifted open if you had the knack. And as Hetty had spent a lot of time wondering how she could fix it, or if she'd have to get the man back, and incurring even more expense, she had developed the knack.

Please don't let the dogs hear me, she thought, and tiptoed up the path and round the side of the house. The smell of early roses scented the air, far stronger now than during the day, and petals fell as she pushed past them. Hetty, anxious that their thorns didn't snag Caroline's clothes, spent precious seconds unhooking them. A bit of drastic pruning was what was called for, she thought. And then changed her mind. As the window-lock was broken, what better defence against burglars than roses? They beat razor-wire any day.

At last, she reached the window and got it open. Climbing in was easy, if undignified, and she managed to cross the room in the dark without difficulty. Congratulating herself on her resourcefulness, Hetty tried the door, but she couldn't open it. All the shaking, pulling and lifting forced her to one conclusion – it was locked. Someone, probably Phyllis, must have discovered the window and locked the door so as to limit a burglar's haul to just one room.

Knowing why it was locked didn't make it any less frustrating. She leant against the door and swore silently. The last thing she wanted was Connor to hear her, think she was a burglar and knock her out. When he found out it was her, he might do something much worse.

She could climb out of the window, go round to the back of the house, knock on the door, and face Connor. But he would be bound to shout, and although the wine hadn't made her drunk, it had given her a headache.

No, she couldn't face Connor. She felt too weary. She switched on one of the table lamps and looked at the sofa. It had served her as a bed before, it could do so again. As long as she got up in the morning early enough. It wouldn't do for Phyllis to discover her there.

CHAPTER NINETEEN

Hetty was woken by birdsong and a noise which could have been made by a male elephant on the rampage coming from inside the house. Both sounds were too loud for her throbbing head. She may not have felt drunk last night, but she certainly had a hangover this morning.

Cursing herself for not waking sooner, she scrambled off the sofa and burrowed about for the plastic bag full of her clothes. If she appeared in Caroline's elegant garments, she'd create even more speculation than she might have done already. It all depended on whether anyone, namely Connor, had realized she hadn't slept in her bed last night. Somehow she would have to get into the rest of the house without him noticing.

It was a lot easier climbing out of the window than it had been climbing in, mostly because she didn't have to worry about snagging Caroline's clothes. She ducked down low, so she couldn't be seen from any of the downstairs windows.

A discreet peep through the kitchen window gave her the impression the coast was clear. She went round to the back door, hoping the elephant noise had been Connor, and that she would find it unlocked. If he'd gone out with the dogs, he would never have locked it behind him.

The dogs, not out, greeted her warmly. Connor, crouching in front of a cupboard searching for something, did not. He straightened up as Hetty came in, looking more than normally haggard. 'Where the bloody hell have you been? I've been out of my *mind* with worry!'

Hetty opened and shut her mouth a few times as she observed that Connor was still wearing the same clothes he'd had on yesterday. The kitchen table was littered with mugs, and a bottle of brandy she'd not seen before stood half empty.

'I rang Caroline, who said she'd dropped you off at the corner

– she's probably phoned the police by now. I phoned Peter, who said he hadn't seen you. For crying out loud, I even phoned Phyllis!'

'Oh, God.'

'So where the fuck were you?'

'In the sitting room.'

Everything he had previously said seemed to have been delivered in a whisper compared with the volume he managed this time. '*Where? Why?*'

'In the sitting room. I got in through the window and the door was locked.'

'Of course it was! I locked it!'

'But why?'

'Because of the damn window! Phyllis cornered me about it only yesterday. She thought I might be able to fix it. But why didn't you use the door to come in by? If it's not a silly question.'

It didn't seem as silly as telling him she hadn't wanted to face him, and why. 'I didn't want to wake you.'

He pushed his hair off his face. 'You needn't have worried. I wasn't asleep!'

'You didn't wait up for me?'

'Yes! But even if I hadn't, you would hardly have woken me up by using the door like a reasonable human being!'

Hetty wished he wouldn't shout so. 'I forgot my key.'

'Then why didn't you knock!'

'I said, I didn't want to wake you.'

'Oh, for crying out loud!'

'So why did you wait up for me?'

Connor gawped at her for several seconds. 'Don't ask *me* questions! You're the one creeping home like a – a –'

Seeing Connor at a loss for the right word, Hetty followed up her advantage. 'An escaped convict? A teenage daughter? Or an errant wife? I'm not any of those, am I? So why were you waiting up?'

This time Connor was ready for her. 'I waited up because I promised Samuel I'd look after you!'

'I thought you just promised –'

He brushed this interjection aside. 'I didn't fill in a form! His intention was that I should see you were all right! Now, why the

206

fuck did you put me through a night of hell by refusing to use the bloody door?'

'I didn't want a quarrel at two in the morning. And, actually, I don't want one now.' It sounded so pathetic, and by avoiding a row last night she'd made things much worse for herself now. Quarrelling with Connor was tough at the best of times. When he was in the right, it was more than her throbbing head could bear. 'Please,' she lifted a hand in a gesture of truce. 'I've got a headache.'

'A hangover, you mean. Caroline told me you'd been drinking heavily. And a hangover is better than you deserve for putting the whole village through all that worry!'

'I didn't put the village through any worry. It was you who did that when you rang them! A rather major piece of over-reaction, don't you think?'

'No, actually – a perfectly logical thing to do. You'd gone out, God knows where –'

'I told you –'

'Did you hell! You said you were going out to a Tupperware party! Did you really expect me to believe that?'

It did seem unreasonable, but could she tell him the truth? No. 'I was with Caroline –'

'But you didn't come home with Caroline, or at least, not right home. Ringing round your friends seemed perfectly reasonable!'

'Ringing people at that hour is never reasonable,' she whispered.

Connor glared at her with so much anger and hatred she almost cringed. 'I think I'm just going to save myself a lot of heartache and kill you.'

Her headache was so bad she was tempted to let him. But her instincts of self-preservation were strong and, hardly aware she was doing it, she'd manoeuvred her way round the room so she was nearly at the inside door. She was just about to leg it, and risk an undignified capture half-way up the stairs, when she heard a car. Connor heard it too.

'But before I do,' he went on, positioning himself between Hetty and her escape route, 'I think you'd better explain yourself to Phyllis.'

Hetty would have preferred to be discovered choking to death,

Connor's hands incriminatingly around her neck. But he was in no mood to be co-operative. 'Look, tell her I'm –'

'Oh, no. I'm not going to lie for you. I'm going to watch you squirm!'

Hetty pulled her clothes straight and scraped her fingers through her hair, and the minute Phyllis appeared she began. 'Look, I'm so sorry about Connor ringing you last night, I don't know how it happened, but he didn't hear me come in and took it into his head that something dreadful had happened to me. Had I known he'd create such a commotion, I'd have woken him.'

Connor's rumble was as threatening as any erupting volcano. 'You know damn well I wasn't asleep. I waited up for you!'

'But I didn't know you were in the kitchen, I thought you were tucked up in bed!'

'That's a bloody lie! You knew I was in the kitchen, which was why you didn't dare come in that way!'

'I didn't ask you to wait up! And I certainly didn't expect you to ring half the county just because you considered I was late home!'

'I was worried half out of my mind, what was I supposed to do?'

'Anything you like! Tear your hair out! Bite your nails! Meditate?'

To Hetty, it appeared that Connor had gathered himself to spring, either forgetting, or no longer caring, that there'd be a witness to her murder. Phyllis may have thought the same, because she cleared her throat loudly, which seemed to change his mind.

'I think I see what's happened here – complete crossing of lines. But do tell, where were you, Hetty?'

For a terrible moment, Hetty thought she was going to have to tell Phyllis and Connor about the Naughty Knickers party, but then she realized that Phyllis was asking where she had spent the night. 'In the sitting room. I got in through the window.'

'But I always lock the sitting-room door. I'd mentioned to Connor to make sure he did too.'

'I know. I mean, I didn't know about locking it. Why didn't you tell me?'

'You weren't around at the time, and I'd only just discovered about the window.'

'Oh.' Hetty had known about it for ages, but it had kept slipping her mind.

'Did you know about it?'

Hetty became vague. 'Oh, yes, I discovered it the other day. I meant to say something to Peter, but I forgot.'

'Don't worry,' said Connor. 'You can tell him now. Here he is!'

'Hetty! Are you all right! I didn't sleep a wink after Connor phoned.'

'I'm fine –'

'Don't lie. You've got a hangover,' murmured Connor.

'Oh.' Peter appeared as shocked by this information as Connor had intended him to be. 'Well, I'm sorry you feel unwell, but you caused everyone a lot of anxiety.'

'I'm the one who should be sorry.' She shot Connor a look that denied her words. 'But it never occurred to me that anyone would worry. I went out with Caroline and got back a bit late. That's all.'

'You didn't appear to get back at all, late, or otherwise,' said Connor. 'She slept in the sitting room,' he explained.

'What?' demanded Peter. 'Why?'

'My question exactly. Tell us, Hetty.'

Hetty decided that before she finally put an end to his life, she would make sure that Connor suffered a headache as bad as hers. Only when it was better, would she deliver the *coup de grâce*. 'Because I knew Connor would pick a quarrel, and I didn't want one.'

'Why would he do that?'

'Because I told him, as you and Phyllis insisted I should, that we knew the house wasn't listed!' Both Phyllis and Peter's jaws dropped gratifyingly. 'Naturally, he wasn't pleased.'

'I'll be damned if I'll be blackmailed!' Connor began.

'To avoid further conflict –' Hetty persisted.

'At two o'clock in the morning,' muttered Connor.

'– I tried to avoid seeing him. And if you lot hadn't all been so hooked on security, I'd've got up to bed easily!'

'Now now, dear, there's no need to get upset. You know security's important. There are valuable things in this house –'

'Are there? Still?' said Connor.

Phyllis glared at him ferociously. He stared back, unimpressed. 'Everything we have done to this house, young man,' said Phyllis, 'has been done both for the good of the house and of your uncle! If Hetty and Peter and I had done nothing in your absence, your uncle would have no decent home to return to!'

Hetty cheered, quietly.

'And as it is,' returned Connor, unabashed by Phyllis's righteous indignation, 'he's got a house constantly bombarded by visitors, allowing no privacy and precious little peace! Please don't expect me to be grateful!'

'Nobody expects that much of you,' declared Phyllis. 'But Samuel is my friend, and I'll do my best to guard his interests.'

'Um – er,' Hetty tried to attract their attention, but they were locked in battle. She wondered if she ought to fill a bucket.

'Blood is thicker than water, Mrs Hempstead!' roared Connor. 'He's my only relative. And, if you don't mind, *I'll* decide what his best interests are!'

'Excuse me!' broke in Hetty. 'Sorry to interrupt and all that . . .'

Connor turned to her, his eyes still on full blaze. 'What?'

'There's a coachload of people just driven up. Are they one of your specials, Phyllis?'

'Oh, hell,' said Connor, 'I'm off.'

'Bugger!' said Phyllis, startling Peter and Hetty. 'They are. I'll have to see to them. But don't think you've heard the last of this, young man.' Phyllis bustled out of the back door into the yard so she could greet her party. Hetty had the weird impression that she was laughing.

Hetty and Connor collided in the doorway, both desperate to escape; Hetty so she could at least get a couple of paracetamol down before she started work; and Connor so he wouldn't be smarmed over by the visitors.

Hetty heard Connor's car drive off soon after, but Phyllis was harder to avoid. Hetty apologized to her again, but surprisingly Phyllis didn't seem annoyed.

'I've never liked Connor, you know that. And his plans for the house are barbaric. But I never realized until now how much he cares about his uncle. You've got to respect that.'

Yesterday Hetty would have been grateful for any sign that Phyllis was warming to Connor. Having them both constantly snarling and griping was like sharing the house with a pair of rival Jack Russells. But today, when she was so furious with Connor herself, hearing him praised, by Phyllis of all people, was intensely annoying.

'I suppose so,' she agreed grudgingly. 'And he's talking about converting those old barns, you know? The ones at the opposite side of the courtyard. So Samuel can have somewhere level, in case he's in a wheelchair. Because even if the house wasn't full of visitors, which it probably won't be, when all the locals have been, there's still no downstairs bathroom.'

'Nor is there. But how on earth are we to raise that sort of money when there's so much else we've got to do?'

'I asked him that. He said he'd get a loan.'

'Did he indeed? He's not quite so bad after all.'

'Don't forget he's planning to pull down the house!' Hetty, her headache still lingering at the back of her neck, was nettled.

'Is he, though? Do you know, I think we might all turn out to be very pleased and surprised by that young man.'

'I hope "that young man" is grateful!' muttered Hetty, but only after Phyllis had gone downstairs to give her lecture on tapestries.

Later, Hetty went to find Peter to apologize to him for being rung up in the middle of the night. She knew he was somewhere about because his car was parked in the yard. She ought to get him to do something about the damn window, too. But she couldn't track him down, and when she finally caught sight of him he was accompanied by Connor. They were talking, man to man.

Judas! thought Hetty, grimly. First Phyllis and now Peter, gone over to the enemy, leaving her the only one out in the cold. Caroline had never joined in the We Hate Connor campaign, or she'd have had a moan to her. But she did give her a ring, to apologize, yet again, for Connor's nocturnal call.

'Oh, that's OK. It was soon after I got home anyway – I wasn't asleep. And I thought it was rather sweet, don't you? Worrying about you when you're out?'

'If he was my mother or my grandmother, maybe, but as he's just some very distant relation I just happen to be sharing a house with, no.'

'He was just a smidge more to you than that not long ago.'

'Well, he's not now. And the worse thing is, Phyllis has started to like him. And I saw him talking to Peter, and I daresay we'll discover that he's going to design and plan the conversion of the barns so Samuel's got somewhere to live that's on the level.'

'I can't really see why you should be annoyed about that. Peter's a super craftsman. You'd be furious if Connor got someone else in.'

Hetty exhaled. 'I know. It's just the mon –' Just in time she stopped herself saying it out loud.

'The what?'

'Oh, I don't know.' Quickly she changed the subject. 'Have you heard when Jack's coming home yet? Will your crotchless panties have arrived by then?'

'Well, Jack'll be home for your ruby wedding –'

'Not my personal ruby wedding, I hope?'

'No, I know. But he will be around to run the bar. I asked him on the phone.'

'You told him about it being on the Sunday?'

'Yes – he said he'd love to help. Which means I can be your Mistress of Ceremonies.'

After her experiences last night, a sudden vision of Caroline dressed as a sort of dominatrix flashed into her mind. 'You'll just wear that black dress we talked about?'

'Of course, darling. What did you think I'd wear? Long black boots and a whip?'

'Of course not!' said Hetty guiltily.

Hetty had asked if Caroline could mingle among the guests during the ruby wedding, making sure everything was going to plan, while she rushed about behind the scenes. It would be impossible for her to arrange the serving of the food, the concealment of the heifer, and worry about where everyone was going to go, and keep her eye on the party. The good thing about Caroline, apart from her stunning looks, was that she didn't want to be paid. Ditto Jack.

Felicity Makepiece was due to visit the next day so Hetty spent all morning making the rooms look larger by removing bits of furniture and clearing surfaces of knick-knacks. But when Felicity arrived, she looked around and shook her head.

'There's nowhere big enough to eat in except the great hall.

And if we eat there, how could you clear it in time for the cabaret?'

Hetty, who had been turning this problem over in her mind for a long time, shrugged. 'You can't really shuffle people out after the meal and ask them to have coffee in the other rooms, or you'll never get them out of the sofas.'

Felicity nodded. 'Oh, dear. I was so looking forward to having the party here. And it'll be difficult to find anywhere else at such short notice.'

Hetty had been looking forward to the huge amount of money the party was going to bring in. She didn't like to point out to Felicity that the numbers she had originally talked about when she first came to look at the house had been doubled. If she lost the contract now, she'd have no choice but to do the honourable thing and kill herself.

'There are the barns,' she said suddenly. 'You could eat in one of them.'

'What barns? I didn't know you had barns.'

'Oh, dozens of them. But there are two directly opposite the back of the house that are being cleared out. They're going to be converted into a flat for Uncle Samuel. One is larger than the other.'

'Let's have a look.'

Felicity loved the barns, in spite of, or maybe because of, the agricultural clutter that almost filled them. 'It's so romantic, like something out of *Cold Comfort Farm*.' Hetty didn't comment. 'You can imagine all the tables laid out, garlands of wild flowers everywhere . . .' Hetty made a mental note to get in an extra flower-arranger for the barn. Their present one specialized in formal arrangements best viewed from the end of an early fifteenth-century aisle. '. . . and, of course, it's the perfect place to present Ruby.'

'Er . . . ?'

'You know, the little heifer. She's so gorgeous. Just born the other day, so she'll still be quite little.'

'And if she makes a mess, it'll be easier to clear up in a barn.'

'Of course! Do you think you'll have time to give the place a coat of whitewash as well as clearing it out?'

'Oh yes, easily,' said Hetty, crossing her fingers. 'And now, are you sure these are the final figures?'

'Oh, yes. My husband says we don't know anyone else.'

Hetty fervently hoped that Felicity's husband was right.

Before announcing this change of plan to Connor or Peter, both of whom would be directly involved and probably uncooperative, Hetty rang Caroline. Fortunately this well-connected lady knew a troop of Cub Scouts, who'd like nothing better than to spend a day clearing out a barn before sloshing a lot of whitewash about.

'The akela's a great friend of mine,' said Caroline. 'He's always keen to get his boys to help the community.'

'This hardly counts as the community . . .'

'Darling, it's employing almost everyone in the village – what else *is* the community? But there's one condition . . .'

'What?'

'You let my Brownies come too.'

'But Caroline, your Brownies have done so much already, and surely their parents won't want their little girls getting all filthy.'

'What century were you born in? Why should the boys have all the fun? I'll arrange it for next weekend.'

Hetty broke the news to Peter first. He was fixing the window. 'How would you like it if I got the barn cleared and whitewashed for you?'

'It depends who's doing it. I don't want Caroline's Brownies within a mile of the place.'

This was disappointing. 'Oh. What about Cub Scouts?'

'They're worse.'

'I thought I'd be doing you a favour, saving you all that work.'

'Why bother? They'll make a huge mess, and I haven't finished the designs yet. There's no great hurry.'

Hetty cleared her throat. 'There is, actually.'

CHAPTER TWENTY

In the end it was Connor who supervised the Brownies and the Cub Scouts. And Hetty was the only one who thought his motive was not so much to do with a desire to be helpful as it was to do with Caroline's insistence that the most practical garment to slap paint around in was a bikini.

'I got it out of *Superwoman*, honestly,' she told Hetty smoothly. 'It's easier to wash your body than to wash clothes. And it's hot work.'

'You're all practicality, Caroline,' said Connor.

Connor and Hetty were still not speaking. Hetty couldn't forget how dreadfully unreasonable he'd been, and was working on hating him. If she tried hard enough, she should manage it eventually.

Connor cooked, Hetty cleared up. They said 'excuse me' and 'thank you', 'good-morning' and 'good-night' – but nothing much else. This should have suited Hetty. There was now no longer any danger that he would say something high-minded and embarrassing about their night of thwarted passion.

For Hetty, it was perhaps unfortunate that Phyllis and Connor had become firm friends; and even Peter, who was working closely with Connor on the conversion of the barns, had started to think better of him. Which somehow again left Hetty with no one. Caroline had always been on Connor's side.

All that time when she was defending Connor against Peter and Phyllis, she had felt as if she had friends even if he hadn't. Now she felt alienated, as if it was her who planned to bulldoze the house and deprive the village of their heritage.

All anyone could talk about in the village was the ruby wedding. Everyone was involved in it, if not directly then they knew someone who was. The catering ladies, whose group had swelled to quite a team, all chattered away, and gave Hetty progress reports on the availability of sheet gelatine in the village shop, or raised-pie moulds in town.

The florists, numbering only two, and quieter, discussed twisted willows and sphagnum moss when they met Hetty walking the dogs.

The champagne, which had started out as vintage, been demoted to ordinary and on down to white wine, had recently been reinstated. Alan Brewster ecstatically told her the various stages of play.

'When her husband found out we were down to Chardonnay he was furious. Said if he couldn't give his guests a decent bit of fizz he might as well sell up.'

'Oh. Well, I am pleased. There must be quite a mark-up?'

'Yes, well, I'll give him a pretty good discount – don't want him finding he can buy it cheaper at his supermarket. But my wine merchant will love me.'

It occurred to Hetty, walking home on that particular day, that everyone was being like she had been at thirteen, planning her first teenage party with her friend. They'd made countless lists, what food, what drink, what music, what games, and who should or shouldn't be asked. But it was her parents who actually got it all organized; who made it happen. Now, she felt like a single parent with a houseful of teenagers.

The loan also isolated her. Only Connor knew about it. She had been forced to accept his right to add the money that he earned to the fund, but she was determined that he wouldn't have to sell his car. It would have been preferable not to have to touch any of his money, but such high ideals were beyond her price range. She'd had to dip into the account quite deeply for the ruby wedding, and they wouldn't get that back until after it was too late. She also needed to find out exactly how much was added. Connor would know, but he was the last person she could ask. She would have to find out by more devious means.

She waited until the house was empty of visitors, and the rain seemed set to keep it empty, and rang the loan company. With a few lies and a bit of deviousness, she managed to get the information she required. The sum was considerably lower than she had feared – Connor had obviously managed to pay off quite a bit of the backlog – but there was still going to be a shortfall. And given that the ruby wedding was only the day before the loan was due to be paid, she had a problem. She couldn't expect Mrs Makepiece to pay immediately, and, even if she did, she would need time for the cheque to clear. Even if she could have asked for the money in advance, they would still be a few hundred pounds short. It wasn't a huge amount: if only there was something else they could sell. Her gaze flicked speculatively over the Meissen figurines. If she thought they were properly insured, she'd have broken one.

Two days before the party, the barn was finished.

'As long as the whitewash stays white, and on the walls, until after the party, it can all drop off afterwards.' Hetty was sweeping the floor with a broom with a two-foot-wide head, which Phyllis called a 'bumper'.

'I don't suppose it'll stay on much longer than that,' grumbled Peter from behind a trestle-table he was carrying. 'Those kids won't have prepared the surface properly.' He lowered his burden. 'Where do you want this?'

'I want one up that end, across the way, as a top table, and the others all end-on to it.' She picked up the end of the table. They were too heavy and too long to be handled easily by one person. 'There's rather a lot of these tables, shall I get some Cub Scouts to help you?'

She was only half teasing. Some strong, if unskilled, labour was needed to help him get them all set up, and at the moment she was the only candidate. And, unskilled though she may be, she was also extremely busy. She glanced at her watch. She had to cycle back down to the village in a minute to check if there were enough young people detailed to serve, sweep, fetch and carry.

'The Cub Scouts are all at school,' said Connor, appearing in the doorway. 'I'll give you a hand, Peter.'

'I'll leave you two to it, then,' Hetty escaped and climbed on to Phyllis's bike, trying hard not to feel resentful.

She called in on Caroline on her way home, for a sneaky cup of coffee and a rest.

'So, how are things?' Caroline shoved a packet of biscuits in Hetty's direction. 'Will it all come together in the end?'

'I hope so. I've managed to borrow enough little round tables for the cabaret.' She'd been so absorbed in arrangements, Hetty had almost forgotten who or what the cabaret was. 'There should be enough trestle-tables, though some people might be awfully squashed. The barn looks lovely.'

'And who's doing flowers for the barn? Presumably you haven't asked Mrs Willbury and her friend?'

'No, they're doing them in the house, but when I suggested they might like to try something freer, for the barn, they looked put-upon and declined.'

'So, will you do without flowers?'

Hetty had a mouthful of Hobnob so she shook her head. 'There are all sorts of hooky things on the wall,' she said when she'd swallowed. 'I'm going to hang jamjars on them and fill them with something frothy and informal to decorate the walls.'

' "Frothy and informal," eh? Like what?'

Hetty shrugged. 'Dunno, whatever comes to hand on the morning. Cow-parsley probably.'

'And the food's all sorted?'

'Yup, enough to feed the starving millions and have leftovers. The drink's all at the shop, cooling. So we don't have to fill our fridge with it. I've borrowed knives and forks and plates from the WI. I've had to buy some more, but I'm sure they'll come in useful. What else?'

'Chairs?'

'Chairs?' Hetty thought. She knew there was something about chairs that was worrying her. 'I know. I've got to pick them up.'

'How are you going to do that? You won't get many on the back of a bike.'

'I know, but for some reason the firm I'm borrowing them from could only lend them if I collected them. Damn.'

'Peter's pick-up would take a few, but how many are they?'

'Two hundred and fifty – or at least I hope there are. I only asked for two hundred, but dear Felicity has invited yet more people.'

'Will there be enough food?'

Hetty nodded. 'According to my catering team, the more people you have the less people eat. It's something to do with not being able to get at the food, or manœuvre your elbows once you have.' Hetty regarded her friend thoughtfully. 'I don't suppose you know a friendly farmer with a cattle-truck?'

Caroline pulled out a file marked *Brownies*. She rummaged through sheaves of paper, badges, innumerable forms and several copies of the *Brownie Handbook*. At last she found what she was looking for. 'Cattle-trucks. Bill Jones. Want me to ask him?'

'If ever you need a kidney or anything just ask me, Caro. I owe you at least one.'

Hetty had hoped to slip up to her room unnoticed. She wanted to run through her lists again and would do it better if half-a-dozen people didn't keep interrupting her, wanting her to do something else. Connor caught her, by the wrist, and pulled her into the sitting room, which happened to be empty.

'Hetty! It's no good avoiding me. We've got to rehearse! You seem to have forgotten we're putting on a show for these people.'

Not forgotten, just pushed to the back of the attic of her mind, behind a lot of other junk. 'I haven't time!' This was true, she hadn't. But it was also an excuse. 'I've been practising.' This was less true. She had done a few exercises, her voice was more or less in trim, but she hadn't decided what songs to sing, and therefore, had only sung a random selection.

'We have to rehearse together! Come along. There's only a few people setting up tables in the hall now.' He took her arm and she found herself going with him.

'I can't practise in front of all these people,' she hissed.

'They're all helpers. There are no members of the public likely to hear you. And think how much worse it would be to not practise before playing in front of two hundred paying customers!'

'Two hundred and fifty,' she muttered, knowing he was right.

Hetty found it very difficult to sing when she was out of sympathy with her pianist. That time, a lifetime ago, when they had sung and played together well had been so wonderful, so natural. They were such a team, instinctively interpreting each other's intentions, moving and flowing like fish in a stream.

Now, Hetty could barely open her mouth. Her voice was tight, her jaw was tight, her breathing shallow and unsupportive. Connor's playing – curse him – was just as relaxed and instinctive as ever.

'This isn't working,' said Hetty. 'And neither am I. I'm sure it'll all come together on the night.'

'Liar. If you were sure, I'd let you get away with it. But you're nervous as hell, you just won't let yourself think about it.'

She wanted to say, 'Whose fault's that?' but this was one she couldn't pin on him. There were two hundred and fifty other people in the queue for blame.

'Sing something you know really well.'

' "Good King Wenceslas"?' She was flippant because she was nervous.

' "Summertime", with not too high a start.' He played a few bars of introduction.

Hetty got through it, and it sounded better towards the end, but it was still not right. 'That was O K. Now, I must go.'

'It couldn't have been much worse and still be recognizable,' said Connor, but Hetty was already half out of the room.

It wasn't that she wasn't keen to put on a good performance – she was, desperately – but she didn't think there was any point in her rehearsing with Connor just at the moment. Her mind was too full of other things. She couldn't sing well unless she was totally involved in the music.

The day of the party dawned magically fair. Hetty saw it from her bedroom and decided that Phyllis was definitely a witch, a white one of course, who had again concentrated her efforts and produced perfect weather for momentous occasions.

She got up, knowing she needed a little time before anyone else was around to check on the final details, do the flowers for the barn, and a thousand other things she couldn't foresee but knew would need doing.

She took the dogs for a long walk. They didn't need a long walk but she did, and together they followed the same route she had taken when she had first arrived, when winter had held the country-side in thrall.

Now there was mist in the valleys, promising a scorching day, spiders' webs glistening from every blade of grass. Dew covered everything, and from time to time a drop would sparkle like a prism, all the colours of the spectrum in a tiny sphere. When she was little, Hetty always thought of these drops as fairies. Some part of her still did.

The woods were cool, would stay cool, alive with birdsong,

pungent with the smell of wild garlic where before there had been bluebells. Twigs crackled under Hetty's feet and she had to restrain herself from picking them up for kindling. She would no longer be at Courtbridge House when fires were needed again. It would be Connor's job to gather kindling.

For Hetty had decided, without even being aware that she was thinking of anything other than bowls of potato salad and bunches of cow-parsley, that as soon as the debt was paid, she would leave.

Her work would be done. Connor was here, for the foreseeable future. He and Phyllis and Peter were all best buddies now and could run the house on a day-to-day basis. And if there were more bookings after tonight's event, there was a whole team set up to deal with them.

Samuel didn't need her. He was going to have a handsome barn conversion, level, convenient, with wide doorways and every aid to disabled living invented. And he might not even end up in a wheelchair. All this preparation was Connor's way of getting him home. Connor's argument was that if they had somewhere sensible for him to live, and paid outside nurses to care for him, give him physiotherapy and get him on his feet, he'd recover far more quickly than he would in hospital. He'd told Samuel of his plans, and Samuel was now working hard on getting stronger.

Connor had got a loan to pay for the conversion quite easily (she had learnt via Peter), and this knowledge galled Hetty unbearably. Maybe he could have got a loan to pay off Samuel's debt quite easily. Unless, which seemed more likely, he had convinced the bank on the grounds that the barn conversions were an investment. Paying Samuel's debts wouldn't be seen like that – not by a bank anyway.

And nor did the dogs, Islay and Talisker, need her. They were happy to walk with anyone who'd take them, sleep with or on anyone who'd let them. Even Clovis, whom she searched for every morning, dreading finding him dead, had Connor on his side. He was the only one who hadn't declared the animal should be put down for sanitary reasons.

And Connor certainly didn't need her. He didn't need anyone, nor, indeed, ever would. He hadn't so much as touched her since his return. At best, what had happened before must have been caused by lust. And now he had that well under control.

It was only by concentrating hard on the beauties of nature that Hetty managed to keep from weeping with self-pity. Fortunately, the beauties of nature were abundant.

She had hardly been back long enough to take off her wellingtons when her mother rang her. It was still only seven o'clock. 'I hope I haven't woken you dear?'

'Oh, no. I've been up since five.'

'Just thought I'd ring and see how things were getting on before you got busy.'

'I've been busy all day so far, Mum. How are you?' This was a hint to her mother that she didn't want to chat.

'Fine, dear, but what I really wanted to say is, do you want a job? A paid one, I mean?'

Hetty realized she really didn't give her mother enough credit. 'Yes I do. What sort of job?'

'Only temporary, I'm afraid, but you might love it and then who knows?'

'What sort of job?' Her mother may be wonderful but she wasn't perfect.

'Running a hotel. In Shropshire, right on the Welsh border. So the owners can have a break.'

'But that sounds rather beyond me. I'm only a glorified typist, you know.'

'You are not! You're running a stately home single-handed! You're an Events Director, a Catering Co-ordinator, all sorts of things.'

'Not actually single-handed, Mum.'

'Nor will you be in Shropshire. There's plenty of staff, just no one to co-ordinate them.'

'I'm not sure –'

'Darling, you must capitalize on your assets. Think of what you've learnt at Courtbridge House? All those skills you never knew you had. I'll tell these people you'll do it, shall I?'

'I really ought to look for my own job –'

'Yes, but they need you as soon as possible. You wouldn't want to let them down.'

'Why not? I don't even know them. Why should I care?'

'The woman's a distant cousin of your father's, dear.'

That seemed to settle the matter.

Hetty called the dogs, found the kitchen scissors, and went out of the back door to the fields. She had to pick flowers for the barns and this might be her only opportunity, even though there was a risk that they would have flopped before the party. She made her way across the field-cum-parking-lot to where the cow-parsley grew high and thick.

As she cut, she thought about her mother, and wondered why she felt obliged to solve everyone's problems, using Hetty as her solvent. Of course she should refuse to run this hotel in Shropshire. Working for distant cousins had proved itself to be thoroughly dangerous.

On the other hand, she did accept that the thought of going back to London to work in an office didn't seem very appealing. And it was not only because she was surrounded by a golden June morning. When she first came here it was still winter, and bitterly cold. She had still learnt to love the place.

God, how miserable she'd been then. How heart-broken, how bereft of any self-esteem. Well, she might still be heart-broken, but at least this time it was for a man worthy of it. And in every other way, she was wiser, stronger and braver. She'd done so much growing up, taken on so much responsibility. In fact, she should almost be grateful to Alistair for putting her in a position where her mother could manipulate her. If she hadn't been jobless just when Uncle Samuel was going into hospital, she would never have come to Courtbridge House.

She gathered her dew-soaked armfuls and made her way back to the house, her jeans and sweater drenched. Leaving Courtbridge House, Samuel – everyone – would be devastating. But not to have ever come would have been a real tragedy. 'You know what they say,' she said to Islay, who was frisking round Hetty's feet with her head on one side. '"It's better to have loved and lost than never to have loved at all." And no, I didn't bring a ball.'

By the time she had finished her flower-arrangements – huge and dangling, looking like shields of hedgerow attached to the walls of the barn – the house was seething with people.

She was making herself a quick bacon butty in the kitchen when Connor came in. 'Hetty!' He swooped on her from behind. 'Come with me.'

Hetty plonked the second slice of bread on top of the bacon, found a plate and followed. He led her into a little room that had previously been full of junk, but which, since the revamp of the house, had become a little sitting room, its pretty bay window a perfect place for two low chairs and an occasional table.

'We need to sort out what we're doing tonight.'

'Not nervous are you?' inquired Hetty through a mouthful of bacon and Mother's Pride.

'No, but we need to know what we're doing if we're not to look like a pair of complete amateurs.'

'Which is what we are.'

'But we don't want to look like amateurs, or we'll have to give the money back.'

Hetty swallowed. 'I suppose so.'

'I've made a list.' He put his hand in his pocket and produced a crumpled piece of paper.

'So have I.' Hetty rummaged in her jeans and found a used envelope, equally crumpled.

They swapped papers, then their eyes met.

'Well,' said Connor, 'it seems we agree on something at last.'

Hetty looked down. She had only made the list the day before, in a rare spare moment. 'Coincidence is a funny thing,' she said.

Connor nodded. 'But total humiliation isn't. We must practise.'

Knowing he was right didn't make Hetty one jot more willing to follow him. She had decided to leave Courtbridge House when the debt was paid, which should be fairly soon. Part of the leaving process was detaching herself emotionally from Connor.

Their rehearsal did not go well. She was tense, she couldn't get her jaw to relax and her breath came in short, panicky little puffs.

'I'll be better tonight,' she promised.

Connor closed the lid of the piano. 'I hope so.'

'I'm just going upstairs to check the Ladies' cloakroom is in order,' said Hetty and abandoned the party of cleaners who were polishing a floor – more, Hetty was sure, for the pleasure of being in such a companionable band than because it needed doing.

Hetty actually had no intention of checking the cloakroom. She knew that the bedroom with the four-poster was in order. She was going to grab a quick shower and a hair wash while she had the chance. But somehow she couldn't bring herself to tell the other women, who were working so hard, that she was going to do something so unproductive.

Caroline had lent her the black dress she had worn to Felicity Makepiece's dinner party. She had a little boxy linen jacket to wear over it for most of the evening, but would wear it uncensored for the cabaret. Knowing she would have very little time to change later, Hetty put on Caroline's bra and black tights under her jeans. She put on some make-up and fluffed up her hair. Now all she would have to do was strip off her outer garments and put on the dress.

It was just as well. The first fifty guests arrived before she had had a moment to get out of her jeans.

CHAPTER TWENTY-ONE

'The downstairs Gents won't flush.' Felicity's husband, whose name, try as she might, Hetty couldn't remember, appeared apologetically before her. 'We have one at home, works perfectly well for family, won't do a thing for strangers.'

Hetty gulped and tried to smile. This was the sort of thing that could turn a comparative success into abject failure. 'Our one is usually fine. I'll come and look.'

She should have asked Peter or even Connor, but finding them would have been a problem, they could be anywhere. The party had taken on a life of its own, and had spread far beyond its original boundaries.

It had been Connor who had suggested, a couple of days before, that if the weather was fine the guests might like to wander out of the french windows, on to the lawn. Everyone had agreed that, as the numbers had more than doubled since Mrs Makepiece had chosen the house for her party, this was a good idea. Only Hetty was negative enough to point out there was no lawn, only an extremely overgrown piece of land, which hadn't seen a mower in its life. Nobody took any notice.

It had been fairly easy, with Peter's expertise, to reinstate the french windows. What was harder was creating something for the french windows to open on to. No one had done anything about that side of the house in the grand restoration. It was a case of out of sight, not on the list of things to do.

But suddenly it had top-priority status. Scythes and whetstones were excavated from one of the many forgotten store-rooms. Connor and Peter honed the scythes to a lethal sharpness, and advanced on the waist-high nettles, thistles, teasels and multifarious umbellifers in the faint hope that there might be grass underneath.

Hetty was sure one of them would lose a hand or a foot during the process. Thus convinced, she took herself off so she wouldn't be the one to have to pick up the severed limb, wrap it in frozen peas and carry it to the hospital.

Fortunately it wasn't a large space, there was something vaguely green growing under the weeds, and nobody so much as cut themselves. The hedge that bounded it made an attractive back-drop. There were no flower-beds as such to worry about. By the time the area had been cut with a Flymo as well, it looked almost lawn-like.

Tables and chairs had been set out on the bits considered level enough. Hetty put cloths on the tables, set candles in jamjars and hung them in the branches of an old plum tree. More candles, in bottles, were put on the tables. A few nibbles in little dishes, and she was almost satisfied. Then she heard the Makepieces' car, and had to dash off to greet them. But her backward glance as she went into the house was very pleasing. The hedge was full of Traveller's Joy and honeysuckle, and filled the little area with scent. As long as the cars, to be parked just the other side, didn't spoil it with their exhaust fumes, it was pleasantly romantic.

That had been an hour and two hundred people ago. Now Hetty hitched up her tight skirt and climbed up on to the lavatory seat, glad that Mr Makepiece had wandered off. She took the lid off the cistern and saw that the coupling had broken, so the chain pulled on nothing. A piece of string and a lot of very fiddly threading and tying later, and Hetty jumped down to test her work. The lavatory flushed noisily, and Hetty gave it a satisfied pat before pulling her skirt into place. It was, Phyllis had told her proudly, when Hetty had first arrived, a genuine Thomas Crapper.

'I've been looking for you,' said Connor. 'Felicity wants you. Come on.'

She followed Connor as he beat a path through the crowd to where Felicity was holding court in the garden.

'There seem to be an awful lot of people, darling. Did I really invite so many?'

'I think so. They don't look like gatecrashers.'

Felicity sighed. 'No, and I do know most of them, by sight, anyway. I'm just wondering if there's going to be enough room.'

'They should all fit in all right.'

'Oh, good. And here's more champagne.' She replaced her

empty glass with a full one. 'I think I'm entitled, don't you?'

A little later, Peter and Connor managed to get the guests' attention and summon them to supper. They picked their way across the yard to the barn, which looked rural and flower-filled enough to gladden the heart of any Thomas Hardy fan.

The trestle-tables had bowls of bread, butter and salad, and bottles of wine all along their centre lines. The guests were to come up, a table at a time, for the substance of the meal. Hetty hadn't had an opportunity to see the barn with all the food set out and, although she knew it would work, she was still surprised at how attractive and appetizing it all looked.

The Catering Corps, as they had become known, had done them proud. They had all put on pretty floral dresses and white aprons, and stood behind the plates of food, armed with serving spoons, ladles and forks. No one would leave the barn un-fed. In fact, few would leave it without feeling thoroughly stuffed.

Glistening pies, quiches, Scotch eggs and sausage rolls were piled next to dainty Italian puffs, tiny wholemeal blinis and filo-pastry baskets filled with smoked salmon. Huge joints of beef, pork and ham, cooked to perfection, were partially sliced. Whole salmons, glazed with cucumber, looking like pieces of modern art, competed with turkeys, boned and stuffed for the starring role.

One glance at Felicity's face as she entered the barn, told Hetty everything she wanted to know. 'You done good,' she murmured to the chief orchestrator of the feast as she moved to her place behind the egg mayonnaise and tiny balls of rice, cheese and vegetables, dipped in breadcrumbs and deep-fried. 'It looks fabulous.'

The woman made a face. 'It ought to. I never want to look at another Coronation Chicken. That's why I'm up the veggie end.' Then, seeing Hetty's face fall, she went on. 'I don't mean it. I enjoyed myself, really I did. I'd love to do something like this again.' She smiled pleasantly as the first guests began to filter in.

'Thank goodness for that,' said Hetty. 'Egg mayonnaise for you, sir? Oh, hello Alistair.' She should have realized he'd be there. Anyone who'd slept under Felicity's roof would definitely qualify for an invitation.

'Hello, Hetty.' He smiled. He'd obviously spotted her from afar, or he wouldn't have come near the vegetarian section. 'So this is what you're doing now. Being a waitress.'

Hetty couldn't think how she'd ever fallen in love with such a snob. She smiled. 'That's right. It's nice to think I've gone up in the world since working for you. Now,' she murmured from between clenched teeth, 'would you like this on your plate, or on your shirt?'

Startled and speechless, Alistair moved on to something more carnivorous, and Hetty explained to her neighbour who he was. 'I shouldn't have said that to him really. But, what the hell, I'm tired.'

'Quite tasty, though,' said her companion, referring to Alistair.

'Yes, but not substantial. Nothing to really get your teeth into.'

'Not like that Connor.'

'Er – no.' Hetty wished she'd never started this conversation. 'Have you tried the blinis? They're lush.'

Hetty had just put a blini where her mouth was, when two women, one obviously the daughter of the other, approached.

'You might possibly be able to save our lives,' said the younger one.

Hetty, unable to speak, nodded.

'We've been terribly let down,' said the older one.

Hetty swallowed. 'Oh?'

'You see, I'm getting married,' said the younger one, 'and the hotel where we were going to have the reception –'

'*And* the evening disco –'

'Had a fire. They had to cancel.'

'I suppose they would have to,' said Hetty.

'*So* inconvenient.'

'It wasn't their fault, Mummy –'

'No, but it's our misfortune. And we've both fallen in love with this place.'

It was too much to hope they wanted to buy it. 'And?' Hetty checked the corner of her mouth with her tongue for traces of sour cream.

'Well, could we have the reception here?'

'Um –' began Hetty.

'We do realize it's terribly short notice,' said the mother.

'But Felicity thought you might be able to help.'

'I'm sure –'

'The thing is, the date.'

'Oh?' Please God they didn't want to get married next weekend.'

'It's August bank holiday Saturday.'

'Oh –'

'Of course, I realize you're likely to be booked up –'

'I'd need to check –'

'It would be *so* wonderful.' The bride-to-be was beginning to look tearful. 'We've tried so many places, and none of them can help.'

'I tell you what!' The mother of the bride-to-be had a brainwave. 'I'll give you a deposit! Would five hundred pounds be enough to secure it?'

'I think that would be fine,' said Hetty. Not quite enough to pay off the loan, but a handsome amount.

The woman dived into her handbag and produced a cheque-book. A few moments later, Hetty tucked it into her cleavage, and suddenly saw the world as a better place.

While the guests ate their first courses, the serving tables were rearranged. Savouries were put on to the table, for those wanting seconds, while most of the tables were cleared for the puddings.

Hetty knew that at some future date, when she was hungry and yearning for something delicious, she would look back on those puddings with regret.

Pavlovas, like Ascot hats, delicate, frilly with whorls of cream, dotted with *fraises du bois*, and clusters of individual chocolate mousses in chocolate cups, blobbed with cream and grated chocolate, snuggled up with bowls of trifle and summer puddings. Pyramids of profiteroles filled with cream and decorated with spun sugar and grapes, charlotte russes, malakofs, basins of fruit salad, mountains of strawberries and pagodas of cream-filled brandysnaps covered every available space. There was even bread-and-butter pudding for those wanting something ostensibly less rich.

But Hetty had neither time nor appetite to taste any of them. After she'd dolloped 'a bit of everything' on to thirty plates, a process that made a rather unattractive mess, she had to arrange for Ruby's appearance. Those guests who still had room had a whole Stilton and a whole farmhouse Cheddar to get through.

Ruby, who'd been happily ensconced in a small stable, surrounded by sweet hay and buckets of calf-nuts, didn't particularly want to have a garland put round her neck. Flowers, in her considered opinion, were to be eaten, not worn.

Peter was supposed to be helping Hetty with Ruby, but she realized he had probably got held up by his job of replacing all empty bottles with full ones. Everyone seemed to be drinking rather a lot.

At last Hetty got Ruby's head out of the bucket and the halter half on. She was just wondering how she would know when to bring her in when Peter appeared, a prettily-dressed child in tow.

'Hi. This is Sophie, she's Felicity's great-niece. Felicity says, can she lead Ruby in to present her to John?'

'Hello, Sophie. What a lovely dress!'

'It's Laura Ashley,' said Sophie. 'I don't like it much. I prefer Clara's dress. It's green. And not frilly.'

Sophie was one of those children who could spot an adult unused to dealing with the young a mile off.

Aware that she was one of these, Hetty did her best. 'But Clara's not going to lead this lovely little calf, is she?'

'No.' Sophie said in agreement. 'But I would have led it even if I'd had a green dress, wouldn't I?'

Hetty gave up. 'I expect so. Now here's what we've got to do.'

She explained to Peter and Sophie that she would fight her way to Felicity's side and ask her for a signal. With luck, John, on Felicity's other side, wouldn't hear what Hetty was saying over the din. Then Hetty would beckon to Sophie to lead in the calf.

It took Hetty a while to negotiate her way to Felicity for their conference, but they agreed that Felicity would signal to Phyllis, who would signal to Hetty and the others when they should appear.

Hetty, heartily relieved that she would not have to lead the calf herself, and thus be the centre of attention, did wonder if it would prove too much for Sophie, who, although strong of character, was relatively puny of build. 'Supposing Ruby pulls her over?' she whispered to Peter, as they waited until Phyllis came to the door to signal.

Peter shrugged. 'Giving an animal as a present is a damn-fool idea to begin with.'

Hetty didn't reply. He was probably right, but it was a sweet thought, even so.

Phyllis appeared at the door. Hetty, Peter, Sophie and Ruby crept up to it, Ruby oblivious of the need to keep quiet, pulling like a train.

There were speeches going on inside. Hetty heard her name being taken in vain, or maybe she was being thanked. There was laughter, applause and, once, a loud drumming on the tables with glasses or bottles. Hetty hoped everyone had eaten a lot, to sop up the alcohol.

Then came virtual silence, which Hetty took to mean that Felicity was making her speech. There was laughter, Phyllis beckoned, and Hetty pushed Sophie forward.

'You're on!'

'What am I supposed to do?'

'Sophie! We've been through all this! Lead Ruby up to Uncle . . . you know! It's simple! Off you go.'

Ruby seemed to have understood her instructions at any rate. She set off at a tremendous pace. Through the doors she went, pulling her pretty dairymaid with her.

An explosion of laughter greeted this entrance, and Ruby, hearing it, changed her mind and headed back towards the door, dragging Sophie behind her.

What Ruby hadn't reckoned on was that so many of the guests would be young, rugby-playing types, who, suitably primed, welcomed the chance of a ruck. There was even a phalanx of Young Farmers. So, as Ruby, followed by Sophie on her stomach, headed for the calf-nuts, five young men tackled her to the ground.

Thus it was that Ruby, a pedigree Devon Red heifer, was presented to her new master in the arms of someone whom he barely knew, but who at least wasn't crying.

'It's a Devon Red, darling!' shouted Felicity over the noise. 'They call them Devon Rubies. And it's our ruby-wedding anniversary!' She didn't actually say, 'Geddit?' but it was implied.

Up until that point, Hetty had had no time to feel nervous about the prospect of singing. She had so much else on her mind, there was no space to spare for anxiety. Now, in the sudden quiet of the great hall, she felt paralysed with fear.

Her limbs would hardly move her as she adjusted tables, made sure there were enough chairs. She fiddled with candles and cloths, not allowing her gaze to venture near the piano, large and threatening at the end of the room.

By the time Connor found her she was shaking, from sheer terror, hunger, and what felt like nervous exhaustion. She stood with her back to the piano, her head in her hands.

'Hetty?' His voice was gentle and for a moment she thought she might cry. 'Are you OK?' She shook her head.

'Come with me.' He put his arm round her and propelled her out of the room into the little ante-room where they had discussed their songs. He took out a flask of whisky from behind a vase of flowers and poured a large measure into a glass. 'Have you had anything to eat?'

Hetty shook her head again, unable to speak, let alone sing. 'Good,' said Connor. 'Drink this.'

Surprised, but obedient, Hetty drank. When she put down the empty glass, coughing slightly, he took her into his arms and kissed her.

It was a long, deep, penetrating kiss, which added to the lightheadedness Hetty had been feeling before. His arms were hard and firm about her ribs, containing her anxiety with their strength. When he finally let her go, she was staggering, but a great deal steadier than she had been.

'Now, slap my face,' he ordered. 'It'll make you feel much better.'

Hetty smiled. 'I don't want to slap your face. I feel better anyway.'

'You won't get another chance to do it.'

'I'll forgo my privilege.'

He grinned back, mischief dancing in his eyes. They both knew this was a suspension of their hostilities, not a truce. 'Good. I didn't really want to appear with a swollen jaw. I'll get my music sorted out.'

'Your music?' Hetty called as she followed him out of the room. 'I thought you couldn't read music?'

He glanced over his shoulder at her. 'I never said I couldn't, I just usually prefer not to. Now, have you got your list of songs?'

This caused Hetty's new-found confidence to waver. 'No.'

'Never mind, I've got mine. Now, let's have a little sing until they come in.'

Connor didn't seem to believe in telling his soloist what she was to sing – instead, he just played a long introduction. His first choice, thought Hetty as she recognized it, was quite apposite: 'It Had to be You'.

Hetty and Connor continued to perform, softly, almost to themselves, while people got into their seats, found their drinks, went to the loo, fetched their wives' handbags, and, to Hetty's secret horror, lit cigarettes.

'Will you be OK?' Connor asked softly as he saw the couple on the front table both light up.

Hetty, who was prepared to blame her entire bad performance – if she gave one – on this couple, nodded. 'I'll be hoarse tomorrow anyway,' she mumbled back, as Connor's musical fingers tiddled about in the upper octaves.

'I think it's time we got this lot to settle down.'

Hetty stopped singing, and Connor began playing more loudly, and gradually the noise quietened.

'You're a genius. Have you done this before?' asked Hetty, out of the corner of her mouth.

'Course. What do you think I am – a fucking amateur?'

This expletive caused Hetty's mouth to open nice and wide for her first song.

Music flowed from her that night. The whisky and Connor's kiss seemed to have released all her tension, so there were no obstructions between how she heard the music in her head and what came out. Her voice seemed perfectly flexible, in tune, obedient to every whim. And in this matter, if none other, Connor was the perfect partner.

It wasn't a large space, as performance spaces go, but it was full of people, who absorbed the sound and were prone to twitching. Still Hetty managed to fill it with sound apparently without effort.

I'll never sing like this again, she thought. Never again would alcohol and kisses seduce her voice into such a relaxed, natural performance. It's like making love with music, instead of bodies. The effect was almost as glorious.

The audience loved it. She and Connor got through their programme before Hetty felt they'd really got going, and were asked for more. They consulted each other, and performed a couple more songs. Then they stopped, refusing all entreaties to continue. They were only an interlude, after all, not the whole focus for the evening. Their applause, Hetty noticed with satisfaction, was almost as loud as Ruby's had been.

'That was wonderful.' Ruby's new owner caught Hetty as she followed Connor out of the room. 'The whole evening's been wonderful. And I want to give you this cheque.'

Hetty demurred, trying not to snatch it from his hand.

'I can remember how hard it is to get a new business going. And if people don't pay their bills promptly your cash flow is all to pot, and you're sunk. So I've written you an interim cheque, something on account to keep you going until you've worked out the final figure and sent us the bill.'

Hetty thanked his departing back and put the cheque to join the other one. Then she went to find Connor.

She found him in the garden, sitting at the one table left there, playing with the wax that ran down the side of the candle.

'You must be shattered,' he said, pulling out a second chair.

'Mmm, but it went well, didn't it?'

'Very. We could set up in business as a cabaret act.'

'But we won't,' said Hetty. There was a tiny silence. This was one of the other things they agreed on.

'Have a drink.' Connor had concealed a bottle and two glasses under a hedge. He eased the cork out with his thumbs. 'It's not terribly cold, I'm afraid.'

'It's delicious.' Hetty closed her eyes. In a minute she would tell Connor about the two cheques, stashed away in her cleavage. But now she felt too tired to talk.

After what they had just shared they couldn't resume hostilities, but nor could they pretend they'd always been the best of friends. Hetty's eyes refused to open. In a minute she and Connor would be interrupted by several dozen people. She'd have to tell him now, while she had an opportunity.

'A man's coming to buy the car tomorrow.' Connor broke the silence. 'He's been badgering me to sell to him for years. It'll be enough to pay off the debt.'

'But, Connor, you don't have to do that! We've earned enough today to pay off the debt, and I've got two cheques –'

'That's not all profit.'

'I *know* that, but some of it is, and –'

'You have to give a cheque four working days to clear. I'll be paid in cash. Phyllis is lending me her car so I can go up to London and get those bastards off our backs for ever. Besides, I owe you about eight hundred.'

'Do you?'

'You sold your car, didn't you? Used the money to make up an instalment? You must have that back.'

Hurt and horrified, Hetty stared at Connor. 'But not *now*! You don't have to sell your car to pay me back for mine. I can easily wait. Anyway, it was only five hundred.'

'It's *my* car, *my* uncle's debt, I can pay it off how I like.'

'But don't you see, this is a quite unnecessary sacrifice! I've got cheques –'

'There's no point in arguing. I've made my decision.' He got up, set his glass down on the table, and stalked off into the house.

Hetty watched him go. She was shaking with anger. He was so insufferably proud and arrogant he'd rather sell his car than accept that the house could earn its keep. Her contribution was worth nothing, simply disregarded. All the hard work, the wheeling and dealing, the anxiety – everything she had gone through had all been for nothing.

At that moment, she hated him, not for changing from the wonderful, inspired accompanist back to the sort of man who didn't care about his heritage, but because he couldn't be wrong.

She was concentrating on getting herself up to her bedroom without losing her temper on the way when Sophie came up, her dress awry and her hair in rat's-tails.

'Ruby's got into the barn and eaten all the flower-arrangements.'

Hetty looked at her blankly. She hadn't a clue who Ruby was. 'Has she? How odd. I hope she isn't sick on the carpet.'

Sophie opened her mouth to explain but Hetty had already left.

CHAPTER TWENTY-TWO

Although aching with tiredness, Hetty couldn't sleep well. Guilt from abandoning the party before the last guest had gone added to her torment. She was so furious with Connor's high-handed dismissal of her achievements she was glad that it would punish him more than her. But after she had slept a bit, and dawn was breaking, she knew she didn't want him to lose the car he loved so dearly.

Of course the car would bring in cash, and he was right about the cheques needing time to clear. And Connor would have money over with which to buy another, ordinary, car. But he wouldn't find another quite so special. Surely there was another way round the problem?

It occurred to her at five o'clock, when she gave up trying to sleep and got up, that what she ought to do was to convince him to put off selling his car, and demand that the loan people wait a few days for the cheques to clear. But she realized, her toothbrush half-way to her mouth, that they would probably refuse. They would be far more interested in getting their hands on Courtbridge House. Which would explain why Connor was so insistent on selling his car. Which, she concluded, was a point in his favour.

Hetty wiped the flecks of toothpaste off the bathroom mirror with her sleeve, wishing she could clear her feelings about Connor as easily. But she couldn't. Love, hate, frustration and pure rage churned about like an emotional soup: it was quite impossible to extract one ingredient and react to it separately.

On the other hand, if the loan was to be paid off, she couldn't waste time wondering if she loved Connor or hated him, wanted him to keep his car, or thought losing it a just punishment. Getting the loan paid off was the important thing, and that needed action, not philosophical introspection. Hetty went back to her bedroom to get dressed, and as she did so an idea came to her so outrageous she rejected it several times before allowing it to develop. But while she was rejecting it, she did put on clean, relatively smart clothes, instead of the jeans and T-shirt she had originally salvaged from her bedroom chair. And having done that it seemed a waste not to go ahead with it. She didn't want to change her clothes again, after all.

She refined the details as she walked home across the fields with the dogs. The beauty of the plan was that Connor had given it to her. He had told her he was borrowing Phyllis's car and taking the cash up to London. Anything he could do, she could do better. She would borrow Connor's car, go and see the under-manager at the bank and ask him for an overdraft for the four days necessary to clear the cheques, and ask for it in cash. Then, cash in hand, she would drive up to London and pay off the debt, then come home again and give Connor's car back. And while he'd never admit he was glad it had been out of the way, and therefore couldn't be sold, in his heart he would be.

And if the under-manager refused her very reasonable request, (and this was distinctly possible) she could just come back and let Connor carry on with his plan, entirely unaware of her interference.

So elated was she by this poem of tactics and method that she happily washed up until seven o'clock, which she judged was when she should leave. Any earlier and she would be hanging around town for hours waiting for the bank to open – any later and Connor would be up. The thought of stealing his car filled her with a dreadful excitement, but the thought of stealing it while he was actually awake took excitement over the edge to terror.

Hetty was determined not to get carried away and make some fatal mistake, like forgetting the cheques. She put on a bit of make-up (London required make-up), brushed her hair, made sure she had the correspondence from the loan company as well as the cheques, then tiptoed out of the house, having left a note stating that she'd gone to see Caroline. It was important that no one miss her before they missed the car. And the car, which had been parked well out of the way of the visiting cars the day before, wouldn't be missed until the man came to buy it.

It was a little nerve-racking, driving through the gate, thinking that at any moment Connor might look out of the window and see his precious car disappearing. And the car felt very strange to drive. She didn't dare stop to walk back and shut the gate until she'd driven the car some way down the lane.

Even having made her escape, Hetty found she couldn't relax. The car, as it turned out, was not only strange but difficult. It was heavy, and seemed to pull to the left. By the time Hetty got to the town her arms were aching. Just as well it was so early, she thought. It meant there were plenty of parking spaces, and she could choose one she could just slide into. She wouldn't have wanted to do much backing and filling in a car that was difficult to steer.

She bought a newspaper and then found the café where Phyllis had taken her the day she had visited the bank. There she indulged in a pot of tea and a scone, still warm from the oven, and settled down to calculate, on a paper napkin, exactly what Courtbridge House owed, and what was owing to Courtbridge House.

She was waiting on the doorstep when the bank opened, and, consequently, didn't have too long to wait before she got to see the manager.

'I need an overdraft!' she declared, sounding a bit melodramatic, even to her own ears.

The bank manager raised his eyebrows, wishing Hetty hadn't refused coffee. He so needed some himself.

Hetty subsided into her role as supplicant. 'You did say that you might be able to help with one if the house became a profit-making concern.' She pulled out two crumpled cheques. 'We would have been in profit before if it hadn't been for the iniquitous rate of interest we've had to pay on Samuel's loan.'

'Oh?' He took the cheques. 'What are these?'

'One's a deposit for a wedding. The final cheque will be huge.' She didn't know this for a fact, but it was a reasonable assumption. 'And the other is part-payment for an event that took place last night. The rest of the money should be coming very soon. Here's what we're due.' She handed him the napkin on which her sums were written.

'When are you expecting the balance of the money?'

'Pretty soon. Mr Makepiece, whose party it was, gave me the

interim cheque because he knows what a bad time small businesses have when people don't pay promptly.'

'That's certainly true.'

'So I don't think he'll keep us waiting long for the balance.'

'No. And I see from your calculations' – he peered at her napkin – 'that you are owed well in excess of the money required to pay off the loan. So why do you need an overdraft?'

She produced the letter from the loan company. 'I need to pay them today. It's the third of June.'

'Tricky. You want a loan to cover the period that the cheques take to clear?'

Hetty nodded. 'In cash.'

'Supposing the cheques bounce?'

'They won't.'

The under-manager considered her proposal and how it might impinge on his career for what seemed like hours. 'OK. As you've done so much to turn round the fortunes of the house, in a comparatively short time, I'll allow you the cash.'

It took an age for the money to appear, but when it did it was in neat paper bands and had the unmistakable smell of new money. Hetty stuffed it into her bag, realizing it wouldn't fit and that she'd have to find something else to put it in, and then rushed round the table and hugged the bank manager. Too surprised to know what he was doing, he hugged her back.

Hetty found the way to the motorway quite easily and, although her arms were aching, the car went well enough. She stopped for fuel and filled up, glad she'd had the forethought to put a wadge of notes in her handbag, for ready use. The rest of the money was in a carrier bag, concealed under a bag of baps and a lardy cake, which she'd bought while waiting for the bank to open.

She was passing the Lucozade bottle on the approach to Hammersmith when it dawned on her that, after she'd returned the car, she would never be able to go back to the house – at least, not while Connor was there. For even if her plan came off (and she had doubts, even now), he would hate her for taking control of the situation, not telling him what she'd planned. It was going behind his back on a grand scale.

Hetty didn't like driving in central London at the best of times, which these were certainly not. To avoid having to, she found a quiet corner of Hammersmith and parked, glad Connor's car had a Krook-lock, praying it wouldn't be stolen while she took the tube into town.

A life-time seemed to have passed since Hetty was last in London, but she still knew her way round the tube system, and, the money still safe under its doughy blanket, she reached the Strand by one o'clock.

All I have to do now, she thought, is find the building. Having bought a copy of *The Big Issue*, she asked the boy who sold it to her the way. He walked along the street with her until they reached it.

'They'd better not all be at lunch, bloody people,' she muttered as she ran up the steps of the building.

They weren't. There was a man there to receive the money, but he was put out to see Hetty and not Connor and did it with bad grace – it would have been so much more satisfying for him if Courtbridge House had been distrained against – handling the plastic bag which contained it with disdainful fingers. True, the lardy cake had oozed a bit, and some of the bundles of notes were rather sticky, but it was all there, as the man reluctantly discovered, when he pedantically counted it.

Hetty paused at the entrance to the tube, suddenly not wanting to go back to Courtbridge. Connor would be so furious with her, as would everyone. No one would understand why she'd found it necessary to get Connor's car out of the way, except perhaps Jack. And he would have expected her to hide it at his house, not drive it to London with a large amount of banknotes riding shotgun.

So instead of taking the tube back to Hammersmith, she went to the cinema. Then she rang Penny, her friend from the office, and agreed to meet her after work. Thus it was seven o'clock when, the worst of the rush-hour over, Hetty got back to Connor's car and, having given a brief prayer of thanksgiving that it was still there and undamaged, set off for home.

It seemed to take for ever to get out of London. The sun was in her eyes most of the time and lack of sleep was catching up with her. Why, after nights of tossing and turning and praying for sleep should it suddenly descend upon her like an inescapable blanket, just when she least wanted it? She fought from under it, but got off the motorway as soon as she could, pulled over, and closed her eyes for ten minutes or so.

Slightly refreshed, she carried on, pulling off bits of lardy cake and bap from the crumpled paper bag at her side. But the car seemed to be getting harder and harder to drive. It didn't want to stay on the road, showing a strong preference for the hedge instead. She stopped worrying about what Connor would do to her when she finally got back – in case she didn't. Being torn limb from limb by the man you loved seemed a better end than hurtling head first through the windscreen, or into the side of a lorry.

She was about twenty miles from Courtbridge, and had just decided that the best thing to do when – if – she finally got home would be to park the car away from the house and slink in when no one was looking, when the car's penchant for hedges became too strong for Hetty. As she steered round a bend, the car went straight on, ploughing past a telegraph pole and not stopping until it was entirely surrounded by hawthorn and covered with late blossom. Hetty jerked against the taut seat-belt and knocked her head on the door pillar.

'Are you all right?'

Hetty opened her eyes and looked directly at the policeman. She felt entirely serene. 'I think so.'

'Anything broken, do you think?'

She shook her head and then the pain came. 'I'm not sure. My side hurts, and I feel a bit muzzy.'

'When did you last have anything to drink?'

Hetty had to think about this. 'About half-past five.'

'And how much did you drink?'

'About half a pint, I suppose.'

'You suppose? And what was it you were drinking, madam?'

'Oh, I had a Grapefruit Henry.'

The policeman's eyes narrowed. 'What's that?'

Hetty found herself having to think hard. 'Grapefruit juice and lemonade.'

The policeman turned his back and mumbled into his radio. When he turned back his expression was stern. 'This car has been reported stolen.'

'Well, it would have been,' said Hetty. 'I stole it.'

'Would you mind if I smelt your breath, miss?'

'I'd rather you didn't, but if you feel you must.'

He felt he must. 'You don't smell as if you've been drinking and, if you don't mind my saying so, you don't look like a car thief.' He began to check her limbs for broken bones.

'I'd mind it a whole lot more if you thought I did look like a car thief. Ouch. But I did steal it,' she added.

'Mmm,' said the policeman. 'The ambulance'll be here in a little while, and I don't think the car will burst into flames, so you just sit there.'

'Is the car badly damaged?'

'Don't you worry about that, dear. You just sit quietly.'

'But I *am* worried. How badly is it damaged? You must be able to tell me.'

The policeman shook his head. 'With luck you won't have to be cut out of it, but it hit a telegraph pole on its way down the bank. I'd say it was write-off.'

Hetty closed her eyes. She'd tried so hard to save Connor's car, and all she'd succeeded in doing was wrecking it. 'Oh, God.'

'There's no point in crying, love. If you didn't want the car damaged, you shouldn't have stolen it.'

He moved away. Hetty could hear him complaining to his colleague that it was a bloody domestic, and that people really should keep their private quarrels off the public highway.

Hetty subsided into an uneasy doze, which seemed preferable to facing the reality of the situation. She was forced out of it when the paramedics came. They strapped her to a board, which was incredibly uncomfortable, and put her into an ambulance.

'Where are you taking me?' she asked, as they secured the stretcher.

'Wheatstone General Hospital.'

'Oh.' Not too near Courtbridge then. And not the same hospital as Samuel was in. This seemed like good news. Would it be possible, she wondered, to go straight to her parents' from there? Could her father possibly come and get her before Connor did? But Connor wouldn't come and get her, would he? He'd go and see about his car. And having done that he'd come back to kill her. She was trying to calculate how long everything would take when her brain fogged over.

243

The casualty department was fairly quiet. A few people sat on chairs, flicking through magazines. One had his foot wound up in a bandage, and another had on a very grubby sling. Two others appeared to be waiting for people undergoing treatment. Hetty, victim of an RTA, was ushered straight in.

It was a relief to get off her board and on to an examination bed, and a greater relief to be rid of the paramedics, who had spent the short journey from the back of the ambulance to the cubicle discussing the damage on Connor's car. They seemed to wonder if it would have much scrap value, or whether it could be salvaged for parts. They might as well have been discussing whether Hetty's vital organs could be recycled, she thought.

A nurse with very cold hands but a warm smile probed Hetty tentatively, having removed her clothes and put her into a hospital gown. 'You'll definitely need to stay in for the night,' she said eventually. 'Just wait here quietly for the doctor.'

Hetty's eyes had just closed again when she heard hard, loud, long strides marching down the Marley tiles. There was a little bit of conversation and then the footsteps came nearer. Hetty hoped against hope that it was the doctor. The curtain was pulled violently aside. It wasn't.

'Are you all right?' Connor was white under his fading tan, sweat glistened on his neck and chest, revealed by his unbuttoned shirt. He hadn't shaved and his hair was wild.

'I'm fine. But the car –'

'So, you're fine are you? Well isn't that just dandy! You're fine and my car is a write-off. God, I know you have reason not to like me, Hetty, but I didn't think you hated me that much. And I didn't think you capable of spite, and spite on such a grand scale! I thought you had enough honour to fight me face to face, not steal what I cared most about and wreck it!'

'I didn't –' Her voice was barely audible.

'Oh, don't crow about getting the debt paid off. I don't want to hear about how you got the cash to do it. What I would like to know is why the fuck you didn't tell me, why you couldn't have just put our differences aside and told me? I could have got the cash to London without having to sacrifice my car to do it.'

'Please –'

'Don't you dare speak to me! You knew how much that car

meant to me, you thought of the one way you could really hurt me, and you used it. By God, if you weren't already in a hospital bed, I'd damn well put you in one myself! You could have been killed! Or crippled for life! Or was that part of your plan too, to have me had up for manslaughter!'

'Manslaughter?'

'Or are you trying to tell me you didn't know there was a problem with the steering?'

'I didn't – how could I have done?'

He ignored her strangled whisper. 'Do you really think that house – any house – is worth the kind of risk you took? If the steering had gone on the motorway you'd have killed yourself and taken dozens with you. It was the most thoughtless, childish, hysterical, half-baked, self-indulgent, idiotic thing to do. Why the fuck didn't you tell me?'

Hetty hesitated a moment to see if he was going to allow her time to answer.

'Well?' he demanded, having deemed three seconds enough.

'I didn't think you'd take too kindly at being woken at two in the morning, which is when I first thought of the plan –'

'Oh, didn't you?' Sarcasm like molten metal flowed over the white heat of his anger. 'You thought I'd take kindly to finding my car gone, just before it was due to be sold, and you missing too? You thought I'd appreciate spending the entire day worried sick, waiting for the police to come and tell me you were dead? Wondering what could have happened to you, what lunatic notion you'd taken into your head about paying off the loan? I had it all set up to do that, you know. But oh no, you couldn't let me, Conan the Barbarian, save the house. It had to be Hetty Saves the Day, and to hell with the consequences.'

'I really –'

'To think I thought . . . Thank God I found out what a stupid, heartless, thoughtless little bitch you are before it's too late!'

Hetty closed her eyes and listened for the sounds of him leaving. They didn't come.

'And when the fuck can I take you home?'

'Not until she's had the gash in the back of her head seen to,' said a woman's voice. 'And been thoroughly tested.'

Hetty's eyes flew open in time to see a diminutive creature in a white coat and a stethoscope reduce Connor to silence. He glared at the doctor, and glared at Hetty. 'So you're a liar as well as everything else, are you?' Then he strode off down the passage.

'God, they're beautiful when they're angry,' said the doctor when the echoes of his footsteps had died away. 'Don't worry, I'm sure he'll forgive you.'

'I doubt it,' said Hetty, 'I killed his car.'

Caroline collected Hetty after a second night in hospital. The cut in her head had been neatly stapled, and no other injuries discovered. The police had told her that Connor was not going to press charges. Probably, thought Hetty, deeply depressed, so he wouldn't have to see her in court. Caroline, who, during Hetty's day of tests, had plied her with grapes, magazines and a bottle of champagne, which they shared with all the staff, was to take her back to Phyllis's.

'It's all been worked out. Your mother will come for you as soon as she can, but you've got to have complete rest for a few days, so you can't go back to Courtbridge House.'

'Why don't you just tell me the truth, Caroline? Connor wouldn't let me within a mile of the place, even if I wanted to go.'

'Oh, no! I don't think he's said anything like that. Although he is still hopping mad, of course.' Caroline shot her a glance as she changed gear. 'You must have been a bit mad yourself, don't you think?'

'At the time it seemed the only logical thing. I didn't want Connor to sell his car. I needed to get to London to pay off the loan. It killed two birds with one stone. I didn't know about the steering fault.'

'I told him you didn't, but I'm afraid he's too angry to listen to reason.'

'I can't blame him, I suppose.'

'And I *think* he minds more about what might have happened to you than about the car.'

'But you can't be sure? Well, I can. He may have felt a moment or two of anxiety about me, but that'll soon be forgotten. After all, I'll get better. His car won't.'

'I'm afraid you're probably right.'

246

Hetty turned to stare out of the window, biting her lip, fighting tears.

'The bank holiday wedding people confirmed,' Caroline went on, observing Hetty's averted head. 'And Mrs Makepiece sent her cheque. Phyllis told me. She's had several other inquiries too. It seems everyone wants to have a rural celebration at Courtbridge House.'

Hetty got her voice under control. 'Oh, good. I'm really, really glad. But I won't be able to go back, you know. Ever.'

Caroline didn't speak immediately. Hetty had half hoped that she would protest and argue and tell her not to be silly. 'Well, not for a bit anyway,' she said eventually.

The following morning, Phyllis came into Hetty's room carrying a tray.

'I rang your mother, as you asked, and managed to persuade her not to come, but she wanted to know if you'd done anything about those people in Shropshire.' Phyllis set the tray down on Hetty's knees. 'I told her I didn't expect you'd done anything yet, and may not for a while. Was I right?'

'Absolutely. And you really shouldn't spoil me like this. There's nothing wrong with me.'

'Tell me that after you've been to the bathroom and I'll believe you,' said Phyllis, handing Hetty a dressing-gown.

Having done this, Hetty was very pleased to get back into bed. 'I feel as if I've been run over by a bus.'

'Jolly lucky you weren't. Connor said the car had a steering fault. You could have been killed.' Phyllis perched on the end of the bed, nearly causing Hetty's cornflakes to spill. 'It was why he reported the car stolen. He knew you'd taken it and wanted you stopped before you – '

'Killed myself?'

She nodded. 'He'll probably come in to see you later.'

Hetty suddenly felt incredibly weak. 'I can't face him. I feel so guilty about his car. Does he know why I stole it?'

'I think so. He told me about the loan, by the way. You poor child. Couldn't tell me about the loan, couldn't tell Connor about the listing. Well, I've told him now. And I *think* he's agreed.'

'Oh, good.'

'Now I ought to cut along to Courtbridge, if you don't mind being left. With Connor out there's no one to open up.'

'With Connor *in* there's no one to open up.'

'He's really a very good man you know, under all that bluster.'

Hetty managed a feeble smile. 'I'm glad he'll have you as a character witness when he murders me for writing his car off.'

Hetty slept for most of the day, glad to be away from Courtbridge House, away from Connor. She desperately wanted to avoid seeing him. She would have to learn to live with her guilt, and it would be easier if Connor's hatred wasn't branded on her memory. She'd seen it once, and that threatened to leave a permanent scar.

Phyllis came back at tea-time. 'I'd better warn you that Connor's planning to come and see you this evening.'

'Oh, God! Can't you tell him I'm too ill?'

'Too late, I'm afraid. Anyway, he's probably had a chance to calm down, now. He might not shout.'

CHAPTER TWENTY-THREE

Connor didn't look as if Phyllis's presence outside the door would be at all inhibiting. His expression was grim. He seemed tired, and there was a frown etched between his brows. If Hetty hadn't found moving so difficult she'd have run away. She hunched down into her pillows, hoping to be camouflaged in Phyllis's floral nightie by the daisies and hollyhocks that bedecked the bed linen.

'How are you feeling?' he demanded. 'And don't,' he added tersely, 'say "fine".'

Hetty licked her lips. 'Better.'

'Why didn't you tell me you were hurt in the accident?'

Hetty felt she could take this two ways. She could accept responsibility for Connor's justifiable anger, or she could find some anger of her own to work on. She took the moral low road. 'So, it's an accident now, is it? I thought you thought I'd done it on purpose!'

'If I thought that at the time I've learnt differently since. I absolve you of trying to commit suicide.'

'What?'

'The car is covered in blood.'

'Oh.' Her feeble spurt of anger subsided and she bit back the word 'sorry', knowing it would result in him laying violent hands on her. Part of her wished he would anyway, in the hope that having shaken her senseless he might take her into his arms, that she might break through his icy fury. The other part, the sensible, this-is-real-life-not-a-Clark-Gable-film part, felt it best to pick her words. 'Head wounds always bleed a lot.'

'I'll have to have it reupholstered.'

'What? The car? But I thought, I mean, isn't it a write-off?'

'No. It's damaged of course, but not terminally. It can be repaired.'

'Then why, I mean, why are you still – why aren't you thrilled?'

'You could have been killed. I don't think that's anything to get excited about.'

'Goodness me, in the hospital you seemed ready to kill me yourself!'

'Squeezing the breath out of you with my own hands is one thing. Having you hurtle through the windscreen of my car is another.'

Breath-squeezing still seemed on the cards. 'I always wear my seat-belt. It was only the back of my head that got cut.'

'No thanks to you.'

'And your car can be repaired, so everything –'

'Oh yes, Hetty. My car can be repaired, the loan is paid off, the house will be listed; and so, from your point of view, and in your words, everything is just "fine". So you can now take yourself off, out of my house, out of my business, and leave me to get on with my life!' He glared at her, his eyes like black ice, hard and unforgiving, then he turned and walked out of the room.

Hetty pulled the pillow over her head and kept it there for a long time.

Caroline came the following morning and Hetty explained to her and Phyllis that she couldn't go back to Courtbridge House and why.

'Bet you don't need me anyway. I mean, I know there's this big wedding coming up, but all the systems are in place. I'd be a bit spare even if Connor hadn't thrown me out.'

'Do you want us to confirm or deny that?' asked Phyllis. 'And I really don't think you should take any notice of what Connor says in a rage. If you wanted to stay.'

'I don't. I really don't.' If she'd felt nothing for Connor she could easily have ignored his wrathful words – after all, it was still Samuel's house, not his. But she loved him. His hatred of her was infinitely painful.

'I'll miss you so,' said Caroline, unwittingly confirming that she agreed with Hetty that Connor really did hate her.

'So, what will you do?' asked Phyllis. 'Get in touch with those people in Shropshire?'

Hetty nodded and explained to Caroline about her father's distant cousins and their desperate need for a break.

'Well, I suppose it's a promotion,' said Caroline. 'Last time you were only a house-sitter. This time, you're a hotel manager.'

'Next time I'll find my own job,' said Hetty. 'But this way, I've got somewhere to stay, and I don't need to go through a long interview process. And I really need to earn some proper money as soon as I can.'

'But how will you get there?' Caroline made Shropshire sound like the Himalayas.

'Public transport,' said Hetty. 'Heard of it, have you?'

Caroline snorted. 'I'll drive you up. I'd enjoy it, and it would give me a chance to check out the talent. I'm still determined to find you a nice man. I had hoped that you and Connor might –'

'Out of the question,' said Hetty, very firmly indeed.

'OK,' said Caroline. 'But do let me drive you.'

As it turned out, Hetty didn't need anyone to drive her. For in front of Phyllis's house, two days later, her car was parked, the yellow 2CV she had sold. Phyllis handed her an envelope through which some keys were protruding. It had her name scrawled on it, and Hetty didn't need to be a graphologist to work out who'd written it, or what mood they were in when they wrote it.

There was a brief note. *Here's your car back. I've had it serviced and valeted. I'm away for a couple of weeks.*

Hetty started to protest, but Phyllis cut her short. 'It's only fair. You sacrificed your car, which you paid for –'

'My parents paid, actually. I must pay them back.'

'– for his heritage. You also risked your life –'

'But I didn't *know* I was –'

'– for his heritage. He's a proud man, Hetty. You must allow him to repay you as he thinks fit.'

Hetty was forced to laugh. 'If he really repaid me as he thinks fit he'd be prosecuted. I hope he didn't pay over the odds to get my car back.'

Hetty got lost three times, in spite of, or because of, the detailed directions given her. It was tea-time when she arrived, and pouring with rain.

The hotel was just on the Welsh border, built in England, but with Wales as the view out of the windows. It was a long, low building, which had been added to over the generations, and was now famous for the level of comfort and cuisine it provided.

At first Hetty was very flattered that its owners, a couple with two young children and a very new baby, should entrust it to her care. But as they showed her around, and she realized how exhausted they all were, with the baby waking five times a night, and the toddlers needing their share of attention, she accepted they would have left a drunken axe-murderer in charge if it had meant they could have a break.

Almost all the staff welcomed Hetty kindly, if a little warily. Only the housekeeper resented her employers for thinking that Hetty was necessary. But the others recognized the owners' need for a holiday, and if Hetty meant they got one, they were prepared to give her a go.

'We haven't had a day off – except to have Suky –' Brenda joggled the baby up and down, 'since we bought the place. We're full quite a lot of the time. You won't get much time off.'

'That's all right. I like being busy.' I find it's just the thing for a broken heart. She added this rider silently. This time her mother hadn't gone before her, telling all and sundry about the state of her emotions.

'So, you'll be all right for a month? We're being lent a house in France. My mother's coming with us to help with the children.'

'Well, I'll let you know how I get on, shall I? I might drive away all your custom, and your staff might hate me. But I should think I could manage for a month without destroying your goodwill.'

'A month would be bliss. We never go away during the high season usually, it's just we're so shattered, and your mother said –'

'I hope she didn't say I had a degree in hotel management, or anything like that?'

'Oh, no. In fact she said you weren't qualified at all, but picked things up quickly, and got on with people.'

Hetty laughed. 'Well, I hope that's true. I'm sure I shall enjoy it.'

Hetty realized that her mother had been right: with the right help, she could manage a hotel. Her method was to ask everyone what their job was, exclaim long and loud at the skill they must have to do it, and then constantly remind them what a good job they were doing.

The chef was Italian, lured to the country by his first job as head chef and the opportunity to be as creative as he liked. Despite being determinedly homosexual, he adored Hetty. He was accustomed to being asked whether marmalade really went well with haddock, not to being told, 'God, you're *so* imaginative! This is *to die* for.' He would do anything for her, insisted she was too thin, and took to making bacon butties and taking them out to her in the garden when he knew she hadn't eaten.

Winning the housekeeper round took more devious methods. Hetty managed to hint to her, without saying directly, that she had been taken on by the Wynn-Joneses more or less out of pity, because she had no other job to go to and needed to be trained to do *something*.

Slowly, Beryl unbent, and gradually learned to appreciate not having to deal with every little staff detail herself. All the girls, who doubled as waitresses or chambermaids as the need arose, were related to her one way or another and gave her no trouble. But that Giovanni in the kitchen was another matter.

Hetty worked long hours, far longer than the job demanded. But doing nothing gave her no pleasure, and while occasionally she walked in the hills, which were truly beautiful, they were the wrong hills, and the view from them was the wrong view.

In the afternoons, when the hotel guests were all about their business, the rooms were done, the tables for dinner were all set, and Giovanni was having his siesta, Hetty worked on clearing a long flower-border, which had once been part of the kitchen garden.

She found it very satisfying work. Llew, Beryl's cousin, teased her that she took as much satisfaction in digging up a whole nest of bindweed roots, white and as thick as twigs, as he did in digging a boiling of potatoes. Hetty accepted he was right. Although she knew she wouldn't be able to plant the bed until she could be sure every tiny fragment of root had been removed, she found the process of clearing extremely cathartic.

While she dug, she worked on her mind, trying to eradicate every little scrap of feeling she had for Connor. But that was a thankless task. Not even bindweed was as resistent to eradication.

The Wynn-Joneses telephoned after the first week. Brenda spoke to Hetty.

'Is everything OK?'

'Fine. I'm getting the hang of it a bit now.'

'Oh, good. The thing is, we may not be able to come back quite as soon as we'd hoped. Paul's got glandular fever . . .' A while later, having been assured that Hetty could cope, Brenda finished, 'And remember, I'm only on the end of a phone if you want me.'

When Hetty put the phone down later she reflected on how life seemed to run in repeating patterns. She'd been sent to Court-bridge House as a stopgap, just for a while until Samuel came out of hospital. That hadn't turned out quite as her mother had promised. Nor had this job. She had been a three-week-holiday stand-in, now it looked as if she'd be there for two months. When she finally got home, she determined to take charge of her life, and not let it take charge of her.

The main holiday season was over, but the hotel was almost as busy with people on autumn breaks. Hetty was tugging with both hands at a briar root one afternoon when she heard a voice behind her.

'I was told I'd find you here.'

Hetty let go of the root and straightened up. It was Connor. She couldn't see the details of him as he had his back to the October sun. But his huge, craggy shape was the same.

For a moment she felt faint, with shock and with longing, and with the desire to fling her arms around him, to feel his solid bulk, just to make sure he was real. Then she remembered how they'd parted, and wished he hadn't caught her wearing a boiler suit and over-large wellington boots, her fingers stiff with earth. Why on earth had he come? It must be to do with Samuel. Her heart started to jump unhealthily, and she pulled off her gardening gloves and gave him a rather formal smile.

'Hello. What are you doing here?'

'It's all right. I haven't come to murder you. Though I doubt if any court would blame me if I did.'

He wouldn't have talked like that if Samuel had died. 'Because of your car?'

'Because you ran away while I was out of the country and couldn't stop you.' His gaze flicked over her briefly, as if making sure she was still intact.

'I didn't run. I was sent. I had very clear instructions.'

'I know. That's partly why I came. To apologize.'

Hetty wished she hadn't referred to their parting. The trouble was, it still hurt. 'A postcard would have done. You didn't have to come all this way to say sorry.' She swallowed. 'Thank you for my car, by the way.'

'I wouldn't have given it to you if I'd known you'd use it to leave me.'

'I thought that *was* why you gave it to me. To give me no excuse to hang around.'

Although he still had his back to the sun and his features were in shadow, she could see him wince. 'Surely you know me better than to take what I say in a temper seriously?'

'No, I don't.'

'Hetty – I do realize I behaved abominably. I shouted and ranted when I wanted . . .'

'You wanted?'

He half smiled, half frowned, ending up with an expression of extreme ruefulness. 'To put you over my knee.'

Hetty was outraged. 'Some apology.'

'I know how dreadful that must sound. What I mean is, if I'd actually touched you, I would never have been able to stop myself – I mean, you would have known – how I feel about you.'

'I got the message perfectly well, thank you!'

'But you didn't! You got the wrong message. And you were lying there looking so pale, with stitches in your head. And I was so worried and frustrated, I just shouted.' He paused. 'I'm making a complete hames of this. The trouble is, I haven't had much practice at apologizing.'

'So I see.' In fact, Hetty had already forgiven him, but she picked at her nails so he wouldn't see it in her eyes.

'There's an awful lot unsaid between us, Hetty.'

His tone forced her to look up. 'Is there?'

'You know there is. But don't worry, I realize this isn't the time or the place to rake over the past.'

'Good.'

'So, what are you doing?' He indicated her border. 'Restoring the kitchen garden?'

'Not really. Only this bed. And probably not for vegetables.

But it was a jungle of weeds, and it's a lovely sheltered wall, perfect for fruit trees and things. It was wasted on brambles and ash seedlings. Not to mention the nettles and convolvulus.' Aware her conversation had become as rambling as the briar rose she had been digging out, she stopped.

'I see.'

Quite what he saw she could only speculate, but she was very aware of her boiler suit. She needed to wear it as protection from the brambles and gardening was hot work: she was only wearing a pair of pants underneath. Without checking, she couldn't remember how many buttons she had undone. A trickle of sweat rolled down the space between her breasts.

Connor had his jacket hooked over his shoulder, and his shirt-sleeves rolled up. 'It's surprisingly warm, for the time of year.'

It was unlike Connor to talk about the weather. Hetty felt he must be giving her a hint. She put a hand casually between her breasts and felt the top button loose between her fingers. 'Yes.'

She turned away from him and discovered her boiler suit was open to the waist. She did up two buttons.

Connor was smiling slightly when she turned back. 'So, restoring things has got to be a habit with you?'

'I suppose it has.' Especially when I'm suffering from a broken heart, she added to herself. 'It is hard work.'

'And hard work is good for you?'

Hetty nodded. It used up lots of energy and helped her to sleep at night.

Connor shifted his feet. Hetty noticed that he'd polished his shoes. It was such an un-Connor-like thing to do, she thought he must be going somewhere else. 'Are you on your way somewhere, or have you time for a cup of coffee or something.'

'I've come to see you. And I'm hoping for lunch.'

Hetty laughed and relaxed, suddenly able to enjoy being with him. 'I expect I can rustle up a tin of beans.'

He grinned back. 'How much longer do you expect to be here?'

She shrugged. 'I'm not sure. The owners have come back, but I think they may offer me a permanent job. It's tough running a hotel when you've got a young baby.'

His eyebrows came together for a moment. 'Will you take it? The job, I mean.'

Hetty shrugged again. 'I'm not sure. I may. They're very good to me and I've got a lovely little flat. It is very beautiful here.' She gestured to the tree-covered hills, which were just beginning to turn. 'Let's sit down for a minute.' She indicated the bench that was placed so guests could enjoy the view.

Connor sat down next to her, but he didn't seem well-disposed to the beauties of nature. Something was bothering him. Hetty suddenly panicked that he was bracing himself to give her bad news.

'Everything's all right, is it? At Courtbridge? Samuel's not – dying or anything?'

'We're all dying, Hetty. And Samuel's doing it a bit faster than the rest of us, but he's nowhere near there yet.'

'What a relief.'

'Even Clovis is still annoying the hell out of everyone, and if ever an animal had outlived its natural span it's him.' He turned towards her, still awkward. 'I just came to apologize, not to give you bad news.'

'So, you haven't got to sell the house to provide an income for Samuel or anything?'

'The house is doing that without having to be sold.'

'But you could still sell it. Later. If you wanted to?' She concentrated on sounding as if this was a good idea.

'Could I? Wouldn't you find some way to stop me?'

'I couldn't drive off with Courtbridge House like I did your car. And as I'm not there, I don't see that I could do anything.'

'You could go there. In fact, I wish you would. Everyone misses you so.'

'Do they? I would have thought they'd have got used to me not being there by now.' Most people had, according to Caroline, with whom Hetty was in regular contact.

'No. There was a big hole when you left.'

Hetty suddenly felt very hot and uncomfortable in her wellingtons. She wanted to kick them off, but they were borrowed and had a smell all their own, which, on a day as warm as this, would waft up to Connor. She curled her toes inside them and felt the grit and dirt that had accumulated. Her feet would be filthy too.

'So, will you come? For a visit?'

Part of her yearned to see Courtbridge House again, to be with everyone, with Connor. But her more sensible side wanted to know why she was even thinking about opening up a wound that had barely begun to heal. 'Oh, I don't think I should. You know what they say, you should never go back.'

'Who's "they"?'

'Oh, you know.' Hetty made a flapping gesture. 'They!'

'I don't think you should let yourself be governed by rules written by people who don't really exist.'

'No, well, I suppose you're right.' *Ask me to come again, and I'll say yes.*

He didn't ask again. 'What will you do, if you don't stay on?'

'Apply for jobs, I suppose. I can't go on letting my mother find me gainful employment with my hapless relations for ever. Or I might go abroad.'

He picked up one of her hands. His were firm and warm. Hetty's instantly became moist with sweat. 'Come and see us first, for Samuel's sake if nothing else.'

'Caroline told me that you've had the barn converted for him. How is he liking it?'

'He loves it. He's so much more mobile, with all the floors being level.'

'He doesn't miss being in the big house?'

'No. He realizes he couldn't manage there even if most of the rooms weren't on show. And he's happy being so independent.'

'What about Phyllis? Is she still helping? Or have you driven her away?'

'Phyllis and I have our moments. But she's still as busy as ever. It's nice now there's a bit more money to spend. We've done awfully well since Caroline became our Events Manager.'

'Don't tell me she's turned Courtbridge House into a casino or anything dreadful?'

'No, but that's a thought . . .'

'Connor!'

'Only joking. But she does have some brilliant ideas. Jack's thrilled. Not only is she earning money, but she doesn't have time to spend much. He wins both ways.' He began fiddling with her hand as if it were inanimate. 'She's applied for permission for us to do weddings – the ceremonies – and not just receptions, which we've got down to a fine art. And we even had a karaoke evening in the great hall –'

'Good God! I bet Phyllis had something to say about that!'

'She said it very quietly. It was one of the Brownie fathers' firm's do, and she knows how much the Brownies help the house.'

Hetty laughed. 'And did you get up and sing, "Great Balls of Fire"?'

'I don't sing, Hetty. I play the piano.'

Hetty swallowed. 'So you do.'

'I miss you, Hetty.'

A trickle of saliva caught her at the back of the throat and she nearly choked. 'Oh? Why?'

'I miss you singing around the house.'

Hetty blushed. 'You could get a canary.'

'Clovis would eat it.'

Hetty had to smile. 'Unlikely. Not unless the canary actually lay down in his bowl. The dogs would get it long before Clovis had a chance.'

'You'd better come instead then.'

It was as flattering an invitation as she was likely to get from him. 'OK,' she said, after a moment. 'But only for a visit. To see Samuel.'

Connor's lashes narrowed in reply, causing Hetty to jump up suddenly. 'Let's eat,' she said quickly.

CHAPTER TWENTY-FOUR

It was misty when Hetty set off for Courtbridge House, and far later than she'd intended. The St Martin's summer had been replaced by frosty mornings and chilly nights. Fires were being lit in the hotel now, and although there were still leaves on the trees, drifts of them were heaped at the sides of the roads, like soggy cornflakes.

She'd dressed carefully, glad that the change in the weather had justified a new pair of boots and an elegant woollen skirt. She wanted to erase from Connor's mind her grubby, *décolleté* boiler suit and smelly wellington boots.

She took the journey slowly, glad she'd arranged to stay with Caroline and wouldn't have to drive back until the following afternoon. It was early evening when she finally arrived.

The first thing she saw that was different was a notice on the gate saying CLOSED UNTIL EASTER. She remembered her horror when she discovered that the house opened at all. It seemed such a long time ago now.

Connor appeared as she was opening the gate. He didn't hug her, but his eyes had a burning quality that made her heart lurch.

'You're late.' He closed the gate behind her and opened her car door.

'I know. I'm sorry,' she said as she got out. 'Last-minute crisis. I did ask someone to ring and say I would be.' She felt desperately shy and unsure how to greet him. If he'd been anyone but Connor she would have kissed him. 'Where are the dogs?'

'Come and see.' He took her hand and led her towards the house. The dogs rushed up the moment they heard her footsteps. She crouched down to submit to the onslaught of licking, yipping and love. She embraced them both, laughing and trying to avoid their warm, dry tongues. 'It's lovely to see you, darlings, but it's your Uncle Samuel I've really come to see.'

'Oh, he's not in,' said Connor. 'Phyllis and he have gone some-where for the day.'

'But I've come all this way to see him!' Heaven forbid that Connor should think she'd come to see him.

He shrugged. 'You're staying the night, aren't you? You can see him tomorrow.'

'But I have to leave early.'

'You've only just arrived, Hetty. Don't worry about leaving yet. Come and see Clovis, he's in the kitchen.'

'That hasn't changed, then.'

But the kitchen had – beyond recognition. It appeared at first sight to be a perfect period restoration.

'Goodness me!' Hetty heaved Clovis on to her shoulder so he could feel near her but not breathe over her. 'I'd hardly know the place!'

'Do you like it? This is what Phyllis describes as a "working display kitchen". What she means is she can fool the public into thinking people actually cook in here.'

'But don't they? It seems a shame. It's so lovely.'

'Don't gush. You sound like Caroline.'

'Shut up and let me look.'

The tat had been replaced by good, solid pieces of furniture. The Formica cupboards with rotting bottoms had been replaced by Peter's handiwork. Shiny copper and brass pans hung from hooks: a Scotch airer hung above the range and from that hung a selection of suspiciously well-ironed glass-cloths and tea-towels. They were there, Hetty could tell at a glance, for show. Heaven help the poor sap who used one.

'I don't believe it! That's a fake *armoire*, with wire netting! Not very authentic for an English country kitchen!'

'*That*,' said Connor, making it clear what he thought of the idea, 'is how it gets to be a "working" kitchen. A bloody great piece of furniture with nothing but knick-knacks in it.'

'So you don't cook in here then? Look, a combination hob! Very posh.'

'I prefer to cook in Samuel's barn most of the time. It's purely functional.'

'So what else has been going on since I've been away?'

Connor took her on a tour of the house, the dogs fussing at

their heels. Nothing else had changed as dramatically as the kitchen, but there were improvements everywhere. The house had lost much of the gentlemanly shabbiness it had had when she had first arrived, but it was still as beautiful.

'Show me Samuel's barn,' she said, after dawdling in the great hall, unwillingly remembering times spent singing there with Connor. 'I'm dying to see it.'

Connor hesitated, as if he realized there was more to Hetty's wish to get away from the hall than just curiosity to see the barn.

'You did convert it, didn't you? You haven't got Samuel locked in a cellar somewhere?'

He frowned slightly at her glibness, then he led the way across the yard while the dogs ran ahead. Hetty attempted a few light-hearted remarks as they walked, but after the first few she dried up. She was finding her turbulent emotions harder and harder to contain.

She'd thought it would be all right, coming to Courtbridge for a visit. But she hadn't known she would be alone with Connor, or she might have listened to the unspecified 'they' and kept away. There was too much unfinished, unspoken business between them – business better left unfinished.

'This is wonderful!' Hetty was grateful to be able to sound and feel so sincere in her praise as they inspected the barn. 'It's perfect. Peter has done a good job.'

'It's mostly maple. It's a light wood and looks nice with the stone walls.'

'It must have cost a fortune!' A second later Hetty wished she hadn't said that. It was vulgar and confrontational. 'I mean –'

'I know what you mean, Hetty. You mean, it must have cost a fortune. And it did. The wide doorways, the ramps, the low sinks. It was expensive. But I thought once Samuel dies, we could let it to people with disabilities.' He scowled down at her. 'At a vastly inflated rate, of course. To ensure I get my money back.'

Hetty wanted to kick herself. 'I didn't mean that! It's just –'

'Just what? I wish you'd say what you mean for once in your life.'

'It's lovely,' she said, lame but sincere.

'Now, there's something else I want to show you. You stay here, dogs. You,' he put his hand on her shoulder, 'come with me.'

It was the coach-house. He led her up the stone steps that went up the side of the building and let her inside.

It was beautiful. But where she'd imagined two rooms – small, but ideal for a holiday home – he had one vast space. It had a light, varnished-wood floor with rugs. There was little furniture but what there was fitted in with the simplicity of the décor. Thick cream-coloured curtains swept the floor. There was concealed lighting somewhere, which gave the impression of sun coming from every window. Two huge sofas were drawn up to a wood-burning stove at one end. Its doors were open and some sweet-smelling logs still glowed faintly within its depths.

Connor piled on more logs. 'Just in time. It gives out quite a lot of heat, but there are radiators too.'

Hetty had noticed them. 'But what about a staircase? Or are people going to have to use the outside steps?'

'Here.' Behind a wooden wall she hadn't noticed at first was a door, which led to a flight of wooden steps that mirrored the ones on the outside of the building. 'The kitchen's downstairs. Come and see it.'

He led the way down the steps, not giving Hetty a chance to ask about the bathroom or the bedroom, which she guessed must be where they had talked about it going, that life-time ago.

The kitchen was tiny, ergo-dynamic and modern, well-lit and practical. Every inch was used. There was a specially narrow dishwasher and fridge. A combination hob slotted in beside a section of slate, presumably for hot pans. Next to that was a shallow porcelain sink, full-sized, but set end-on, to save more space. There was an oven somewhere, and Connor pulled out what looked like a drawer to create an extra working surface. There was also a satisfyingly deep window-sill, which had pots of basil and coriander on it. It was as different from the Courtbridge House kitchen as possible.

'So, what do you think?' There was a certain tension in his attitude.

'It's – amazing. Did Peter design it, or did you get someone in?'

'I designed it. Peter built it.'

Hetty was impressed. 'And have you been living here?'

Connor nodded. 'I sold my flat in London.' If he'd been anyone else, she would have thought he looked a bit shamefaced. 'It's handy for Samuel. He has a buzzer he can press if wants me. And I can't stand living in the house when it's open to the public.'

'But Connor, think of the rent you could be getting for this. It would be perfect for honeymoon couples.'

'It wasn't ready for this season.'

'But you could let it out over Christmas. You could charge anything you like. It's such a perfect love-nest, with the wood-burning stove and things.' She coughed suddenly, as she realized she was expressing her own dreams out loud. 'How are you going to pay for it, if you don't let it?' she added, and instantly wished she hadn't.

Connor scowled. 'Because, Miss Money-Grubber, we'd get much more if we let the big house, for people who want to bring their whole families together for a traditional country Christmas in a stately home. And Samuel and I do have to live somewhere.'

Hetty sighed and looked out of a tiny slit window, which was set in the thickness of the stone. The huge chestnut tree in the yard had long since lost its leaves, and now its branches were tearing about in a wild semaphore, no doubt telling her to shut up and mind her own business.

'I'm sorry, Connor,' she said, still staring at the tree. 'I had no right to say that. It's none of my business any more.'

He came up behind her and laid his hand on her shoulder.

'It's OK. I only just thought of that Christmas thing, because you challenged me. Yet again.'

What did he mean? They'd always argued, but surely she hadn't challenged him? But she didn't dare turn round and ask him, in case he read her feelings and didn't return them. He was being very nice to her, but that was probably just remorse, for having been so angry with her before.

'It's a good idea, though.'

'Yes – I'm becoming quite the ideas man, now you're not here. Now, you go upstairs and sit by the fire while I go and start the potatoes.'

'But I'm having dinner with Caroline!'

He shook his head slowly. 'She had to go out this evening. But she will be in later, if you want to stay the night with her.'

'But I was going to spend the evening with her! That was what was planned!'

'Why don't you ring her? The phone's upstairs, by the window. I'll bring us some drinks when I've put the potatoes on.'

Confused, Hetty trotted upstairs and found the phone. She dialled the number, prepared to ask some penetrating questions about the morality of setting up her friend without consulting her. Caroline answered remarkably quickly.

'Hi! Hetty! Where are you?'

'In the coach-house. Caroline –'

'It's to die for, isn't it? Straight out of a mag, only nicer. That man's got taste.'

'It's a love-nest, Caroline.'

'Nothing wrong with that, is there? Are you going to sleep with him?'

'I came to visit Samuel and found myself set up for a night of passion!'

'That's all right, isn't it? You still love him, don't you?'

Hetty lowered her voice, in case Connor could hear. 'Yes, but I've no idea how he feels about me. For all I know he still hates me for what I did to his car. He hasn't so much as kissed me.'

'Then kiss him! And as for hating you, you know what they say about it being the next best thing to love?'

'Caroline, you're impossible!'

'No, just manipulative. And romantic. If he wants to wine and dine you, let him. And if you don't want to sleep with him, he's not going to force you, and you can come here. Now, if you don't mind, there's a really good film just starting. Byee.'

Hetty regarded the receiver with hurt surprise, and was still holding it when Connor appeared with a tray.

'So what did Caroline say?'

'That there was a really good film starting.'

'So you're staying then?' Connor turned away, so Hetty couldn't see if he was pleased or sorry.

'For supper, yes.'

'Good. Now,' he handed her a glass, 'whisky, and something to eat.' He handed her a plate with some water biscuits spread with hummus. 'Come by the fire. The sofa's very comfortable.'

Hesitantly she moved from the austerity of the stool by the

telephone to the downy luxuriance of the sofa. 'Oh. It's a sofa-bed!' She smoothed her hand over it, glad she'd found something positive to say. 'You could put another couple up in here, if you wanted to.'

'I suppose so. I can't see myself wanting to, though.'

'Of course, I haven't seen the bedroom yet. You may have put bunks in it.'

'I haven't. Just the one bed.'

He sat down next to her – unnecessarily, as there was a perfectly good sofa the other side of the fire. They sipped in silence. Then they both started to speak at once. 'What were –' she began, but stopped abruptly.

'Sorry, do go on,' said Connor.

'No, you. I was only going to ask what the visitor numbers were in the end.'

He looked at her in bemusement. 'I haven't the faintest idea. You'd have to ask Phyllis.'

'So, what were you going to say?'

'I was going to ask you if you knew Jack and Caroline are thinking about having a baby?'

She took a sip of her whisky. She did, but if she told him that it would leave them without a topic of conversation again. 'It takes more than thinking, doesn't it?'

'I expect they do that anyway. I'm just wondering how Court-bridge House will do without its Events Manager.'

She lowered her glass, horrified lest all this buttering up was because he wanted her to come back and work. 'Are you offering me a job?'

'Good God no!' He was equally horrified. 'Whatever gave you that idea?'

Hetty shrugged, hurt and relieved at the same time. 'I just wondered why you brought the subject up, if you didn't have an ulterior motive.'

'Just making conversation. You wouldn't be nearly as good at it as Caroline. You don't have her brass neck. Nor her contacts.'

'I'm sure I could develop a brass neck and contacts.'

'Do you want to?'

'Not particularly, no.'

266

'Then don't. More whisky?'

'No thanks. I've got to drive to Caroline's.'

He got up, presumably to fetch the whisky. 'She's not expecting you early.'

'I thought she was expecting me for dinner? She told me yesterday she was going to make chocolate mousse. My favourite.'

'She made the mousse. It's in the fridge.'

An excited panic enveloped her. If only she thought he loved her, she would have been ecstatic. 'Oh.'

'You don't have to stay the night or anything. I've got a key if Caroline's gone to bed. I just wanted to give you dinner.'

'Well, you can. But why are you so keen to give it to me?'

'Well, not because I think you're likely to die of malnutrition.'

'Why then?'

'Why do you think?'

'I don't know, that's why I'm asking. Conversation isn't exactly pouring from us now. How are we going to keep it up for another four hours or so?'

'My trouble is, I'm really better at shouting than communicating. Perhaps we should have another drink.'

'Do you think it'll help?'

'It might.'

'Then go ahead. I can't, but don't let me stop you.'

'But I've got a really nice bottle of wine to go with dinner.'

'I shouldn't have had the whisky. I can't have any more.'

'You *could* stay the night.' There was nothing in his expression to give her any hint of an ulterior meaning.

'On the sofa?'

'Wherever you like. Courtbridge House has seven bedrooms fit for habitation.'

'Seven? There must have been some clearing out done. Which rooms are bedrooms now?'

'Don't change the subject.'

'Please let me. The other one wasn't getting us anywhere.'

'I just want you to know that you can stay. Without obligation,' he added.

'What about Caroline?'

'Ring and tell her you're staying the night.'

Hetty couldn't think what she should do. If she told Caroline she was staying the night she was committed to doing so. 'You could drive me to Caroline's?'

He shook his head. 'I had a drink before you came.'

So much for not putting pressure on her to stay. 'If you were a gentleman, you'd've abstained.'

'If the moon was made of green cheese, pigs might fly. I am not, never have been, or never will be, a gentleman.' He looked down. 'You know that perfectly well.'

She knew nothing of the sort, but agreed with him anyway. 'I suppose so.'

'So, do I open the wine, or what?'

'I could take a taxi to Caroline's.'

He got up. 'You could.'

'One of the Brownie fathers has a taxi.'

'Naturally. I should think Caroline could produce her own Yellow Pages consisting entirely of Brownie dads.'

'You don't sound very pleased. I give us a solution to the problem and you go all grumpy. Not hard for you, of course.'

He leant his arm against the piece of maple above the stove which acted as a mantelpiece. 'You can't expect me to be pleased. I've planned a particularly good dinner to give you and all you can think about is going. Not very flattering.'

'If you want flattery you've asked the wrong girl to dinner.'

'I don't want flattery, and I've asked the right girl. The trouble is, now I've got her here, I don't know how to handle her.'

Handle – that sounded encouraging. 'Oh?'

'She's not my usual type. I usually go for sophisticated blondes. I don't love them, and they don't love me. It suits us both. When I leave, we neither of us have any regrets.' He paused. 'But when I am away from you, I regret every minute.'

Hetty bit her lip as she frantically tried to work out the subtext and failed. 'Should we order the taxi now?'

'No,' he said firmly. 'Come with me.'

Hetty knew she should feel relieved that he didn't declare his intention to carry her off to bed the moment they'd finished the chocolate mousse. Indeed, she felt disappointed.

Fortunately, this rogue emotion was blown away by the wind that hit them the moment they left the coach-house. He held her hand and pulled her across the yard into the main house.

'I wonder if that piece of string is still holding the loo together,' she said. 'I must go and see.'

Hetty took the opportunity to run her fingers through her hair and make sure her mascara hadn't fallen off.

Connor waited impatiently until she emerged, then he took her to the great hall, and switched on the lights. 'Better, don't you think?'

'Mmm. Much more atmospheric. Did you do it?'

He nodded. 'Neither Phyllis nor Peter seem to care much about lighting.'

Hetty shot him a teasing glance. 'You're really quite artistic for a – whatever you are.'

'I'm a civil engineer.'

Hetty snorted rudely. 'Engineer, maybe.'

He scowled and opened the piano. 'I bet you haven't had a good sing for ages.'

He started playing and, after a moment, Hetty realized it was one of her favourite songs. Unfortunately its words were about as politically incorrect as they could be. She'd always refused to sing it with him before.

Now, because of the whisky, and for want of anything better, she found herself humming along to Gershwin's music, and, gradually, the words of 'A Woman is a Sometime Thing' emerged from her mouth, reluctantly at first. Then she managed to forget she was a white female with feminist leanings and let the music carry her away.

Having broken the ice, Connor led her through all her favourites and, as her voice freed itself, so did her inhibitions. They may not be able to communicate in the normal way, but they were good at this.

They sang for about half an hour, after which Hetty was exhausted, not having breathed properly since the last time they had sung together, at the ruby wedding. Then Connor looked at his watch. 'Come on. I must see about dinner. But first, there's one last thing I want you to see.'

CHAPTER TWENTY-FIVE

He led her to one of the side barns and switched on the light. His car gleamed beneath it.

'You've restored it! It looks wonderful!' She turned to him. 'I'm so glad. I felt so dreadful wrecking it when all I meant to do was stop you selling it.'

He took hold of her hands. 'I know. And restoring it was sort of symbolic. I thought, if I got my car back, I could get you back.' He looked down at her hands, to avoid looking at her directly. 'If I ever had you in the first place.'

Hetty wished he'd just shout at her. At least then she usually managed to understand him. 'Did you do the work yourself?'

He released her hands. 'No. That would have taken far too long. It took long enough as it was.'

'Oh?'

'I made myself wait until it was finished before coming to see you.'

'Why?'

'I thought you needed time to forgive me. I behaved so abominably. I thought if I gave you time to forget, I'd have a better chance of . . .'

'Of what? You accuse me of not saying what I mean, but you're worse.'

'Am I? Well, I told you communicating isn't my strong point. I'm far better at cooking.'

Hetty despaired. Twice he'd nearly declared himself, told her that he cared about her. But until he actually came out with it, she couldn't take it on trust. She'd been hurt before.

'You'd better get on and cook, then. Having forced me to agree to eat it!'

Connor's eyes narrowed unnervingly. He took hold of her shoulders, turned her round and marched her out. 'Come on then.'

★

He opened the doors of the stove and restacked it with logs. Hetty drew the curtains and lit the table lamps, which gave the huge room a more intimate feel.

'You need a few screens, to make it more cosy.'

'You can do anything you like, of course. Now, will you be all right here while I cook? Would you like to use the bathroom or anything?'

'Actually, I don't know where the bathroom is.'

'Don't you? Didn't I show it to you?' She shook her head. 'It's up that little flight of stairs, through the bedroom. Help yourself. I must get on with supper.'

When Hetty saw the bedroom she knew why Connor hadn't shown it to her. It had honeymoon written all over it. The bed, which took up almost the entire space, was a four-poster, lightly draped with muslin curtains. On either side of it, table lamps, which had come on when she flicked on the wall switch, glowed invitingly. On a chest at the end of the bed, which was almost the only piece of furniture, was a huge vase of lilies. Their scent filled the room with delicate eroticism. On the floor by one side of the bed was a tray with a couple of glasses and a bottle of champagne. There was probably a concealed sound system somewhere set to play the right kind of romantic music. And, no doubt at all, Connor would be well provided with condoms.

But did Connor intend to seduce her or didn't he? Surely if he had, he wouldn't have been so reluctant to show her the bedroom. But if he didn't, why buy lilies and champagne?

One thing was certain – her body yearned for his. More than anything she wanted his arms around her, his naked skin against hers, the slight roughness of his hands against her flesh. She closed her eyes, supporting herself by one of the bedposts, inhaled the lilies and indulged in a moment's dreaming. She could almost feel his hands on her breasts, her waist, her hips. Then she straightened up and made her way to the bathroom.

This too had been prepared. Expensive bath oils, candles, soap, and huge, fluffy towels made their function clear. The bath was on the small side for sharing, but there was a very large, comfortable-looking bath mat.

But Hetty was by no means sure she would let Connor have his evil way with her, even if it was her evil way too. She'd been badly hurt before. Even without sleeping with him, Connor was taking a long time to get over. If she let him make love to her properly, his mark would be on her, possibly for life. No, the next time she let a man make love to her, she would be absolutely certain that he loved her. And this time, she would recognize a false promise made only to get her clothes off a mile away.

She made her decision and washed her hands, marring the gleaming porcelain of the sink and ruffling the towels. Did Connor know, she wondered, that new towels never dry you properly? If not, it was her duty to tell him.

She marched downstairs to the kitchen determined that nothing would persuade her to let Connor even suggest they should sleep together. She would sleep on the sofa-bed, in front of the fire, and she would sleep alone.

Connor was doing something to two little rounds of meat. He was concentrating, and a lock of hair had fallen down over his face. When he heard Hetty and glanced up, he looked flushed.

'You can see why I didn't show it to you, can't you?'

'What?'

'The bedroom. I knew it was a bad idea. But Caroline convinced me . . .'

'Yes?'

'That I should make everywhere as attractive as possible.' He looked Hetty directly in the eyes. He was ashamed. 'The bedroom is way over the top. But you're not to feel pressured.'

Hetty, who had been, and had been buoyed up by her indignation, felt the metaphorical steam hiss from under her, leaving her weak and vulnerable. 'No.'

'Anyway, I hope your appetite's in good form?'

'It will be when it sees what it's getting to eat. That looks delicious. Can I help?'

He opened his mouth to say no, but thought better of it. 'You could chop some parsley. It's already washed, over there.'

'I always use frozen parsley.' Hetty found a knife.

'I know you do. I don't.' He busied himself with some carrots and an orange before he looked up again. 'No, not that knife!' He took it out of her hand. 'And not like that!' With a different knife he made a few cross cuts into the parsley, which got the bunch under control, and then started chopping up and down at an amazing speed, pulverizing it.

Hetty giggled. 'You take food far too seriously, you know. It's only food.'

Connor growled. 'This isn't food. It's filet mignon cooked to a turn with red wine and herbs. So if you're just going to make frivolous remarks you can go away.' His glance took the sting from his words. 'I need to concentrate, and I can't with you here.'

'You never minded me in the kitchen before.'

'Much bigger kitchen. And this is different.'

She didn't ask him why it was different. 'If you're turning away a good galley-slave . . .'

'I am. There's a television in the little cupboard in the corner, by the fire. If you just open the doors, you can watch it.'

'Can I have another drink?' She didn't want to leave him. She wanted to watch him work his magic on the vegetables, see knives disappear into a blur of activity.

'No. It'll spoil your wine. I don't want you drunk.'

'You've changed your tune! A while ago you were pressing strong drink on me.'

He looked at her, his eyes full of a scary combination of lust, disapproval and promise. 'Go on. Shoo.'

Hetty made her way upstairs and slouched on the sofa, coming to the conclusion that she was very contrary. She was offended by his preparations for her seduction, and yet when he chased her away, she didn't want to go. She wanted to provoke the very thing that she should be fleeing from. It would definitely have been safer to have had dinner with Caroline. She found the television, but couldn't interest herself in either a game show, a gritty northern soap, or a documentary about koala bears who had syphilis.

She went back down to the kitchen. 'There's absolutely nothing on television. Are you sure I can't help?'

He was slicing carrots into hair-fine sticks with terrifying dexterity. 'Not if you want to be sure of keeping your fingers.' He gathered the carrots into a colander and rinsed them under the tap.

'Well, can I just stay in the corner and talk to you?'

'No.'

'Honestly! For someone who's set their bedroom up like a brothel' – it was a slander on the tastefulness of the room, but never mind – 'you might be a bit more conciliatory!'

'I told you, the bedroom was all Caroline's idea.'

'I think if Caroline wanted to seduce me she would have mentioned it before now.'

Connor laughed. 'I think you'll find that Caroline is fairly hooked on testosterone and all its tiresome side effects.'

'Speaking from personal experience, are you?'

'What sort of a question is that?' His eyes glittered alarmingly. 'Now, do you want to eat tonight or don't you? If you can't find anything on television there are some books under one of the windows.'

'Improving, are they?'

'I can't speak for the books, but the dinner won't be unless you get out of here!'

Hetty departed slowly. Having been thrown out of his kitchen for a second time didn't oblige her to hurry.

They ate on a small folding table in front of the fire. Connor said he would have preferred them to eat at a proper table, but that he hadn't organized one yet. Peter was going to build one when he had time. 'And the kitchen is no place for a romantic dinner.'

'I don't suppose the guests will mind not having a dining room.' Hetty broke off a bit of bread. 'This is delicious. I could eat the sauce with a spoon.'

'But do you mind not having a dining room?'

'Why should it matter if I mind or not?'

He put down his knife and fork. 'Because I want you to like it!'

'But why? I'm not involved with Courtbridge House any more. Does it matter what I think?'

'Of course! It was your idea to convert the coach-house in the first place.'

'For holiday lets, not as a home.'

'But do you like it as a home?'

'I love it. It's beautiful . . .'

'But? You prefer the main house?'

'No – yes. I don't know. It's like comparing oranges with apples.'

'And which do you prefer? Oranges or apples?'

274

Hetty felt helpless to say the right thing. 'Fruit salad?'

He gave her a smile that she hoped was lecherous. It might have been irritated. 'I haven't got fruit salad. How's your steak?'

'If I fished for compliments, I'd get told off. It's delicious,' she added.

Connor looked down. Instead of his usual bland acceptance of praise, he seemed pleased. 'Good. I . . .'

'You?'

'I chose it very carefully,' he finished.

'That wasn't what you were going to say.'

Connor took a breath. 'I was going to say that I really wanted this meal to be good.'

'You always do. You care about everything you cook. What's so special about this meal?'

'If I told you that, you might run away.'

Hetty's stomach dipped and lurched, and she wondered if she ought to run away while she still could.

'What about Caroline's mousse?' Connor took her plate and stacked it on his own.

Hetty shook her head, glad to be able to give a straightforward answer. 'Connor, I'm stuffed. I couldn't eat another thing.'

'Nor could I. What about coffee and brandy?'

She shook her head again. 'No thank you. But don't let me stop you.'

'Oh, don't go all polite on me, I can't bear it.'

'Sorry.'

'Hetty!' She bit her lip, feeling sheepish. 'Tell you what. Let's get this table out of the way and finish our wine in comfort. These chairs may be aesthetic, but they're not very comfortable.'

Somehow, Hetty found herself sitting next to Connor on the sofa in front of the fire, a glass of wine in her hand.

'All right?' he asked.

'Actually, I'm awfully hot.'

'Take off your jacket, then.'

She had meant him to move the sofa a little further away from the fire, but she found herself leaning forward so he could help her out of her jacket.

'And your boots.' These came off before she realized he intended to remove them. 'That's better. Now you can curl up properly.'

He took her feet on to his lap. 'Lie back and relax, Hetty. You don't have to go anywhere.' He took her feet between his hands and gently began to stroke them.

Hetty closed her eyes. She didn't have to go anywhere. There were seven bedrooms and a sofa-bed to protect her virtue, and it was hard to stay tense with her feet being massaged, but a corner of her brain tried to stay on top of the situation.

Connor placed her feet tenderly on the floor and moved closer to her. He put his arm round her shoulder. His hand felt hot through the thin silk of her blouse. His closeness reminded her that she was wearing a vest, of the most passion-killing type. Should she make an excuse and go and take it off?

'I need to talk to you, Hetty.'

'Talk away, I'm not stopping you.' Although if he'd given her a choice, she'd have gone for a bit of kissing.

'Are you sure you like this house?'

'How many times do I have to tell you? I love it.'

'Because I did it for you. I tried to make this place into a home you'd like.'

'Did you? Why?'

'Don't be so dense. This is very hard for me. I'm not used to expressing my feelings.'

Hetty closed her mouth, but her whole body was tense with uncertainty.

'I want you to know how much you mean to me.'

'I thought I was a thorn in your side who interfered with your life and wrecked your car.'

His lips narrowed with irritation. 'Are you being deliberately stupid? Surely you knew I only said those things because you could have been killed? Finding you alive when I'd been waiting all day to hear you'd had a fatal accident was such a relief, it came out as anger, surely you realized that?'

'As you said, Connor, communication isn't your best thing.'

'Oh, hell! I love you, Hetty. I love you with my heart and soul and body. There's nothing I wouldn't do for you, nothing that you could do that would make me stop loving you. You could take my car and crash it into a wall if you wanted.' He frowned. 'As long as you weren't hurt.'

'And as long as the car could be repaired?'

'No. No caveats.' He suddenly looked very serious. 'But I realize I don't have much to offer you – or anyone. I'm saddled with Courtbridge for ever. At the moment my job takes me out of the country for quite long periods. And, having spent all I earned on my last contract and the profit from my flat on this place, I don't have much money.'

Hetty moistened her lips. She'd heard the most beautiful words in the world. It was a situation of the utmost delicacy. It was imperative that she say the right thing back. The wrong thing said now could ruin her life for ever. She gave a little sigh. 'In that case, don't say another word. I won't have anything to do with you unless you can prove to me you're a millionaire.'

He gave her a horrified glance and then descended, flinging his body on to hers, pressing her mercilessly into the softness of the sofa. 'You bitch,' he muttered before silencing her protests in the time-honoured way.

A little while and a thermal vest later, Connor sat up. He was naked to the waist and was just about to tackle Hetty's bra when he paused.

'I haven't rushed you, have I? Caroline said that if I just swept you off to bed everything would be all right, but I wasn't so sure.'

'Why?'

'Because you've been hurt before, and I'm not just after a one-night stand here. I love you and I want to marry you. You may need to think about it.'

'I'll think about it, I promise.'

'Then could you hurry up and get on with it? I'm quietly dying here! I know living together first would seem a more sensible idea, but I feel living where we – I – do, we should perhaps obey the conventions.'

Hetty struggled upright. 'Run that by me again?'

'Which bit? Me quietly dying, or getting married?'

'The bit about you obeying the conventions. I mean, those aren't words I expected to hear from the Connor I know . . .' a tiny pause, 'and love.'

'Did you say what I think you said?'

'Yes.'

'Then I think we should go upstairs. There are clean, line-dried sheets on the bed and the pillows are pure down. And I know how you hate waste.'

Hetty was a little anxious that moving would make her want to change her mind. But she needn't have worried. The sheets were initially cool on her skin, but Connor was warm, providing all the heat she needed. She wallowed in his body, his deep, hairy chest, the hardness of his muscles and his intense masculine odour. She could have lain in his arms for ever, except that lying was not what he had in mind.

He stripped off her bra and pants in great haste, but Hetty forgot to feel shy, the look in his eyes as he scanned her body told her she was beautiful. He was more restrained than she would have been. Her instinct would have been to fling herself on him and make love without further ado. But Connor had other ideas, he wanted to make love to each part of her individually. First it was her chest, tantalizingly close to, but not touching, her breasts. He circled where the veins showed blue, he brushed his face against where flesh covered bone in a thin layer, his emergent beard making its presence felt. It was only when she pushed her fingers into his hair and forced him that he turned his attention to her breasts.

No longer able to stay passive under his onslaught, Hetty rolled him on to his back and used her breasts to tantalize him. She grazed his chest with her nipples, she sat astride him and kept herself almost out of reach.

It was his turn to be assertive. He rolled her on to her back so he could run his hands up and down her sides, which he did vigorously, making her laugh. And then changed his tactics and paid delicate, particular attention to the inside of her thighs.

Hetty forgot about being proactive, she just let her body follow its instincts, and Connor's instructive hands. He taught her a lot, and she loved every little lesson.

When they lay satiated in each other's arms, Connor said. 'What about some chocolate mousse? Caroline will be so offended if we don't eat it.'

Hetty giggled. 'I wouldn't eat it to spare Caroline's feelings, but I would like some.'

'And there's another bottle in the fridge. I'll get it.'

He did have a marvellous back view, Hetty decided. His spine was a delicious valley between hills of muscle, which tapered down to his waist, and from there to his buttocks, firm, well-shaped and powerful.

She took the opportunity to go to the bathroom and tidy the bed while he was gone. While she was plumping the pillows she found a packet of condoms. She was holding them anxiously when he returned with the tray.

'We forgot something,' she said, half expecting him to be angry. He'd been so insistent about taking precautions before.

Connor got into bed beside her. 'That's all right. It just means you'll have to marry me, in case you're pregnant.' He pushed a lock of her hair behind her ear and cupped her cheek with his hand. 'I didn't know how much I loved you before. I didn't know that worrying about someone, thinking about them all the time, combined with wanting to make passionate love to them on top of the piano, meant you loved them. Now,' he took a spoonful of mousse and cream and carried it to Hetty's mouth, 'open wide.'

She ate the mousse and licked her lips. 'More, please.'

'Not until you say yes.'

'What to?'

'What do you think? You stupid woman.'

'I may be a stupid woman, but not so stupid that I'll say yes to something I haven't actually been asked.'

'What do you mean? Oh, did I forget to ask you? Will you marry me, Hetty?'

'If you give me another spoonful of mousse.'

'If you marry me, I'll give you all my worldly goods and the moon and stars as well.'

'The mousse will do to be going on with.' It would do to let Connor know how romantic she thought he was. 'After all, if you're going to keep me for the rest of my life, it wouldn't do to let me go hungry now.'

'Close your eyes and open wide again then.'

'Oh!' she exclaimed. 'There's something hard. What is it?' She took it out of her mouth and looked at it.

It was a ring, garnets and pearls set in pink-coloured gold. 'Here, let me wash it for you.'

He took the ring and rinsed it in his champagne glass. 'It's a family piece. Antique.' He slipped it on to her finger and it fitted perfectly. 'You don't have to have it if you don't like it, of course. I may have promised you the moon and stars, but if you want a socking great diamond you'll have to wait until I've been away again.'

She looked at the ring sparkling in the candlelight. 'It's perfect. Will you have to go away a lot?'

'A bit, to start with. But with luck, I may be able to get consultancy work without going abroad so often. Will you mind being on your own?'

'I'll cope. As long as you always come back to me?'

'No fear of that not happening. You've got me now, you're stuck with me. Are you sure you like your ring?'

'It's the prettiest ring I've ever seen. I love it almost as much as you. Does Samuel know you took it?'

He squeezed her shoulder tightly. 'Of course. He dug out a box of jewellery from some cupboard and said, "Here, if you're going to ask the girl to marry you, you'd better have a ring to put on her finger."'

He sounded so like Samuel. 'I think we should have some more champagne. To celebrate.'

Connor took away the bowl of mousse.

'Later.'